AFTER THE RAINBOW

The South African dream becomes a murderous nightmare

By

M.W. Griffiths

Copyright © M.W. Griffiths 2025, all rights reserved

MEIRION WYN GRIFFITHS

Book One: Spring 2012

Please note, this is a work of fiction. Names, characters, places, and incidents are products of the author's imagination or are used fictitiously. Any resemblance to actual persons, living or dead, events, or locales is entirely coincidental.

ONE

Feeling exhausted after another stressful day at the office, Jabu failed to notice the white double cab in his rear-view mirror that had followed him for most of his journey home. He also failed to spot the strategically placed dried mud splattered over the double cab's number plate. No, Jabu was preoccupied with the late dinner date he'd arranged with the attractive young PA who had just started working with him in the accounts department. All he needed was a quick nap, a shower, and a change of clothes, and he'd be a new man again.

As he drove off the highway and took the ramp to the intersection leading to his suburb, Jabu Maponya was oblivious to the talk show blaring on his radio. The hosts discussed news stories that were no longer news to most South Africans: crooked politicians, corrupt cops, shady civil servants and fraudulent deals done by unscrupulous businesspeople had become the norm.

Jabu was also oblivious to harried commuters' relentless, aggressive honking of horns. Like himself, they were eager to leave the strains of trying to earn a living behind them for another day. After finally edging his way through the intersection, he accelerated down a quieter road, relieved that he was on the last leg of his journey through the jacaranda and acacia-lined avenues.

Turning onto his street, he slowed as he spotted a neighbour jogging along the pavement. He smiled and held up his thumb, approving of the man's efforts, before turning onto his driveway. As he pressed the remote control, the heavy cast iron gate trundled open along its rail.

Driving the last few metres into his property, Jabu was suddenly aware of some loud, inexplicable activity behind him. The shrill screeching of brakes followed a terrific roar of an accelerating engine. He looked in his rear-view mirror as the white double cab drove up and struck his rear bumper, pushing his car forward slightly.

Jabu's first thought about this unexpected presence was that maybe a friend had followed him into the property before the gate closed. But it was reckless. Crazy. Confusing.

As he turned around in his seat and looked over his shoulder, the driver and the passenger doors of the double cab opened simultaneously, and two figures wearing dark clothing leapt out. It was at this precise moment that Jabu realised they were wearing balaclavas. The first pang of fear shivered down his spine.

Balaclava One lunged forward, grabbing Jabu's throat through the open driver's window with his gloved hand as he screamed at him to get out of the car. After a struggle to release his seat belt, Jabu didn't feel his legs carry him as he exited the vehicle. He was also unaware that he'd just pissed in his pants. Balaclava One then dragged him away from the car and pushed him against the garage door before ramming the barrel of a 9mm pistol into his mouth, forcing the cold steel barrel into the back of his throat. Jabu felt the stinging pain as the front sight scratched the roof of his mouth.

Balaclava Two quickly jumped into Jabu's car, revving the engine wildly and screaming at his accomplice to hurry up. But Balaclava One didn't reply. With the cold professionalism of a seasoned criminal, he pulled the trigger. The garage wall behind Jabu's head exploded in blood spatter, along with shattered fragments of bone, brain tissue and skin. Jabu's knees buckled. He was dead before he hit the ground.

Balaclava Two revved the engine again as Balaclava One jumped into the double cab. Then, both vehicles exited the driveway as fast as a standing reverse start would allow. As they started to speed off, both Jabu's car and the double cab came close to colliding with the jogger who, on hearing the single shot, had walked back cautiously towards Jabu's house.

As he looked up the drive and saw the body slumped against the bloodied garage wall, the jogger immediately grasped the shocking finality of the situation. And in the few seconds it took him to realise that he needed to identify the white double cab's number plate, both vehicles were already more than a hundred metres away as they disappeared around the corner into the next street.

The first emergency vehicle arrived at the scene from one of the many private armed security companies that constantly patrol the more affluent suburbs of South African cities. The hopelessness of the incident was immediately reported back to the control room. Within a few minutes, the first police car arrived, followed needlessly by an ambulance.

Within thirty minutes, the street was clogged with all manner of emergency vehicles and unmarked police cars, their blue strobing lights penetrating the increasing darkness of the early evening.

The police detectives – all hard-bitten and profoundly cynical – knew there was little they could do to identify those responsible. But they still went through the motions, pacing their way around Jabu's slumped body, looking for any apparent forensic evidence. All they discovered was one empty 9mm brass casing. But having been ejected from the most ubiquitous handgun calibre in the country, it hardly instilled confidence that this was valuable evidence. As for the bullet, it had passed straight through Jabu's head before the lead fragmented against the garage wall, rendering it useless for ballistic testing.

Police barrier tape cordoned off the scene. Forensic investigators dusted for fingerprints. Photographs were taken. DNA samples were extracted. All the detectives and forensic technicians went through the various processes, knowing that, in reality, it was a futile exercise. After all, this was just part of the wholesale criminal slaughter that had become an everyday occurrence in South Africa, a country reborn with much hope and optimism a little over two and a half decades earlier. Jabu was just another casualty in the low-grade civil war of criminality that had now overwhelmed the country.

Just another senseless hijacking, probably by amateurs, the cops mumbled between themselves. The real pros didn't kill because they were so adept at terrorising victims into immediate compliance: *'Get out of the car . . . Leave the keys in the ignition . . . Don't make any sudden moves . . . Stay calm . . . Drive off . . .* Another day at the office.'

To the investigators, Jabu was just another hijacking victim. Another death. Another statistic. Poor bugger. And they all knew the shocking truth: of the two million plus crimes reported the previous year, barely seven in a hundred had ended in convictions. South Africa had become a Mecca for criminals: rapists, burglars, fraudsters, murderers and car hijackers plied their trades with impunity.

By the time Jabu's corpse was being zipped up in a black plastic body bag and hauled unceremoniously into the back of the municipal mortuary van, both his car and the white double cab were over two hundred kilometres north of the scene. They were far enough so that the sky's countless stars were not dimmed by the ambient lights of Africa's most industrialised city.

The vehicles drove off the quiet country road at an undistinguished junction and onto a badly potholed dirt track winding through farmland. Manoeuvring slowly for several kilometres in the darkness, the two hijackers eventually found what they were looking for: a homemade sign crudely nailed to a pole that read: *'Fourie Plaas'*. And scribbled underneath was a message for anyone who cared to read it that stated the main gate was a further two kilometres away: *'Fourie Plaas. Geen inskrywing volg pad na hoofhek 2 km!'* The farm gate was open, and they drove through before continuing towards a barely discernible speck of light far into the blackness.

After negotiating a few hundred metres of rough ground, the two vehicles arrived at the source of the light: a hastily prepared construction site in the middle of an unremarkable field, on which stood an ancient, rusted mechanical digger with a large steel scoop in the front and a heavy bucket at the back. Sitting in the driver's seat was a young black man wearing overalls. Next to it was a newly excavated hole of around five square metres dug deep into a slight incline.

Jabu's car was driven to the hole's edge before the driver got out. The digger's engine coughed and spluttered into life. The black man and his white partner began a cursory search of the car. On finding nothing of value, the white man held up his thumb, and the digger inched forward and started pushing the vehicle as far into the hole as it would go.

The digger then lumbered around to the side of the hole, and the heavy steel scoop pushed around a ton of soil onto the roof of Jabu's car. Repeating the action, it took several minutes to bury the vehicle, removing it from the world as if it had never existed.

TWO

'Boere Baroque' was how one of the more derisive marketing industry pundits had described the three-storey edifice that housed South Africa's largest independent communications and advertising group, Janse-Mashele.

There was no understated architectural elegance and clean Bauhaus lines for this company. Instead, it was a brash, nouveau riche gaudiness topped by a miniature St Peter's style glass dome held aloft by mock Doric-style pillars.

The bling continued inside the building. Visitors walking through the oversized glass doors were confronted with a cavernous reception area that housed an assortment of lavish fittings and fixtures. These ranged from the Persian silk carpets strewn over the highly polished marble floor tiles to the large ornately framed mirrors that created the appearance of yet more space. Flanking the ground-floor reception area were two broad semi-circular staircases that swept up either side of the interior and wound their way up to the executive floor. And housed directly above that was the glass dome that bathed the area in a blaze of light.

The staff referred to the staircase on the right as the Janse stairs, while the left side was named the Mashele stairs. The reason for these monikers was that each partner habitually used their own staircase. So, it had become something of a tradition at Janse-Mashele: contrived folklore that was meaningless drivel to people not connected to the company but treasured by those whose names were emblazoned on signage throughout the building. And, just in case a visitor might miss seeing any of those logos, one-metre-high letters spelling out JANSE-MASHELE were carved into the teak fascia that ran the length of the reception desk.

Behind the counter sat two glamourous-looking and well-spoken receptionists. For Janse-Mashele, brand image was everything. It was what the company traded in and what it owed its considerable success. So, it was hardly surprising that the company would hire two ex-models to welcome clients and suppliers.

'Good morning, sir, can I help you?' asked the red-haired receptionist as she flashed a dazzling smile worthy of a toothpaste commercial.

'Hi, yes,' replied the young man awkwardly. 'My name's Daniel Steyn, and I was hired last week, so I guess I'm starting today.'

'Oh, wow. That's great. Welcome, Daniel, my name's Sue-Ann, and this is my friend and partner in crime, Thandi. Hey, Thands, this is Daniel, and he's joining the company today.'

'Hi, Daniel', said Thandi with equal enthusiasm. 'In which department?"

'Strategic planning.'

'Oh, Joe Robinson's department, lucky you. Joe's such a character; he's hysterical', continued Thandi. 'I'll call Debbie, Joe's PA, so she can come and fetch you.'

Looking around in awe, Daniel Steyn soaked in the hustle and bustle and the creative energy that seemed to ooze from every pore of Janse-Mashele.

After university, Daniel had spent a gap year in London, earning money through an assortment of unskilled jobs, mainly labouring on construction sites, and because of his large, athletic build, working as a somewhat reluctant doorman at a West End nightclub during the weekends. But now, Steyn was eager to start a real job to challenge his well-honed intellect and satisfy his ever-growing ambitions. So here he was, on the first rung of a ladder destined to reach the heavens. Securing his first job at a blue-chip communications group like Janse-Mashele made him incredibly proud, while it made many of his old college friends more than a little envious.

Debbie Peters, the strategic planning department PA that came to collect him, was in her mid-forties, slim and attractive, even though - in Daniel's mind - her makeup looked as if it had been applied with a trowel.

As they climbed the Janse stairs to the first floor, she lost no time getting familiar with her department's new addition. 'So, you're the fresh meat for this year, hey? Better watch out at the Christmas party. A few chicks around here will be trying it on with you, boytjie', she said in her distinct southern suburbs accent, the roughness amplified by a raspy smoker's timbre that became evident as she chuckled at her jokes.

'God, I'd forgotten that you were such a big bastard', said the ruddy-faced Joe Robinson by way of re-introducing himself to the young man he had offered the position of a junior strategic planner just two weeks previously.

'Hi Joe', replied Daniel as he extended his hand. 'It's great to be here, finally'.

'Well, don't be too bloody keen now. You can't be showing the rest of us up. Never forget that in this department, we pride ourselves on our scepticism and our total refusal to accept anything at face value. To be a good strat planner, you need to question everything. Everything, understand? Now let me show you around and introduce you to some damn fine people.'

The rest of the morning was spent with his new colleagues, drinking copious cups of coffee while listening to Old Joe regale everyone with ancient industry yarns that he always reserved for occasions such as when someone joined the department. Being a consummate storyteller and a master of sardonic humour were two reasons why Joe Robison was one of the most popular characters in the company.

Daniel's arrival was also an excellent excuse for Old Joe to pull out the company plastic and treat everyone in the department to lunch at the local pizzeria. Daniel noticed that Old Joe consumed only a liquid lunch, courtesy of South African Breweries, as everyone devoured their pizzas.

Throughout the rest of the afternoon, Old Joe introduced Daniel to the client list, which mainly comprised state-owned organisations and government departments.

'Why so much government business?' asked Daniel as he skipped through the endless pages of the company's weekly status through an administrative document that monitored each stage of the projects as they were guided through the system.

'Well, we're kind of good at it', was Joe's non-committal reply. Then, with a conspiratorial wink, he added: 'And let's just say we're good at knowing the right people.'

Daniel was also impressed by the company's casual approach and lack of corporate formality. 'Oh, that's typical of the ad industry, always has been, always will be', explained Joe. 'All that pretentious posh stuff is strictly for the TFUs'.

'TFUs?' asked Daniel.

'Yes, TFUs, Those Fuckers Upstairs', replied Old Joe. 'Those pompous wankers who like to have their arses wiped for them', he rambled, much to the delight of everyone within earshot, especially Debbie, who seemed to hang on Joe's every word.

As everyone was about to leave for the evening, Joe whispered some friendly parting advice to Daniel: 'Remember what I said, my boy. Be sceptical and never accept anything at face value, whether it comes from a client, the TFUs, or me.'

THREE

Spotting the gleaming black S-Class Mercedes as it glided up to the foyer of the Pretoria Sheraton, the hotel doormen immediately snapped to attention. They hurried to open the door for the lone passenger in the back seat. Then, reaching for his oversized briefcase, Lwazi Ndlovu curtly instructed his driver. 'Hang around. The meeting shouldn't be more than a couple of hours; then we can call it a night.'

'Yes, Chief', replied the driver, making eye contact with his boss through the rear-view mirror.

'Oh, do me a favour", continued Ndlovu, 'Call me on my cellphone in exactly two hours so I can make an excuse to get out of there.'

'No problem, chief.'

Stepping out of his official car, Ndlovu nodded in response to the deferential greeting he received from the black-uniformed doorman. After three years as director-general of a government department, he had gotten used to such treatment. And, as far as he was concerned, the more they fawned, the better.

He barely acknowledged the smiles from the concierge on entering the hotel lobby as he made his way towards the reception desk. Then, ignoring any pleasantries with the young clerk, he got straight to the point. 'The name's Ndlovu. I have a suite booked for tonight.'

The clerk typed in Ndlovu's name and examined his computer screen. 'Ah... Yes, sir, here it is. Just the one night? No luggage?'

Ndlovu expressed his irritation about being questioned with a look of disdain: 'My private secretary booked it. It's for a private business meeting'.

'Of course, sir', replied the clerk, realising his indiscretion. 'Is there anything you'd like from room service? Anything I can do?'

'Yes, I'd like a bottle of very chilled Moet and some snacks sent to the room. I'm going to the bar first.'

"The wine and snacks will be sent to your room immediately, " replied the clerk, handing over an electronic keycard.

Ndlovu turned away, making a point of not thanking the man.

The bar was boisterous that evening. A large trade delegation from Shanghai was staying at the hotel, and many of them were working their way through the hotel's comprehensive menu of rare malt whiskies, secure in the knowledge that their embassy would write off the tab as diplomatic entertainment.

The usual coterie of African Union diplomats also held court. As they sipped 20-, 30- and 50-year-old scotch and cognac, they loudly conducted their diplomatic business in French, English and Portuguese – the colonial languages of Africa.

Ndlovu pushed his way through the crowd. Even though he enjoyed the sumptuous five-star elegance of the Sheraton, the sandstone structure of the hotel made him feel strangely uneasy. It was similar to the stone used to construct the Union Building. The imposing neoclassic parliament building was the official seat of government that housed the president's office, which stood scarcely two hundred metres away.

Ndlovu spent much of his time at the Union Building, usually grilled by parliamentary portfolio committees on the various aspects of his responsibilities. A task he detested as – invariably - awkward questions would be asked concerning the multi-billion-rand projects under his control. And always the thorny, probing queries from members of oversight committees - the government bodies that dealt with budgets and cost overruns and the massively lucrative government tenders that would be awarded to the rich and powerful, thus making them even richer and even more powerful.

Ndlovu scanned the room and quickly recognised the person waiting for him. With long, straight black hair, the immaculately groomed young black woman, wearing a tight-fitting cocktail dress, sat alone.

Even though she had never met Ndlovu before, she recognised him immediately. His photograph occasionally appeared on the social pages of the most exclusive magazines she studied avidly. He'd often be featured arm-in-arm with his socialite wife of thirteen years. And both would be enjoying the trappings of success at events reserved for the elite of society: the politicians, media personalities and business executives who were strictly A-list.

'Fashionably late, I see', her opening gambit was usually the same whenever she met her gentlemen friends for the first time. Knowing they were formidably powerful, she liked to make it evident from the outset that she was not intimidated by power and wealth. She relished being in the company of influential men.

'My apologies,' he replied, smiling and approving her as he sat. 'I hope you didn't have to wait for long.'

'Not too long,' she replied, emphasising the 'too' with a slight hint of mischief.

He shrugged his shoulders in response. Ndlovu prided himself on making snap assessments of people's characters when meeting them for the first time. On this occasion, he detected a slight English accent. He also sensed abundant self-assurance, the poise and the grace of someone who benefited from an elitist private education. Probably the daughter of returned exiles, he thought, activists and dissidents – like the Tambos and the Sisulus - the cream of the anti-apartheid movement who escaped the lethal claws of the Pretoria regime's security apparatus. Ndlovu was impressed.

'Melanie', she said, offering her right hand across the table.

'Lwazi', he replied as he shook her hand gently, admiring her long, French-manicured nails.

'Lwazi', she said. 'I hate to get down to business . . .'

'Eight thousand for the night', he interrupted. 'Cash, I assume?'

She smiled diffidently. She always liked to create the perception that discussing money with her gentlemen friends was vulgar. Of course, the truth was something else. She loved the money. She did what she did purely for the money. But she had also realised that her clientele did not want to face up to the fact that she was a high-class escort, regardless that she was highly exclusive and expensive. They wanted the mistress' experience without courting someone with dinners, dates, and the usual time-consuming ritual. This arrangement was far more convenient for men like Ndlovu, who had busy schedules and demanding wives and had the means to pay for a woman like Melanie.

'Of course, we can do all that in the room. You have booked a room, I take it?'

'Yes', he replied, 'A suite. Shall we find out if it's to our liking?'

As they walked into the suit, the champagne and the snacks were laid on a side table. Dropping his briefcase, Ndlovu pulled off his jacket and undid his tie before opening the wine and pouring it into crystal flutes. "I take it you will join me?"

'Yes, please. I love all things French, especially champagne.'

'So, is the room to your liking?'

'Not too shabby', she replied, again flashing a mischievous

smile as she admired the luxury a five-star hotel could lay on for its pampered guests.

Ndlovu made his first move by kissing her lightly on her lips. She responded in kind. But as he pushed his tongue into her mouth, she broke away abruptly. 'Why don't we have a drink first?' she asked with a look of faux innocence.

'Of course', he replied as he handed her a glass. 'Cheers', he said with a smile.

'Cheers', she replied as she took the glass and sipped the cold wine.

Again, Ndlovu made a move. They kissed passionately for a moment before she gently pushed him back a second time. 'Darling, I'd like you to shower for me and freshen up a little. It's been a long day.'

'Why don't you take a shower with me?' he suggested.

'Later', she countered. 'You shower now, and I'll have a nice surprise waiting for you', she teased as she lifted her skirt to reveal the top of her fishnet stocking.

He immediately smiled. 'Don't go away now, will you?'

'I'll be here waiting', she replied, kissing him again playfully.

As soon as she heard the glass door closing and the shower taps being turned on, she grabbed her handbag and pulled out a small bottle. Twisting off the cap, she poured the contents into her hand, small blue and white capsules. Selecting two, she quickly replaced the rest into the bottle and placed them back into her bag. She then twisted the capsules to separate the two sides and carefully poured a small amount of white powder into Ndlovu's glass. As she topped up the champagne, the powder dissolved immediately.

Work over, she unzipped herself out of her dress, revealing expensive, erotic lingerie, before spreading herself on the bed.

Within a few minutes, Ndlovu was back in the room, a bath towel tied around his waist. As he examined her body, he allowed the towel to drop, exposing his nakedness.

'Oh, you are a naughty boy', she said with a broad smile. 'You're very keen, aren't you?'

'Well, looking at you, there isn't a man in the world who could blame me.'

'Before we get started, let's have a toast.' She handed Ndlovu his wine, grabbed her glass, and held it up for the salute before swallowing it in one gulp. He followed suit before leaping onto the bed and lying next to her. Then, disregarding any niceties, he started exploring her taught, slim body with his hands before kissing her on the neck.

Within minutes, the lovemaking came to a sudden halt as the increasingly groggy Ndlovu suddenly and without warning passed out, spread-eagled on the bed.

'About bloody time,' she whispered to herself as she struggled to extricate herself from under his body and rearrange her lingerie that Ndlovu had partially removed. 'Right, Mr director-general, let's see what you are made of', she whispered again.

Working quickly, she grabbed his briefcase, which she discovered was locked. But a quick search of his pants pockets soon produced a set of keys, one of which fitted the lock.

Opening the bag, she pulled out a thick stack of files. On the cover of each was printed a government department crest. And above that, the stamped words in large black letters: Strictly Confidential. After quickly flicking through the files, she grabbed her cell phone from her bag and made a call. It was answered immediately. 'It's me. Yes, he's out like a light. I have all the papers. Okay, see you now.'

Her work for the evening was over, and she poured herself

another glass of champagne before getting dressed. Within a few minutes, there was a gentle knock on the door, which she opened to let in a male colleague. He was carrying a small bag, out of which he pulled a hand-held portable scanning machine.

There was barely a word spoken between them as they were both well-versed in the task at hand. The man carefully removed the staples that held the files together before guiding the wand-like scanning machine over each page while she carefully re-stapled the pages back together. It took them no more than fifteen minutes to scan every page before returning the files to the briefcase. And fifteen seconds to strip Ndlovu of his wallet and his Omega watch. Then they both left, leaving Ndlovu alone in his stupor.

FOUR

It was just after 2:00 am when the swing doors at the Pretoria General Hospital's trauma unit were rudely shoved apart as two paramedics pushed the trolley that carried the unconscious Ndlovu. With an oxygen mask covering his face, the scene left no one in any doubt about the seriousness of his condition.

'What have we got here?' asked the nursing sister at the admittance station as she started typing the details into a PC.

'Don't know for sure,' replied the first paramedic. 'Some guy was found passed out on his hotel bed. His vitals are all over the place. BP is extremely low at 48 over 70. Breathing is very shallow. He may have taken an overdose. There was alcohol on the scene, but we don't know how much he drank, but we can't wake him up for dear life.'

'There were no signs of the usual drug use, but we think he's going to need a stomach pump in case he has taken an overdose,' added his partner.

'Right', replied the nurse as she continued to fill in the automated admittance form. 'I'll get the doctor on call straight away.'

Within minutes, a young, tired-looking intern, assisted by two nurses, examined Ndlovu. He started by re-checking his vital signs before extracting blood samples for the pathology lab.

As they worked, two other people walked through the trauma unit foyer. Both were journalists for *The Telegraph*, a daily publication that – appealing to the lowest common denominator – modelled itself on the more lurid Fleet Street tabloids: sex, scandals and anything remotely salacious.

Braam Van Ass and Themba Dube were a team noted for their ability to squirrel a scoop out of a tiny hint of evidence. And if the piece didn't pan out as they hoped, they could always write it any way they wanted. As seasoned hacks, they were not averse to adding a little fiction to colour some facts. After all, why let the truth get in the way of a good story? Corrupt politicians, celebrities cheating on their spouses, dodgy businessmen defrauding their shareholders - Van Ass and Dube covered it all and did so with aplomb.

Their first port of call was the nursing sister who had admitted Ndlovu. 'Yes, gentlemen, can I help you?' she asked.

'Hi, Sister. We're from The Telegraph. We hear the guy they've just wheeled in was picked up at the Sheraton in Pretoria. We wondered if you could tell us his name?' replied Van Ass.

'No, sorry, it's against hospital policy to give information on patients to anyone other than close family.'

'Come on, Sissy', implored Dube, playing the – we're-both-black-and-we-were-both-raised–in-the-township familiarity card. 'The public out there needs to know what's happening in this country.'

But the sister was having none of it: 'Why don't you two get the hell out of here before I call security', she countered, raising her voice with every syllable.

'We can make it worth your while', said Van Ass in his broad Afrikaans accent as he took his wallet out of his jacket pocket and slapped it down on the counter in front of the sister.

'What are you going to try and bribe me?' she shrieked.

'Let's not put it like that,' said Van Ass. 'Look, sister, you work bloody long hours. You help people. For Christ's sake, you save people's lives, and what do you get at the end of the month?

Fock all, right?'

Even though she considered Van Ass's tone coarse and aggressive, she could hardly argue with his logic.

'So for just a bit of information that won't harm a soul, you get a couple of hundred bucks to buy something nice for yourself. You know, a small treat for all that hard work. Now, where's the harm in that?'

Egged on by his partner's persuasiveness, Dube delivered the coup de grâce in hushed tones: 'Sissie, we also serve the public. People have a right to know what's going on in this country. That's all there is to it. People talk to us all the time. The security guys at the hotel said that this dude arrived at the hotel in a big fancy car with government plates. Then, three hours later, his driver and some security guys find him half dead in his room. All we need to know is what's wrong with him. 'Some important guy like this ends up in a hospital, and people are concerned. They need to know the truth. Don't you see? And as my bro says, where's the harm in that?'

By this stage, Van Ass had already extracted two one-hundred-rand notes from his wallet. 'We don't know what's wrong with him at this stage', said the sister, looking up and down the corridor before she quickly snapped the money out of Van Ass's hand. 'The doctor suspects that he may have taken an overdose, or he may have been drugged or something.'

'You mean poisoned?' asked Dube excitedly.

'Fock me! This is serious shit', exclaimed Van Ass.

'But as I said, we don't know anything for sure. That's just speculation from an incredibly young, and if you ask me, a very inexperienced intern. We'll only know for sure when we get the toxicology results.'

'Fock met', said Van Ass, 'it's like something out of a movie script'.

'Yeah, let's get out of here, Braam, my bru; we've got some copy to knock out.'

Glancing at their watches, they both realised they were too late for the early printed edition, but if they hurried back to the newsroom, they could squeeze a scoop for the online edition. The reporters thanked the sister and left.

FIVE

Few people familiar with the company would argue against the widely held belief that Macdonald Mashele was the biggest reason Janse-Mashele had enjoyed such spectacular growth over the previous six years.

Mashele's most significant talent, over and above his street-smart intelligence, was his beguiling charisma, which he used to considerably effect in winning people over within minutes of meeting them. Young or old, rich or poor, avant-garde or conservative, all who met Mashele would swear to his sincerity. His legendary charm had made him one of the most well-connected figures in the South African communications industry.

He was wealthy and successful, and - unlike his partner Henk Janse - he was not shy about sharing his wealth. In the most lavish way imaginable, he entertained friends, acquaintances, clients, and anyone who could be of any value to him. It was a largess that knew no bounds. But over and above his popularity, Mashele had the one commodity that virtually guaranteed business from any government entity in post-apartheid South Africa: struggle credentials.

By the late 1980s, as a teenager growing up in Soweto, the sprawling township Southwest of Johannesburg, Mashele had quickly established himself with his peers as a naturally talented leader. He ran with a gang that spent much of its time trying to bait the apartheid authorities - acts of defiance that usually involved throwing rocks at patrolling armoured vehicles. But when they could lay their hands on some fuel, they graduated to petrol bombs, which required a swift disappearing act into the township's narrow streets and alleyways.

Although he regarded his exploits as no more than a high-risk, high-adrenalin game, Mashele's quick-thinking intelligence and street smartness were soon recognised. Subtle overtures were made to him by local activists with links to the UDF - the United Democratic Front - the coalition of civic, church, student and workers' organisations with the shared aim of making the country ungovernable.

When approached to work for these activists, Mashele didn't need to be asked twice. The first tasks assigned to him were that of a low-level courier, a messenger who carried tiny pieces of tightly folded paper that he handed to nameless, shadowy figures who barely acknowledged him. He had guessed that these messages related to the protests constantly flaring up like bushfires throughout the townships. Telephones were still a rarity in township homes during the 1980s – except for those who worked for government entities. Besides, the few pay phones situated throughout the townships were often tapped by the authorities, so messengers like Mashele were vital for efficient communication amongst the organisers.

Being dedicated to the cause, Mashele soon impressed his handlers with his reliability and capacity to keep his mouth shut – regardless of the situation. On two occasions, he had been picked up by the security forces and questioned. The cops were aware that the anti-apartheid groups used youngsters as messengers, but catching them had proved a near impossibility, and small pieces of paper could easily be discarded, literally under a cop's nose.

The first time Mashele's luck ran out was on a sweltering summer evening in the mid-1980s. The ongoing labour unrest, classroom revolts, rent strikes and consumer boycotts – the easiest and most effective non-violent tactics that ordinary people could use against the apartheid regime – had started to frustrate the ruling powers. Eventually, the protests resulted in some faceless, nameless securocrat ordering the police to: 'Teach the black bastards a lesson they won't forget.'

That particular night, it seemed that half of the township was ablaze. And fanning the flames were columns of yellow police Casspirs that snaked their way through the streets, the V-hulled, landmine-resistant army troop carriers designed for the border wars. But they had been adapted for use by the security police as the struggle came closer to home. Carrying 14 men high off the ground and with narrow windows that bristled with the barrels of rifles and shotguns, these steel-skinned leviathans were a menacing presence in the narrow township streets.

Mashele had just been unlucky that night – wrong time, wrong place, as they say. In his attempt to dodge a police patrol, he ran as fast as his legs could carry him around a street corner when he was confronted with a Casspir that had pulled over for the cops to have a smoke break.

Leaping out of the vehicle's side door, an overzealous corporal – more out of a sense of reckless fun to impress his mates – managed to grab Mashele and wrestle him to the ground. Then he roughly rammed Mashele's head as close as it would go next to one of the Casspir's massive wheels. But even with the engine revving alarmingly and the driver's foot teasing the vehicle's clutch, which would have made any other fifteen-year-old buckle, Mashele refused to answer any of the cop's shouted questions.

But then came a stroke of luck, the kind of luck that would come to personify Mashele in his adult life. The sharp sound of automatic gunfire suddenly rang out from a neighbouring street, which quickly had the cops climbing back inside the vehicle before driving off to find more of an adrenalin fix than an under-weight teenage boy could ever provide.

The next occasion when Mashele was captured was due to a vigilant informer – an *impimpi* – they were called in township parlance. He had spotted Mashele once too often that day.

Thrown into the back of a police van, the security cops took him to the notorious John Forster Square police station in downtown Joburg. Knowing full well that the terrorists used youngsters to carry messages, the police were hell-bent on traumatising into submission any boy they suspected of being involved in anything political. It had started with a few slaps and kicks, which Mashele could take in his stride. But then the situation changed to something far more harrowing.

The handcuffed Mashele could hear the screaming long before the two constables dragged him to the bottom of the stairs in the police station's basement, which housed the holding cells. It was a relentless, high-pitched scream that barely waned in its intensity.

Waiting for him in front of an open cell door was a large, pot-bellied warrant officer. In his thick Afrikaans accent, he shouted into the cell: 'Hey Jacob, we've got a visitor for you.'

A group of junior constables gathered in the passage were chuckling at the officer's comments. They were in awe of their superior - a master craftsman in torture. 'Yes, we have a little terrorist here who is thinking of joining you fokken MK skelms. Now, we need to educate our young friend, don't we, Jacob? We must show him what he can expect when we catch him.'

MK stood for *Umkhonto we Sizwe* or *The Spear of the Nation*, the armed wing of the African National Congress founded by Nelson Mandela, amongst others, when the revolutionary gloves came off after the Sharpeville massacre in 1960. Of all the anti-apartheid movements, MK would have been the organisation most youngsters like Mashele would have aspired to join. These were serious guys: the guys who fought back, the guys who planted bombs, the guys who attacked police stations with RPGs, and the guys who could do significant damage to the oppressors.

But, as Mashele was hauled in front of the open door of the cell, the figure that confronted him was anything but heroic or defiant. Instead, stripped naked in the empty cell was a middle-aged black man strung up with chains attached to his wrists that hung from the ceiling. With his arms stretched apart, he was suspended high up so that the tips of his toes could barely touch the ground – an agonising torment in itself. A steady flow of blood dripped from his nose and his mouth. And his eyes were so swollen from the day's beating that they were both virtually closed.

Mashele felt the sudden urge to vomit. He tried to look away from Jacob and keep his head down, staring at nothing as if that would make him invisible. He could see Jacob's blood spattered on the warrant officer's shirt, and he noticed the strange-looking rubber rod that the cop held in his gloved, ham-like hand. The warrant officer grabbed Mashele's jaw and forced his head up so that he had no choice but to look at the pitiful sight in front of him.

Squeezing Mashele's chin, the warrant officer continued with the lesson: 'So this, my little black friend, is what happens to people who want to fock with my people,' he said, holding up the rod. Mashele could see the two metal electrodes at the end of the shaft. 'This, my little friend, is what happens to you.' Suddenly a bluish spark flashed from one electrode to another, which caused Mashele to piss in his pants.

Pulling his young prisoner behind him, the warrant officer entered the cell and stuck the end of the rod between Jacob's testicles. As he pressed the button on the handle, Jacob's body immediately stiffened and contorted itself in a series of violent jolts and jerks. The screaming started afresh.

Terrified to the depths of his being, Mashele's knees almost buckled under his weight. And he could feel the tears rolling down his cheeks. He had never experienced such wanton, sadistic cruelty. It was beyond the realms of his imagination that anyone could show such callous disregard for any living creature, let alone a fellow human being. It was, to his young and innocent mind, inexplicable.

The warrant officer started showing off to his audience by gently teasing and caressing Jacob's body with the cattle prod before pressing the button that thrust several thousand volts of electricity through skin, muscle, bone and organs. Much to the glee of the constables, the warrant officer paid particular attention to Jacob's testicles, anus, penis and nipples.

Mashele was oblivious to the passage of time, but eventually, the warrant officer began to feel tired, and the constables started getting bored. One young officer was ordered to get rid of Mashele. Then – without a word uttered to him – Mashele was frogmarched up the stairs before being thrown out of a rear entrance of the building.

Even though the trauma he'd witnessed in the cells resulted in weeks of sleepless nights, Mashele refused to be weakened by the ordeal. On the contrary, the entire experience caused him to redouble his efforts to do whatever was needed to help rid the country of such injustice. But it also made him obsessively cautious; the sight of poor Jacob was the cost of his carelessness after being spotted by the impimpi. And it was a sight that was indelibly etched into his consciousness.

After several months of deftly dodging police roadblocks and army patrols, Mashele was trusted with more important duties. When asked to think of ways to help raise funds for the local branch of the movement, his latent entrepreneurial skills came to the fore.

He had hit on the idea that quickly became profitable for the movement and hugely exciting for him. It was to smuggle large amounts of marijuana from Swaziland. This small independent kingdom nestled between Mozambique and the

Eastern Transvaal and Natal provinces in the eastern corner of South Africa.

The modus operandi for these smuggling missions was pretty simple. Remove the tyres from a car's wheels, fill them up with as much compressed marijuana as possible, and then re-inflate the tyres before fixing the wheels back onto the vehicle. The car's handling may have been rendered suicidal, but for Mashele, the satisfaction of being searched and allowed through numerous police roadblocks was immense.

Besides, the profits were enormous. The market for the end product had been relatively easy to establish. Virtually any nonconformist-looking white student in one of the more liberal, English-speaking educational institutions could be considered a customer. The apartheid regime had a tight stranglehold over the entire population. As grossly inhumane as it was for the black population – permeating and dictating every aspect of their lives – it also affected the white population. Most whites bought into apartheid's gravely warped ideology. And through skilful and relentless propaganda, as well as the full compliance of the most influential civil society institutions, they were happy to conform. But for some freethinking, liberal-minded students, smoking a joint was a way of pushing back, of cocking a snook, of saying *fuck you* to a shameful establishment. It was also a welcome respite from the fiercely conservative, suppressive, Calvinistic attitude that was the apartheid order of the day.

Moral or ethical issues of drug use never entered Mashele's mind. These were long-haired, scruffy, neo-liberal white kids from middle-class families. And regardless of how much they protested their hatred for the apartheid system, they had still benefitted handsomely from it: schooling of a far higher standard than anything a kid like Mashele would ever have experienced; extra coaching on manicured sports fields; and black maids to wipe their juvenile arses. So no, Mashele had no pangs of guilt that he was selling drugs to white kids. As he surmised, they had plenty of money and fuck all sense. Besides, it was hugely profitable. And that was all that mattered.

As for the proceeds of this enterprise, they were split roughly into thirds. One-third was ploughed back into the business to replenish stock and to cover expenses. One-third was donated to the local activists, who always covered his back. And the remaining third was deposited into Mashele's savings account at the Post Office.

That money was then reinvested in Mashele's most significant asset: his developing intellect. By the early 1990s, Mashele had saved enough to pay for a Bachelor of Commerce degree course at the same university that had become his primary market: the University of the Witwatersrand or Wits as it was more commonly known.

For the first time in his life, Mashele was rubbing shoulders with the young, white elites of the country. But it was hardly on a similar footing. While his peers were studying Commerce 101, Mashele already had his PhD in street-smart. Within three years, all the hard work and the sacrifices made - such as forfeiting anything that resembled a social life - finally bore fruit. Macdonald Mashele, Bachelor of Commerce, had come of age.

After university, finding his first job had become a far easier proposition than Mashele had imagined. With the dismantling of the apartheid regime, political and economic changes had fast overtaken events. And fortune was finally on the side of the young, gifted Mashele-types of the country. *The Winds of Change* that Harold Macmillan, the British Prime Minister, had cautioned the apartheid government in the 1960s, were now blowing a hurricane of positivity that permeated every nook and cranny throughout the country. With South Africa finally becoming a democracy - and, for a while, even becoming the darling of the Western world - multi-national companies were desperate to hire the best and the brightest black graduates. And few were better and brighter than Mashele.

His first job after leaving Wits was as a junior client service executive with one of the larger multinational advertising agencies. As he was on the first rung of the ad agency ladder, Mashele's duties included the tedious tasks his superiors would avoid: taking notes at client meetings and translating them into contact reports before writing up the client briefs.

No matter how complex or demanding the task, Mashele performed it to the best of his abilities. He also had an irrepressibly cheery disposition and willingness that exceeded expectations - qualities that quickly made him popular with all his senior and junior colleagues.

He soon became the 'go-to guy' for any tricky task. If demanding clients threw their toys out of the cot for whatever reason, Mashele would charm them in no time. If production costs for a TV commercial had suddenly gone way over budget, Mashele would explain.

His rise through the ranks was meteoric. Within a few years, his confidence, charm and intelligence made him a formidable player in the industry. And because he worked in the business of establishing and cultivating a brand image, Mashele also made sure that his name regularly appeared in relevant industry publications. This he did by hiring a small PR company to promote himself and paying them from his meagre salary.

The thought of an individual hiring a PR company was a typical outlandish Mashele idea. But it paid off. Within a few years, he was established as one of the most marketable young executives in the industry. Whenever a senior position became available in one of the blue-chip agencies, Mashele's name was sure to be mentioned by most head-hunters. So, Mashele moved from agency to agency for another few years, upping his salary, reputation and influence with every move.

Then, unexpectedly, Henk Janse called him. They knew each other by name and reputation but had never met. Something that Janse was determined to change.

"Macdonald, I have an interesting proposition for you. One that I think will interest you greatly." Janse had said once the pleasantries had been dispensed with.

Mashele would later joke about Janse's hard, guttural Afrikaans accent by exclaiming: 'Henk Janse made me an offer I couldn't understand.'

But it was the start of a partnership that would result in considerable success for both of them.

SIX

Henk Janse was already on his way to work as the sun broke over the horizon. He had always been a pre-dawn riser; it had been drummed into him growing up on a small family farm in the Northern Cape. Although referred to as a farm, it was no more than a dry, dusty patch of scrubland located on the edge of the Kalahari Desert.

As three generations of the Janse clan could confirm, with barely enough grass to sustain no more than a few emaciated sheep at a time, the family farm produced nothing but hardship.

Growing up dirt poor had some significant side effects on Hendrik Stephanus Janse. The most obvious being that it had made him value money to the point of obsession. Even now, at the stage of his life when he had accumulated vast amounts of wealth, he still detested the thought of parting with even trifling amounts.

Another emotional scar that Henk Janse carried from those early days growing up in the scrubland of the Kalahari was apparent in his relationships with people. He was emotionally close to no one, not even his wife of ten years.

Growing up so poor, he had been forced to walk barefoot to primary school, summer and winter alike. And if being a victim of such grinding poverty wasn't bad enough, he also had to endure being ridiculed and humiliated relentlessly for it by his peers. That crushing shame had haunted him throughout his life. But he would never let it show. Being in complete control of his emotions was something Henk Janse had learned to master early in life. He could be the essence of charm and thoughtfulness with someone he thoroughly despised. He never showed his hand, never gave anything away.

So here he was, an extremely successful businessman running one of the country's largest and most profitable communications agencies, of which his was the first name above the door.

Starting his own business had been Janse's ambition since his adolescent years when he first became aware that he possessed a level of intelligence superior to most people he had encountered up until then. With it came the additional realisation that he despised being told what to do by people he felt were inferior to him in terms of intellect, cunning or ruthlessness, which was how Janse felt about most people who had any influence on his life. From his teachers during his school years to the thuggish corporals and the drill sergeants he served under during his national service days in the army. By the time he obtained a bursary to get into the University of the Free State to study commerce, most of his lecturers and professors had fitted that description, too.

Standing on the first rung of his career ladder, with the position of junior executive in the sales and marketing department of the government-run Maize Marketing Board, Janse loathed his superiors and his colleagues alike. They were dull men in grey suits and grey shoes who lived grey lives. Men who had succumbed to the semi-torpor existence of civil servants with guaranteed employment throughout their working lives. And guaranteed pensions beyond that.

After two uneventful and uninspiring years of an administrative grind, Janse started to recognise an opportunity that would soon put his career on a northward-bound trajectory.

The National Party, which ran its apartheid hegemony that permeated every aspect of society, had an obsessive attitude towards agriculture. Of course, this was hardly surprising because Afrikaners always have and always will feel a powerful affinity with the soil. Farmers - or boere as they referred to themselves - were the backbone of the National Party. So, all the various produce marketing boards were given extremely generous budgets to promote their harvests to consumers.

The reason for this was based on the premise that you couldn't have people eating rice and pasta when millions of hectares of land were being cultivated for maize. When good rains in the Western Cape resulted in a bumper crop of wheat, extra consumer demand for bread, pasta, cereals, and confectionery products had to be stimulated so that prices and profits didn't fall.

Having dealt with the Maize Marketing Board's advertising agency, Janse quickly realised that there was much money to make. All he needed to do was to pull the right strings with the right people. It all boiled down to ingratiating himself with those who would be grateful for the extra, under-the-table income that Janse could provide.

By the time he resigned, the foundations for Janse Promotions had been laid. And the next 20 years were spent building the business by getting to know more people of influence.

And Janse shone. He was, after all, a man of the soil himself – a Northern Cape Boere. He also understood the business, and he knew the consumers. He excelled in running a tight operation as he was also versed in cutting corners on expenses while bilking additional profits out of the budget of any project. Above all, despite his awkwardness in social gatherings, he knew how to entertain his clients through hunting trips.

Up until the demise of the apartheid system in the mid-1990s,

Janse had done very well in milking the system. He was also smart enough to realise that dramatic changes permeating every aspect of the country were inevitable. With the right Black partner, there was no reason his method of acquiring business had to change just because the regime running the country had changed. He just needed a smart, cunning black partner to front the company who was, like himself, not overly concerned about morality, integrity, and other bothersome traits. And in the gifted Mashele, he found the perfect choice.

The new organisation, Janse-Mashele, didn't need to solicit new business in an industry that was perennially overtraded. All the clients they needed came knocking on the company's door. Adopting an arrogance that would be the envy of the industry, Janse-Mashele also turned clients away if the budgets were not large enough to be plundered with impunity. The company also fired clients who insisted on a master-servant relationship that demanded too much of the staff's time and energy. Managing the workload was crucial for profitability; the less time spent on one client meant more billable time spent on other clients.

Not that the company cared about the welfare of the staff in any way. If people worked too hard and burned themselves out, a reason would be found to fire them before suitable replacements could be hired. Talent was just a commodity to be bought and then dumped when it was no longer of any value.

As he drove down to the expansive underground parking area in the Janse-Mashele building, Henk Janse could see a lone car parked in the furthest corner from his designated spot. He was the second of the company's 350 staff complement to arrive that morning. Being at the office early was another game he played to keep his employees on their toes. That other car belonged to the enigmatic Petrus Smit - the person Janse needed to speak to.

Janse walked into Smit's windowless office with a wry smile. It always amused him how his highest-paid and most trusted employee chose an office barely larger than a broom cupboard. A tiny space tucked away in the warren-like maze of corridors that constituted the company's financial department. 'Good morning, Petrus. What news have you got for me?'

'Morning, Henk', replied Smit, as he turned his burly 130 kg frame around from his computer screen to face his boss. 'I believe Macdonald had a busy night last night,' he stated matter-of-factly. 'I picked up that there was some activity in Pretoria. His people were out playing games.'

'Oh yes, he mentioned something to me yesterday.'

'Any news on that other issue?' Asked Janse.

'No, nothing at all. It seems the police still have nothing in the way of leads. The only theory they have right now is that it was probably some amateurs who got scared and shot him in panic.'

'Amateurs? They could well be right there', agreed Janse as the slightest hint of a smile trembled in the corners of his thin mouth.

SEVEN

"Top Government Official Poisoned by Criminal Syndicate!" screamed the banner headline in the online edition of *The Telegraph*. The story continued in an equally sensational style:

> "Late last night, a critically ill Mr. Lwazi Ndlovu, director general in the Department of Communications, was admitted to the Pretoria General Hospital in what appears to have been an attempt on his life through poisoning.
>
> "It is alleged that Mr Ndlovu, 44, had been targeted by one of the various crime syndicates operating within the several state-owned enterprises his department oversees. The avowed anti-corruption campaigner was known to be investigating several senior managers at these companies. And it has been revealed by sources that cannot be named at this point that his efforts were making life uncomfortable for those with much to hide, especially in awarding tenders.
>
> "At this stage, the chemical substance used to poison Mr Ndlovu remains unidentified, and investigators are waiting for the toxicology report, which may take several weeks.
>
> "On learning the news, the minister of communications, Ms Lerato Khumalo, issued a brief statement: "We were deeply shocked on hearing of this dastardly attempt on the director general's life.
>
> "Mr Ndlovu is a crusader against corruption, and we will continue to support his gallant attempt to clean up our government-owned companies of this cancer. The DG is

> *a splendid example of what a public servant should be: courageous, scrupulously honest and dedicated to serving South African citizens.*
>
> *"Our thoughts are with him and his family right now, and we are praying for Mr Ndlovu's speedy recovery."*

'Courageous, scrupulously honest and dedicated to fucking high-class hookers in five-star hotel suites at the South African taxpayer's expense,' laughed Mashele as he handed the newspaper over to Janse.

When both partners were in the office early, they invariably shared a pot of coffee while having a catch-up meeting. It was a routine that usually included checking any of the agency's work that appeared in the national dailies, be they advertisements, press releases or planted stories.

'One of your more imaginative stories, I take it,' commented Janse dryly as his narrow, piercing eyes began scanning the article.

'One of these days, I'll be nominated for a Pulitzer Prize for fiction.'

'Did the JM-Plus guys organise this for you?' asked Janse, referring to one of Janse-Mashele's less well-known subsidiaries.

"They organised the journos, but I organised the girl myself. The old honey trap still works a storm, especially if your dick rules your head.'

'A crusader against corruption?' scoffed Janse. 'That's a bit over the top, isn't it?'

'Oh, I don't know. It has a certain ring to it. The alliteration makes it more memorable to the man in the street. We could build the whole campaign around that.'

'So, what's the payback?'

'Well, to save his job and, no doubt, his marriage, he'll need to help us keep the Post Office account for another three years. We'll have to go through the usual tender process, but we'll write the terms and conditions ourselves, eliminating all the other players, so it's in the bag.'

'That's all well and good, but are you going to get them to increase the budget?'

'I'll make sure he does. We have that R50 million Post Office awareness campaign that has been on hold for the last six months. That can kick in immediately. And let's see what else he can put on the table.'

'Well, push him,' said Janse.

'Just a small matter of remunerating a couple of journos and a sub-editor,' said Mashele. Two fifty k each.'

'Three-quarters of a million rand to kill one fokken story? Do these journos think we're fokken mugs or something?' blasted Janse.

'Killing the story will add at least fifty million to our billing, so what's the big deal?'

'Fokken outrageous crooks, these old hacks,' muttered Janse as he walked out of Mashele's office. 'I'll get Smit onto it.'

EIGHT

Smit closed his laptop and pushed his chair back from his desk before stretching his almost two-metre frame and yawning loudly. He had been working at his desk for ten hours without a break. But – as was evident from the worn-out numerals on the keyboard of his desk calculator – he was used to arduous work.

Smit's diligence and uncanny eye for minutia were two of the few personal qualities that people working at Janse-Mashele readily acknowledged. They were less respectful when describing Smit's other stand-out characteristics, like his obsessively secretive nature and the social awkwardness that would have him blush bright crimson to his hairline if anyone engaged him in any pleasantries.

He was an unfriendly, enigmatic character to his colleagues who barely engaged with anyone. Not a smile. Not a greeting. Not a kindly word. Some of his co-workers had even suggested that he suffered from Asperger's Syndrome. But his sycophantic laughter at Henk Janse's sarcastic jokes put paid to that suggestion. More often than not, the only time he addressed the staff in the finance department was when he discovered some infraction - a misplaced decimal point, a misclassified expense, or an imperfect calculation on a spreadsheet.

After spotting an oversight, Smit would pounce on his hapless victim. Then, in a cold, sneering voice, calculated to be heard by most people working in the department, he would point out that such ineptness would never be tolerated before adding that one would be fired regardless of the labour laws that had prohibited such arbitrary action.

Other than Henk Janse, few were aware of Smit's dark past. On completing an unremarkable school career, followed by a college accountancy course, Smit, like most young Afrikaner men of the time, found sheltered employment as a civil servant. After an initial training course, he was assigned to the finance department at the Ministry of Defence. It hadn't been a particularly exciting or interesting career choice. It was just a solid, steady nine-till-five job in which Smit ensured that the minuscule portion of the defence budget he was responsible for was accountable and put to its intended use.

Although considered dull and taciturn by his colleagues, Smit began to be held in some esteem by his seniors. It was a reputation he had earned through his diligence in performing every task given to him unfailingly and for never questioning the reasons for doing them. Smit would never complain if the task demanded longer than eight hours daily. Or if it necessitated a tedious, uncomfortable journey to some fly-infested covert military camp deep in the African bush along the country's borders.

After several years of steadily toeing the line, Smit had worked his way up to middle management before being given the opportunity to transform his life.

In the late 1980s, due to the increasing internal and external political and economic pressure that the apartheid government was facing, it formed a highly classified organisation called the Civil Cooperation Bureau.

As a government department, the CCB sounded innocuous enough. The very mention of its name conjured up scenes of well-mannered civil servants obliging the citizenry with whatever bureaucracy that was required. The cynical reality, however, was that the Civil Cooperation Bureau was anything but civil.

Comprising ex-special forces and security police personnel, these were the renegades and the mavericks who found it difficult to conform to the rigid discipline of the military. So, they became useful in other ways: assassinations through shootings, stabbings, beatings and bogus burglaries to plant incriminating evidence were grist to the mill for the CCB.

But now and again, the most warped operatives prided themselves on being more creative in their homicidal pursuits. Like emptying a bottle of a cholera bacterium into the primary water source for an MK training camp in some neighbouring country. Sending a letter bomb to an exiled dissident. Forcing a delinquent journalist to drink copious amounts of alcohol before sending him on his way in a car that had its accelerator wedged to the floor. Or - as was a much-publicised case at the time - the hanging of a baboon foetus from a tree in the garden of Archbishop Desmond Tutu's official residence in Cape Town. It was an act of supreme stupidity done in the outrageous hope that the rebellious cleric would somehow become bewitched and alter his meddling ways.

Being part of this secret organisation significantly boosted Smit's meagre self-esteem. As an organisation of hit squads that operated in small cells spread throughout the country and in neighbouring states, it was self-funded through criminal enterprises that ranged from bank robberies to fraud to protection rackets for nightclubs and bars in the larger inner-city areas. Smit's job at the CCB was to handle the finances for Sector Six, the division responsible for operations within the borders of South Africa.

Like some venomous spider's long, spindly legs, the CCB comprised eight operational sectors. And each spun its murderous web in the shadows where dissident forces gathered. Most of these locations were in neighbouring countries such as Mozambique, Zimbabwe, Botswana, Lesotho and Swaziland. But they were also found further afield in countries such as Zambia, Tanzania and Angola. And because anti-apartheid activists were working throughout Western Europe, and especially in the United Kingdom, deep-cover CCB operatives attempted a variety of nefarious ways to discredit them.

For Sector Six, Smit was the guardian of all the share transfer certificates for the intricate network of front companies bought to provide cover. One of those companies was a small, little-known PR and advertising agency called Janse Promotions.

By the late 1980s, the CCB was exposed in the media by a small group of courageous investigative journalists, and the organisation was hastily disbanded. This came as a cataclysmic shock to Smit as he found himself jobless for the first time. Putting him in a more severe predicament was that his prospects of gaining new employment were severely compromised due to the years he had spent running the finances of the largest sector of the CCB organisation, which could never be revealed in his resume. Furthermore, the securocrats who had previously sat on the executive level of the CCB - as well as the politicians who patted them on the back every time an enemy of the state was eliminated – quickly went to ground, and all links to the organisation were strenuously denied. So, Smit was hardly able to request a reference.

Other than being unemployed, he was also unemployable. When Janse made Smit an offer to come and work for his company, it was a lifeline for a desperate man. It was also an act that immediately cemented Smit's unquestioning loyalty to Janse for life. Of benefit to Janse was that Smit also possessed some confidential CCB files regarding indiscretions made by certain captains of South African industry. Material based on those who had kept mistresses, or who enjoyed the company of rent boys, or had developed pharmaceutical habits, and so on.

Then there was the biggest prize for Janse: Smit's ready source of ex-operatives who were willing enough, and by now impoverished enough, to do anything asked of them for modest remuneration. If someone needed a little persuasion to conform to Janse's way of thinking on any particular issue, then the means to achieve that had now been secured. If Janse needed tabs to be kept on any specific person – who he was talking to, what he was saying on the phone, what and where he had salted away far from the prying eyes of the revenue services – the means were now at his disposal. And if Janse needed someone eliminated, it could also be arranged.

To help legitimise Smit's covert network, Janse started a new company called J-Plus. Later, when Mashele joined the company, the name was changed to JM-Plus. It was a small and little-known PR subsidiary. The company was staffed by a team of ageing ex-newspaper men who had worked for the publications that supported the apartheid regime. Having been caught on the wrong side of history, they were unemployable in the mainstream media. So, just like the ex-CCB operatives, they were immensely grateful to Janse and Smit for their livelihood. And they were always willing to do what was asked of them to create disinformation, damage reputations, and assassinate characters.

Through this private network of unnamed, unseen, shadowy operatives, who would never be hampered by unnecessary traits such as compassion, morality, or honesty, Smit had given Janse the means to rewrite the rules of the game.

NINE

As Mashele walked into the private hospital room, the massive bouquet he carried in both arms impressed the usually contemptuous Ndlovu.

'Lwazi, my brother, how the hell are you?'

Ndlovu made a feeble attempt to sit up in his bed. 'Hey, Mac, good to see you, my friend.'

Mashele tossed the flowers onto the bottom of the bed before embracing Ndlovu gently.

'So Lwazi, what the hell happened?'

'Oh, man. Where do I start?'

'Start at the beginning.'

'Okay, but please not a word of this to a living soul.'

Mashele held his hand over his heart. 'You don't have to tell me that.'

'No, of course not. Anyway, I had a meeting with this lady . . .'

'And don't tell me,' Interrupted Mashele. 'She turned out not to be a lady at all?'

Ndlovu shook his head. 'No, she was a bitch. She drugged me. Dropped something into my drink, and while I was out cold, she stole my wallet, watch, and stuff. Thank God she didn't steal my briefcase as I had a lot of sensitive papers in there.'

'Who was she?'

Ndlovu looked embarrassed. 'She was some woman I had met on some dating website. You know, those websites for people looking for affairs.'

'Jesus, Lwazi. Why didn't you get yourself a hooker?'

'She was an escort. Beautiful too. She started texting messages about us getting together, and, well, I booked a room at the Sheraton, and then the bitch almost killed me. How did you get involved in all this?

'When you were taken to the emergency room, a couple of reporters were sniffing around, and when they sussed out who you were, they thought they'd hit the Jackspot. So, they contacted one of my people to strike a deal to bury the story. Obviously, we paid them off.'

'Hell, Mac, I don't know how to thank you.'

Mashele smiled. 'Oh, I do.'

'Yes. I suppose the Post Office budget should take care of that.'

'That will pay for getting you off the hook. Then there's the story we put out there about you being drugged by a crime syndicate.'

'That was good.'

'Thank you. That was my idea.'

'Still got that magic touch, hey Mac. Even my wife was impressed with me after reading that story.'

Mashele laughed. 'See what I can do for you. She wouldn't have been so impressed had we not stepped in, would she now?'

'So, let me approve that R50 million budget for that Post Office campaign you presented a while back. That should take care of things.'

'Yes. But I also thought that as the SABC is under your wing, we could do some work for them. A bit of rebranding, maybe?'

'Well, some radio channels could do with a revamp.'

'And the TV channels?'

'Okay, but just one channel, though. I can't have you guys hogging all the work. You're going to piss off your competitors, and eventually, the trouble they'll cause will end up with fingers pointing at me. I've told you this before, Mac: get too greedy, and people will make mischief for you and me.'

'Let me worry about that,' replied Mashele. 'You just worry about getting 100% healthy so you can get out of this place and get back to work so that you can approve all of our costs.'

TEN

Mashele walked into Janse's office for the usual morning conference and found his partner irritated and sullen.

'What is it with you that you must be so flash with money?', barked Janse as he stood before the window watching the staff arriving at work three stories beneath him. 'Was that a new Ferrari I saw you driving into work this morning?'

Mashele was taken aback by the sudden condemnation. 'What's bugging you?' he asked defensively.

'Your bloody flamboyant ways of spending our hard-earned money' was Janse's curt reply.

'That's the difference between you mulungus and we darkies', replied Mashele as he composed himself. 'We like to celebrate our wealth...'

'Fokken showing off is more like it.'

'Yes, it is showing off. We like showing it off. You drive the top-of-the-range AMG Mercedes, and what do you do? You have the AMG letters taken off the car. Everyone who knows anything about cars can see the four exhausts, and they'll know it's an AMG. So what's the point of that?'

'The point is that you don't want to show off your wealth to clients. You don't need to advertise your success. You don't want them to think that you're doing so well. They get ideas that their money is paying for your Ferraris while they're driving around in Toyotas. They start to think that we're charging them too much.'

'Bullshit. Black people respect people who have succeeded in life. They're not jealous or resentful. They like to see people succeed. And the measure of that success is material goods, like Ferraris, Bentleys, and even AMG Mercs. Besides, we have something far more important to discuss than me buying a Ferrari.'

Janse grunted a half-hearted agreement. 'So what's on the agenda?'

'A new client in the form of the Department of Correctional Services. They'll call for ad agencies to pitch for a big new awareness campaign.'

'Why?' asked Janse, perplexed, 'Are they looking to recruit new inmates.' He chuckled at his rare but feeble attempt at making a joke.

'It looks like the minister is losing his grip. He's way behind on most of his deliverables. The media are on to him like a pack of hyenas, and he's getting his arse kicked in the cabinet. He's worried he could be out of a job the next time the president has a reshuffle.'

'So he thinks that some ad campaign will help him?'

'He doesn't think it'll help; he's convinced it will help because I did the convincing. I had dinner with him last night. I may add that he told me about the problems he's facing, all because of his incompetence and laziness.

Janse sat back in his chair, warming up to his partner's latest sales exploit. 'So what exactly did you sell him?'

'That we do a big campaign based on his department's success. The new prisons being built, the amount of prisoners being reformed, the prison gangs being broken up, all that kind of stuff.'

'Is any of this true?' asked Janse.

'Of course not, we just need to be creative with the issues', said Mashele with a smile. 'I also told the minister that we must do lots of PR to build his personal profile. Hell, in a few months, he'll have his name on the presidential honours list for services to the nation. Either way, it'll help build up his power base for a while. And help us to build up our bank balance.'

'How much are we talking about?'

'I've convinced him that we need fifty million for the rest of this year and double that over the next fiscal as a maintenance campaign.'

Janse smiled. The thought of another fifty million rand to this year's balance sheet would look good. And the profit margin – especially the unofficial profit margin – would look even better. 'But surely, as a government account, we'll have to go through the tender process and pitch for the business against other agencies?'

'Yes, but I told the minister we could help his procurement people write the tender's terms and conditions. You know, the usual stuff: It must be an agency of a particular size, billing-wise. It must have a high percentage of local ownership and broad-based black economic empowerment credentials. I'll get Joe Robinson to work things out so that we'll win the pitch before it even happens.'

'Just don't tell Joe too much. He's too cynical for his own good at times.'

'I'm always discreet', replied Mashele as he gulped down his coffee and got up to leave.

ELEVEN

As he settled into his new job at Janse-Mashele, Daniel felt his confidence growing each day. He loved the casual, non-conformist nature that typified the industry - especially the irreverence of the arty types that populated the creative department. Young people dressed uniformly in torn jeans and t-shirts who swore incessantly and argued passionately for their work. And they were led by what Daniel considered to be highly strung and opinionated creative directors who built their well-remunerated careers on their ability to win industry awards. It was an all-or-nothing attitude driven by high-octane egos.

Review meetings – at which creative work would be evaluated before being presented to the clients – often erupted into loud, ill-mannered mayhem. People would scream insults. Layouts would be ripped up in fits of anger. Egos would be bruised.
And, as always, Old Joe would be found at the epicentre of the argument, questioning some art director's choice of fonts for a headline. Or criticising a copywriter's proposed tagline. Daniel suspected that Old Joe wasn't too bothered about the subtle nuances of graphic design. It was more of a case of being provocative because he loved the cut and thrust of the reviews; the louder and more aggressive, the better, as far as Joe was concerned.

But Daniel also quickly gained the respect of his colleagues, especially when he stood up to Joe and sided with the younger creative people. He also caught the eye of several young female art directors and designers.

That morning, a large team had been summoned to a meeting room to discuss a new client. Present were creative people, client service executives, media planners, production people, and administrators who trafficked the work through all the different departments. There was a sense of anticipation in the air as this new client's identity had been kept firmly under wraps.

With such a large contingent of people, the residue of half-eaten snacks, breakfast pastries, muffins and an assortment of coffee mugs quickly transformed the table into a clutter of paper and cardboard. Excited voices spoke over each other as people took their seats. Joe entered the room and sat at his usual spot, at the head of the table, next to the flip chart.

'So, Joe, what shit are you briefing us on today?' asked a young copywriter who relished goading Joe into a robust debate on any topic under the sun.

'Good morning, Sipiwe, replied Joe with a broad grin. 'And good morning to the rest of you juvenile rabble that purports to be a creative department.' Joe's caustic humour was immediately countered with a barrage of good-natured jeers and insults.

Looking at the mess on the table, Joe continued his provocative style. 'Did your mommies pack nice snacks for you today? Oh, that's sweet. Then are you little kiddie-winkies going to have a little zizz after playtime?'

'Fuck off back to the old age home, you rancid old wanker.' shouted a dreadlocked art director, much to everyone's amusement.

'Jesus Christ, Mpho, hasn't the health department condemned that mop on the top of your head yet? Rats are breeding in that thing. Christ, you're a one-person bubonic plague distribution mechanism.'

As the raucous laughter continued, the door opened, and Macdonald Mashele swept into the room like a performer taking the stage. 'Well, this is just what I like to see in our morning briefings', said Mashele. 'People enjoying themselves. And people who are glad to be here. I firmly believe that happy employees make for productive employees. And that pleases me no end.'

As people settled down, Joe turned to his boss. 'Well, Mr Mashele, sir. To what do we owe the auspicious occasion of your presence in a new client briefing?'

'Joe, Joe, please', protested Mashele. 'You make me feel like I'm stuck in some ivory tower. You know I've always been a man of the people.'

As his eyes quickly darted around the table, Mashele quickly spotted an unfamiliar face. 'Ah, and you must be Daniel?' asked Mashele. 'Joe's new right-hand man?'

'Yes', replied Daniel diffidently.

'Let me introduce myself. My name's Macdonald Mashele, but everyone calls me Mac, everyone other than Joe, who pretends to be obsequious towards me. He likes to take the piss, does our Joe.'

'Hi Mac', replied Daniel. 'It's good meeting you.'

'Likewise,' replied Mashele as he enthusiastically shook Daniel's outreached hand. 'You know Daniel, you can learn lots of good stuff from Joe. But there's also a lot of shit stuff you need to ignore', said Mac, much to everyone's amusement, including Joe's.

Mashele clapped his hands to get everyone's attention. 'Right, you lot, let's get down to business—or new business, to be more accurate. And, people, it's an exciting piece of new business. Something no agency has ever handled before, I may add. So, the creative opportunities will be immense.'

Mashele could sense the excitement building in the room, especially amongst the creative staff: the designers, art directors and copywriters. 'So, with a budget of more than R50 million, we need to promote all the great work being done by the South African Department of Correctional Services.'

Joe, who could barely contain his disbelief, was first to speak: 'Are you serious, Mac? It's not April Fool's Day, is it?'

'Yes Joe, I'm deadly serious', said Mashele, who expected a lot of cynical flak from his head of strategy.

'But why does the Department of Correctional Services want to advertise? Are they looking for new customers or something?'

'The Department does crucial work. And it isn't just locking up crooks. The campaign I'm visualizing will be about incredible human-interest stories. Stories of hardened criminals – murderers, rapists, hijackers, robbers - that have had their lives transformed so that they have become useful members of society.'

Turning towards the creative guys, Mashele – the spin master – continued with an infectious zeal. 'Guys, think of the TV commercials you can make. Please consider the awards you can enter because that's what I want you to do. Win awards with a series of TV commercials that can be potent mini documentaries. Hey Mpho, can't you see it in your mind's eye? A moody, grainy, black-and-white footage of some guy – some thug – with arms covered in tattoos – breaking down in tears as he recounts the pain and suffering he has caused to innocent people. Can you see it, Mpho?'

'Can you see it, Sipiwe? Brad? Jane? Can you guys see what I'm seeing? Prisoners are begging for forgiveness from their victims. Prisoners are turning their lives around. Prisoners are getting another shot at life - a normal life.'

By now, everyone in the room was enthralled by Mashele's vision. This was a man who knew all the hot buttons to press. He also understood what motivated creative people working in ad agencies like Janse-Mashele: big-budget TV work and creative freedom to chase the elusive advertising awards that could establish careers and double salaries overnight.

Even Joe was astonished. Not by the thought of creating award-winning work for some incongruous client but by Mashele's extraordinary skill in manipulating a roomful of intelligent, educated people who should have known better. Joe thought that Mashele had, in a few short minutes, created an atmosphere in the room that surpassed enthusiasm - it was more like religious fervour!

'So, can I count on you guys to get us onto the stage at Cannes next year? ... Can I rely on you guys for the Grand Prix at the Loerie Awards? ... Can I rely on you guys for gold at the New York Festival? And a gold medal at the D and AD awards in London. Well, can I?'

Every question Mashele asked was answered with a resounding 'YES' that got louder and louder until it became a rhythmic chant. In Joe's mind, it was a bizarre, excessive display of teamwork better suited to a rugby team psyching themselves up for an especially tough fixture than a team of office workers about to start a new project.

'Now, guys', shouted Mashele over the euphoria. 'We need to get ourselves organised. Joe and Daniel will lead the process by researching and finding the insights for the communications strategy that will allow you creative guys to get the creative juices flowing.

'For you media planning guys, we're looking at an overall budget of fifty bar, so think about ten bar spent on production and the rest on media. And as I said, this must be heavy TV and radio because we must have maximum emotion for this campaign.

'And you traffic ladies, I want some serious arse-kicking from you so that we are ready long before deadlines. No last-minute panics . . . Okay? Let's get to it, guys, and review some ideas by next week. We need to move on this ASAP!' Then, as quickly as Mashele was up from his seat, he was out of the room.

Joe turned to Daniel and said: 'So old son, looks like we must send you to the clink for a short stretch. That should get you to behave.'

TWELVE

As soon as the music track accompanying the opening title sequence reached its giddy crescendo, the TV show cut to the opening shot of a young, beautiful black woman standing in front of ornate wrought iron gates that led to an opulent estate.

With a beaming smile, she addressed her audience: 'Good evening and welcome to this week's episode of . . . From Rags to Riches. This series showcases the lifestyles of some of South Africa's most successful individuals. The men and women who have pulled themselves out of the morass of poverty to reach great success through hard work, dedication, and talent . . . From Rags to Riches is the series that serves to inspire us all!

'Tonight, we feature a man renowned for his remarkable advertising, PR, and communication achievements. His expertise has greatly benefited many of the top South African consumer brands, as well as several government departments and state-owned enterprises. That man is Mr Macdonald Mashele.'

The on-screen image cut to a photograph of a smiling Mashele.

Cutting back to the young woman, she continued her dialogue. 'Join me, Evelyn Bokang, inside Mr Mashele's sumptuous home to discover the secrets of his incredible success.'

The scene then cuts to a wide establishing shot of Mashele and Evelyn sitting on oversized couches in a large formal lounge before cutting to a close-up of Evelyn. 'First of all, Mr Mashele, thank you so much for allowing us into your beautiful home and your life.'

'You're very welcome, Evelyn. It's a pleasure to have you here', replied Mashele graciously.

The rest of the programme featured Mashele's palatial home full of his extravagant possessions: his art collection, his fleet of Italian and German supercars, his conservatory overflowing with rare orchids. His climate-controlled wine cellar fully stocked with rare Cape, Bordeaux, and Champagne vintages. The industrial-sized kitchen full of every appliance imaginable.

The cameras then explored other parts of the house with lingering, slow panning shots of bathrooms fitted with gold-plated taps, heated toilet seats and Louis the XIV reproduction furniture.

And the ultimate in Mashele's arsenal of brag factors: his dining room that featured the most expensive wallpaper in the world. At $23,000 a square metre, this outrageous folly had been an idea that Mashele had plagiarised from a magazine article about some Russian billionaire oligarch who boasted such décor at his London home. The thought of one square metre of his dining room wall costing the equivalent of an average family sedan had delighted Mashele.

The programme continued with Mashele's voice describing how the experience of growing up amid crushing poverty had inspired him to seek a better life through educating himself—Mashele's dialogue, juxtaposed with visuals of his unadulterated extravagance, made for spellbinding television.

Mashele, a Harley Street specialist in spin-doctoring, then completed his life story by recounting his struggle credentials. In such situations, he was always purposefully vague and spouting his ready-made fiction about the need to maintain discretion. Of course, this was no more than a fallacy that made his activism sound far more significant than it had been.

As one would expect, no mention was made of his Swaziland wholesale smuggling operation. Neither was there a word concerning his successful career as a drug peddler to students.

With his immense talent for self-promotion, Mashele would soon mobilise an army of blog writers to create the necessary hype about his success. While the memory of this episode of *From Rags to Riches* remained fresh in peoples' minds, his public relations people would be badgering newspaper editors and radio producers to keep Mashele's success story top of mind. Column inches in newspapers would be procured, as would airtime nationwide on radio stations. With Mashele's well-oiled machine jumping into action, it would take no more than a couple of days to get the whole country talking about his success.

But then, as the programme ended, one viewer was stunned into silence about the whole affair. As the end titles rolled up on the screen, Henk Janse gripped the top of his whisky tumbler so hard that the glass shattered, inflicting a lacerated thumb. But his smouldering rage was such that he didn't register any pain or notice the blood dripping onto the carpet.

THIRTEEN

As was his nightly routine, Joe pulled into the car park of his local bar, *'The Fiddler'*, to relax with a few beers after work. Having no one to go home to, other than a cat that was far too aloof to be considered a companion, Joe enjoyed the convivial atmosphere and the friendly bar staff. Besides, the food was greatly more edible than Joe's paltry efforts in the kitchen.

'Good evening, Gordon, me old mate', said Joe as he parked himself on his usual stool.

'Ah, good evening, Mr Joe', replied the barman as he grabbed a glass and filled it with Joe's favourite draught. 'And how are you tonight, Mr Robinson?'

'Same as always, Gordon, same as always. But what's the bloody use of complaining, hey? Doesn't get you anywhere, does it?' It was the same banter every night, but Gordon still chuckled politely.

'There you go, sir', said Gordon as he handed over the beer. 'That should make life a bit more palatable.

'Cheers, Gordon, just what I need.' He quaffed down half of the beer in two gulps. 'May as well pour another one, Gordon', he said as he swallowed another big mouthful.

'There was a young lady here yesterday who was asking for you.'

'Really?'

'Yes, a youngish black lady. She said she knew you through work . . . Or something along those lines.'

Joe looked baffled. It wasn't every day that a youngish black lady was enquiring after him. 'Really, what did she look like?'

'Oh, around mid-twenties, slim, well-dressed, well-spoken, and attractive, she asked me to give you her card with her number. I have it here somewhere,' Gordon turned and started scratching behind the bar. 'Here it is,' he said as he handed it over.

Joe examined the card: *Judith Maponya LLB, Candidate Attorney. Barker Ngubane: Attorneys at Law.* 'Hell, I don't know any lawyers, and I've never heard of Barker Ngubane.'

'She said to get you to call her as soon as I gave you her card,' added Gordon.

Joe picked up his cell phone and was about to dial the mobile number listed amongst the contact details on the back of the card when Gordon handed him the cordless landline phone instead. 'She asked me to get you to use this instead of your cell phone,' said Gordon with a distinct *don't-ask-me* shrug of the shoulders.

Utterly baffled, Joe dialled the lady's number. He smiled as he realised that Gordon, watching his every move, was just as curious as he was. A tired female voice answered by the third ring: 'Hello, Judith Maponya speaking.'

'Hello Judith,' replied Joe in a perky voice he usually reserved for those times when he flirted with women. 'It's Joe Robinson speaking; I believe you've been . . .'

Before he could even finish his first sentence, Judith interrupted him in excitement. 'Oh Joe, thank you so much for calling me. I appreciate it. I know you don't know me, but I need to talk to you about something very important.'

'Oh, I see from your card that you're a lawyer. Did some distant old aunt in Australia die and leave me her estate?'

Ignoring his feeble attempt at humour, Judith continued: 'I

need to speak to you urgently. I can't talk on your phone. I will come and see you. I take it you're at the bar. Can you wait for me? It'll take me about twenty minutes to get there.'

'Okay,' replied Joe guardedly. 'If you know where I drink, surely you know where I work?'

'Yes, Janse-Mashele. But I can't call you or see you there.'

'Why all the cloak and dagger stuff?'

'Look, Joe, I'm sorry, but it has to be this way. When I see you, I'll explain everything.'

'Okay', said Joe. 'See you in twenty minutes then,' he replaced the phone on its cradle and turned to Gordon. 'While I'm waiting, better have another beer, me old mate.'

It was more like thirty minutes by the time a harassed-looking young woman entered the bar and made her way to Joe. 'Hi, I'm sorry I'm a bit late, she muttered breathlessly. 'I had to take a round-about way to ensure I wasn't followed,' she continued.

As she took her jacket off, Joe saw she was an attractive young woman in her mid-twenties, as Gordon had guessed. Although smartly but conservatively dressed, Joe could also see that Judith was no slave to designer labels.

'Followed? Jesus Christ, what is going on here? I mean, you won't speak to me over the phone . . . '

'Please, can we go and sit down somewhere quiet,' countered Judith with a firm but not unkind sense of authority that belied her young age. Much to Gordon's disappointment, they moved to an alcove as far away from earshot as possible.

As they sat down, Judith lost no time explaining her situation: 'Okay, my name is Judith Maponya. My brother was Jabu Maponya. He worked with you at Janse-Mashele?'

'My God, of course . . . Poor Jabu . . . Oh, Judith, I don't know what to say. It was a terrible thing that happened to Jabu. Life's just far too cheap for these bastards who will kill someone for a car...'

'Jabu's death wasn't a hijacking,' interrupted Judith. It was plain murder... A professional hit made to look like a hijacking.'

Joe almost choked on his beer. 'You can't know that Judith', he stammered, 'I mean, you can't know that for certain.'

'Oh, but I can, Joe. Jabu told me many things about Janse-Mashele that could put certain people away for a long time.

She took a deep breath to calm herself. 'Jabu had only worked at Janse-Mashele briefly when he discovered that some senior management people were involved in fraud. Apparently, they were defrauding everyone: clients, shareholders, the government, the revenue service – everyone.'

'That's a hell of a serious accusation, Judith.'

'Anyway, over a few weeks, Jabu collected a shoebox full of documents – copies of invoices, receipts, bank statements, spreadsheets, and all that kind of financial stuff. He called it his insurance policy.'

'Okay,' said Joe cagily on hearing this hard evidence.

'Then Jabu did some stupid things. He started to steal money from the company. He opened a false bank account and began to channel Janse-Mashele's money into that account.'

'Good God.'

'I told him, pleaded with him to stop it. I told him that it was so wrong. But he wouldn't stop. I think he became addicted to the money and the thrill of stealing it. He believed that because the management of that damn company was a pack of thieves, it wasn't stealing in the true sense of the word. He was taking money that they had stolen anyhow.'

'Did he tell you how Janse-Mashele was stealing this money?'

'Yes, he came across invoices for some ads that the company ran overseas on behalf of the government. I think it was something to do with the trying to attract foreign investment into the country.'

'Yes, TISA, Trade and Investment South Africa, we did a campaign for the Department of Trade and Industry', explained Joe. 'Know it well, worked on it myself.'

'Well, according to Jabu, someone was managing the finances on the client side, and they were approving payments for ads that should have been placed in foreign newspapers and magazines. The thing was that those ads never appeared in any publications.'

'That's out-and-out fraud', said Joe with a sigh. 'Christ, that campaign had a R60 million budget.'

'Jabu said that the closer he investigated it, the more fraud he discovered. So, he started making copies of invoices he knew to be fraudulent. Then, as I said, he started to steal money for himself.'

'Oh Jabu, you bloody fool', whispered Joe sadly.

'You must understand Joe, Jabu, and I were not raised like that. Our parents were God-fearing, churchgoing, respectable people. They sacrificed so much so that Jabu and I had a decent education, universities, and all that.

'Anyway, I pleaded with him to stop stealing this money . . . I told him it would be a matter of time before they found out. Then he'd lose his job and his reputation. But he believed he had so much information about their crimes that they wouldn't dare do anything to him.'

'The insurance policy?'

'Yes, that shoebox with all those papers', agreed Judith. 'Jabu said that if anyone troubled him, he could negotiate his way out of it.' The tears started to well up in Judith's eyes. 'Do you know, Joe, one of the last things that Jabu told me was that he was bulletproof.'

'Oh my God.'

She picked up a napkin to wipe away the tears streaming down her face, 'Well, he wasn't bulletproof, was he? He couldn't stop that bullet that ripped through his head.'

Joe took a big gulp of his beer. 'Okay, I heard rumours that Jabu was having some trouble with the company. There was nothing concrete, you understand, just rumours. But if someone works in the finance department of a company and gets into some trouble, it's natural to assume they've got their fingers in the till . . . But, Judith, dear, that doesn't prove that it was an intentional murder. Or prove that anyone at Janse-Mashele had anything to do with it . . .'

'The day before he was murdered, Jabu told me that they'd found out about him stealing. That someone called Smit had threatened him.'

'Oh God, yes, it would be Smit.'

'This Smit guy told Jabu that he would be in big trouble if he didn't repay all the money he had taken. That's when Jabu told him about all those invoices in the shoebox and threatened to expose all the fraud.'

Joe was silent for a few seconds, his mind preoccupied with the thought of Smit – all two metres of him – looming over Jabu and uttering threats in his shrill, effeminate voice.

'I have a question for you', asked Joe, 'Why me? Why are you telling me all this?'

'Jabu mentioned you. I remember him telling me that you were the only senior person in the company who stood up to the management. He liked and trusted you. He also said you were the only one that had any integrity.'

Joe was flattered. 'Okay. But I still don't understand why you're talking to me. You should be talking to the police or the newspapers.'

'There are certain high-ranking police officers that Janse and Mashele have in their pockets. It's the same with the National Prosecution Authority and the Department of Justice. They also have half of the newspapers in this country at their beck and call. And that's my big problem, Joe... I don't know which half is straight and which half is on Janse-Mashele's payroll.'

'Oh Jesus', groaned Joe.

'I work in a law firm, so I know how these things work. If an honest person lays a complaint using all the right channels against bad guys like these people, I can assure you that ninety-nine times out of a hundred, no action will be taken. Nothing. Zilch.'

Joe took another swig of his beer.

'Even in the rare cases when charges are laid, the police case dockets just disappear. It happens time and time again. It just seems that everybody has a price. And right now, here in South Africa, the going rate is as cheap as hell.'

They both sat in silence for a few seconds.

'I just don't know who to turn to, Joe. There's something else; maybe I'm paranoid, but I feel I am always being watched. That my phone calls are being listened to. And that I'm being followed. That's why I took the long route here tonight.'

'Look', said Joe. 'From knowing what I know about certain people in Janse-Mashele, especially our friend Smit, I wouldn't be surprised if they had some private eye following you or tapping your phone or something. They have some subsidiary that hardly anyone knows anything about. It's called JM-Plus, and it's like a dirty tricks department. I've heard rumours that they make use of private detectives, and I have no doubt they're evil bastards. So, you must be careful. The other thing is Jabu's insurance policy. Do you know if they found it?

'No, they couldn't have. Jabu gave it to me for safekeeping. I have it in the strong room at the law firm where I work. It's hidden amongst a mountain of files, so it's safe.'

'Clever girl. Now we need to think carefully about how to bring these bastards to book.'

FOURTEEN

Email to All Staff

From: The Office of Macdonald Mashele

Subject: The tragic death of Jabu Maponya

My dear colleagues and friends,

The Maponya family has just informed me that the funeral for our late colleague and friend, Jabu, will be held at Westpark Cemetery in Melville this coming Saturday at 11:00 am.

Even though Jabu was relatively new to the company, he was still a highly valued member of the Janse-Mashele family, as are you all. He was also a well-liked young man who was diligent in his work and charming towards everyone who met him.
We will, therefore, celebrate Jabu's life and mourn his passing with a wake at the company bar on Friday night, starting at 4 pm. And I expect that you will all show up.

I also appeal to as many of you as possible to attend Jabu's funeral for the sake of Jabu's family and friends, who must have been traumatised by his tragic and senseless death. Your attendance will comfort them as it demonstrates that Jabu was a popular and respected individual by his colleagues.

So, let's give Jabu the send-off he deserves on Friday night, and please all attend his funeral on Saturday morning.
As I am sure you will all approve, Janse-Mashele will pick up the tab for the cost of the flowers for the funeral.

Warm regards,

Mac

FIFTEEN

'A few dahlias and a spray of fucking daffodils,' slurred Old Joe disdainfully as he read the email on his computer screen.

'Oh, I think it's a very decent thing for the company to do.' Replied Daniel as he carefully nursed his beer. Over his first few days at the company, he had already ascertained that keeping up with Old Joe in the end-of-the-day beer-swilling stakes was not an option. 'It shows that the company is caring and sincere', he continued.

'I agree with Daniel', said Debbie, who was not showing the same circumspection with her large glass of white wine. 'It's a nice gesture, and it helps the family out.'

'Oh yes', replied Joe in his most caustic tone, 'They cared a lot for Jabu. They cared a lot about the rumours that he was fiddling the books. And they were very sincere in getting rid of that slight problem.'

'Come off it, Joe', laughed Daniel. 'You're not telling me that Janse-Mashele had someone bumped off for having their fingers in the till.'

'Yes, Joe, for fuck sake', agreed Debbie as she blew her cigarette smoke through the open window. 'That's outrageous and beyond belief, even for you. And besides, you're only saying this because you're pissed from that long lunch you had.'

'Outrageous, yes. Unbelievable? Well, the jury in my mind is out on that one, my dear Debbie.'

'Besides, how do you know all this stuff?' asked Daniel.

'I know because people talk. And I have friends in the accounts department. Always befriend those who dole out the loot.'

Both Daniel and Debbie looked unconvinced.

'Look, it may be just a rumour', continued Joe. 'But the story is that Jabu had encountered some corruption or other, and he'd mentioned it to a couple of people. Then, he decided that if his bosses were stealing money, he'd get in on the act himself. It may be just a rumour, but as rumours go, it's plausible.'

Daniel chuckled, which antagonised Joe.

'The fact is, having your fingers in the till is not advisable at Janse-Mashele. The management here takes a dim view of anyone who tries to steal any money they've already stolen from our clients.'

'Committing fraud is one thing, but then having someone murdered, Christ, that's a bit extreme, don't you think?' asked Debbie.

'Well, Janse does have his fucking pit-bull Smit, who is pretty extreme at the best of times.'

'Who is Smit?' asked Daniel.

'That's the dark prince himself. He's the company Gollum who lives in a hole in the ground in the deepest, darkest recesses of this building.'

On seeing Daniel's mystified look, Joe's flippancy diminished: 'Smit is an enigmatic figure if ever there was one. He runs the finance department, where he bullies the rest of the bean counters. And he doesn't answer to anyone but Janse. I suppose you could call him Janse's right-hand man as he does all the big man's bidding.'

Joe took a long swig of his beer before continuing: 'Smit is also rumoured to run JM-Plus, a bunch of very dodgy PR people who get by through writing disinformation and getting the lies published in the press by bribing journalists. This is Janse's black ops department.'

'Smit also keeps a beady eye on every cent that goes through the entire group. That's why poor amateur thieves like Jabu don't stand a chance of getting away with having their fingers in the till. And that's because they're all being watched by a much more accomplished thief like Smit acting on behalf of the biggest thief of all, Janse.'

Joe paused to collect his thoughts and to finish the beer in the can. But after hearing footsteps in the corridor outside his office, Joe suddenly felt unnerved. The idea that Smit might be listening to him scared him to his core, so he quickly made light of the subject. 'Of course, it's unbelievable, you dickhead. It's all bullshit, just a product of my overly furtive imagination', he exclaimed loudly enough for his voice to carry. He paused for a moment to listen for any sound. But there was nothing but the distant hum of the rush hour traffic on the highway.

'Now pass me another beer, young man, and be prepared to learn a thing or two about the finer virtuosities of strategic planning', he said before burping loudly.

'Charming', said Debbie as she lit another cigarette and blew the smoke out the window.

'Furtive imagination indeed', whispered a visibly shaken Smit through his gritted teeth as he walked away from the passage leading to the strategy department.

SIXTEEN

The high, pale-yellow brick walls of the maximum-security prison were intimidating enough, even for someone like Daniel, who was never inclined to break any laws.

The institution had undergone an official name change with the demise of the apartheid regime. From the prosaic Pretoria Central Prison, it had officially become *Kgosi Mampuru II*. This name commemorated an African revolutionary leader of the Bapedi tribe who was hanged within the prison walls in the late 1800s. But for most people living in Pretoria, it was always called C-Max, which referred to the jail's maximum-security wing.

The fact that it was the country's only hanging prison for many decades - which went into extreme overdrive during the rebellious 1980s and early 90s - gave Kgosi Mampuru II an unnerving sense of eeriness.

Escorted by two uniformed senior Department of Correctional Services officials, Daniel's passage through to the inner sanctum of the prison – the high-security section that housed the most dangerous and disruptive long-term prisoners – was surprisingly easy. It was not the usually long-drawn-out affair that ordinary visitors had to undergo: the body searches, the pat downs, the electronic security wands, the sniffer dogs with noses sensitised for illicit drugs, the explosives trace detection devices and x-ray machines and metal detectors.

As he accompanied the two officials through a maze of endless corridors, each indistinguishable from the last one, Daniel's nasal passages were assaulted by the overpowering, pungent stench. It was an astringent combination of industrial-strength disinfectant and floor polish. Also, each door unlocked before them and locked again after them was accompanied by a deep steel-on-steel clanking and a heavy metallic echo reverberating around the walls of each section they passed through.

But Daniel's uneasiness was also matched by a growing sense of excitement. Here he was, working on the first major assignment of his budding career, thrown into the deep end, as Joe had insisted. But Joe had also done much to assist Daniel, such as pointing him in the right direction regarding the background desk research. Together, they pulled out the relevant statistics that dealt with prisoner rehabilitation, which were shockingly low figures. Correctional Services desperately needed correction because of wanton corruption, ineptitude, overcrowding and lack of resources. Not that it mattered, as Janse-Mashele could massage, manipulate, and spin any statistics into some thought-provoking, emotive narrative that appeared impressive to anyone who didn't interrogate them too closely.

Now, all that Daniel needed to do was conduct field trips to prisons with varying security classifications to get a clearer picture of the department's work. The people that Daniel dealt with were friendly and helpful. They were excited at the thought that their efforts in dealing with the prisoners would be depicted in the media in a positive light for a change. Of course, the fact that this exercise in bolstering their cause would come with a R50 million price tag had not been mentioned to any of them.

Before he could meet any prisoners, Daniel was subjected to a briefing from the senior wardens. They explained to him how he should behave. That he was not to talk to any prisoner, he came across in the passages. He could only speak to those inmates who had been selected for interviews. Four wardens would escort him throughout the visit. And he had to obey their every command, especially in the unlikely event of some disturbance or protest. If that occurred, Daniel would be ordered to sit tight and wait to be evacuated to a secure area by a crack team of specially trained officers armed with batons and electric shields.

Eventually, after a quick tour through one wing of the prison, Daniel ended up in a small interview room where he received another briefing. This time, one of the department's communication specialists spoke with little enthusiasm about the various rehabilitation courses offered to the men in its care. With a parrot-like tone, the official droned on about the *Victim/Offender Dialogue Programme* designed to break the cycle of crime. The *Healing through Art Programmes* were intended to bring some sense of tranquillity to inmates by exploring their latent creativity and, of course, all kinds of *Literacy and Post-School Education Programmes*.

After that, Daniel was finally allowed to quiz selected prisoners, who were well-versed in what must be said concerning all the official programmes that had already been mentioned. These were mainly Category C inmates who enjoyed the least privileges, such as far less family visits and phone calls.

Also, most of the stories the prisoners had to tell bore striking similarities: growing up in abject poverty in the townships. Being part of a dysfunctional family due to a dead or absent father; having little or no opportunity for a decent education; joining a gang; dabbling in drugs; being unemployed; having little or no prospects of ever being employed in a decent job; getting involved with petty crime; graduating to more serious crimes; acquiring a gun; getting caught by the police; being sent to jail. A wretched waste of a life.

Some prisoners were shy and distant, and Daniel found it tiresome to prise any meaningful information out of them.

Others were happy to chat, even though Daniel suspected they enjoyed a break from the usual grinding routine.

The one thing that struck Daniel was the ordinariness of all the inmates he met. Talking to men who had committed severe and, in many cases, violent crimes such as murder and rape, they were no different to your colleagues at work, the people you pass on the street, or the people you find standing next to you at the supermarket check-out.

Towards the end of the afternoon, Daniel was introduced to a tall, almost skeletal, heavily bearded man called Riaan du Plessis. A lifer serving time for multiple murders, kidnapping, grievous bodily harm, burglary, robbery and a litany of lesser crimes, Du Plessis had already served 22 years in C-Max.

From the moment he laid eyes on him, Daniel was intrigued by his demeanour. More than that, he took an immediate liking to the man. Du Plessis was humble and polite to the point of gentleness. He also possessed a sense of dignity that belied the fact that he had murdered several people in cold blood as an assassin employed by the security forces during the struggle. There was also an aura of calmness that emanated from the man. An inner peace became apparent when Daniel had to halt the interview several times as the small dictaphone he had brought kept pausing of its own accord.

'This place teaches you to be patient', Du Plessis said to Daniel. 'Everything slows down when you come to a place like this. And being locked up for twenty-three hours out of twenty-four, the days are long and the nights even longer.'

When Daniel had asked him about his rehabilitation, Du Plessis had been remarkably frank and candid: 'For the first few years in this place, I was a bitter man - a very bitter man. You see, unlike all my ex-bosses, the generals, the civil servants, and the politicians who ordered all the killings that I, and people like me, committed in the name of a ruthless, nasty political system, we were left to carry the can on our own. And what did they do? They ended up living comfortably on their big farms and mansions. Those bastards were living like millionaires. And knowing that they had got away with it made me a resentful and twisted man.'

Not trusting his defective recorder, Daniel scribbled notes as fast as his hand allowed.

'And something else that made me resentful was the brainwashing that my family and I had been subjected to about Africans. They convinced us that the blacks were inferior to us whites in every way. And oh, how we lapped it up. We even believed that the other whites living here in South Africa – the *uitlanders* and the *rooinek Engelse* - were also inferior to us Afrikaners. Then, slowly, I started to realise that all these negative feelings and resentment were eating me up inside like some big, cancerous tumour. It was consuming my life and would eventually kill me.'

'Do you think you'll be released someday?' asked Daniel.

'No, I don't think so. You see, there are guys like me in this place who, after serving twenty-five years of a life sentence, start thinking about getting out. They think about nothing but parole . . . or medical parole, and stuff like that. In a way, the rejections keep adding to the bitterness. So, as far as I'm concerned, I'm okay with them carrying me out of here in a pine box. It isn't as if I had a wife and children out there. Both my parents have died. I have a younger sister somewhere in Port Elizabeth. She wrote me off a long time ago. And a half-sister, Brenda, that I hardly know. He chuckled that was a big scandal in the Du Plessis family. My father, the devoted NG church parishioner and a lifelong apartheid devotee, had an affair with Brenda's black mother. But that's another story. So, no, I don't think I will ever be released. The best I can look forward to is a transfer to a low-security prison one day when I'm too old and too arthritic to jump the fence. It'll be nice to feel the sun's warmth on my face again.'

'So how did you come to terms with being locked up here for the rest of your life?'

'Look, I didn't have some miraculous, religious experience; I didn't wake up one morning thinking I had found God or anything like that. And I didn't find the Holy Ghost sitting on the end of my bed. I go to the chapel here on Sundays because it helps break the routine, but I'm not religious. No, it was a slow realisation that when life deals you a bad hand, you must still make the best of it, regardless of your circumstances. Maybe it's a survival instinct; I don't know.'

'And did that realisation help you come to terms with the crimes you had committed?'

'You know, Daniel, I did some unspeakable things, things that weigh heavily on my conscience and things that I will carry with me to my grave. And if apologising to the people whose family members I killed would make any difference, I would apologise to them a million times over. So yes, coming to terms with what I did has been the most important part of my rehabilitation.'

'And did the prison system help you in any way?'

'After I came to terms with all that bad stuff, I decided to study. Before prison, I had never gone further than my school-leaving certificate, so I started doing correspondence courses through UNISA, and it took me a few years to get my first degree.'

'Your first degree?' replied Daniel, impressed, 'How many have you got?'

'Being in maximum security means you have a lot of time on your hands, a hell of a lot of time. My first degree was a BA in law. A couple of years later, I got my BSc in psychology, then an MSc in the subject a few years later.'

'Wow, that's impressive', said Daniel. 'So, tell me, Riaan, how do you feel about being part of our publicity campaign about the work the department is doing to help rehabilitate inmates? Would you agree to tell your story before a movie camera?'

Du Plessis chuckled. 'I'm too old and ugly to become a movie star. But if whatever I have to say can help anyone, especially the people that I have caused pain, then I am willing to do anything.'

Daniel smiled and stuck his handout. 'Thank you, Riaan. I think you're going to help many people.'

SEVENTEEN

'Are you out of your fokken mind!' screamed Janse down the phone.

Mashele turned down the volume on his in-car hands-free device as neighbouring drivers who were also waiting for the traffic lights to change were beginning to stare at him in his open-top Porsche.

'Are you completely fokken mad, or is your fokken ego so big that it's clouded your judgment?'

'Hey', barked Mashele as his anger rose. 'Calm down, for God's sake. I know what I'm doing.'

'Oh yes', countered Janse', you know what you're doing all right. You're fokking up my company; that's what you're doing.'

'Let's get a few things straight', said Mashele, raising his voice for the first time in years. 'One, it isn't your company anymore. I own forty-nine per cent of it . . . And second, you don't give me orders . . . And thirdly, you do not talk to me in this white baas bullshit tone of voice. Get it?'

'I'll talk to you in any damn way I please, Mashele, because you're nothing without me. You're nothing but a dumb fokken black. I warned you about this . . . '

Being referred to in such an offensive, racist way came as a crushing shock to Mashele. It was an attitude of hatred that personified the depth of apartheid intolerance and so-called white superiority. Every time he heard racism uttered in anger, and especially when it was said in a broad Afrikaans accent, his thoughts were immediately hurled back to that police cell where Jacob, the forgotten MK freedom fighter, was so sadistically tortured in front of his eyes.

Mashele was so stunned that he couldn't even think of a reply, so he switched off the phone, cutting Janse off in mid-sentence.

As he drove away, he realised in that instant rush of anger, disgust, and hatred that his partnership with Janse was over.

He pulled the car over into a layby and caught his breath. Then, as soon as there was a gap in the morning traffic, he turned his car around and returned home. He wouldn't be in the office today; he would be far too busy planning a war.

EIGHTEEN

Smit sat next to the large window of the Pretoria coffee shop, thumbing through the contents of a thick A4 envelope, when he spotted Fourie driving into the car park in his double cab. As his responsibilities in the CCB never extended beyond paper pushing, he always envied the guys who worked in the field. And he had always aspired to be included in their ranks. Not that intelligence gathering was glamorous in any way. As any operative would tell you, ninety-nine per cent of the time, it was pure drudgery. But to Smit, it all sounded much more appealing than working a calculator for ten hours daily.

Fourie walked into the coffee shop and shook his head in disdain when he saw the indiscreet table in front of a large picture window where Smit had chosen to sit. He ignored his client and found a table in the darkest, most distant corner of the cafe.

Smit, realising his carelessness in making himself so conspicuous, picked up his cappuccino and, spilling a good deal of it, walked across to Fourie's table with a sheepish half-grin on his face.

'Why don't you stand on a fokken pedestal and shout your intentions for the entire world to hear?' was Fourie's gruff way of greeting.

Although a good 50 kgs heavier and three-quarters of a metre taller, Smit had always been intimidated by the compact, wiry-built Fourie, even returning to their days together in the CCB. And he had always been even more unnerved by Fourie's icy-cold blue eyes that projected an aloof, almost hostile demeanour.

'So, what do you want to talk about that's so urgent?' asked Fourie.

'I've got a big job for you', was Smit's reply, trying to impress. 'A very big job.'

'Okay, so tell me about it.'

'We need someone else silenced.'

'You mean you want me to kill someone else for you.'

Smit winced on hearing his intentions stripped of their softer euphemisms. 'Yes, that's right. We need someone out of the way.'

'Who?'

'Another person who works for the company. It's a man called Joe Robinson.'

'Tell me about him?'

'Well, he's in his early sixties, and he's not a healthy person. He drinks too much and smokes too much. He's overweight and hasn't exercised in decades. He's the type who could easily have a heart attack or a stroke at any moment if you ask me.'

'Ja', replied Fourie with a hint of disdain. 'But no one will ask you, will they, Mr Smit? You're not a doctor. You're not a pathologist. And besides, I don't do poisons or anything like that; too unpredictable and, most of the time, too easy to trace.'

'Well, we can't be having another hijacking', said Smit before lowering his voice. 'It's going to cause people to be suspicious.'

'No, but there are other ways. A burglary gone wrong; a mugger who oversteps the mark; a drunk in a bar who picks a fight and goes for the jugular with a broken bottle.'

Smit shivered at the thought of such naked, brutal violence. 'I think my people will insist on a more natural-looking death.

The Jabu Maponya incident, although very well done, is still too fresh in people's minds. And if something else happens to a member of staff, that's violent . . . Well, you know, people talk, don't they? People make up stories, you know what I mean.'

Fourie looked unmoved. 'Ja, okay, I'll need to think about it. What information have you got for me on this Robinson guy?'

Smit pushed the large envelope across the table. Fourie opened it just wide enough to see the wodge of papers and official company photographs of Joe Robinson.

'Everything you need concerning the target is there, ' whispered Smit. 'His address, the details of his car, the pubs, bars, and restaurants he frequents, his work routine, office hours and the like. It's all accurate because I compiled it myself.'

'I'll be the judge on whether it's accurate or not', scowled Fourie. 'I do my own recces and my own research on every job.'

'Oh, of course', stammered Smit. 'I just thought it would help you'.

'Thanks, but no thanks', replied Fourie coldly as he stuffed the envelope inside his Jacket, zipped it up, and rose to leave. 'I'll be in touch'. Before Smit could reply, Fourie was out of earshot and, within a moment, out of the coffee shop.

NINETEEN

For days after meeting with Judith Maponya, Joe couldn't take his mind off what had happened to Jabu. The sheer terrifying horror the poor guy would have experienced during those last few seconds. And the cold-blooded callousness of those who had ordered the hit. The more he thought about it, the more his hatred for Janse and Smit festered like an open, gangrenous wound.

Joe also realised that he had been extremely careless and cavalier in shooting his drunken mouth off at work. He was sure that someone had been lurking outside his office when he told Debbie and Daniel about those he held responsible for Jabu's murder. He had been stupid to open his big mouth. And silly to get so drunk. He vowed never to be that reckless again and to trust no one – friend or foe alike – with Judith's knowledge about Janse and Smit's fraud. Or at least not until he could help Judith collect all the evidence that would make an ironclad case that would see Janse and Smit spending the rest of their miserable lives in prison.

He bought two cheap cell phones with pay-as-you-go contracts so that he and Judith could communicate without fear of anyone eavesdropping on their conversations. They met in coffee shops well away from their usual haunts. And they took long, indirect routes whenever they needed to drive to clandestine meetings.

It was helpful that Judith was a lawyer – even if she was only on the first rung of the legal ladder - at least she knew the right questions to ask. But the problem they had revolved around who to ask. Sure, there were some honest cops, but how could they distinguish them from corrupt officers? Their first port of call should have been the Hawks, South Africa's specialist crime unit that investigated any case of corruption, organised crime and commercial crimes over R100 000. But members of this unit, with its official, wordy title of the *Directorate for Priority Crime Investigation,* had also been tainted by accusations of being pliable.

The Hawks was the unit that had taken over from the Scorpions, a highly efficient, FBI-trained investigation unit that had boasted an unprecedented prosecution rate of around 90%. But the unit became a victim of its success. Scorpion officers had been prone to tipping off the media before raiding the homes or the offices of high-profile wrongdoers so that those who stood accused would be arrested in a glare of publicity. The Scorpions were effective, but they were also flashy. And regardless of the good press that seemed to follow their efforts, they were despised in certain political quarters. In 2008, the entire unit was disbanded amidst enormous controversy and media clamour. The liberal-minded press and the opposition parties firmly believed it was a ploy to protect prominent and corrupt ANC politicians. Many of those in the senior ranks of the ruling party who lobbied for the disbanding of the Scorpions were themselves being investigated by the unit for serious corruption.

The Hawks never enjoyed the same confidence level with the general public as their predecessors. It was a cynicism fuelled by an increasingly strident media. And because Joe was an avid consumer of the liberal media, he had disregarded the Hawks without a second thought.

Joe's other option was the media itself. But he knew that even though there were investigative journalists who stood firm on the front lines in battling criminality, Janse-Mashele's cancerous influence still metastasized far into that industry.

The same applied to the National Prosecution Agency, the NPA, which had also been embroiled in various controversies regarding its lack of impartiality.

Even Judith's law firm had done some contractual work for Janse-Mashele, so even her colleagues couldn't be fully trusted. But Judith had persuaded Joe that there was an advocate that her law firm often engaged when they needed a criminal law specialist. By all accounts, he was a man of high integrity who was also well known for his aversion to the corruption permeating every aspect of life in South Africa.

Advocate Bernard Van Rooyen SC was an imposing, towering figure. He was also almost as wide as he was tall. On meeting him at his ramshackle chambers, Joe was immediately impressed by the chaotic state of Van Rooyen's office. Disorganised piles of case files stood next to waist-high stacks of legal documents, and every shelf buckled under rows of dusty old law books. Joe was also impressed with Van Rooyen's appearance. Judging by the ruddy cheeks and a bulbous nose covered in a criss-cross maze of capillaries, this was a red wine drinker equal to his prodigious consumption.

Judith did most of the talking, briefing the seasoned advocate professionally and dispassionately, without referring to her own flesh and blood.

After listening intently and inspecting some of the financial documents in the shoebox, Van Rooyen finally spoke. 'The most important evidence you have against these people is right here in this box', he exclaimed in his deep baritone voice. 'All these copies of allegedly fraudulent invoices. But this in itself can only prove fraud. It may suggest a motive for murder, but you have nothing that proves murder. The fact is everything you've told me here today is nothing more than hearsay and conjecture. And to be brutally honest with you, even the most junior counsel would make mincemeat out of you in two minutes flat.'

Van Rooyen saw that Joe looked ready to explode angrily while Judith looked crestfallen.

'Now', continued Van Rooyen, adopting a more optimistic note. 'The best option is to nail them on this hard evidence. The invoices for the frauds committed against Trade and Investment South Africa were made as part of that international campaign you mentioned, Joe. All that can be verified is by checking through the back issues of the publications mentioned on these invoices. I would say, in conclusion, you have a simple but strong case. And judging by the number of invoices we have here, they'll never get away with any claims of clerical errors. This is fraud on an industrial scale, and every anomaly we find on these invoices will become a charge in and of itself. So, looking at this pile of invoices, I guess we're probably talking about a few hundred offences.

'But surely, that's not nearly enough for what those bastards did', grumbled Joe.

'Look, fraud of this nature is still a severe charge with a minimum sentence of fifteen years. The point is that when someone's looking at the daunting prospects of a fifteen-year stretch, they become quite happy to cut a deal with the prosecutors. We just need to give them half a chance of an indemnity or even a reduction in the sentence offered to them. In my experience, all niceties like loyalty and fidelity to friends and partners quickly fall by the wayside. And people will talk until the cows come home to save their skins.'

For the first time during their meeting, Joe smiled. 'And I know exactly who the first of these murderous bastards would want to save his skin.'

The advocate continued. 'This needs to be our strategy to bring these guys to book for the far more severe charges of pre-meditated murder and conspiracy to murder, either of which carries a compulsory life sentence.'

Joe's smile turned into a broad grin: 'Now you're talking'.

'Look, Judith and Joe, we still need to be realistic. Before we can get a case like this to the courts, we must have the NPA firmly on our side. And if what you say about Janse-Mashele is true, then once we make overtures to the NPA, chances are they'll soon know about it because the NPA leaks like a sieve.'

'You must know who the good guys are at the NPA?' asked Judith.

'Oh yes, replied Van Rooyen. 'Despite what you read in the papers, there is still a core of honest, dedicated lawyers working within the structures of the NPA. I know them well and have battled them in many courts for years. So don't worry about that. I would be delighted to help you ensure that this case gets prosecuted. And I'll be glad to do that on a pro-bono basis.'

Judith and Joe shook the advocate's hand and thanked him profusely.

'The first few nails in Janse's and Smit's coffins', said Joe.

TWENTY

Of the thirty-two cemeteries spread throughout greater Johannesburg, Westpark is one of only nine that can still accommodate the departed. It's a growing problem exacerbated by the fact that from a cultural point of view, cremation is not an option for most Africans.

Nestling underneath the rocky outcrop of hills known as the Melville Koppies and spread over thirty-three acres of gently undulating knolls, Westpark is densely populated by large Jacaranda trees. Trees that are perennially pleasant to the eye, but as it was springtime, they looked even more striking as they were ablaze with lavender flowers. And adding to the spectacle, the early spring rains had transformed the brown-yellow lawns, burnt by the harsh winter sun, into bright, fresh hues of emerald.

By 11:00 that Saturday morning, the temperature had risen to 31 degrees, and the people who arrived to mourn Jabu Maponya's passing had already discarded their jackets and ties.

The turnout, as is typical of African funerals, was considerable. Over two hundred people crowded around the freshly dug grave where Jabu would spend eternity. And the mourners were bolstered by a large contingent of colleagues from Janse-Mashele.

The church service that had started three hours earlier in Soweto had been avoided by most of the white people attending the graveside service. The paranoia of township violence was still prevalent in the minds of many of them a good twenty years after the struggle had ended. And, if truth be told, most had little idea that the people living in the sprawling township were more neighbourly and community-spirited than they could ever hope to experience in their high-walled suburbs.

One person who had attended the church services was Macdonald Mashele. The soulful singing of the church choir had deeply touched him. However, the ladies who made up the choir regarded the service as especially poignant, as Jabu's mother had been a fellow member for forty years.

After a vigil that lasted throughout the night with Ma Maponya, Judith, and extended family members from far and wide, the choir reconvened at the small Soweto church at the start of the service at 8:00 am. It had continued singing the most rousing hymns and psalms for another two hours.

The service at Westpark was the conclusion of the day's events. The priest invited everyone to gather closer as the coffin was carried up to the side of the open grave. During this polite jostling, Joe Robinson caught Judith's eye as she sat on one of the plastic garden chairs laid out for the immediate family. But there was no more than a momentary half-smile of acknowledgement between them, as they had agreed beforehand to be strangers to each other.

As the large crowd of mourners settled, Joe felt a looming presence behind him. He turned and was taken aback to find Smit standing there. They exchanged glances but no word of greeting.

Throughout the service, Jabu's mother sobbed quietly, which brought tears to the eyes of many of the mourners. But the closer the priest came to the end of the service, the louder her weeping became. As the priest concluded with the funeral prayer, he raised his voice: 'Sure and certain hope of the resurrection to eternal life through our Lord Jesus Christ, we commend to Almighty God our brother Jabu . . . '

The finality of losing her only son rendered her inconsolable.

'And we commit his body to the ground ... earth to earth ... ashes to ashes ... dust to dust ...'

By now, Jabu's mother was howling in anguish.

'The Lord bless him and keep him; the Lord make his face to shine upon him and be gracious unto him and give him peace ...'

Before the priest could conclude with 'amen', Jabu's mother collapsed in a wretched heap as she watched the coffin being lowered into the ground. Judith and her relatives struggled to help Ma Maponya regain her composure.

With nothing left to do, the congregation broke up, and people made their way through the tree-lined avenues. Affected deeply by Ma Maponya's grief, everyone was stunned into a respectful silence.

Everyone, that is, except for Smit. He turned to one of the ladies who worked in the finance department. 'Well, good job it's a Saturday, or we'd have to close down the company for half a day.'

On hearing Smit's comment, Joe was incensed. He sidled up to the man who towered over him and whispered through clenched teeth: 'How dare you make jokes about Jabu Maponya, you bastard ... I know what you and your fucking crooked friends did to Jabu, and you're all going to pay for it ... You're going to go to prison for a very long time, Smit, you are pathetic, fucking mammy's boy.'

Smit, apoplectic with rage, merely stared back at Joe in silence.

TWENTY-ONE

It was on the second ring that Fourie picked up his cell phone, but on seeing Smit's name on the screen, he let it ring a few more times to irritate his client.

'Ja?' he said eventually.

'It's me, Smit. Listen, you need to move on that job we discussed during our last meeting.'

Fourie could sense the anger in Smit's voice: 'I'll do it when I'm good and . . .'

Smit cut him short: 'You'll do it when I fucking tell you', he screeched down the phone. 'I'm the one paying your fees.'

Fourie was taken aback by Smit's sudden burst of anger: 'Oh, will I now?'

'Yes, you will. I want him taken out straight away. A.S.A-Fucking-P. And there's something else, too.'

'Okay?'

'I don't just want him killed; I want his miserable fucking memory dragged through the mud. I want him embarrassed and humiliated. I want you to make Joe-Fucking-Robinson look like a fool. Do you hear me? I want people to see him in the worst light possible.'

'Such as?'

'Oh, for fuck sake, use your imagination, man. Plant some child porn on his computer. Hide some drugs in his home, where the police will find it. I don't know. I'm paying you to come up with something. But like I said before, you must make it look like a suicide, do you understand?'

'Ja, well, what can I say, Mr Smit?' said Fourie, with a hint of sarcastic emphasis on the honorific. 'It's clear as a . . .'

Smit hung up on him before Fourie could finish the sentence.

TWENTY-TWO

After his argument with Janse two days earlier, Macdonald Mashele was still incensed with rage. For years, he had tolerated much of Janse's self-serving, aggressive, and uncouth behaviour. But Janse's outrageous racism had finally worn him down. In Mashele's mind, the staggering level of hypocrisy angered him most. Janse portrayed himself as the respectable God-fearing type who went to his Dutch Reformed Church every Sunday morning. And he prayed to God before every meal. But as far as Mashele was concerned, Janse didn't have a Christian bone in his body when it came to black people.

Mashele was also annoyed with himself. For far too long, he had looked the other way when Janse made comments that were paternalistic at best and bullying at worst—snapping at waiters or car guards who weren't attentive or deferential enough, screaming and shouting at secretaries, tea ladies and cleaners for some imaginary infraction.

Then, there was his aloofness and air of superiority. When talking to Mashele, there were always subtle jibes. Janse would refer to Mashele's black associates as *'your people'* as if they were a different species. And he would snap out *'you blacks'* as if spitting a grape pip.

Janse, he knew, was a product of the apartheid system and that paternalistic arrogance and white supremacy were deeply rooted in Janse's DNA. He would never socialise with black people. And he would only invite them to his home if there were obvious business benefits from such an occasion.

Since the argument, there has been no contact between

the two. No early morning briefings over coffee. No phone calls. No emails. There were no attempts at an apology or reconciliation. Not that Mashele would have been interested in patching things up. His feelings were far too bruised. Mashele's future working relationship with Janse would be based on a sham, a gossamer-thin veneer of respect, and a cauldron of hatred.

Mashele would only go into the office when his PA, Monica, phoned him to say that Janse had left for the afternoon, which, as was his habit, was usually around lunchtime. He also kept a wide berth from Smit, who he knew never to trust.

Mashele spent most of his time at home, where he held court with trusted friends and colleagues who came to sympathise with him and help him plot his way through Janse's mess.

One thing was sure: Janse-Mashele would soon make way for *Mashele and Associates.* And Mashele was pleased that there was no shortage of associates who were more than ready to support him - emotionally and financially - to the hilt.

Mashele also spoke to several clients during this time. Nearly all of them agreed immediately to move their business to Mashele's new venture once all the contractual issues with Janse-Mashele were ironed out.

One of Mashele's visitors during this time was an old college friend who shared a similar background. David Tlale, like Mashele, had also been a gang member and a messenger in his youth. He ran through the streets of Soweto, dodging police and army patrols, delivering whatever was needed to support the struggle.

Like Mashele, Tlale had also done well for himself. But unlike his ostentatious friend, Tlale could hardly flaunt his success. He was the deputy director general of the National Intelligence Agency, the domestic branch of the State Security Agency, the counter-intelligence organisation that protected the Republic from any foreign or domestic threat.

Sitting in the oversized patio, Tlale picked up the cognac he had been nursing and sniffing for a good deal of the evening: 'Hey Mac, take a walk with me. I want to see your garden'.

'What are you talking about, David? It's just a load of flowers, trees, and bushes. You've never taken an interest in my garden before . . .' Mashele stopped talking immediately on seeing Tlale hold an upward-pointing index finger close to the centre of his lips.

They walked into the middle of the main lawn at the back of Mashele's property.

'We need to be careful', whispered Tlale.

'You sure you're not being dramatic?'

'Mac, before we do anything, I will order a team of my guys to come and sweep your home, office, car, and anywhere and everywhere you spend any time. Even your toilet.'

'Sweep?' asked Mashele.

'Yes, sweep for electronic listening devices.'

Mashele looked confused.

'Bugs, wires, phone taps', said Tlale. 'You know when they bug your office or home or tap your phone?'

'Oh, come on, that sounds like something out of the movies', protested Mashele.

'Christ, Mac, you seriously need an urgent wake-up call because, for such a clever guy, you are so naïve. There's an army of private detectives in this country who can be bought for next to nothing, and this is the kind of stuff they do. And from what you're telling me, Janse's the kind of ruthless slimeball who's likely to hire these lowlifes.'

'But do people really use bugging devices to spy on people?'

Tlale chuckled as he swirled the cognac and scrutinised the tears flowing back down on the inside of the glass. 'You would be surprised. Let me get my people to do some basic sweeps and see what happens. If we find nothing, great, let's move on. No damage has been done. But if we do find something, you'll better understand what you're up against.'

'Okay, if you think we should do it, let's do it.'

'Hey, I'll even assign a name to the operation. How about *Operation Pissed Off*? Or *Operation Fuck-You-Janse*', laughed Tlale.

'How about *Operation Suffer?*' countered Mashele. 'Because that's what I want that bastard Janse to do.'

'No, I've got it', said Tlale, as he downed the last of the cognac and looked around the garden. 'The perfect name that sums up this place and sums up your naivety towards all things covert: *Operation Green.*'

TWENTY-THREE

AFFIDAVIT

I, Joseph George Robinson, hereby declare that the information herein is true, correct, and complete to the best of my knowledge.

I am an adult male, South African citizen, ID Number 4906125718184, and I make this Affidavit of my own free will.

Since January 5, 2006, I have been the director of strategic planning for the communications, advertising and marketing group of companies collectively known as Janse-Mashele.

As a senior executive at Janse-Mashele, including a company executive committee member, I have had close contact with all of Janse-Mashele's clients. The reason for this is that strategic planning forms the primary introductory function of the process of producing advertising and public relations campaigns.

Furthermore, I have played an integral role in gaining and acquiring new business for the company and its various subsidiaries.

Approximately 70% of Janse-Mashele's considerable revenues are earned from government clients. The 2011 turnover (or "Billings" as they are referred to in the industry) was R1.4 billion. This includes numerous central government departments, various provincial governments throughout the Republic, and several State-Owned Enterprises (SOEs).

Since I started working at the company six years ago, while performing my function as head of strategy, I have witnessed the following incidents of gross irregularities and illegalities in the way that Janse-Mashele has conducted business with its government clients, which includes tender irregularities, graft, bribery, and corruption.

To be more specific, I hereby swear that on the dates stipulated herein, that I witnessed, first-hand, the following:

1. On or about September 15, 2009, prior to tendering for the Department of Transport's Road Safety Campaign, including the Christmas Anti-Drinking and Driving Campaign, senior executives from Janse-Mashele, namely Henk Janse, the company CEO, Macdonald Mashele, MD, Petrus Smit, Financial Director, and myself, attended an all-day clandestine meeting with senior personnel from the department. This included the director general, Mr Aubrey Ndlovu, and deputy director general, Mr Hannes van der Merwe.

    1a. This meeting was held in a private conference room at the Blenheim Spa in Sandton. The purpose of this meeting was to brief Janse-Mashele on confidential strategic issues related to the objectives of these campaigns and to share confidential research findings. This meeting contravened the Public Finance Management Act and infringed the rules and regulations governing tenders by the State. The sole purpose of this meeting was to provide Janse-Mashele with a clear but unfair advantage for winning the Department of Transport business.

    1b. The information traded that day allowed Janse-Mashele to demonstrate superior knowledge and understanding of the department's objectives during the formal pitch presentation that was followed three weeks later, on October 5, 2009.

1c. After the meeting had concluded, informal conversations continued over drinks. During this time, I overheard a private conversation between Janse-Mashele's managing director, Mr Macdonald Mashele, and Mr Aubrey Ndlovu, the department's DG, in which a bribe of R2 million was solicited by the DG and agreed to by Mr Mashele. Moreover, I distinctly heard that this payment was to be made in the form of a property – a holiday apartment to the value of R2 million on the beachfront in Durban – and that it was to be purchased in the name of the DG's long-term civil partner, Ms Bridget Tshabalala.

1d. In October 2010, it was announced in the trade press that Janse-Mashele had been successful in securing the Department of Transport account. This account was worth in excess of R120 million in billings. After a hotly-contested four-way pitch between rival communications groups, Janse-Mashele was successful due to what the Department of Transport's press release stated as "*a combination of creative excellence and outstanding strategic insights.*"

1e. Copies of all relevant documents, including my notes from this meeting, are included in Appendix A of this document.

2. On or about July 28, 2010, Janse-Mashele was engaged in the pitch for the South African Post Office (SAPO). I personally wrote the conditions

of the tender that were then supplied to the procurement officials of that organisation in contravention of the Tenders Act of 1994.

2a. My actions aimed to manipulate the tender procedure by writing the terms and conditions to eliminate competing communications groups from the tendering process. This was achieved by providing effective barriers to entry for competing agencies, thus giving Janse-Mashele an unfair advantage in acquiring the business.

2b. I did this work on the express orders of the CEO of Janse-Mashele, Mr Henk Janse.

2c. On August 12, 2010, the terms and conditions of the SAPO Tender for Advertising and Communications Agencies were duly published and distributed to all interested parties. The terms and conditions in the document were identical to those I had written and then submitted to the SAPO procurement department.

2d. The terms and conditions expressly eliminated non-South African-owned communications groups from participating in the pitch process. It also stipulated that only 100% South African-owned communications companies were eligible to apply.

2e. The Terms and conditions also eliminated smaller, South African-owned communications companies by stipulating that only communications groups with billings (annual turnover) above R500 million could apply. This eliminated all but three contenders, with Janse-

Mashele being the most viable option.

2f. By September 1, 2010, it was announced that Janse-Mashele had been short-listed for the account, along with two other agencies.

2g. By October 15, 2011, after a three-way pitch process, SAPO announced that Janse-Mashele had successfully won SAPO's R70 million marketing and communications budget.

3. On or about 18 June, 2011, after several meetings had been conducted with senior South African Broadcasting Corporation (SABC) personnel (an existing client), the proposed budget for the broadcaster's advertising campaign, which had been stipulated as R150 million, was inflated to the sum of R210 million. This occurred through a series of fraudulent interventions by Mr Henk Janse, the company CEO, and Mr Petrus Smit, which resulted in substantial bribes being offered to senior SABC executives, the details of which are included in Appendix B of this document.

4. On numerous occasions, Janse-Mashele received irregular and illegal commissions in film production fees that contravened the contractual agreement between the company and many of the aforementioned government clients.

4a. The contracts between both parties stipulated that a monthly fee would be paid to Janse-Mashele in lieu of all work done and that no additional monies would be payable to the company through production or media commissions.

4b. However, these agreements were consistently

and continually broken as kickbacks of between five and ten per cent of the production budgets were demanded from film production companies.

4c.These payments were disguised as *"Early Settlement Discounts"*. I believe these transactions were criminally fraudulent, over and above violating the agreements.

Finally, I realise full well that my involvement in the aforementioned cases of bribery and corruption makes me guilty of contravening the Prevention and Combating Corrupt Activities Act because, as a person of authority within the Janse-Mashele organisation, I witnessed acts of corruption in excess of R100 000 being committed, and failed to report them. I now fully accept responsibility for my actions and admit my guilt for these offences.

Signed here in..................................at the city of........................... On the......day of...................2012.

.....................................Joseph George Robison.

Joe stopped typing on his laptop. What he didn't understand about legalities and the legal mumbo-jumbo required for an Affidavit, Judith could knock it into shape some other day. At least he had most of the basics down.

He rose from the kitchen table to get another beer from the fridge. As the ice-cold lager slipped down his throat, Joe was suddenly taken by the realisation of the six years of his life he had dedicated to Janse-Mashele. And there it all was, made up of diaries, notepads and old flash drives stacked up on his kitchen table, next to the half-eaten cheese sandwich that was his meagre supper.

Six fucking years thought Joe. How could I have been complicit in those ongoing acts of criminality for so long? So, what did I get out of it? Nothing more than getting to keep my job. And while I was doing that, I knowingly helped those crooks plunder and pillage as much money as they possibly could. I knew about the bribes to those sell-outs, the civil servants and executives who ran the SOEs. They were no more than traitors who enriched themselves when they were supposed to serve this country's people.

He took another large gulp of his beer. Well, at least he was finally doing the right thing. It was just so tragic that someone had to lose his life before he - Joe Robinson, who should have known better - could eventually unearth some integrity.

In the morning, he'd call Judith on their newly acquired, clandestine cellphones about safely emailing his Affidavit to her freshly acquired covert Hotmail address. Christ thought Joe; he never thought he'd be involved in cloak-and-dagger skulduggery at his age. He downed the rest of the beer and turned in for the night.

TWENTY-FOUR

E-mail to: Deputy Director David Tlale

From: Agent 324, Covert Counterintelligence Unit B5

Date: 05:09:21

Subject: Operation Green

Good morning, Sir,

Concerning the above-named operation, we have conducted a preliminary sweep of several rooms in the subject's house, his vehicles, and his offices at Janse-Mashele House. The findings are as follows:

- Remotely activated spy mobile phone software was found to be operational in both phones used by the subject: A Samsung S20 and an Apple iPhone 11.

- Electronic listening devices were discovered in the lounge, bar, dining room and patio of the subject's home.

- During a sweep of the subject's office at his place of employment, we discovered devices placed under the desk, inside all landline handsets and in the light fitting above the conference table.

- Illicit phone tapping devices were discovered on all three landlines operating at the subject's property, plus the fibre-optic broadband line. These devices were found in the landline junction box located on the subject's street.

- Three of the motor vehicles most extensively used by the subject, a Porsche 911 GT3, A Ferrari 458 Italia, and a Range Rover HSE, also tested positive for listening devices.

As per your orders, we have neither disturbed nor deactivated these devices in any way or form. So, whichever party or parties that have the subject under surveillance are likely unaware of our discoveries.

Finally, I would like to add that the concealment of these devices was of a far higher standard of professionalism than we usually come across in industrial espionage cases. Also, the devices used are of a more sophisticated nature than the technology in common use. In other words, whoever has the subject under surveillance is someone trained to the highest professional standard, possibly from a government agency.

My unit awaits your orders before taking any further action.

TWENTY-FIVE

Joe yawned loudly as he negotiated his car through the dense early evening traffic. It had been a long day, and he was tired. Since the incident with Smit at Jabu's funeral, he had been sleeping poorly; even worse than usual. Losing his temper and telling Smit what he thought of him still preyed on his mind. And he was angry with himself for losing control and revealing his intentions.

Even though he was sure no one else could have heard what he had said, he knew Smit would now be plotting against him. And if Smit could have a man killed, who knows what might happen to him? Joe just hoped he would have enough time to get to Smit before Smit got to him. Judith and Advocate Van Rooyen had his Affidavit, highlighting a litany of cases that needed investigation. They also had the content of Jabu's shoebox, which was more than enough to convict Smit.

But losing his temper like that at the funeral? That was plain bloody foolish. Joe felt that whatever had happened from then on, he had thrown away the surprise element. For days, he had fantasised about seeing Smit's face at the moment of his arrest. Fraud, corruption, racketeering, and money laundering were all charges that could conceivably be laid against him. Joe had also lain awake at night, wondering what kind of expression Smit would have on his face as he stood in the dock while the judge read out his sentence. He'll cry. The bastard would cry, Joe thought. He'll cry like a fucking baby. And God, I will enjoy watching that big bastard being brought down to size.

With luck and hard work, they may even be able to pin that

murder charge on him. Van Rooyen was right. We need to scare Smit with the fraud charges so that they can force him to testify against Janse. Maybe he gets 12 years instead of 15, thought Joe. Fuck it, let's be generous and compromise a little to get Smit to spill the beans to convict Janse.

As Van Rooyen had pointed out, any one of those charges carried a minimum 15-year sentence. And the threat of 15 years would make even the toughest crook think twice about saving his boss out of loyalty. So, the only option would be to cut a deal with the prosecutors.

But Smit wouldn't just talk, thought Joe. He would squeal - squeal like a baby. Then Janse would be nailed. The bastard would spend the rest of his life in some filthy little cell where some gang of animals would be queuing to gangbang him up the arse. A thought always brought a large grin to Joe's face.

He was still smiling as he drove into his townhouse complex. As he stopped at the boom gate, the security guards who staffed the guardhouse greeted him. 'Hello, Mr Joe. How are you tonight?'

'Hello, J Edgar', replied Joe to the man who shared the same name as the director who dominated the FBI for over fifty years. Joe knew the names of all the security guards at the complex, and each one had a Joe-inspired variation. 'How many felons have you arrested today?'

Edgar laughed, even though he'd heard the same joke a few dozen times. 'Today, I arrest 12.'

'Only twelve, you're working half days again?'

'As always, Joe's quip had all three of the security guards in peals of laughter. You youngsters don't know the meaning of hard work.'

'Well, you can sleep easy tonight, Mr Joe. The A-team is here to look after you.'

Joe laughed as he inched his car slowly underneath the raised boom, 'Thank you, J Edgar. I always sleep easy because of you guys. You have a good evening now.'

Living in such a complex was perfect for Joe as he was far too disorganised to manage domestic issues like mowing a lawn, washing the car, or securing a home. Paying someone to do all that crap for you had always been Joe's thinking. Besides, living in a smart housing complex like this meant that the electric fences, the CCTV cameras, the burglar alarms, and the infrared beams were on the high outer walls where you didn't have to look at them through the lounge window. And some residents, like Joe, didn't see the need for additional security measures. There's a guardhouse with an excellent team of guys caring for that. The place is like C-Max. And it should be considering the levies I have to pay.

It would be impossible for anyone not trained as part of a crack undercover security unit to break into the complex.

Driving to the parking spot in front of his house, Joe was surprised to see his cat waiting for him. 'What are you doing here, boy? Have the mice kicked you out or something?' The cat meowed some indifferent reply while licking his paw.

As Joe unlocked the front door, he again tried to reason with the feline: 'Well, are you coming in or not?' But after another long, plaintive meow, Joe turned his back on his moody friend: 'Well, fuck you then. Hunt for your own bloody food.'

Joe threw his car keys on the hallway table before entering the kitchen. Being a creature of habit, he switched on the TV to catch up with the news channels. He then grabbed a cold beer from the fridge before pulling his laptop out of his briefcase to go through all the emails he hadn't addressed during the day. Especially the ongoing hotmail conversations he shared with Judith.

He downed about half of the content of the beer bottle in one go before looking at his laptop screen as it was booting up. Joe thought one of the most frustrating things in the world was waiting for the infernal computer to boot up. And the more sophisticated they became, the longer he felt he had to wait before being able to use the bloody things.

Something unusual caught his eye. There was some movement on his monitor that he'd not noticed before. He leant forward and peered at his screen; when he saw his reflection before this dark, moving object, he suddenly realised what was happening: someone was standing behind him.

By the time he sensed the two hands coming down on each side of his head, the cord was already drawn tightly around his throat. The blinding shock and terror took his breath away. And the searing, lacerating pain around his throat was unbearable.

Desperate to breathe, he tried to lash out, but his flailing arms merely swatted the air. He attempted to kick backwards. And even though he felt a weak, glancing connection on a shin, the blows seemed to strengthen his assailant's resolve. The increasing pressure on the ever-tightening cord was crushing Joe's windpipe.

Then, the assailant made a final Herculean effort, which lifted Joe off the ground and shook him like a rag doll. Whatever strength Joe still possessed immediately deserted his body.

As the cord tightened even more, Joe's lungs felt like they were about to explode. Then the blackness came. First, big black blotches in front of his eyes. Then, an all-enveloping blackness to which he surrendered until he finally passed out.

Even though Fourie had sensed Joe's strength slowly ebbing out of his body, he continued applying the pressure by pulling on the cord with all his strength. Fourie understood well that during strangulation, the victim would pass out in around 15 seconds. But it would then take as much as several minutes before death through asphyxiation would finally be achieved.

Eventually – after he was satisfied that Joe was finally dead – Fourie relaxed his hold on the wooden dowels on each side of the cord and pulled off the black balaclava. If he had had the choice, he would have used steel wire to garrotte his victim – a cheese cutter was perfect for the job. Even though it was messier, at least it was quicker as it sliced through the soft tissue and constricted the carotid arteries, which would starve the brain of oxygen, resulting in death in just a few minutes. But there were sound reasons why he had to use the cord.

He rested on the kitchen floor momentarily to catch his breath. The irony wasn't lost on him. At least he could catch his breath, unlike Joe, whose open eyes bulged out of their sockets.

He unravelled the cord from the dowels. He had a firm plan in place, and he couldn't allow the adrenaline that was by now pumping through his body to cause him to make some stupid mistake. Besides, he needed to move quickly before the blood started pooling in the lower extremities of Joe's body, which is a tell-tale sign that a corpse has been moved post-mortem. Even the undertrained, underpaid, under-resourced and overworked forensic technicians in the police would spot that anomaly without too much trouble.

But first, Fourie needed the tools of his trade. Opening the back door, he grabbed a rucksack he'd hidden in the bushes when he arrived earlier. After stripping the body of clothes, Fourie rolled it over onto a rug before pulling it down the hallway and into the lounge. It wouldn't do to drag Joe's body around the house as scuff marks could easily be left on toes and heels.

At the doorway between the lounge and the study, Fourie carefully lifted Joe's body so that he could prop it up on its knees before balancing it against the door frame. Then he tied the cord around the door handle and made a slip knot, which he carefully placed back around Joe's throat so that the section of cord that had been faintly stained with blood was positioned over the fierce welt that had been left around Joe's neck. Fourie then carefully let Joe's body slump forward so that the cord tightened around his throat as it supported the weight of his body.

Then he pulled out the contents of the rucksack: pictures of children in sexually suggestive positions, which he placed on the floor around Joe's body.

As slapdash and ill-trained as the police forensics units had become, even they would recognise autoerotic strangulation. A self-inflicted form of suffocation intended to heighten sexual arousal and orgasm by cutting off the blood supply to the brain, or hypoxia, as a medic would call it.

It wasn't a form of death they came across every day, but the signs were clear enough to make this an open-and-shut case. The victim was engaged in some masochistic sexual activities, and he evidently lost consciousness before he could pull the cord that would unfasten the slip knot. There would be a hurried autopsy, followed by an inquest some weeks later before an official finding would be announced *'Death by Misadventure.'* Open and shut case.

Fourie went through the house one last time to ensure he had not overlooked anything. Then, silently, he let himself out through the back door before disappearing into the darkness.

Book Two: Summer 2012

TWENTY-SIX

The sign on the gate left no one under any illusion that a carefree stroll through this stretch of land would have been ill-advised. *'Ingozi Amabhubesi'*, *'Ingozi yeeNgonyama'*, *'Gevaar Leeus'* and *'Danger Lions'* made the point succinctly in South Africa's four most spoken languages. Even illiterates were catered for with a graphic image of a male lion's head with a gaping mouth exposing ferocious canines.

But that was how the farm's owner, Sarel Gerhadus Fourie, wanted it: no prying eyes and no one poking around his property looking for a job or scrounging food or looking to rob him. Fourie had no time for people, be they black or white, rich or poor. He only had time for his cats.

Running a lion breeding programme was far less labour-intensive than most forms of farming. So, Fourie didn't require an army of labourers. He had a couple of trusted workers who had been with him for many years. This form of game farming also afforded him plenty of time off to pursue his main line of work as an enforcer for an exclusive, enigmatic group of clients who could afford his considerable fees.

Besides, establishing the breeding programme had not been a financial strain for him, nor had it required specialist expertise. Fourie had more than enough land, a farm owned by the family for generations. All he and his workers had to do was fence it securely into various sections that separated each mature male and his harem of females from other males. Plus isolated areas for females to give birth far from the rest of the pride.

As for the running costs, other than the odd fee from the local vet to tranquilise them so they could be sutured after a nasty fight or to extract a rotten tooth, his biggest cost was for the steady supply of food. Fresh meat usually arrived on four legs in the form of donkeys and ponies that had spent a lifetime pulling coal carts in the townships that bordered every city. At least Fourie had the decency to shoot them before his workers skinned and butchered them.

With no breeding season, the farm was assured a constant stream of cubs, with one female producing a litter of anything between one and six offspring every two years. The result of the programme was an increase of around sixty and eighty cats annually that needed feeding until they were around two years old.

As much as he admired these creatures for their physical strength, hunting skills, and majestic looks, Fourie never harboured any sentimentality towards his lions. To him, they were a commodity, a valuable source of revenue of around four to five thousand US dollars per female and a couple of thousand more for a mature male.

On reaching adulthood, the lions were sold to hunting farms catering to wealthy foreigners. Usually European or American, they tended not to be unduly concerned about how they could acquire the ultimate hunting trophy to hang on the walls of their mancaves.

Even though this was Fourie's only source of legitimate income, he had little respect for his customers. It wasn't hunting at all, more like murder with a high-powered rifle in an enclosed area that was otherwise known as canned hunting.

In Fourie's eyes, only the laziest weaklings would ever participate in this form of lion hunting. After all, it required no more effort or skill than to sit in an open-top off-road vehicle driven into a fenced enclosure about the size of a football field.

Then, after having the selected creature pointed out to them, they just had to aim through telescopic sights before pulling the trigger. The entire hunt would often be over in minutes without the hunter leaving the vehicle.

Shooting lions this way also had its challenges. Most of these so-called hunters lacked the shooting skills to ensure a clean kill. The required shot needed to be either straight-on to the centre of the chest or side-on, approximately one-third of the way down from the lion's shoulder. Once the animal was dead, the carcass would be propped up with its head held high and its front paws stretched out. At times, small sticks placed inside the animal's mouth would keep its jaws open to reveal the ten-centimetre-long canines that had never posed a threat to those who had just shot the creature to death. Then, with the proud-looking hunter crouching next to the animal while holding his rifle, the all-important photograph would be taken; usually, a snapshot highlighting a split-second of primal exhilaration that would provide the hunter with a lifetime of bragging rights. And the fiercer the animal looked, the better it could perpetuate the illusion that the quarry had been tracked and stalked in the boundless wilds of Africa.

Dead lions also produced additional revenues through the ever-increasing markets in the Far East, especially Vietnam, China, and Thailand. The populations of these countries have an insatiable appetite for remedies of no medical value that consist of crushed bones, teeth, claws, and the organs of large cats. This misguided market had turned its interest to lions after all subspecies of tigers from India to Siberia had been rendered virtually extinct through poaching. So, there was never any shortage of agents ready to exploit every lion they could find. And it was all perfectly legal - not that Fourie cared much for legalities anyway.

Fourie sat inside his Toyota double cab as his two workers, Nelson and Willem, struggled to lift the head of a dead carthorse so they could feed a rope around its neck.

'Come on, put your fokken backs into it,' he shouted impatiently at the guys, 'I don't have all day.'

Then, after the rope was thrown over a branch of a tree above the horse and attached to the front bull bar on the pick-up, Fourie reversed a few metres back, which hoisted the carcass up into a position that made it easier for the men to start skinning the animal.

'Come on, Nelson, what's the matter with you this morning? You're like some little girl.'

'This horse has been dead for too long', protested Nelson, 'Eish, it's too tough to skin. It's not coming away nicely like a freshly killed animal.'

Nelson, a Zimbabwean, had known Fourie for many years. During the Rhodesian Bush War, he had been an Askari, a ZANLA fighter captured and turned by the Rhodesian forces. Fourie, a young South African Special Forces officer, had been seconded to the Rhodesian SAS's counterinsurgency unit, and both he and Nelson served together, operating clandestinely behind enemy lines.

After the war, in which Robert Mugabe's ZANU party, the political master of ZANLA, was victorious, most Askaris moved south to join various units in the South African Special Forces. As hardened fighters, they had been feared and reviled in equal measures by their people, so they had little option but to escape the retribution that would have been inevitable.

'Are you getting too old for this job, Nelson?' Maybe we should hoist you up and skin you before feeding you to the fokken lions.'

'You can't do that, baas', said Willem, through a toothy grin, 'Nelson is so old he'll just give them a stomach ache.' With this, he laughed uproariously at his joke. Nelson reacted by glowering at his younger colleague.

Even Fourie flashed a rare smile. 'Ja, Willem, you're probably right. Nelson would be so tough it would be like eating ten-year-old biltong.'

Willem's screech of laughter was interrupted by Fourie's ringing phone.

Oh, fokken Smit again, thought Fourie as he looked at the screen. He let it ring a few times before taking the call. 'Ja', he said curtly.

'It's me,' whispered Smit on the other end of the phone.

'Speak up, man, I can't hear you.'

'I can't', replied Smit. 'I'm in a meeting at the police station. I need to know where else you hid the child porn so that we can get the story right.'

'I've told you time and time again. I downloaded about a dozen pictures onto the man's hard drive in the office. That's it. No more. Do you understand?'

'Okay, that's all I wanted to know,' replied Smit before the phone went dead.

'Fokken old woman,' muttered Fourie under his breath as both his workers grabbed the skin that had separated from the withers of the horse and started to wrench it off using all the strength they could muster.

TWENTY-SEVEN

As the news of Joe Robinson's death spread throughout Janse-Mashele, the level of distress was profound. People filed out of their offices and assembled in the lobby, meeting rooms, and canteen. A pall of disbelief and despair permeated through the gathering crowds. Many of Joe's colleagues were in tears, numb with shock, and no one was in the mood to work. No one, that is, except for Smit.

It wasn't that he didn't care one of the most senior colleagues in the company was dead; he was positively revelling in it. He could hardly conceal his delight at the demise of Joe Robinson. And what made it even better for Smit was that Robinson's memory would soon be tarnished with the most unacceptable taboos imaginable: sexual perversion involving child pornography. Smit was so elated by the situation that he continuously fought the urge to break out in giggling fits. That paedophile idea to discredit Robinson had been a stroke of genius. And fuck Fourie, he thought, he'd claim the credit for it. Suddenly, a sombre-looking Janse barged into his office. 'So, it happened them?' he asked in hushed tones.

'Well, it had to be done and done quickly', replied Smit defensively.

'Jesus Christ, I can't believe he's dead. I know he was a troublemaker with a big mouth, but we also had a lot of good times. What are we telling people?'

'At this stage, there's not a lot of information. His cleaner found his body at around seven 'o'clock this morning. Apparently, he had hanged himself. She phoned the emergency services, but he had been dead for hours.'

'Hanged himself? So, it was made to look like a suicide then?'

Smit chubby face broke into a broad grin. 'No . . . not suicide as such. We arranged something far more imaginative.'

'What the hell are you talking about?'

'Look, the police haven't finished investigating the scene yet, and of course, there hasn't been a post-mortem, and we're not supposed to know any of this', whispered Smit. 'But it wasn't a straight suicide. We made it look like a sexual thing.'

Janse was dumbstruck: 'A what?'

'It's called autoeroticism or something like that', said Smit, blushing in embarrassment. 'Apparently, people choke themselves until they nearly pass out. And, you know . . .'

'No, I don't know', said Janse, raising his voice in frustration.

'Well, they get off on it . . . '

'Get off on it?'

'Yes. Apparently, it's a big turn-on for perverts. A sexual thing . . .'

'Jesus Christ!' exclaimed Janse. 'What kind of a twisted mind would do that sort of stuff?'

'The Joe Robinson type, I suppose', replied Smit, barely able to suppress a giggle.

'For fuck sake, pull yourself together, man.'

'Well, it's even more perverted than that', smiled Smit.

'How the hell can it be?'

'It's what Joe Robinson was looking at before he choked himself to death.'

'What, pornography or something?'

'Child pornography', replied Smit.

'Jesus... Why the fuck did you do that?'

Smit stood his ground, expecting some protest from Janse, who was even more prudish than he was. 'Look, the quicker Joe Robinson is forgotten, the better. We don't want people being too sympathetic and asking questions. You know how people put dead people on a pedestal? Make them out to be saints. And Joe Robinson could have caused us big trouble. You know, he was always shooting his mouth off.'

'But child porn? Jesus, whose idea was that?'

'Well, mine, actually', said Smit. 'We had to discredit him somehow.'

Janse gazed at his finance director with almost a smile of appreciation. 'My God, Petrus, you're either cleverer or more devious than I ever imagined.'

'I just do what needs to be done', replied Smit with a self-righteous shrug of the shoulders.

'Call all the staff together right now, and let's meet in the lobby. We're going to have to confirm his death formally. And we need to get our senior people to speak to our clients before the newspapers get hold of the story.'

'What about Mashele? Have you spoken to him about this?'

'Fuck Mashele', said Janse. 'He's still sulking after the mouthful I gave him. Just get all the staff together, and we say anything about this perverted stuff.'

'Of course not, we're not supposed to know, anyway', protested Smit. But he needn't have bothered because Janse was already out of the room before he'd finished his sentence.

'Ungrateful bastard', whispered Smit.

TWENTY-EIGHT

'Please, can everyone make their way to the main lobby of the building on the ground floor for a crucial all-staff address by the CEO, Mr Janse. Please leave whatever you're doing and go to the lobby immediately; thank you.' The blaring public address system wasn't often used at Janse-Mashele, so the announcement immediately gained everyone's attention.

People went to the company's entrance lobby in small, silent groups, and the cavernous space only took a few minutes to fill up. Janse stood on the top floor balcony, watching his staff congregate below him. Then, from a nod given to him by Smit on the ground floor, he started making his way down the stairs.

Everyone knew that Janse was not in the same league as Mashele as a public speaker; he was stilted and unemotional. But what he lacked in polish was made up for by his tell-it-like-it-is, earthy approach, intensified by his guttural Afrikaans accent.

'Colleagues, some may have heard the terrible news concerning Joe Robinson by now. I want to confirm that, even though we don't have any details at this stage, it is true that Joe is, tragically, no longer with us. He died sometime during the night.'

There were audible gasps and a few loud sobs from the staff. Many people started to weep openly.

This bizarre scene greeted Daniel as he walked up the stairs from the underground parking area with his laptop bag strung over his shoulder. He had been held up that morning with an accident on the highway. After thinking he could sneak into the building unseen, it felt surreal to find the company's entire staff complement standing before him. Even though he could see Janse, whom he had never met, standing halfway up the stairs addressing everyone, he couldn't immediately grasp what the CEO was saying.

'Here is what we do know at this stage. Joe's body was found early this morning at his home by his domestic worker, said Janse.

Joe's body? Daniel's mind was swirling with all kinds of inexplicable thoughts. But he couldn't bring himself to piece the information together to reach the obvious conclusion. It just couldn't be real.

Janse continued in his solemn tone. 'The emergency services were called, and by the time the paramedics arrived, he was pronounced dead at the scene.'

Dead at the scene – oh my God. Dead at the scene. Old Joe, dead at the scene! None of this made sense. None of it!

'The police have confirmed this. As I said, that is all we know at this stage, but as soon as we receive more information, we will share it with you. And please don't listen to or spread rumours about Joe and how he died. Please be patient and wait for the facts to be established. That's all I have to say right now. I will keep you informed of developments.'

As the gathering slowly started to break up, the realisation finally struck Daniel. 'Joe's dead? What the hell happened?' asked Daniel to no one in particular as he turned to the person beside him.

'Yes, Joe Robinson was found dead this morning', replied Petrus Smit in a matter-of-fact tone. 'You are Daniel Steyn, aren't you?' You worked with Joe in strategic planning.'

'Yes, that's right', replied Daniel, recognising Smit and remembering how Joe despised him.

'So why are you so late getting to work?' snapped Smit.

Daniel was stunned by the harshness of Smit's tone and by the insensitivity. 'How can you ask me that now? I've just come in and heard that my boss and my friend is dead, and you ask me why I'm fucking late?'

Red in the face, Smit leant his two-metre bulk forward towards Daniel and whispered through clenched teeth. 'I took shit for that little fucker Joe Robinson for years. But I'll never take shit from a young arsehole like you. Do you understand? You watch your step, Steyn, if you don't want to start looking for another job.'

Daniel stepped back and stared defiantly into Smit's eyes before turning around and silently going to his office.

TWENTY-NINE

'Please don't listen to or spread rumours about Joe and how he died..." Janse's voice sounded tinny as it blared out of the small digital recorder in Mashele's hand. He rewound the track and pressed play for the eighth time that night as he pondered over Janse's speech: 'Please don't listen to or spread rumours about Joe and how he died...'

Mashele was alone in his breakfast room, one of the few rooms declared free of listening devices, when Tlale's security agents conducted the electronic sweep of his property. Monica, his PA, had discreetly recorded Janse's all-staff speech concerning the news about Joe's death to keep him abreast of events at the company.

'Please don't listen to or spread rumours about Joe and how he died...'

But how did he die? And why would anyone spread rumours about Joe's death when no one even knew the cause of death? It seemed evident to Mashele that Janse knew more about Joe's passing than he was letting on. Maybe he had some prior knowledge about Joe's demise? What could Janse be concerned about, suicide? Or the shame of suicide? But why should that be of concern to Janse? Someone taking their life, while always tragic, was hardly a rare occurrence in the advertising business.

With its punishingly long hours and brutal competitiveness, the industry tended to grind people down. Even those who were mentally tough and had the stamina of ultra-marathon runners could eventually find themselves flagging by the wayside. Eventually, their efforts would no longer be appreciated; their energy levels diminished, and their once-rapier-sharp ideas blunted through the cynicism that would inevitably creep up as they reached their middle years.

Compounding the problems was that the profession attracted a particular type of individual, the mercurial, sensitive, creative type, who could quickly slump into black periods of self-doubt and uncertainty when their ideas were rejected too many times. That was when the emotional baggage they carried became a real burden. And many would resort to the two crutches that seemed to prop up the industry: recreational drugs and alcohol. As Old Joe once quipped to Mashele, emotionally, this industry had more baggage than OR Tambo International during the Christmas season.

But then, Joe was well into middle age, thought Mashele. Christ, compared to everyone at the company, Joe was ancient. And everyone knew that Joe liked his beer more than he probably cared to admit. But was he depressed? Was he mentally unstable? Was he tired of his job? Was he tired of his life? If he was, Mashele thought, Joe did an Oscar-winning performance in concealing it from the world. Sure, Joe was a drunk. But he was primarily a happy drunk who functioned brilliantly on every level. No, Mashele was sure that Janse was somehow involved with Joe's death.

As he pondered Janse's probable involvement in Joe's demise, he strolled aimlessly through the ground floor of his house. Entering his study, he examined his favourite piece of furniture, the large rosewood desk that dominated the room. Moving his chair from behind the antique bureau, he lowered himself to the floor and manoeuvred his way into the kneehole so that he was lying on his back looking straight up the underside of this quarter ton of ancient wood. In the semi-darkness, his eyes focussed on the small, innocuous-looking black plastic device attached to the desk's corner joint. The news that his office, several rooms in his home, and vehicles had been bugged with listening devices shocked Mashele. Now he understood why his friend David Tlale had called him naïve. He was under no illusions about Janse's lack of moral fibre, but it never crossed his mind that Janse would stoop so low as to spy on his partner. Even though he felt violated and angry about this underhanded intrusion into his life, Mashele was pleased that the bugging devices remained where they were placed. By feeding disinformation, one piece at a time, Mashele had a secret weapon in the war of attrition that he would now be waging against Janse. He smiled at the thought of how to turn the tables on Janse and start manipulating him like Janse had always manipulated others.

Mashele did not doubt that Smit was also deeply involved in a conspiracy against him. As Janse's toadying sycophant, Smit worked for Janse only, not Janse-Mashele, which paid his generous salary. Smit was Janse's go-to man for dirty tricks of the filthiest variety. So, neutralise Smit, Mashele thought, to weaken Janse. But how? The man had no life outside of Janse-Mashele. And, other than Janse, he didn't seem to have any friends within the company either. If anything, Smit was an unpopular figure derided by people throughout the organisation. Mashele had often heard and paid no heed to many snide, backhanded remarks by colleagues that ridiculed Smit. Comments ranged from Smit's penny-pinching ways to his effeminate mannerisms and fawning obsequiousness towards Janse.

Old Joe Robinson had despised Smit more than anyone, thought Mashele. But Joe's death meant losing what could have been a valuable ally to Mashele. Also, besides liking Joe for his maverick, don't-give-a-damn attitude, Mashele had always admired Joe's razor-sharp intellect. He had arguably been the company's most valued senior executive. He was also respected and admired by virtually all the clients because of the value he unlocked in their brands. Yes, his untimely death had been a massive blow to the company. But now that he thought about it, there was none of the usual panic he would have expected to emanate from Janse's office when something serious threatened the company's status quo. Instead of the usual bluster that seemed inevitable when something didn't go according to plan, Janse took the shocking news about Joe in his stride. That wasn't like him, thought Mashele. The fact that Janse sounded quite level-headed when he made that speech – polished even – was just not like the Janse he had known for several years.

Mashele collected his thoughts to compose his to-do list for the following day: first, call Tlale to ensure that Joe's death would be appropriately investigated. Second, swallow his considerable pride and return to work. Third, humbly apologise to Janse, after all, what was that line about keeping your friends close and your enemies closer?

Mashele was just about to press the play button on his recorder for the tenth time that night before he realised that he probably wouldn't be the only one listening to it if he did.

Thank you, Mr Tlale, he whispered to himself.

THIRTY

The Mortuary and Forensic Services building stood on Hospital Street, Hillbrow, which was convenient considering that Hillbrow was probably the most violent neighbourhood in greater Johannesburg. Bodies had a habit of regularly appearing on the streets as victims of random stabbings or shootings or from muggings, robberies or drug deals that had gone awry. Sometimes, they were women beaten to death by partners who were too drunk or too stoned to know what they were doing. And, ever so occasionally, the bodies even came from above, thrown off the balconies of high-rise buildings occupied, reputedly, by gangs of West African drug dealers who needed to remind their clientele that liberties such as non-payment for pharmaceutical services rendered would not be tolerated.

The dull-yellow fluorescent lights illuminated featureless corridors that reeked of extra-strength disinfectant inside the grey, nondescript mortuary building. Every Wednesday, students from the nearby Wits medical school milled through the corridors, pacing towards their assigned autopsy theatre for that day. Many of the students were apprehensive about being exposed to some of the harshest lessons of life, lessons that left most of them as pale as the cadavers they watched being examined.

Braam Van Ass and Themba Dube strolled into the building with the confidence earned over many mortuary visits made throughout their careers. To them, it was home turf. They greeted the disinterested security guys with a nod and a cursory 'Howzit'.

Dube had received an early call from one of his more lucrative off-the-record clients, one of the shadowy staffers from JM-Plus. It was a tip-off about the death of one of the Janse-Mashele staff members. For his usual fee, split with Van Ass, Dube was glad to help put a lid on the story if that was what the client required.

Their first stop was the enquiries desk on the ground floor, an area usually surrounded by small family groups who were deep in shock and fraught with grief. Calling people to come in to identify the body of a loved one was a tragic drama that played itself out several times a day at the country's busiest mortuary. The attendants had quickly learned that to remain sane, they needed to be as emotionally detached as possible.

Van Ass and Dube were also impervious to the plight of the people trying to comfort one another. They waded through the crowd and walked up to the reception desk. 'Howzit chief,' said Van Ass in a matter-of-fact, cheerful way as he held up his press accreditation ID card. 'One of your vans brought in an elderly guy early this morning, a Joseph George Robinson. He was found dead at his home in Sandton.'

The mortuary attendant nodded and looked at his computer screen at the list of names entered that day. Even though it was still early, the list was already long.

'Yes, we've got him here. The pathologist is doing the autopsy this morning, so you're going to have to wait, gents.'

Who's the pathologist?' Asked Dube.

The attendant looked back at his computer screen. 'Dr Vickram Pillay.'

'And has he got a crowd of students with him?' asked Dube.

'Today is Wednesday, and every Wednesday, the Wits students spend time here as part of their coursework,' answered the attendant pedantically.

'How long before Dr Pillay takes a break?' asked Vann Ass.

'I couldn't tell you that.'

'He takes a lunch hour, surely?' ventured Dube, desperate to add as much lurid sensationalism to the story as possible. *Man Found Dead at Home* was hardly the angle to earn him a National Press Club Award.

Van Ass held a fifty rand note between his fingers. 'Look, friend, if you can help us get to see Dr Pillay as soon as possible, we can make it worth your while.'

The attendant looked around to ensure he wasn't spotted by any of the bereaved, whose numbers seemed to be swelling in the corridor. 'I'm sure I can get a message to him when he takes a break,' said the attendant as he discreetly pocketed the banknote. 'Best you guys wait in the reception area. Who shall I say is looking for him?'

Dube passed his business card, which displayed the Telegraph banner. 'Thank you, my friend,' he said with a smile.

After sitting in the reception lounge for an hour listening to the sobs and quiet weeping from various families that had gathered there, Van Ass and Dube were fast losing patience at the non-appearance of Dr Pillay. But then, on seeing four med students in green scrubs feeding coins into a coffee machine, Van Ass decided on a new tack. He walked over to them: 'I'd be careful about drinking coffee from this machine', he said with a smile.

'Of yeah, why's that?' asked a fresh-faced blonde woman in her early twenties.

'Well, rumour has it that a couple of customers had the cappuccino and ended up in a fridge in the basement.'

The students sniggered politely, except for the blonde, who had the air of sassy confidence that comes with being a straight-A student all her life. 'Oh really, I hear they use the espresso when they run out of embalming fluid.'

'Not quite', replied Van Ass, enjoying the contest. 'They've swapped them because the formaldehyde tasted better than the coffee.'

The blonde cracked half a smile, 'We don't often get comedians in here.'

'Don't suppose they get too many nice-looking blondes here either?'

'Steady on', she cautioned. 'We have to spend one day a week here as part of our course.'

'Yes, I gathered', replied Van Ass. 'You're all from Wits, aren't you?'

'Yeah, fourth year', replied one of the blonde's friends.

'I'm Braam Van Ass, and this is my partner, Themba Dube, we both write for The Telegraph.'

'So, you're with the gutter press, are you?'

'No, we write for a quality broadsheet', corrected Dube as he battled to hide his irritation with the banter. He hated it when Van Ass started flirting with virtually every half-decent-looking woman under the age of forty.

'Broad shits more like it', declared the blonde. The sudden burst of laughter from the students elicited disapproving looks from some family members.

As the students composed themselves, Dube took advantage of this sudden change in mood: 'Were you guys working with Dr Pillay this morning, by any chance?'

'Yes, we watched him performing three autopsies', said the oldest-looking student who wore thick-rimmed glasses.

'Did you witness the autopsy of a Mr Joseph Robinson?'

'He must have been the last cadaver they wheeled in, the oldish white guy', answered another student.

'How could you know it was him for sure?' asked Van Ass.

'Well, it wasn't what you'd call a demanding medical

challenge', replied the blonde. 'He was the only white male to have an autopsy this morning by Dr Pillay. The other two were black women.'

'So, what went down in the autopsy?' asked Van Ass casually.

'Do you really want to know?' asked the blonde with a hint of haughtiness. 'Well, as it was a suspected death by strangulation because of the ligature marks on the deceased's throat, you understand. Dr Pillay also pointed out the blood spots in the eyes, as well as the slight frothing at the mouth and petechial haemorrhaging, all of which were indications of death from asphyxiation.'

Seeing that both Vann Ass and Dube were looking increasingly uncomfortable, the blonde was well in her stride. 'Dr Pillay made a V-shaped incision right here', she drew her finger up to the front of Van Ass's neck. 'So, he could examine the throat.'

Van Ass resisted the urge to swallow.

'Dr Pillay then pointed out to us the ligature marks, the bloodshot eyes, the severe soft tissue bruising and the fracture to the hyoid bone, which is a horseshoe-shaped bone that supports the tongue, located right here.' This time, she indicated the position of the bone by poking at Van Ass's prominent Adam's Apple.

'So, he hung himself?' asked Dube.

'No, paintings get hung on the wall, the laundry gets hung on the line', replied the blonde with far too much condescension for Dube's taste. 'I think the word you're looking for is hanged.'

'So, they've got us chasing a suicide', said Van Ass.

'Well, that's not cut and dry either', said the bespectacled student. 'Dr Pillay and the cops were talking about a sexual thing.'

'A sexual thing?' repeated Van Ass, trying to stifle his growing excitement at the first indication of a salacious story.

'Who said it was sexual? And where did the cops come into the story?' asked Dube.

'Dr Pillay was halfway through the autopsy when a couple of detectives walked in. They started whispering amongst themselves, but we could still overhear them. They were definitely talking about a sexual thing. Dr Pillay saw that we were listening, so he asked us to leave.'

'Damn pisser', added the bespectacled student. 'Just as things were getting interesting.'

With the prospects of a big story lurking, Dube and Van Ass's moods quickly brightened. But just then, a loud, booming voice with a slight Indian accent interrupted the conversation: 'Are you the gentlemen from The Telegraph who wanted to talk to me about Mr Robinson?'

Both Dube and Van Ass turned around to face a tall, gaunt Indian man dressed in green scrubs underneath a heavy plastic apron that stretched from his knees to his upper chest.

'Yes, are you Dr Pillay?' replied Van Ass.

'Yes, I am, but you realise that I cannot give you any information about the deceased or the circumstances of his death until we have spoken to his family members first.'

'Well, we don't know if Mr Robinson had any close family members.'

'It doesn't make any difference. You should know better than asking me these kinds of questions. And I certainly hope you haven't been quizzing these students?' He looked at each of the group, but the blonde woman's blushed cheeks were a blatant betrayal. 'Right, back to work, the lot of you', he commanded, and the students quickly made themselves scarce.

'Really, guys, you should know better than trying to get information from students. They don't know anything anyway. I am thinking of calling your editor about this.'

'Okay, Dr', protested Van Ass. 'But you can give us the name of the detective in charge. Come on, Dr, you can do that.'

'Lieutenant Gideon Buthelezi was here this morning with a colleague, so I assume he's leading the case.'

'Ah, we know the Lieutenant well,' said Dube. 'He's an old friend.'

THIRTY-ONE

Mashele took a deep breath as he stepped onto the stairs leading towards the executive floor. The few staff members he had encountered as he walked up from the underground parking area had been genuinely excited to see him back. Buoyed by this spontaneous show of loyalty and affection, Mashele added a slight bounce to his step.

As he walked to his office, Monica, his PA, welcomed him with a hug. 'Janse's alone in his office. I don't think he's expecting you,' she whispered as she straightened his tie.

'Right,' said Mashele. 'There's nothing like the present to get things done.'

Janse was momentarily stunned to see Mashele walking into his office, and in shock, he spilt some tea from his cup. 'Good God, the prodigal returns,' said Janse amidst nervous laughter. 'I didn't expect to see you today. How are you, Mac?'

'I'm good, thank you, Henk. I thought it was time we talked.'

'Yes, of course', said Janse as he wiped the tea off his newspaper. 'So, what do you have in mind,' replied Janse cautiously.

Mashele sat down opposite Janse. 'Let me get straight to the point, Henk. We have built a great partnership over several years, benefiting both of us. It's been a true win-win situation.'

'Yes, it has,' admitted Janse guardedly.

'And you know that with this terrible news about Old Joe...'

'Yes,' interrupted Janse. 'That was a hell of a shock to us all.'

'Yes, well, it kick-started the realisation that whatever was said between us, however much we pissed each other off, our partnership is too important to have it destroyed because of an argument. If we both walk away from this, we both lose.'

'Yes, I see what you mean.' He was nodding his head slowly. Janse was relieved that Mashele didn't ask for an apology. Janse loathed, making apologies. On the surface, everything Mashele said made sense, but he was always suspicious of any show of magnanimity. It wasn't part of his personality, and it was a quality that he viewed with suspicion when others displayed it.

Janse finally spoke after a long silent pause, with an occasional nod. 'You know, Mac, what you say makes much sense. And I also want to say how much I appreciate you coming here this morning. It takes a brave man to stand up to his responsibilities like you have done today. I respect you for that.' Janse held his hand out by way of a truce.

Mashele, ignoring Janse's condescending tone, accepted his partner's hand and shook it vigorously.

'So, what do we know about Joe?' asked Mashele. 'What happened to him?'

'We're still trying to find out. Petrus has a friend in the police who told him that Joe had hanged himself.'

'God, suicide?'

'Well, not really. We know that it's more complicated than that.'

'I don't understand.'

At that moment, an excited Smit walked through the doorway. But, seeing Mashele stopped him in his tracks, and his beaming smile quickly changed to a look of astonishment.

'Good morning, Petrus,' said Mashele cheerfully. 'You seem incredibly happy about something.'

Smit fidgeted awkwardly with some files he was carrying.

'Oh . . . it's just some budget figures,' stammered Smit as his face blushed to a bright shade of crimson.

'We were just discussing that terrible news about Joe,' said Mashele.

'Oh, yes, terrible news,' agreed Smit.

The awkwardness in the room was palpable until Mashele hauled himself up from the chair. 'I'll let you, gentlemen, discuss your budget figures. I'm sure I have much work waiting on my desk.'

Mashele walked out of Janse's office, pleased with himself and his mission accomplished.

THIRTY-TWO

Two floors below, Daniel sat in his office looking at a series of cellphone photographs his colleagues had uploaded onto the company server. Pictures of Joe during happy times at various Janse-Mashele events: Christmas parties, staff leaving parties, new business celebrations, and birthday lunches. And Old Joe was the central figure in all the shots. Always with a beer in his hand, Joe's warm, mischievous smile radiated out of Daniel's laptop screen.

It had started as a wonderful gesture from one of the creative directors who collected some long-forgotten pictures of Joe and organised them in a file, which he uploaded onto the company server. Then, staff members added another large stack of photos. Then, with some simple but stylish editing, one of the art directors assembled all the images into a coherent video with long, lingering dissolves between shots. And as a finishing touch, he laid it over Camille Saint-Saëns's *The Swan*, a slow, haunting classical piece that seemed at odds with the happy bonhomie of the visuals. The choice of music was a reminder of a drunken evening when Joe had confessed to a group of young colleagues that he loved the music of nineteenth-century French composers. He then regaled them with a spontaneous lecture on the Romantic period's poetry, painting, and music. That was the thing about Joe, thought Daniel, he always surprised people. And Daniel hadn't even known him that long.

When Janse had called everyone together and announced Joe's death, a pall of black depression had descended over the company. All semblance of work came to a halt for the day. Many people went home. Some sat in groups gossiping while others made for the nearest pub for a liquid lunch to honour Joe's memory, which was the only way he would have approved.

Daniel had joined the latter group. With everyone speaking in hushed tones, what had started as a sentimental affair soon became a raucous occasion as people began recounting some of Joe's more outrageous exploits. Daniel drank so much that the afternoon passed in a blur of laughter. And by early evening, when someone sober enough to call for a taxi to take him home, the day's events had already been consigned to oblivion.

The following morning, as he nursed his hangover, the occasional flashback provided clues as to what had transpired. He cringed at the thought of trying to persuade one of the receptionists to join him at his apartment before bursting into tears at her rejection. He was also embarrassed by the fact that he had vomited over one of the girls in the accounts department.

His office door opened, and Debbie walked in. 'So, you made it in then', she said, her voice raspier than ever after the alcohol and the cigarettes from the previous evening. 'God, I feel rough as shit.'

'Ditto.'

'What time did you get home?'

'Haven't a clue.'

'So, I take it you didn't get your rocks off last night?' Debbie giggled.

'Oh please', protested Daniel.

'Well, it wasn't for the want of trying.' Seeing Daniel wincing, she softened her approach. 'Hey, don't be too hard on yourself, you were pissed, everyone was pissed. No one gives a shit. Except for that little lass in accounts. Shame. She didn't smell of roses after you puked over her dress.'

'For Christ's sake, don't even mention it, or I'll throw up again.'

'Old Joe would have loved it, though. Bless him. That was the best thing we could have done to honour him.'

'Yeah, you're right, the old bugger would have enjoyed himself last night. So, did you ever see Joe chatting up the females?'

'No. He wasn't the flirting type. But I tried it on with him one night. He may not have been a looker, but I was fond of him. So, I tried to chat him up myself.' She snorted a half laugh, 'God, what a fucking disaster that was.'

'What happened?'

'I really shouldn't be saying this, but it was after one of the Christmas parties I was a bit horny, and I tried it on with him. And although he was just as pissed as I was. He told me straight. He was sorry, but he couldn't do it.'

Daniel looked puzzled.

'You know he couldn't get it up. He couldn't get a hard-on.'

Daniel chuckled. 'Oh, well, he'd had a skin full of beer, so it couldn't have been surprising.'

'No. No, it wasn't that. He sat me down and told me in the nicest way that he had a medical condition, some vascular disease so that he couldn't perform sexually. He was impotent and had been for years.'

Daniel thought about how little he knew Joe. 'Poor bugger', he said after a long pause.

'Yeah, poor bugger', agreed Debbie.

Suddenly, the silence was broken by the irritatingly cheerful ringtone of Daniel's cellphone.

Before he could answer it, Debbie stood up. 'I'll get you some aspirin and some coffee. You look as if you could do with both.'

THIRTY-THREE

Lieutenant Gideon Buthelezi, a thirty-year police veteran, was sitting with a group of colleagues in the staff cafeteria at the Sandton Police Station, having an early lunch. He had been on the job since the early hours of the morning after being called to a suspicious death in a townhouse in Sandton.

Buthelezi took a bite of a hamburger big enough to require both hands. Tomato sauce and meat juices dribbled down the side of his wrist and stained his shirt cuff.

Although the staff cafeteria was off-limits to the public, seasoned crime reporters – who enjoyed a semi-symbiotic, love/hate existence with the cops – were usually given the courtesy of a blind eye.

'Hey, howzit, Lieut', said Dube with enough enthusiasm to signal to the wily Buthelezi that they were searching for information instead of providing him with any.

'Howzit Bru', replied Buthelezi, irritated that his free time was about to be hijacked.

'Lieutenant Buthelezi', jeez man, how long has it been?' enquired Van Ass.

'Cut the shit, you two. What are you after?' He took another large bite of his hamburger, the stain on his cuff growing by the second.

'We believe you're working on the Robinson case?'

Buthelezi looked nonplussed. With a caseload that ran to well over one hundred investigations, including several murders on his hands at any given time, remembering some detail from a single case was usually an optimistic stretch.

'The body that was found in a townhouse here in Sandton this morning', said Van Ass.

'Oh, yeah, the dead weirdo we found this morning . . . Sick bastard . . . Or should I say sick wanker', which prompted some nervous laughter from the other detectives sitting around the table.

'So, what can you tell us about this guy?' asked Dube, puzzled about Buthelezi's sudden hostility towards Robinson.

'Look, we have too much on our plates to worry about perverts. And he's one dead pervert that won't bother anyone again.'

'Luit, we don't understand. What is it you're telling us?'

'This guy was a fucking paedophile. He was wanking to pictures of naked little kids when he strangled himself.'

'Good fucking riddance too', interjected one of the detectives at the far end of the table to the approval of his colleagues.

Dube and Van Ass were still at a loss about what the cops were discussing. 'Christ, we were told this was a suicide', said Dube.

'Do you want the fancy name for it? It's auto-erotic strangulation. It's when these weirdos try and strangle themselves almost to the point of passing out. Apparently, it's a big turn-on. Know what I mean?'

It was evident from the reporters' facial expressions that they didn't know what Buthelezi meant. 'Auto-erotic strangulation', recited Van Ass as he wrote it on his notepad.

'That's right. The problem is, some of them pass out and end up killing themselves, continued Buthelezi, who had by now given up on his hamburger.

'You've come across this before?' asked Dube.

'It's a big no-no. A big taboo that no one ever talks about, but we see it from time to time, more so in the last ten years or so thanks to the internet... But it's nearly always swept under the carpet when we come across it.'

'How come we haven't heard of this?' asked Dube.

'Look, when we come across the corpse of some guy who has killed himself, it's already a huge shock to his loved ones. So, more often than not, we just say it's suicide. The wives and mothers shouldn't torture themselves, thinking that their loving husbands or sons took their own lives because of depression or something. It's better than the shame of killing themselves because of their weird sexual tastes. But the worst part of this bastard was that he was into little kids. There were pictures of little girls and little boys all over the place. Fuck, you think you've seen it all.'

'So, this one won't be recorded as a suicide then?'

'By the time the coroner gets around to this one, it'll probably be recorded as death by misadventure. And leave it at that.'

'Okay, thanks a lot, man, I appreciate your help.' Dube got up from his chair. 'Excuse me, guys, but I've got to make a call.'

Walking to a quiet corner in the cafeteria, Dube pulled his cellphone from his pocket and pressed the redial button on the number on his screen that had started the investigation earlier that morning. 'Hi, look, we've found out about your Robinson guy. And it's not pretty. Something called auto-erotic strangulation. The cops tell me that it's when guys . . . Oh, you know about it . . . Okay, but hang on, it gets worse. By all accounts, he was masturbating to kiddie porn, so your man, I'm sorry to say, was a paedophile.' Dube was suddenly aware of the silence at the other end of the phone . . . 'Hi, you still there? . . . 'Okay, we can try and put a lid on this, but you know what people are like when there's a mention of a paedophile . . . Someone's going to talk, either one of the cops or someone at the morgue . . . Burying this story is going to be hard, if not impossible . . . Is that what you want us to do . . . Okay, call me back then. Bye.'

Van Ass looked at Dube with a look of expectation. 'So?'

'So, he's going to speak to one of his bosses and call me back right now.'

'Fock, you're right about it being hard to put a lid on a story like this. Look at these cops here; they all know reporters and can all do with a couple of hundred bucks finder's fee on the story.'

Dube's phone rang. 'Yes?' he said before it rang a second time. 'Are you kidding me? Dube looked shocked. 'Are you sure, are you 100% sure you want us to do that . . . But he was one of your guys? . . . No, fine, hey, you're the boss . . . If that's what you want us to do, we'll do it.' He switched off his phone.

Van Ass was on edge: 'What did he say?'

'You are not going to believe this. The client doesn't want the story buried; he wants it splashed all over the front page.'

Van Ass was incredulous: 'What?'

'That's what he said. He also said some shit about dragging Robinson's name through the mud. Make as much noise about this story as possible. And don't hold back naming Janse-Mashele.'

'Fock it,' said Van Ass angrily. 'We must get back to the newsroom if we're going to break this story.'

THIRTY-FOUR

On entering the creative department meeting room, Mashele was greeted warmly by the extended team. It was 10 a.m., the time set aside for reviewing the concepts for major campaigns before the labour-intensive work could progress to a slick state of readiness for client presentations.

'So, what are we talking about today?' asked Mashele as he sat.

'Mac, before we start, can I ask you something?' Asked a young art director as she looked sadly at the empty chair - Joe's chair.

'Of course, you can, Susan, fire away.'

'We were just wondering if you've heard anything more about what happened to Old Joe', she replied.'

'No, I'm afraid I haven't. But I know Petrus Smit was talking to the police this morning, so I assume there's some investigation. I promise we will share everything with you as soon as we hear anything concrete. What did Henk say yesterday about being patient?'

The murmurs of agreement swept around the room.

'Okay, what are we reviewing this morning?'

'The campaign for the Department of Correctional Services campaign', replied Daniel.

'Of course, I've been looking forward to seeing this work. Remember what I said in our last meeting: if you creative guys don't sweep all the awards with this campaign, I'll personally fire the bloody lot of you', said Mashele, adding a needed touch of levity. 'So where do we start, Daniel? You've written the strat. Do you want to run it past us?'

'Yes, of course', said Daniel as he switched on the projector, and his PowerPoint presentation came to life on the screen.

'Oh, and I believe you did a stretch for us inside C-Max?' said Mashele, again to laughter around the room.

'It was one hell of an eye-opener', replied Daniel. 'And I sure wouldn't want to spend real time there.'

Daniel expanded on his experience at the prisons he visited as he clicked through his slides. He spoke at length about some of the characters he'd met. Yes, there was an abundance of men who had committed the most heinous crimes imaginable. But these men, with the department's aid, were turning their lives around for the better through various educational courses and psychological therapy.

Daniel spoke passionately and clearly about how he believed the campaign should be developed creatively. Emotion was the critical factor in winning over the hearts and minds of a population that had, for years, been battered relentlessly by violent crime. But, he cautioned, the main objective of this campaign was not to elicit sympathy for the perpetrators of these crimes, which most people would reject. The aim is to demonstrate how a government department was working hard to ensure that prisoners had the means to change their ways so they could be helpful to society and not just rot away in prison.

'The campaign's heroes are the people working for and running the Department of Correctional Services', said Daniel. 'Not the prisoners in their charge.'

Daniel then spoke about the impact that Riaan du Plessis had on him. 'This guy is an ex-security services operative who has murdered several people on behalf of the apartheid government. Now, he is genuinely remorseful about the crimes he committed. But he knows he doesn't deserve anyone's sympathy. The system has helped change him from what he was, a murderous thug, to having a master's degree in psychology. So, the system needs to be lauded, not du Plessis.'

'I think you've nailed it, Daniel', said Mashele. This is impressive stuff. What are your thoughts on the creative executions?'

'We need a simple TV campaign in which we interview some of these prisoners. Let them tell their stories very humanly about how the facilities and the staff have helped them change. Who knows, by the time they're eventually released, they can become useful members of society and not vicious criminals who will re-offend.'

After Daniel, the creative directors took everyone through a series of storyboards illustrating the keyframes for the commercials they planned to produce.

At the end of the meeting, Mashele stood up and showed his appreciation by clapping his hands loudly. 'This is magnificent work', he said with unbridled enthusiasm. 'God, I'm so excited by this campaign. We will have to sell this, guys', he said as he looked at the client service team. 'And if the clients don't buy this campaign, I'll machine gun the bloody lot of them.'

The room erupted into laughter.

'At least then you'll have plenty of time to get some more degrees in C-Max', said Daniel.

'Ha! Shouted Mashele, I'll have a PhD by the time I'm finished there.'

As the laughter died, Mashele summed up what needed to be done and by whom. They discussed the order of the presentation. And Mashele approved all the costs required to make the presentation as dynamic as possible. No expense spared on this one, he said. Then, as always from the consummate gentleman he was, he thanked everyone for their hard work.

Mashele had a simple philosophy on how to sell a big-budget campaign. Pre-sell it to the most critical decision-maker on the client side a day or two before the formal presentation. His logic was simple. Firstly, it allowed him to have a comfortable, discreet session where he could use his extraordinary powers of reason and his abundance of charm. Secondly, having a private meeting gave the client time to mull over the campaign so that when their team saw the work in the formal presentation, which everyone believed was for the first time, they could comment intelligently and eruditely about the proposed work. Thirdly, it allowed Mashele to talk confidently about extracurricular payments. Mashele went directly to his office to call the Minister of Correctional Services.

THIRTY-FIVE

The rain was pouring hard as Daniel was driving home later that evening. Even though Joe's death still dominated the conversation, it had been a surprisingly good day. Mashele had enthusiastically approved the Correctional Services review, and everyone was excited. It seemed that things were slowly getting back to some semblance of normality.

As the traffic inched along the main drag close to Daniel's home, it puzzled him how the Johannesburg traffic always slowed to a crawl whenever it rained. When he had lived in London, where it rained incessantly, he couldn't remember a single downpour affecting the London traffic flow. Maybe the Brits are just more used to it, he thought.

Daniel looked to the side of the road to see a familiar face, the local newspaper seller. He was a friendly young lad, and Daniel often enjoyed snatches of conversations with him when he bought the evening paper. The lad smiled and waved to Daniel, who returned the gesture. It was then that the headline of the paper suddenly caught his attention. He pressed his foot on the brake.

'AD EXEC DIES EXPOSING HIMSELF AS A PAEDOPHILE! Screamed The Telegraph's banner headline through the transparent plastic cover, held high in the young lad's hand.

Daniel was so stunned he was oblivious to the hooting taxi behind him. He was also unaware of the other drivers screaming and shouting obscenities at him for stopping in the middle of the road for no apparent reason. One particularly aggressive woman caught his attention by hooting her horn beside his car. As he turned to look at her, he could lip-read her mouthing two syllables: *'arse-hole'*. Daniel switched on his hazard lights and pulled over to buy a newspaper.

There was no time for small talk with the paper seller that evening. Seeing the subhead confirmed Daniel's worst fears: *Top Janse-Mashele executive dies in a sordid sex act involving child porn.* Daniel took a long, deep breath to compose himself before reading the article.

'A well-known advertising executive and a senior manager at the renowned communications group, Janse-Mashele, was found dead early this morning at his Sandton townhouse. Joe Robinson, a 64-year-old strategic planning director, was declared dead at the scene.

'His domestic worker discovered his naked and trussed up body in what one senior police officer described as: 'Probably the most sordid scene I have ever had the misfortune to witness'. Mr Robinson is believed to have strangled himself during a little-known sexual act referred to by psychologists and sexologists as auto-erotic strangulation.

'This hazardous practice involves impeding the air supply to heighten sexual pleasure. Although infrequently reported, it has been rumoured that several celebrities have suffered death through this sub-category of sexual masochism. The most famous are Michael Hutchence, the lead singer for the Australian rock band INXS, and Hollywood actor and martial artist David Carradine.

'However, according to police detectives, the most disturbing aspect of the scene was the abundance of child pornography found at Mr Robinson's home.

The detective in charge of the case, Lieutenant Gideon Buthelezi, said that no foul play by any other parties is suspected.

'Asked for comment, the financial director of Janse-Mashele, Mr Petrus Smit, issued a statement.

'Joe Robinson worked here at Janse-Mashele for several years, and

during this time, no one suspected that he had this dark, perverted side to his character.

'As soon as I heard about these allegations about the pornographic material of children, I briefed members of the Janse-Mashele IT department to examine the company server and Mr Robinson's desktop computer for any illegal material. We find Mr Robinson's behaviour to be distressing in the extreme, and we will cooperate fully with the police investigations.

'You think you know people, but obviously, this dark and sordid side of that man has come as a tremendous shock to all of us at Janse-Mashele.'

Fucking Smit must love this, thought Daniel.

'Police are investigating further, and anyone with any information needs to contact Lieutenant Buthelezi of the Sandton Police Station urgently.'

THIRTY-SIX

Petrus Smit giggled as he read the article for the eighth time that night. There were specific phrases that he could now recite by heart. He was even more thrilled when the story featured on the national TV news channels. Even though the detail was highly sanitised compared to the more sensational print media, it was still a big story in the making.

Smit was so excited that when he finally went to bed, he couldn't sleep. His mind was buzzing with thoughts of getting his revenge on Robinson. Yes, Old Joe wouldn't be so popular in the company now. And yes, there wouldn't be any more tears shed for a man regarded as a sexual deviant of the worst kind.

Tossing and turning through most of the night, Smit thought about Fourie. Even though he hated the man for his lack of respect and despised him for his arrogance, Fourie was still the consummate master of his chosen profession.

When he awoke, he was delighted that the radio stations had picked up on the news. The story, spurred on by social media, was abuzz with lurid details. Auto-erotic strangulation was by far the most used hashtag of the day on Twitter accounts throughout the country.

It also seemed that radio reporters were hunting down every qualified sexologist for their take on this taboo subject. Clinical psychologists – be they university academics or practising professionals – were being lined up with talk show stations explaining this deviant behaviour and encouraged to go into the most lurid and sensational detail.

The attitude towards paedophilia - the label now attached to

Joe – was, however, markedly different. Angry callers flooded the airwaves with demands that paedophiles be castrated. The more intelligent callers referred to chemical castration, whereas the less intellectually gifted demanded the physical variety. 'Preferably with a blunt knife!' said one elderly lady. 'And yes, she would gladly cut the bastard's pecker off herself. And do so in public if she could.'

Listening to the radio in his bathroom, Smit laughed so much when he heard the old lady's comment that he nicked himself shaving. He was astonished that all this media frenzy had started with his phone call to one of his most trusted PR men at JM-Plus, who had then called one of his tame reporters. The sense of his power overawed him as he drove to the office that morning. He felt invincible.

But, as usual, he battled to contain his emotions whenever he experienced euphoria. And it always manifested itself in an embarrassing, high-pitched, girl-like giggle. No, he thought, today he'd have to try his utmost to be angry, disgusted, shocked, sickened, appalled, and horror-struck by the disclosure of Joe Robinson's reprehensible character.

That, he thought, should make for good copy to be given to the JM-Plus man to use in the following press release to be distributed to the media to keep the story fresh in people's minds. He recited the line again loudly in his car. 'I am so angry and disgusted and shocked and sickened and appalled and horror-struck by the disclosure of Joe Robinson's reprehensible character.' He screeched with laughter as he drove through the boom gates at Janse-Mashele.

THIRTY-SEVEN

Daniel also heard some of the comments on the radio, which is why he switched it off and drove to work in silence. He felt depressed. The memory of the man he knew and admired was in the process of being systematically and utterly destroyed. And he was also beginning to doubt Joe. How could he not have noticed that Joe was like that? How could he fail to see the signs? Like the fact that Joe didn't seem interested in women in a sexual sense.

The silence ended when his cellphone started ringing. He picked it up, not caring about the R1,000 fine for using a cellphone while driving a car. 'Yes', he said with little or no attempt to be polite.

'Hi, is this Daniel?' said a female voice in an African accent. 'My name is Judith Maponya. Like you, I was a friend of Joe's.'

'Oh, really', he said cautiously. 'Well, what can I do for you?'

'Listen, we need to get together urgently. We need to talk.'

'What's there to talk about, Joe's sexual preferences?'

'It's all lies, Daniel. Lies, I tell you. You must listen to me. Those bastards at Janse-Mashele had my brother Jabu murdered. Joe was helping me to nail them. Hard evidence shows that Janse and Petrus Smit defrauded their clients for years. They murdered my brother, and I'm pretty damn sure they murdered Joe, too.'

Daniel was stunned into silence.

'Hello... hello... Daniel... are you there?'

'Yes, sorry. Just hang on a minute... I need to pull over.'

Judith could hear Daniel's car coming to a halt, and the hand brake being pulled before Daniel returned to the line. He sounded more receptive: 'Okay, I don't know what you're saying or who you are, but I do know that Joe had his enemies at Janse-Mashele. When and where do you want to meet?'

'Today. Preferably now.'

'Okay, I'm on my way to work. Where are you?'

'I'm at the Willows Coffee Shop in Sandton, do you know it?'

'Yes, of course. How will I recognise you?

'I'm wearing a beige suit and a white blouse, and I'll hold a copy of Business Day.'

'Okay, I'm on my way.'

'Great. I'll be waiting for you.'

Daniel walked into one of Sandton City's more elegant coffee shops within twenty minutes. Even though it was full of the usual crowd of young, trendy executives, it was quiet. Most clientele sat alone on the communal tables, engrossed with their laptops or iPads. Daniel spotted the elegantly dressed Judith almost at once.

'Hi, I'm Daniel', he said as he held out his hand. 'I'm sorry, I didn't catch your name?'

'Judith . . . Judith Maponya.'

'I'm deeply sorry about you brother. Jabu's death happened just before I started working at Janse-Mashele, so I didn't know him, I'm afraid. But I remember Joe telling me he had a friend in the accounts department. I assume he was referring to Jabu.'

'Probably. Thank you for coming to meet with me. I was scared that you might think of me as insane.'

The conversation was interrupted as the waiter came to take Daniel's order of a double espresso. Judith declined a second café latte.

'God, I cannot believe the insanity of the last forty-eight hours', said Daniel. 'And I don't know which is the biggest shock, Joe's death or all this stuff about him being a paedophile and this auto-erotic shit that everyone's talking about.'

'Look, the information I want to share with you is extremely dangerous. First of all, I don't believe Joe killed himself; I'm convinced he was murdered because of this information. And I know for a fact that this was the reason they murdered my brother Jabu.'

'But the newspaper articles all said that he had accidentally strangled himself when that auto-erotic thing went wrong. And that there was no foul play.'

'I don't believe it. Joe told me that Janse-Mashele has a covert subsidiary that hardly anyone knows about, which spreads disinformation that damages the reputations of their enemies and competitors.'

'Yes, JM-Plus, Joe mentioned it to me, too.'

"Also, Daniel, I'm a lawyer; in my job, you get to know when people are lying to you or have something to hide, and I am convinced that Joe wasn't anything like how he has been depicted in the media. Joe had a big heart. He had integrity.'

Again, the conversation halted when the waiter delivered Daniel's coffee.

'Okay, Judith, I agree he was a great guy with integrity, and I really liked him. And I don't want to believe all this crap being said about him. But do you know what? It's pretty bloody convincing.'

'Well, that's because the people who killed him are extremely smart and ruthless.'

Daniel swallowed most of the espresso in one gulp, slightly burning the roof of his mouth. 'I don't know ... what is this all about?'

'Okay, Daniel, let me start from the beginning. My brother, as you know, worked in Petrus Smit's finance department, and while he was there, he unearthed a massive scam. Smit and Janse were defrauding clients for millions.'

'Could he prove this?'

'Yes. Jabu had all the hard evidence: copies of invoices, receipts, bank statements, spreadsheets, and financial stuff. And it was for fictitious work. Advertisements were supposed to be placed in foreign publications for one of the government agencies, but in reality, they never appeared. I told Jabu that he had to report it to the authorities. But stupidly, Jabu decided to get in on the act himself.'

'It was probably TISA, Trade and Investment South Africa, which is part of the Department of Trade and Industry.'

'Yes, TISA, that's it.'

'Janse-Mashele still has the account. Shit', said Daniel as the realisation suddenly dawned on him. 'Things are making sense now; I remember one evening after work when Joe mentioned something. Yeah, it was just before Jabu's funeral, and Joe was extremely pissed off when he heard that Janse-Mashele was paying for the flowers. It set him off in a hell of a rage. Then he hinted that Jabu knew something and that he was dipping his hands in the company cash register. And I didn't believe him when he said that Smit and Janse had had Jabu killed. Joe had been out for lunch, and I thought he'd just had a few beers too many.'

'God, I begged Jabu not to be so stupid. But he became greedy and arrogant, thinking he could get away with it because of all the evidence he had. He called it his insurance policy.'

'Where is all that evidence now?'

'It's safe and staying where it is until I am sure it's not going to the wrong hands. These people will stop at nothing to save themselves. They're utterly ruthless.'

'But all this still doesn't explain what happened to Joe. The police said that Joe strangled himself.'

'Look, Daniel, because I deal with criminal law, and I can tell you right now that forensic pathology is in complete shambles here in South Africa. There are only forty trained specialists in the country, and they must handle over 80,000 medico-legal autopsies a year. Do the arithmetic, that's two thousand cases per specialist per year. Or five or six autopsies a day, seven days a week, without a single day off in twelve months. And here's something else. If the cause of death is not immediately obvious, like a gunshot wound or an axe in the head, an autopsy can easily take five hours or more. So how precise can these specialists be?'

'Hell, yes, when you put it that way', conceded Daniel.

'That's right, and it's not like CSI on TV when these medical sleuths agonise over a particular case until they crack it. In this country, right now, unless there are obvious clues, these people can only do the basics; they go through the motions because they don't have the time. If there's a murder case where the forensic evidence is complex, then by the time it gets to court, the chances are high that the evidence will be compromised. This means people are literally getting away with murder.'

'My God. So, what do we do about it?'

'Well, we must get a private forensic pathologist on the case. Someone who has the time to investigate the evidence properly.'

'Joe and I had been talking to an advocate who was helping us on a pro-bono basis. I need to chat with him and get his advice.'

'So, what do you need from me?' asked Daniel.

'I need someone inside Janse-Mashele, someone I can trust. Joe thought the world of you and spoke of you often. He said you had integrity.'

Daniel finished the dregs in his coffee cup. 'As I said, I don't want to believe this crap that's being written and spoken about Joe. He was better than that.'

'If you agree to help me, I must give you this.' Judith pulled a cellphone out of her bag. 'Whenever you need to talk to me, my number is stored here.'

Daniel looked surprised. 'This is a bit melodramatic, isn't it?'

'No, it's not', insisted Judith. 'Joe and I never used our own phones when we needed to talk. Please, Daniel, you must understand these people are dangerous abd they also have the resources and the wherewithal to follow you, tap your phone, and read your emails and text messages. This is real, Daniel. These are the kinds of things that the bad guys are doing right now.'

Daniel took the phone and placed it inside his Jacket pocket. 'Okay, we'll talk then. 'Thanks, thanks for trusting me.' Said Judith as they shook hands before Daniel left.

THIRTY-EIGHT

Mashele's return to the company had been much more straightforward than he had expected. Most of the staff had been welcoming and supportive. And, to Mashele's surprise, Janse had even been conciliatory. He may not have been gushing with magnanimity, but he had made a concerted effort to confer with Mashele on a few big decisions. He also agreed with Mashele's suggestion that the company hold an extraordinary executive committee meeting to discuss the situation surrounding Joe's death.

The exco members, who were mainly heads of departments in the parent company and managing directors of the various subsidiaries - all except JM-Plus - were gathered in the main boardroom, sipping coffee and chatting when Mashele entered. He greeted his colleagues and engaged in some small talk and general banter. After a few minutes, it immediately stopped as Janssen entered the room.

He addressed his senior colleagues before taking his seat at the end of the ten-metre-long oval table: 'Good morning, ladies and gentlemen. Shall we call this meeting to order?'

After everyone had taken their seats, no one could fail to notice the one empty chair that made Joe's absence more palpable.'

'Thank you for taking the time out of your busy schedules for this meeting. Now, with this awful business about Joe Robinson, some issues need to be discussed. And as you can imagine, they will not be pleasant.'

Some of the people shifted in their seats.

'The first issue we must discuss is the possible reputational damage to our Janse-Mashele brand. Brenda, this is your area of expertise. Can you share your views?'

Brenda Isaksson, the diminutive, bookish-looking head of PR, spoke confidently. 'Good crisis management dictates that we are open, honest, and quick to respond to the media about any issue. And that we do not attempt to ignore it or brush it under the carpet.' She turned to look directly at Smit: 'Petrus, you were interviewed by The Telegraph?'

'Yes', replied Smit defensively.

'As the head of PR communications at Janse-Mashele, please refer any queries from the media to me and let me manage them. We can't have everyone commenting willy-nilly.'

Smit, although irked, kept his silence. He glared at her, thinking she was a rank amateur compared to his private team at JM-Plus.

Brenda Isaksson continued: 'Look, it's one of these shocking situations you can never plan for. However, I don't believe this will harm the company because paedophilia and sexual perverts are being exposed all the time in the media, usually for downloading kiddy porn from the Internet. They can be doctors, lawyers, sportsmen, anything. People we would regard as perfectly respectable are being exposed, so there was nothing unique regarding Joe Robinson.'

'So, what are you suggesting?' asked Janse.

'We need to be proactive in distancing ourselves from Joe Robinson as much as possible to negate any damaging rub-off on the Janse-Mashele brand.'

Smit felt an intense urge to giggle but suppressed it by faking a coughing fit that momentarily broke the PR boss's train of thought. Smit mumbled a half-hearted apology and sipped some water.

'We also need to get involved with some other measures that show a caring side of Janse-Mashele', continued Isaksson. 'I was thinking that we make a sizable donation to one of the charities that deal with sexually abused children as part of the company's corporate social investment.'

There was an immediate murmur of approval from around the table.

'Or that we do some pro-bono work for one of those charities,' she continued.

'The pro-bono work is a particularly promising idea', interrupted Janse. He was always enthusiastic about options that cost the company nothing more than the time of some staff members. 'Brenda, you must identify a suitable charity and approach them for permission. And Mac, we'll need a strategy before we open the brief to all the creative staff.'

'But we can't shift any of the paying jobs out of the system', insisted Smit. 'Everyone working on this must give up their evenings or weekends.'

'Next on the agenda, we'll need to discuss a replacement for Robinson,' said Janse.

Mashele noticed that the once friendly monikers of 'Old Joe' and even plain 'Joe' had now been discarded and replaced by the more detached and impersonal 'Robinson'. It seemed that the demonisation of the man was complete.

Janse continued. 'I want you all to write a list of potential candidates so that we can draw up a shortlist. I do not want to rely on headhunters, which will cost us a fortune. So, please give me suggestions for the people you can vouch for or have worked with in the past. Okay, that's it from my side. Is there any other business to discuss here?'

Smit, the only exco member who emulated Janse's formal tone in such meetings, cleared his throat before addressing the meeting: 'Yes, Mr Chairman. I want to raise an issue concerning the staff levels at the strategic department. This department is overstaffed at the junior level. And recommend that we cut a couple of staff members who can't add much value to the company's bottom line.'

There was a slight murmur of disquiet at this ruthless talk of retrenchments in a department that had just recently experienced trauma. But it was quickly silenced when Janse spoke up.

'Who do you have in mind?'

'Well, there's that fellow Daniel Stein for one. Then there's ...'

'Daniel Stein', interrupted Mashele, his voice raised in exasperation. 'That young guy is a brilliant asset to this company. I'll go even further and say he's the most talented young planner I have come across in years. You must be mad to want to fire him.'

Smit's face turned a deep crimson at Mashele's stinging rebuke. 'Well, I also thought that when we eventually find the replacement for Joe Robinson, that person will want to hire his or her own people.'

'That is complete and utter nonsense', countered Mashele. 'If we use your logic, then every time a head of a department leaves the company, we have to fire everyone working in that department. Where's the sense in that? Besides, you should know better than anyone in this room, as HR reports to you that you can't fire anyone for spurious reasons with our labour laws. No, sorry, Petrus. You're mistaken, and your logic is warped.'

The ever-prickly Smit recoiled in anger at Mashele's comments. But before he could stammer a reply, Janse spoke up. 'Petrus, I don't think we need to discuss this now. And as Mac feels so positive about this young man, let's leave it at that.'

He looked around the table. 'As there is no other issue that needs to be raised, then this meeting is over. Thank you once again.'

THIRTY-NINE

Things were not going well for Fourie. A bow-hunting owner of a chain of hardware stores from Idaho had killed a black-maned male lion in Zimbabwe. The hapless lion had been lured illegally into a fenced-off enclosure outside Hwange National Park. Then, to make matters worse, the lion had turned out to be a feline celebrity. Mambo wasn't just a big attraction to the many thousands of visitors to the park; he was also being tracked and studied by researchers from a British university. After the international media had picked up on the story, the floodgates of outrage quickly opened. With this kind of publicity, Fourie was paranoid about what could happen to his thriving business.

Even though Fourie didn't care for canned hunting, he cared very deeply about his income. And such a hugely emotional media clamour against canned hunting would inevitably mean pressure applied to African governments who would, in turn, apply pressure on professional hunters to end the practice. Fourie rolled up the newspaper that carried the Mambo story into a tight ball before throwing it into his braai fire.

'Pinko-liberal fokken hypocrites', he whispered to himself as the paper caught alight. He took a mouthful of brandy and coke, his sixth of the evening. He knew he was drinking too much, but he didn't care. It seemed stories were vying for people's attention on the front pages: Mambo and Robinson. And both were linked to him in various degrees.

Even more worrying was that his undercover work was beginning to dry up. His only active client now was Petrus

Smit—a man he despised, and assassination was hardly a service that could be advertised. Killing Joe Robinson had been the first job since the Maponya murder, and he felt he had undercharged on his fee.

Whereas the Maponya murder was straightforward, killing Joe Robinson had been complicated. It had taken a lot of time to reconnoitre Robinson's townhouse complex and find the only spot along the exterior walls the security cameras didn't cover. Then, there was the issue of deactivating the electric fence and causing a diversion so that he could scale the wall. Then, the murder itself and making the strangulation appear like a self-inflicted act. Then all the child porn had to be sourced. All those issues had increased the risks involved, and he hadn't charged enough.

How the mighty have fallen, he thought to himself as he downed the content of his glass. One minute, a captain in an elite unit in the security forces, heading a covert cell of agents; the next, relegated to doing the dirty work for the likes of Petrus Smit. He poured himself another brandy and coke.

Petrus Smit was the root cause of his problems. He had been broke before, even unemployed, but he had never lost his self-respect, and he had never had to pander to some sly, cowardly lowlife like Smit. But what could be done? Kill the bastard, but first, drain him of every cent he possessed. Blackmail him? He knew that Smit feared him, but he also knew that Smit had ample evidence against himself. But how could he get back at Smit without incriminating himself? One thing was sure; Smit would never have the guts to inform on him because he knew he'd be dead. And he knew it would be nasty.

He picked up his cellphone and made a call to Smit. It rang twice before Smit picked up. 'Yes, Fourie? Is that you?'

Fourie kept his silence to unnerve Smit.

'Fourie... Fourie, what is it you want?'

Fourie could hear the anxiety rising in Smit's voice. 'You owe me money.' Fourie slurred down the phone.

'Owe you what?' protested Smit indignantly. 'I've paid you for every job you've ever done for me. What the hell are you talking about, man?'

'You owe me more money for the last job. The Robinson job.'

'I paid you what we agreed. You asked for fifty thousand, and I paid you fifty thousand.'

'Yeah, well, it wasn't enough. Not half enough for what I had to do for you, you big bastard.'

'What the fuck is the matter with you, Fourie. Are you drunk? ... You are, aren't you? ... You're fucking drunk.'

'Yeah, well, I'm not drunk enough. And you're not paying me enough. I kill people for you, and it's all over the newspapers. I don't need that kind of heat.'

'Look, Fourie', said Smit, softening his stance. 'There won't be any comebacks on you, so there won't be any heat. You do a job for me, and I pay you. You can't come to me after the fact and demand more money. That's not how things work.'

'You want to know how things fokken work? Here's how they work. You pay me another fifty grand, or I'll fokken do the next job on you. Do you know what I mean?'

'Fourie. You're drunk, and I'm putting the phone down right now.'

'The next time you see me, you're going to pay me another fifty grand, do you hear?'

'Fourie, we had a deal, and I have honoured my side of that deal. I am hanging up now.'

'Honour? What the fok do you know about honour? You slimy bastard. I had honour; I had a rank that everyone looked up to and respected ... I served a cause ... Do you know what that fokken means, well do you Smit?'

Smit finally plucked up the courage and switched his phone off.

Fourie threw his cellphone far into the back of his overgrown yard. He then poured himself another brandy, this time disregarding the coke. He downed it in one before slumping back in his chair as the tears of self-pity and self-loathing started to flow down his cheeks.

FORTY

'Okay, everyone quiet on set . . . We are about to start shooting . . . First positions everyone.' The assistant director's booming voice interrupted the numerous conversations from the various small groups of people spread around the film set.

Using the garden behind the Kgosi Mampuru II Prison as a convenient and secure location, film crew members mingled with the Janse-Mashele production and creative team. And the numbers were swelled by the large and primarily uninvited group of Correctional Services personnel helping themselves at the craft tables laden with snacks and beverages.

'First positions, everyone', reiterated the assistant director and the film crew quickly snapped to attention.

'Roll sound.'

The boom operator responded to the order: 'Speed.'

'Roll camera.'

As the whirring sound of the film speeding through the 35-mm Arriflex camera increased, the camera operator also reacted to the order. 'Speed', he replied.

'Ready for take one, tag it.'

The clapper-loader held the electronic clapper board for the camera lens to record the shot for the editor's benefit. 'Take one, scene one!' He shouted before exiting the scene.

'Marked' shouted the camera operator.

And action', commanded the assistant director.

The camera was mounted on a dolly - a heavy mobile platform

on rails - and was pushed by the key grip, usually the biggest and strongest crew member on set. He worked alongside the camera crew, headed by the director of photography, who sat on a stool mounted on the dolly behind the camera.

The opening shot consisted of four seconds of dialogue in a smooth-flowing tracking shot that moved in an arc around the subject: Category C prisoner Riaan du Plessis.

Riaan looked nervous. 'Even though I have been a prisoner for the last 22 years, I have not been idle . . .'

'And cut!' interrupted the director, who sat alongside the DOP on the dolly. 'That's very good, Riaan. You were just a tad hesitant, but not to worry, even the most experienced actors bugger things up on the first take. The most important thing is to keep looking straight at the camera lens. Don't forget you're engaging with the audience at home, and when you look straight into the camera, it's like you're looking straight into their eyes. Okay?'

'Yes, I will try my best, ' replied Riaan. The make-up lady applied more face powder to remove the shine from his balding head caused by the heat of the tungsten lights bearing down on him. He looked uncomfortable at being fussed over.

Daniel and Riaan could only nod a greeting to each other from a distance as the film crew and the agency personnel had been warned that fraternising with any prisoners was strictly forbidden. The call time for the shoot was 30 minutes earlier than usual so a senior department official could brief everyone on the protocols. They were determined to maintain strict segregation between the heavily guarded prisoners and everyone else on the set.

'Back to first position, everyone', barked the assistant director like a drill sergeant on a parade ground.

Daniel always imagined that the film director would do all the shouting on a film set. But the director's role was focused entirely on the subject matter rather than guiding the process and the crew, which was the assistant director's function. Daniel sat on directors' chairs under a canvas gazebo, watching all the action on a video monitor connected to the camera.

'Scene one. Take two . . . And action!'

'Even though I have been a prisoner for the last 22 years, I have not been idle . . .'

Daniel was impressed with Riaan's performance. He came across as natural and sincere. And on hearing the whispered comments from the agency creatives, Daniel could also sense their approval.

There was no precedence for a serving category C prisoner to be the subject of a TV commercial like this, and permission had to be granted by the minister in person. But as this was the minister's pet project, designed to enhance his teetering career due to his glaring incompetence, the entire process had been fast-tracked with extraordinary efficiency.

Although it was not the norm for strategic planners to be present on set during the filming process, Daniel had made a special plea to the head of TV production and the creative director. He was close to this job and had wanted to be involved with the production. Besides, he'd never been on a film set before and was fascinated by the process. Daniel's enthusiasm impressed everyone, and they quickly agreed to include him on the film set.

After several takes, the director seemed satisfied that he finally had what he called 'the bankable shot'. 'But let's have one for Lloyds', he added, referring to the old film industry cliché of having one final take for 'insurance' purposes.

Daniel was fascinated by the director's and the DOP's diligence. It seemed they had endless patience working with a non-professional actor. Daniel also enjoyed the attention he, his agency colleagues, and the clients were getting from the on-set caterers. Cappuccino orders were constantly sought, and large platters of toasted sandwiches were liberally distributed.

After a few hours of repetitive action, Mashele joined his colleagues on set. He sat in one of the canvas director's chairs next to Daniel and enjoyed a lively banter in hushed tones with his colleagues as they watched the action on the monitor. Sometime later, the assistant director announced there'd be an early lunch before the art crew and props master would prepare the set for the next scene.

As everyone made their way to the caterer's marquee for the buffet, Mashele grabbed Daniel by the wrist and whispered to him. 'Hang in there for a moment, Daniel', he said. 'I need to chat with you privately.'

Mashele then waited for the last of the stragglers to leave before he looked Daniel in the eye and asked him bluntly: 'Why does Petrus Smit want you fired?

Daniel was shocked by the directness of the question. 'Are you kidding me?' was the only way he could respond.

'I wish I was. But Petrus Smit has it in for you, and I am intrigued as to why.'

'We had words', explained Daniel. 'The morning I heard about Joe's death when everyone assembled at the reception and Henk Janse made his speech.'

'So, what happened?'

'I was a bit late coming in that morning. I walked in when the CEO was about halfway through the announcement. I was stunned to hear that Joe had died ... I was in shock, I suppose. Joe meant a hell of a lot to me ... Then Smit started having a go at me for being late ... My friend and boss had just died, and he was so fucking petty.'

'Well, he's hardly a diplomat', opined Mashele with his usual tinge of irony.

'He hated Joe', said Daniel. 'He said something like he'd taken so much shit from that little fucker Joe Robinson, but he would never take shit from a young arsehole like me. He then threatened to fire me.'

'Why do you think he and Joe hated each other so much?

'Well . . . I suppose . . . I can't really say.' Daniel hesitated as he realised that he had already revealed more than he should have done. He attempted to check himself: 'What I mean is that I don't know that much.'

'Of course, I understand. But I want you to know that I have a high regard for you, Daniel, and I will protect you from Smit. So, don't worry, okay? Now, let's see what they have for lunch. Lobster and Kobe beef, I bet, judging from the production budget.'

FORTY-ONE

From the moment he'd hung up on Fourie's call two days earlier, Smit plunged into panic. He hadn't slept. He hadn't eaten. And his stress levels were so high that he started to double up on his blood pressure medication. In his mind, Smit had interrogated every permutation of every point he could remember Fourie making during his drunken tirade. He was scared to the core of his being.

One thing was for sure: with Fourie being so emotionally unstable - and most likely an alcoholic - Smit realised that he couldn't afford to antagonise the man further. He also realised he had little choice but to pay him the extra fifty thousand. It worried him that this was the thin end of an extortionate wedge: fifty thousand today, a hundred thousand tomorrow, a million next week? Also, Fourie was still extremely useful to the operation, and replacing him would be impossible.

Worst of all was the threat that Fourie had made to his life. He had sensed Fourie's contempt towards him building for some time. But he hadn't realised it was rooted in such hatred. Smit cringed at the thought of being stalked by one of the most ruthless psychopaths imaginable. He was a maniac with the knowledge and the means to eliminate virtually anyone he wished.

Over those two days, his paranoia about his safety had grown extreme. He double-checked the locks on his property. He would continuously be looking through the windows for any strangers who may be loitering in the street. He changed his route to work. He left the office early in the evenings to avoid driving home in darkness. He slept with his ancient .38

Special revolver beside his bed every night. And he grabbed the weapon every time he heard the slightest noise.

Smit also realised he would have to share his predicament with the other man he feared: Janse. Of course, Janse knew about Fourie but had always refused to be drawn into any face-to-face meetings with the ex-security forces killer. All the dirty work was for Smit to take care of.

Smit walked into Janse's office and closed the door behind him, a sign that Janse took to mean something furtive was on the agenda. 'Morning, Petrus. Why are you looking so tired? Are you working too hard?'

Smit sat down in front of Janse. Again, Janse noted that this was not Smit's usual behaviour. If Smit had something to say, he said it on his feet, with little or no time for small talk or pleasantries.

'Henk, we have a bit of a problem', said Smit in a hushed tone.

'What is it now?'

'It's our friend Fourie.'

'Jesus Christ, Petrus. You know I don't get involved with that side of things', said Janse indignantly.

'But you have to get involved. Just hear me out.'

'He's your contact. I don't know him. I've never spoken to him. I've never laid eyes on him. You do. If you have a problem with him, you'll have to sort it out, for fok sake.'

'Look, Fourie is getting out of hand.'

'What do you mean?'

'He phoned me a few nights ago. He was drunk and aggressive. He said we had to pay him more money for the . . . 'Smit dropped his voice to a barely discernible whisper, 'for the Joe Robinson job.'

'Fokken hell', exclaimed Janse through gritted teeth. 'You told me that this Fourie guy was dependable, and now you tell me he's a drunk who's shooting his mouth off?'

'He's gone off the rails. Who knows, maybe it's the booze, maybe killing people for a living has finally got to him.'

'You say he wants more money, how much?'

'Another fifty thousand.'

'Okay, that's nothing, and we're not in any position to argue with the man.'

'No, we're not. We must pay him the fifty grand. But it worries me that he will be even more demanding.'

'That depends on who we need to get rid of.'

'No, I don't mean Fourie will raise the price for every job he does for us. I'm scared that he might start blackmailing us.'

'You mean blackmailing you.'

'I mean blackmailing us. Fourie knows all about Janse-Mashele. Christ, he's killed two of our employees for us', replied Smit, showing some rare dissent against his boss.

'Okay, okay', said Janse dismissively. 'First things first, we pay him the fifty grand to get him off our backs. Then, we need to get some JM-Plus people to help us get a grip on things. We must play it by ear on this Fourie matter. Call him and offer to pay the fifty grand and see how he reacts.'

'Okay, I will do it today.'

'What else is happening with this Joe Robinson thing?'

'There'll be one more story from us in the paper over the weekend. We found more kiddie porn on his hard drive.'

'You mean you put the porn on his hard drive. There's too much fuss about his death. All you had to do was to get rid of him, not get the whole fokken country talking about him.'

'But he's hated, despised. No one will bother looking into his death.'

'You sure about that? Are you sure that no one is going to think that maybe this is all bullshit?'

'Look, Fourie has always been professional.'

'Professional? He's becoming a fokken lunatic, and you tell me he's professional? For Christ's sake, Petrus, how do we know he didn't fok up? How do you know he didn't make some mistake?'

Smit was lost for words.

'Who was close to Joe?'

'Daniel Stein', replied Smit. 'And maybe Debbie Peters, his PA.'

'Right, that's where we start. I want them watched very carefully. I want to know who they meet, who they speak to on the phone, who they email, who they send SMSs to, everything. Do you understand? We have got to get a grip on this thing.'

'I'll speak to the JM-Plus people today', replied Smit.'

FORTY-TWO

As the phone rang, Daniel awoke from a deep slumber. He was baffled by the unfamiliar ringtone. It rang continuously, giving him time to collect his thoughts until he remembered the phone Judith had given him. He jumped out of bed and retrieved it from a Jacket pocket that he had dumped on the couch in the lounge the previous evening.

'Hello', said Daniel.

'Were you asleep or couldn't you find the phone?' asked Judith.

'Sorry, guilty on both charges.'

'Well, good morning anyway. Have you got plans for today?'

'Good morning. No, just a few chores, the usual Saturday stuff. Why do you want to meet up or something?'

'Yes, I want you to meet that advocate I mentioned who was advising Joe and me. He wants to chat to us both about bringing a private pathologist for a second autopsy.'

'Okay, good. When and where should we meet?'

'He suggests we meet at Carlo's at Melrose Arch. Do you know it?'

'I do'.

'Great, we're meeting him at eleven. I call him now to confirm. See you there.'

Daniel felt awkward as he drove into the vast underground car park at Melrose Arch. His eight-year-old Toyota looked decidedly third-world as he drove past gleaming Jaguars, Porches, Range Rovers and Maseratis. As a shopping centre,

Melrose Arch catered to the cream of Johannesburg society.

While he walked through the mall, it seemed to Daniel that the centre was populated only by impeccably groomed fashionistas carrying shopping bags emblazoned with the names of the most exclusive European fashion brands. This was why I don't shop here, thought Daniel.

He walked across the square to Carlo's, a Mediterranean eatery considered one of the more stylish pavement cafés in the northern suburbs. Daniel walked past the queue that seemed a permanent feature outside the restaurant at weekends. Scanning the crowded dining area, Daniel spotted Judith sharing a table with a rather large, middle-aged white man. Judith spotted Daniel and waved.

'Hi Daniel, thanks for joining us. Let me introduce you to Advocate Bernard Van Rooyen.'

Daniel held his hand out as Van Rooyen spoke with a mouthful of food. 'Excuse me for filling my face, Daniel, but I missed breakfast this morning. And by the way, friends call me Bernie.'

Daniel looked at the half-eaten omelette that seemed to burst with every filling imaginable. 'No problem. Hi, Bernie, good to meet you.'

'Would you like to order something to eat, Daniel? Can't get Judith to eat a damn thing, no wonder she's wasting away.'

Judith smiled as she modestly sipped her lemon tea.

'No, I'm fine, thank you', replied Daniel. 'Just a coffee will be good.'

Van Rooyen caught the attention of a nearby waiter and ordered Daniel's coffee before launching into the purpose of the meeting. 'So, you were Joe's colleague at Janse-Mashele?'

'Yes, and his friend.'

'Awful business this', conceded Van Rooyen. 'Judith believes that Joe's death is not what it seems. What do you think?'

'I don't know for sure. I hadn't known Joe that long, but I found him to be principled, honourable, and honest - brutally honest, at times. Joe is also a flawed character in many ways. He drank too much; he could be irritable and rude. And he lacked any semblance of diplomacy or discretion. So Joe may have had faults by the truckload, but he was a hell of a likeable and popular guy. I'm no psychologist, but I find it hard to imagine that someone who can be living a massive lie - as a paedophile and a sexual pervert - could be as gregarious and extrovert and uninhibited as Joe. I don't know; it's just a silly theory, I guess.'

'Not silly at all', said Van Rooyen, wiping his mouth with a napkin.

'Of course, a theory, no matter how plausible, is still just a theory. It isn't hard evidence', said Judith.

'Absolutely, it wouldn't stand up in a court of law for one minute,' said Van Rooyen. 'But our job now is to find the hard evidence that Joe didn't die as had been reported. And this means that we need the services of an independent forensic pathologist and an experienced private investigator to look into the case.'

Van Rooyen paused as he devoured more of the omelette. 'I have looked into the case. Joe's body has been moved from the morgue in Hillbrow to a funeral parlour in Rosebank. Joe's closest relative is his niece, Janice Retief, from Hout Bay in Cape Town. It seems that Janice is the daughter of Joe's younger sister, Gloria, who passed away about five years ago. I have spoken to her, and needless to say, she is extremely uncomfortable about the events surrounding Joe's death. Even though she hadn't seen Joe since her mother's funeral, she is flying up to Joburg in the next few days to take care of the arrangements, which she insists on being as discreet as possible. The good news is that she agreed to sign the permissions we need for a second autopsy.'

'Will they have to move Joe's body back to the morgue for the second autopsy?' asked Judith.

'No, the autopsy can be performed at the funeral home. Dr Nel can do whatever she needs to do there and then. She will also take whatever samples she needs back to her lab in Pretoria for testing.'

'Dr Nel?' asked Judith.

'Dr Hanlie Nel, a forensic pathologist, based at the medical faculty at my old alma mater, Tukkies', said Van Rooyen, referring to the University of Pretoria. 'Dr Nel is quite brilliant and extremely meticulous. If there is a whiff of suspicion, Dr Nel will get to the bottom of it.'

'Is there anything else she needs to know? Anything you can think of that will help Dr Nel?' asked Judith.

'Yes,' replied Daniel. 'There is something that crossed my mind the other day', he paused to collect his thoughts.

'Well, out with it', said Van Rooyen impatiently as he deposited another large forkful of omelette into his mouth.

'I can't think of a subtle way of saying this', he said as he looked apologetically at Judith. 'But Joe, I was informed, couldn't get or maintain an erection.'

'Really?' said Van Rooyen, intrigued by this new development. 'Who informed you of this, and how dependable is your source?'

'It was Joe's PA, Debbie Peters, and I'd say she's absolutely dependable. She told me that she was with Joe after some drunken party, and it seems that they had many of those at Janse-Mashele.'

'Lucky them', interjected Van Rooyen with a smile.

'Anyway, Debbie said that she stayed the night at Joe's house because it was so late and that she tried it on with him. But Joe had explained to her that he had some medical condition that made him impotent.'

'That's interesting', said Van Rooyen as he mopped up the remains of his omelette with half a bread roll. 'Not sure what Dr Nel will make of it, but I would have thought she needs to look at it thoroughly.'

'There's something else that Debbie mentioned,' added Daniel. 'Because of this condition, his doctor had prescribed some course of drugs that reduced his sex drive to zero so that, apparently, he never even thought about sex. Debbie said that Joe called it a self-inflicted chemical castration. So, if that was true, how could this auto-erotic strangulation thing be true.'

'I don't know the answer to that, Daniel. But I'm sure Dr Nel will have a look at it. I will call her first thing on Monday morning and brief her.

'I think we must also subpoena Joe's doctor for his medical files.'

'Excellent call, Ms Maponya. My people will be on the case on Monday morning.'

Two tables away, a young couple was settling their bill in cash. As they got up to leave, the man carefully picked up his folded newspaper that was concealing one of the tools of his trade: a long-range, high-sensitivity pen microphone.

FORTY-THREE

On that Saturday afternoon, Mashele had invited a few friends for lunch, a few by Mashele standards being around fifty VVIP guests. As always, the planning had been impeccable, with food prepared by one of the finest fine dining caterers in town. The wine cellar had been restocked, and an army of servers patrolled the lawns, liberally dispensing Crystal Champagne. It promised to be a momentous affair.

'Mac' shouted the Minister of Correctional Services through the crowd of friends gathered on the back lawn. 'Mac, come here and let me greet you as the younger brother you are to me'. The minister threw his arms around Mac, enveloping him in a tight bear hug. 'My God, the work you guys have done for us is truly out of this world. Do you know that I had a call from the deputy president himself to congratulate me and to say he thought we were doing an excellent job!'

'Oh, that's great news, and I'm glad you're happy with our service, Mr Minister. We have also had a good response from the media, but we'll put that in a report for your department, plus the market research results of the consumer reaction to the campaign. From what I hear, the top-line results look positive.'

'Excellent, I look forward to reading that report. Is there anything else we can do to help with this process?'

A slight boost in the media budget so that your TV commercials are flighted more often is always good. You know the SABC charges like a wounded buffalo. And there are no discounts for government departments.'

'How much is a slight boost, Mac?'

'Twenty-five to thirty million will buy us another significant media burst of exposure.'

'I'll talk to the DG on Monday morning and get him to take action on everything. But keep up the excellent work. I'll see you just now. I want to say hi to my old friend, the Botswanan ambassador.

'Still hustling, hey Mac?' Mashele turned around to see David Tlale smiling at him.

'Hello, my old friend', said Mashele as he hugged Tlale and slapped him on the back. 'And how have you been?'

'Well, a bit disappointed that you haven't called me about Operation Green.', said Tlale before dropping the level of his voice. 'I mean, we sweep this place for you and identify all the bugs, and you've stopped sharing all the fun of shafting Henk Janse. Don't tell me you're planning to fuck the guy up without my help.'

'Hell no', laughed Mashele. 'I just don't want to rush things. And don't worry, I'd never deprive you of the fun of teaching some racist old bastard like him a lesson he'll never forget.'

'Good, so what are you thinking of doing with him?'

'Well, you'll know all about the Joe Robinson incident?'

'The guy who worked for you who killed himself by doing that auto-erotic whatever?'

'Yes, that's the guy.'

'What the hell kind of perverted people do you employ at your company?' laughed Tlale. 'I mean, that's one hell of a scandal.'

'Well, Joe Robinson was a bit of a lonely old lush. But he was a great strategist, one of the best in the country. He was also a rude, prickly bastard, but I liked him and think he liked me. He certainly didn't have much time for Janse or his poodle, Smit.'

'So, what does this Robinson guy have to do with getting back at Janse?'

'Call it a feeling or intuition or something, but I reckon there's more to Joe's death than what's been reported in the press. Something happened, and Janse and Smit are involved.'

'What makes you think that?'

'Just reading between the lines of what Janse had to say when he announced Joe's death to the staff. It seemed as if he knew more than he was giving away.'

'Do you think they had something to do with his death?'

'Yes, I do. There's something else. We have this young fellow who works for us who was very close to Joe; his name is Daniel Stein. Daniel and I have been working together, so I have gotten to know and like him. We were chatting the other day, and he started to say something about the incident but then checked himself. I think he knows something about what happened to Joe, and he doesn't or can't talk to me about it. Maybe he's scared of our friends. Maybe he doesn't trust me.'

'Maybe we need to get him to trust you?' suggested Tlale.

'What do you mean?'

'Well, if he knows something he's not supposed to know, and if he's scared of Janse and Smit, then we need to keep a close eye on him. Maybe if we find out that he does have something to fear from Smit and Janse, and if you warn him of it, that sounds like a clever way for you to build trust with this guy. There's also a chance he might say something in a phone call or mention something in an email or an SMS.'

'So, your guys will be discreet? Daniel won't know we're tapping his phone and reading his emails?'

'Hell, yes, they'll be discreet. They'll be watching him day and night, and Daniel won't have a clue that he's under surveillance. My guys are good.'

Mashele grabbed two glasses of Christel from a passing server and handed one to Tlale. 'I like that idea. Like it a lot.'

'I also think we should put some of our surveillance people on him to keep an eye on him from a safe distance. Who knows, maybe we can find out what he knows.'

'Okay', said Mashele. 'Let's give it a go.'

FORTY-FOUR

One of Temba Dube's favourite ways to spend a Sunday morning was a leisurely brunch alone at one of Parkhurst's cosy cafés on 4th Avenue. Of course, it was more enjoyable if he had his by-line on a meaty story in that day's Sunday Telegraph. And complete bliss if one of his stories made it to the front page. This was such a morning.

'More Kiddie Porn Found on Pervert's Computer', screamed the banner headline.

Dube read the story he had checked several times after he and Van Ass had written it. But the excitement of reading one of his stories in newsprint was much more satisfying than reading it on a computer screen.

'On Friday, more revelations came to light concerning the sensational demise of Joseph Robinson, the advertising executive who was found dead at his home earlier this week. As was reported, Robinson had allegedly performed a taboo sexual act called auto-erotic strangulation, or auto-erotic asphyxia, as it is known by medical and psychology professionals.

'This extremely dangerous practice involves cutting off the air supply to the brain using a rope or a cord around the throat to heighten sexual pleasure during masturbation. Although infrequently reported, it is allegedly common within underground sadomasochistic circles.

'The most disturbing aspect of this case, however, was the discovery of child pornography at the scene of death.

'These illicit images are believed to have been downloaded from the Internet. An unnamed source attached to the police's Family

Violence, Child Protection and Sexual Offences Unit suggested that such pornographic material is available on what is referred to as The Dark Web, which requires specialist software to access.

'This is the cesspit of the Internet, which is available to every pervert who has a computer and the expertise to download the software', said the source, a senior police officer who cannot be identified for professional reasons.

'In a story that has rocked the advertising industry as 64-year-old Robinson had been a well-respected figure employed by the leading communications group, Janse-Mashele.

'The Sunday Telegraph can now exclusively reveal even more disturbing developments.

'Late on Friday evening, after a thorough investigation by Janse-Mashele's IT personnel, additional pornographic material featuring young children was unearthed on the hard drive of Robinson's desktop computer.

'Most shockingly, it is alleged that the pictures included children estimated to be as young as five or six years old.

'We were all extremely shocked to find this hidden material', said Petrus Smit, Janse-Mashele's financial director. 'It was the most disgusting and awful images I have ever seen. And my colleagues – many of whom are parents – were very distressed to see this material.

'Mr Smit continued: 'When we at Janse-Mashele were first alerted by the police to Robinson's crime, we vowed to do everything in our power to investigate our computer system to ensure that Robinson didn't use our equipment for his disgraceful ends. I am grateful that our IT people, who worked tirelessly throughout the night, have been able to help the authorities to bring an end to this awful situation.

'As was reported by our sister publication, The Telegraph, earlier this week, the country has been rocked by the revelations of this paedophile.

'The detective in charge of the case, Lieutenant Gideon Buthelezi of the Sandton Police Station, had commented that the autopsy conducted at the Hillbrow Mortuary indicated what he and his colleagues strongly believed, that Robinson's death was self-inflicted. He also stated that with no other parties were involved and no foul play suspected, the case would not be investigated further. The date for the inquest into Robinson's death will be published in the coming weeks.

'The cesspit of the Internet. Not a bad line, thought Dube. His smile grew when he looked around and saw that many of the café's clientele were absorbed by the story.'

FORTY-FIVE

Janse was walking to his car in the underground car park when he heard the echoing footsteps of someone running down the stairwell behind him. As he turned around, he saw a dishevelled-looking, red-faced Petrus Smit.

'What the hell are you running like that? Christ Petrus, you're so bloody unfit you'll do yourself an injury, said Janse.

'Henk, we have problems', replied Smit, sweating and trying to catch his breath.

'What now?' said Janse with little attempt to hide his irritation.

Breathing heavily, Smit dropped his voice to a whisper. 'As you know, our friends at JM-Plus had their private investigators put Daniel Stein under surveillance. They've just sent me this disc of a conversation he had with some people, and you need to hear it.'

'Oh, for fok sake. Let me listen to it in the car on the way home, said Janse as he unlocked his Mercedes and threw his briefcase onto the passenger seat.

Smit handed him the CD. 'They're up to something, and it could hurt us.'

'Let me listen, and I will call you from the car.'

Even before he had driven through the boom gates at the entrance to the building, Janse had inserted the CD and pressed the play button. Initially, it was just a cacophony of indiscernible ambient noise, a barrage of voices talking over each other. Then, slowly, the sounds settled and became more focused on a single conversation.

'Hi Daniel, thanks for joining us. Let me introduce you to Advocate Bernard Van Rooyen.'

'Excuse me for filling my face, Daniel, but I missed breakfast this morning. And by the way, friends call me Bernie...'

Janse listened avidly as the rest of the conversation at Carlo's played out. Around forty minutes later, he was on the last leg of his journey home to Pretoria when the recording ended abruptly. Janse pressed the phone button on the Mercedes command system touchscreen and searched for Smits' number before calling him. Smit answered after the first ring.

'Yes, Henk?'

'First, what do we know about this Judith woman Daniel Stein was talking to?'

'The woman is Jabu Maponya's sister; she's an attorney.'

'And this advocate, Van Rooyen?'

'He's a senior counsel, big in crime and corruption cases, and he used to do a lot of work for the NPA, and he does some human rights work for NGOs and that kind of thing.'

'Okay, most of what they were talking about is complete bullshit that would be impossible to prove. Van Rooyen admits that himself. But there is one area where we could be vulnerable: this talk about a second autopsy. We have to stop that from happening at all costs and stop it sooner rather than later. Do you understand?'

'But you can't just march into a funeral parlour and take a body. And how are we going to get rid of it?'

'Use your imagination, man. Blow the funeral parlour up or swap his body with another one that's to be buried tomorrow. I don't care. We pay these JM-Plus people a shitload of money. Now they need to start earning it.'

'Okay, I'm going to call them right now.'

'Just remember, if there's another autopsy on Joe's body, we'll be in deep trouble. Without the body, they're in deep trouble as they won't be able to prove anything. Talk to those guys at JM-Plus, call me first thing tomorrow morning, and let me know what you're planning.'

Janse ended the call as he had started it: devoid of pleasantries.

FORTY-SIX

The text message from Tlale had been vague but intriguing. *'Meet me at the bar in the Hyatt, Rosebank, for a drink at six pm.'* No reasons. No explanations. Just be there. But Mashele was happy to cancel the last couple of meetings he had scheduled that evening.

As Mashele walked through the hotel foyer, its lavish interior was a constant reminder of why this establishment could boast a lengthy list of visiting heads of state as pampered guests. There was a flurry of pleasant greetings from the attentive front-of-house staff as he made his way to the open-air terrace wine and cigar bar, where he immediately spotted Tlale languishing under a large palm plant and smoking an enormous cigar.

'What is that thing in your mouth? Asked Mashele. 'It'll take you a month to smoke something that big.'

'Cuban, Double Corona. And no, the connoisseurs reckon on two and a half hours of smoking time. That's without rushing it, of course. You can't rush a good Cuban. Can I get you one?'

'No thanks, couldn't think of anything worse. A drink, though, would be good.'

Tlale flagged a waiter and asked for the whisky menu. Mashele ordered a large Royal Lochnagar 12-year-old only because he had never tried it before, and its exorbitant price was an obvious indication that it should be part of his repertoire. As they settled down to serious business, Tlale held out his hand and silently mouthed the word 'phone'.

Mashele surrendered his iPhone and watched in fascination as his friend opened the back of the handset and extracted the SIM card.

'There, we can talk now', said Tlale.

'You're getting carried away with this James Bond stuff, aren't you, David?'

'Not at all. In fact, after what I'm about to tell you, you'll be doing it regularly.'

'Is it about Daniel?'

'Yes, it is. Now, you know about JM-Plus?'

'Of course, it's one of our subsidiaries. But I don't have much to do with the people working there. Janse and Smit - especially Smit - deal with them. From what I hear, they're a bunch of old PR farts. But they're rather good at burying news stories or spreading a bit of disinformation here and there. They've helped me a few times but never with me briefing them directly. It's always gone through Janse and, I presume, Smit.'

'They probably are a bunch of old farts. But we think they're dangerous old farts.' Tlale paused to puff at his Double Corona, sending plumes of smoke high into the air above him. 'They're all ex-journalists but not the nice pinko-liberal guys who worked for papers like the *Rand Daily Mail* and the *Mail and Guardian*; these were all pro-apartheid establishment guys. And they were at the beck and call of some nasty lowlifes in the old security services.'

'Christ, I suppose that's why they've been kept far away from me.'

'They also have quite a few private investigators doing most of the work for them, as well as ex-security police and army intelligence guys from the dirty tricks brigade from the bad old days.'

'It makes me worry about who I've been dealing with for all these years.'

'You need to worry seriously about Smit.'

'Why, do you have something on him?'

Tlale puffed hard to revive his nearly extinguished Double Corona. 'Let me tell you a story', he began. 'You'll remember when the apartheid regime and all their securocrats were on their last legs. Well, all kinds of nasty vermin came out of the woodwork. These animals were paid big money to cause as much chaos and shit as they possibly could.'

'How could I ever forget it?' replied Mashele.

'They were all security personnel, cops, and army special forces; death squads who went about fanning the flames between the different players, like the ANC and Inkatha, by bumping people off, usually the key players on both sides.

'Now our friend Mr Smit, who's so polite and always goes to church every Sunday morning, worked for the Department of Defence as an accountant. He had a nice nine-to-five civil service job, but then he was transferred to some shady department. Remember the CCB?'

'The Civil Cooperation Bureau or something?'

'That's right. The CCB consisted of a bunch of spooks that officially didn't exist. But believe it or not, even spies and assassins need accountants. I mean, even they have to account for their expenses.'

Mashele shook his head and chuckled at the absurdity of what Tlale was saying.

'It was an attractive offer for Smit. Think about it. You have the most God-awful, boring desk job as an accountant, and next thing you're on a James Bond movie set during a low-grade civil war.'

'God, but he must have loved it', said Mashele

'I'm sure he did. If knowledge is power, Smit - without anybody realising it - amassed quite a bit. He knew who the local operatives were, where their safe houses were located, and where they worked. He even knew where they shopped and what takeaway meals they ate. Smit was the guy who was checking all the payments. So, he made a lot of contacts in the dark arts of skulduggery.'

'Which made him valuable to Janse?'

'Absolutely.'

'So where does Janse fit in?'

'We know that the CCB bought into a bunch of front companies to give these operatives some cover, and we believe that Janse's first company was one of them.'

'And what's the story about Daniel? How does he fit in all this?'

'I believe your instincts about Daniel were correct. It's obvious he knows something which is dangerous for him because he's under surveillance by these JM-Plus guys. We know there's a tap on his cellphone, and they're probably monitoring his emails. But they also have a tail on him.'

'Christ, this is like some movie.'

'As we discussed at your garden party, I have ordered my people to watch him physically and electronically.

'So, Daniel's having his phone tapped by both sides?'

'Something like that. Look, it's no big deal these days. Go and Google spyware and you will have a wide choice of software to buy to listen to people's calls, read their text messages, and track them to about ten metres anywhere on the planet. Of course, what we use is far more sophisticated.'

'Well, I imagine it would be.'

'The bottom line, Mac? As we chatted before, you need to win Daniel's confidence by warning him about this JM-Plus business; it is the smart way to go.'

'Okay, I'll chat with him.'

'But you both have to be seriously discreet. Okay, Mac? These guys are not playing games, and people could get hurt.'

'Okay, sir. Now, do I have to sit here for another two hours while you finish that damn stinking thing?

'Of course, so you better order more drinks, hadn't you?'

FORTY-SEVEN

Peter Dube was in his shirtsleeves eating his lunch, with a tea towel tied around his neck as a makeshift bib.

He had to be careful about his appearance. As he sat in the workshop flanked by stacks of coffins in various stages of completion, Pricilla, his receptionist, came to find him.

'Just received paperwork concerning Joseph George Robinson and a request for cremation', said Pricilla.

'That's the guy all the newspapers have been writing those terrible stories. The pervert?' asked Dube as he finished the last of his toasted cheese sandwich. He could never eat lunch at his desk in his plush office. It just wasn't done to have the smell of food wafting around when you were meeting with a bereaved family to discuss the arrangements for the burial or cremation of a loved one.

'Yes, apparently, his family has requested that he be cremated as soon as possible.'

'As soon as possible? I suppose they want to get rid of him after all that scandal. Let me see the paperwork.'

Pricilla handed over the file.

'Death certificate looks okay; autopsy report says there were no medical implants or a pacemaker to be taken out. We don't want to blow up the crem, do we now?' said Dube with a chuckle.

Priscilla ignored the joke, which she had heard a few dozen times over the years she and Dube had worked together at the *Angels of Peace Funeral Parlour*.

'What else have we got here, the receipt for the fees . . . The burial order and cremation forms A, B, C, D, and E . . . blah, blah. . . Clearance Certificate from the Medical Referee appointed by the crematorium authorities, blah, blah . . . The medical declaration from Dr Pillay, the pathologist at the morgue . . . Confirmatory medical declaration from a Dr Smithson, also at the morgue. . . I see he had no metal replacement knees or hips . . . And what's this?' he asked as he picked up the last sheet of paper in the file. 'Affidavit from Janice Retief, Next of Kin to Joseph George Robinson, Deceased.'

'Read it. It's from his niece with instructions for the disposal of the body. It's incredibly sad,' said Pricilla.

Dube continued reading aloud. '*As Mr Joseph Robinson's closest living relative and next of kin . . . blah, blah . . . I wish to place on record my wishes for the disposal of my uncle's earthly remains. With all the necessary paperwork enclosed, I request that his body be cremated as soon as possible. It was also my uncle's wish, as an avowed atheist, to have a secular ceremony, with no religious service being part of the cremation. Due to my personal circumstances, neither I nor any members of my immediate family will attend the cremation.*

Yours Sincerely, Janice Retif, blah, blah, blah, Hout Bay, etcetera, etcetera.'

'It's so sad when someone dies and there's no one to give you a send-off', said Pricilla.

'Hell, yes', agreed Dube. 'Not even a priest to be present? When I go, I hope to God it's not like that.'

'Well, if you did what they say he did, you could argue that he deserves his lot. Dumped like some dead mongrel dog that's been run over in the streets.'

'Yes, I suppose you're right. Best call the crematoriums to see which one can handle it quickly.'

'I have done', said Pricilla. 'Brixton can do it at three o'clock tomorrow.'

'Okay, tomorrow it is.'

FORTY-EIGHT

'Complete and utter bullshit', said Debbie, her rage building. 'Did you read that trash in the *Sunday Telegraph* about Joe? I mean, it was a complete joke. Joe didn't know one end of a computer from the other, and they claimed he was downloading software to access the dark web. Christ all mighty, Joe could barely access his emails.'

Debbie and her two colleagues, also PAs who worked in the client service department, had been asked to help set up one of the boardrooms for a significant new business presentation. All they knew was that it was for one of the large Korean car manufacturers whose business Janse-Mashele had pursued for months. And they had been told that it was all hush-hush.

Preparing the boardroom was a humdrum routine: distribute Janse-Mashele-branded notepads and pens, ensure fresh coffee and tea on the hotplate, and ensure enough mineral water and glasses for all the attendees. And the most critical task was to double-check that the PowerPoint presentation was ready and that all the equipment was in working order. Janse-Mashele was unforgiving of any last-minute glitches.

'We know you were close to Joe, Debs, but all this talk about him is making us feel uncomfortable', said the younger of the two other PAs.

'Don't be so fucking naïve Mpho.'

The PA gasped in horror; no one had ever spoken to her with such aggression.

'That's enough, Debbie, ' shouted Jennifer, a woman of similar age and effrontery to Debbie. 'Stop trying to defend Joe, for

God's sake. Just accept it that he was a sexual deviant and probably a child molester.'

'Fuck you, Jennifer! What the fuck do you know about Joe?'

'What do I know about him? Read any newspaper in the country; it'll tell you all you need to know. How can you defend someone like that, a fucking sex maniac and a pervert?'

'Stop calling Joe a pervert, you bitch', screamed Debbie with as much venom as she could muster. 'You don't know anything.'

'Oh, really?'

'Yes, really! Joe couldn't possibly be a sex maniac because he had a medical condition that stopped him from getting a hard-on!' shouted Debbie.

Mpho was wide-eyed as she sat on one of the boardroom chairs.

Jennifer was also momentarily speechless. But then she quickly gathered her wits before resuming the attack. 'How would you know that Joe couldn't get a hard-on? Or are you just a disgusting pervert like him?' screamed Jennifer at the top of her voice.

Without thinking what she was about to do, Debbie slapped Jennifer so hard across the facegthat she was thrust backwards towards the hotplate, where she knocked over two full jugs of coffee, burning her legs in the process. She screamed in pain as the blood poured from her nose.

At that instant, Debbie, Mpho and the sobbing Jennifer realised they were no longer alone in the room. All three turned around to see the client service team standing in the expansive double doorway next to four conservatively dressed Asian gentlemen. Everyone was stunned into silence.

Debbie burst into tears before pushing through the crowded doorway and storming to the nearest ladies' bathroom.

When the news of the altercation reached Petrus Smit, Debbie was back in her office. And Smit was on his way to confront her.

She was also inconsolable. Daniel was trying to calm her down and offer her some support.

'I have never slapped anyone in my adult life. Oh, my God, why was I so stupid? But I couldn't stand there and ignore Joe's name being dragged through the mud like that. When someone dies, their name is the only thing they have left. And Joe's name is being destroyed through what I know to be lies.'

Smit burst into her office. 'Daniel Stein, please leave this room.'

'For God's sake, can't you see the woman is upset?'

'Not as upset as the woman she hit. We've had Jennifer taken to the hospital with probably a broken nose and severely burnt legs. Get out of this office, Stein, before you find yourself in serious trouble.'

Daniel patted Debbie on the shoulder as a futile mark of solidarity before leaving her to her fate with Smit.

'Now, Debbie, there are stringent labour laws in South Africa that prohibit a company from terminating someone's employment. It's usually a long and slow process. There are, however, certain instances where someone can be summarily dismissed. And committing an act of violence towards a colleague in the workplace is one of those reasons.'

'Oh my God, you're firing me, aren't you?' said Debbie as she realised that her ten years at Janse-Mashele were about to end.

'Debbie, I am sorry, but I have no choice but to ask you to leave Janse-Mashele immediately. You will be paid your salary until the end of the month and any holiday pay due to you. Please pack your personal belongings and leave the company now.'

Debbie started crying quietly, but Smit ignored it. 'I also need you to give me your office keys and car park access card'.

'Bastard', muttered Debbie in between sobs. 'You are a heartless bastard. You lied about Joe.'

'That will do, Debbie. Don't say things that you'll regret later.'

'But you lied about him, didn't you? You know perfectly well that Joe could barely switch on a computer. Did you have something to do with Joe dying?'

'That will do, Debbie. Best you shut up right now and don't say another word. Don't make any more trouble for yourself because I can quite easily persuade Jennifer that she needs to press criminal charges against you for assault.'

'There are so many lies about Joe and about the way he died because Joe was impotent. It was a medical impossibility for him to get an erection. I know because he told me that himself.'

Smit was taken aback. 'That's . . . That's enough Debbie'; he stammered.

'You can't scare me, you bastard. No wonder Joe despised you. He said you were nothing but a dishonest, slimy shit.'

'Grievous bodily harm; that's the charge we can lay on you . . . And that will mean a prison term. Do you understand me? Now shut up and never say another word about Joe fucking Robinson. You're fired now fuck off out of this company', shouted Smit. He was red in the face and had saliva drooling from his mouth. He turned around and marched out of Debbie's office.

FORTY-NINE

Operation Green

Transcription of SMS Messages:

Sent by: Daniel Stein 084 112 7891

Received by: Judith Maponya 086 768 9325

Message sent: 09:10.12. 19.54

Hi J. Looks like that bastard Smit has been on the warpath again. He's just fired Debbie, Joe's PA. She was involved in a row about Joe with a colleague, and things got physical. After Smit fired her, I could hear the slanging match between them, and Debbie told him about Joe being impotent. Knowing what Smit and Janse are capable of, I fear for her.

Transcription of SMS Messages:

Sent by: Judith Maponya 086 768 9325

Received by: Daniel Stein 084 112 7891

Message sent: 09:10:12. 19.58

Hi D, I hate to say it, but Smit is well within his rights to instantly dismiss anyone who resorts to violence at the workplace. I wish she hadn't said anything about Joe's impotence. That's evidence we need to keep under wraps. Try not to worry too much about Debbie, not even Smit would be stupid enough to harm her, considering what's happened.

Transcription of SMS Messages:

Sent by: Daniel Stein 084 112 7891

Received by: Judith Maponya 086 768 9325

Message sent: 09:10.12. 20.04

Yes, I suppose you're right. What can I say? It's been a very long week. Shit, it's also been a long period of my life! What are you up to tonight?

Transcription of SMS Messages:

Sent by: Judith Maponya 086 768 9325

Received by: Daniel Stein 084 112 7891

Message sent: 09:10:12. 20. 08

I'm at my mom's house in Soweto, and I thought I'd spend the weekend with her and spoil her with a shopping trip tomorrow. She's not doing too well since losing Jabu. What are you doing?

Transcription of SMS Messages:

Sent by: Daniel Stein 084 112 7891

Received by: Judith Maponya 086 768 9325

Message sent: 09:10.12. 20.04

What a good girl you are for looking after your mom. As for me, I have some correspondence to do, and then I'll stick something inedible into the microwave and maybe fall asleep in front of the TV. Cheers for now. Chat soon, D.

FIFTY

To Prisoner Riaan du Plessis

Block C

Kgosi Mampuru II Prison

Pretoria

Dear Riaan,

I hope life is treating you well (sorry about the terrible pun).

I just thought I would drop you a quick line to fill you in on the developments with our campaign. I am sorry we didn't get a chance to chat during the film shoot. I suppose those running Correctional Services had their reasons, but it was hellishly frustrating as I looked forward to connecting with you again.

I also wanted to let you know that you were great on camera, and my colleagues were impressed with your performance. The commercial has been on TV for a few days already, and I believe the minister is so happy that he's ploughed more money into the media budget. Everyone in the country is going to get to know you, Riaan. They will be on TV several times daily on the three SABC channels over the next month or so.

I don't remember seeing any TV sets in your prison wing, and I never thought to ask if you had access to a TV. I hope you do so that you can see yourself on screen. Who knows, a new career may beckon when you eventually get out!!! If you don't get to see it, I'll be happy to ask the authorities if a special dispensation can be made so I can see you and play the commercial on my laptop.

Please feel free to drop me a line anytime. As a penfriend, I

value your wisdom and unique take on life.
Keep well, and I hope to hear from you soon.
Sincerely, Daniel.

FIFTY-ONE

It had been a busy Monday, and Daniel was packing up when his clandestine cellphone – what he called his cloak-and-dagger phone – rang.

'We have a problem. A big problem.' Daniel immediately caught the sense of anxiety in Judith's voice.

'What is it?'

'Joe's body has already been cremated.'

'What? But we were going to do a second autopsy? How the hell did that happen?'

'I have no idea at this stage, but I'm going to Bernie's chambers. Can you meet me there? The address is the Fifth Floor, The Chambers Building, Paul Kruger Street, Sandton.'

'I'm on my way', replied Daniel.

What should have taken twenty minutes to drive to the building, which housed Van Rooyen's office, took a frustrating hour and a half through the rush hour traffic. Sandton probably had the most chaotic traffic in the country as the one-and-a-half million workers drove in and out of the northern Johannesburg suburb twice a day.

As he was led into Van Rooyen's cluttered office, he found both lawyers sitting around the conference table with two other people: a tall, athletic-looking black man in his mid-thirties and an attractive middle-aged white woman.

'Hey Daniel, you made it', said Judith with a welcoming smile.

'Yes, sorry, but the bloody roads around Sandton are becoming impossible.'

'Not to worry, make yourself comfortable', said Van Rooyen as he pulled out a chair. 'Now let me introduce you to a couple of my colleagues who will assist us in this matter concerning Joe.'

Van Rooyen turned to the woman: 'This is Dr Hanlie Nel, the forensic pathologist from the University of Pretoria.'

Dr Nel offered a friendly smile as she held her hand to Daniel: 'Hello Daniel, it's lovely to meet you', she said with a soft Afrikaans lilt.

'Dr Nel, nice meeting you', replied Daniel.

'Please call me Hanlie.'

'And this fine specimen is Jackson or Jacks Msimang, ex-SAPS and a senior investigator at the Directorate of Special Operations', said Van Rooyen.

'The Scorpions?' asked Daniel, referring to the independent investigations unit disbanded by the ANC government in 2009 under highly controversial circumstances.

'Yes, but I promise you there was nothing glamorous about my days in the Scorpions as people seemed to think. I spent most of my time wading through company spreadsheets with a calculator in my hand. These days, I work for the likes of Advocate Van Rooyen as a private investigator.'

'Well, it's good to meet you both', said Daniel.

'Now, Daniel, before you arrived, we were discussing some developments in this case when the bastards went ahead with the cremation, even though we had an application for a second private autopsy with the Medical Referee. By the way, he is the doctor checking out all the applications and giving final permission for any cremation. He's the officer in charge who the provincial government has appointed. Jacks, would you please expand on what you discovered today?'

'Yes, of course. I spoke to the funeral director, Peter Dube, of *Angels of Peace* Funeral Parlour in Rosebank. And he had everything he was supposed to have to go ahead with the cremation. He said all the official documents looked good. He gave me copies of everything he had. And yes, it all looked legit. It also included an affidavit from Joe's niece, Janice Retief from Hout Bay, requesting that the cremation be carried out as soon as possible.'

Van Rooyen interjected: 'When we called Joe's niece this morning in Cape Town, the poor woman had no idea about this affidavit and categorically denied ever writing one. She told me she was packing her bags to fly up here to Joburg to take care of all the arrangements. What could the poor thing do except cancel her flight?'

'Mr Dube was shocked and quite distressed when I told him it was a forgery. And the Medical Referee had granted the second autopsy.'

'Tell Daniel and Judith what you found yesterday', said Van Rooyen.

'I also looked into the evidence that was discovered at the scene of Mr Robinson's death and read the reports written by the senior detective. There was no evidence of any other party involvement, no sign of forced entry, and no fingerprints of anyone other than Mr Robinson and his housekeeper.

'But here's the strange thing, the pornographic photographs of children thrown on the floor around the body? Well, I looked at all of them, and they were printed on ordinary photocopy paper. From what I could see from the photographs the forensic technicians took and what I saw when I went over to Mr Robinson's house earlier this afternoon, Mr Robinson didn't have a printer. And believe me, you don't go to Minute Print down the road to have material like that printed.'

'Could they have been printed at the office?' asked Daniel. 'You know, late at night when everyone's gone home?'

'Could be', replied Jacks. 'But retrieving any material printed on a commercial office printer is also possible. They all have hard drives and record the material they print.'

'Okay, I see what you mean', said Judith. 'But it's still circumstantial.'

'You are quite correct that it's circumstantial. But there is more evidence. Hang in there, it gets better', said Van Rooyen with a self-satisfied smile. 'Do go on, please, Jacks.'

'I believe we do have some hard evidence. Of all those kiddie porn pictures, not one single fingerprint was detected on any of them.'

'Not one fingerprint', added Van Rooyen dramatically as if he was trying to sway a judge in one of his court cases. 'Not Joe's fingerprints. Not anyone else's fingerprints. Now, isn't that interesting?'

'Whoever handled those photographs did so wearing gloves. And Mr Robinson was not wearing anything on his hands when his body was discovered, concluded Jacks.

'My God', said Judith, tears welling up in her eyes. 'So, all that terrible stuff of Joe being a paedophile must be rubbish. And all those shocking photographs were planted?'

'It's beginning to look that way, isn't it?' said Van Rooyen. 'But there's more. Hanlie, would you please share your thoughts.'

'Daniel, I believe you told Bernie that Mr Robinson was impotent and that he was on some medication to reduce his sex drive?'

'Yes, that's right. The lady who was Joe's PA told me in confidence.'

'Right, I spoke to Mr Robinson's GP, a Dr Deighton, at the Sandton Medical Centre. He was accommodating. First, he confirmed that Mr Robinson was undergoing treatment for a vascular disease, which led to him being impotent. Now I will try and avoid being too technical...'

'Yes, please Hanlie', stressed Van Rooyen. 'Explain it as if you were talking to a five-year-old or a judge; they both have similar levels of competency to grasp complex medical evidence.'

'Okay. Vascular disease is a condition where the vascular system - the blood vessels - restricts blood flow to the body's organs. That simple enough for you advocate?'

'Perfect. Do continue.'

'A vascular disease is usually caused by coronary heart disease, or type two diabetes, high blood pressure, obesity, or high levels of cholesterol. It seems Mr Robinson had every one of those conditions. In most cases, it is treatable with drugs and a change of lifestyle. But according to the results of the tests that Dr Deighton had done, it seems Mr Robinson was a pretty severe case.'

'How did Dr Deighton treat it?' asked Van Rooyen.

'Well, he told me that because of the vascular disease, Mr Robinson also suffered from a venous leak.'

'In English, please, Dr', corrected Van Rooyen.

'To keep an erection, the penis must store blood. If the veins in the penis cannot prevent blood from leaving the penis during an erection, a man will lose that erection, which means he becomes sexually dysfunctional or impotent.

'Dr Deighton also said that he had prescribed a course of drugs called Cyproterone acetate. Now, this is a class of drugs called antiandrogens, which have several uses. However, in this case, it was used to block the action of the male hormones to reduce the number of androgens in Mr Robinson's body. In other words, it took away all sexual feelings and urges.'

'Is that hard evidence? Or could it be construed as a medical opinion open to interpretation?' asked Judith.

'Good question,' said Van Rooyen. 'I'm sure a good defence team would argue that maybe he stopped taking the drugs. After all, being prescribed drugs by your doctor is one thing, but taking the drugs as directed is something altogether different.'

'Well, that would be simple to ascertain. Blood samples were taken, so we need to wait for the toxicology report to confirm that the Cyproterone acetate was still in his system.'

'Now, that is hard evidence', said Van Rooyen with a mischievous wink aimed at Judith.

'Yes, it is, and there's more,' said Dr Nel. 'I'm a bit like Jacks here in that I've left what I believe to be the best hard evidence until the end'.

'Come. Come, share it with us', implored Van Rooyen impatiently.

'Okay, but this is superficial as hell at this stage. A theory, but I think it can be substantiated and withstand rigorous cross-examination.'

'Theorise away, Dr Nel', Van Rooyen was getting more excited.

'Okay, well, the autopsy was conducted by Dr Pillay at the mortuary in Hillbrow. I read his report, and something struck me immediately. Dr Pillay says that when he examined the throat area around where there was severe bruising and soft tissue damage, as one would expect, he found that the hyoid bone was broken.'

Dr Nel paused when she realised she faced three blank facial expressions.

'Okay, let me explain why this is significant. The hyoid bone helps to support the tongue and elevate the larynx when you talk or swallow. It's suspended above the larynx and is anchored by ligaments to the bones in the skull.

'A fracture to the hyoid is considered rare in cases of hanging.

I've checked it out with some research papers. There was an extensive research study done in India a few years back on the bodies of people who had died due to judicial hangings, and the conclusion was that less than one per cent of those deaths resulted in a fractured hyoid bone.'

'So, what causes the hyoid bone to fracture?' asked Van Rooyen, sitting on the edge of his seat by now.

'Manual strangulation', she murmured softly.

Everyone in the room was stunned until Judith started sobbing quietly. Daniel stood up, walked to the table's other side, and offered a comforting hug.

'My God', said Van Rooyen, wistfully. 'My God, but these people are evil.'

Daniel took a deep breath as he felt himself choking up. 'Can I ask you something, Dr?

'Of course you can, Daniel.'

'How can we prove this? Joe's body is gone. There's nothing left to examine, so how do we prove it?'

'What we still have to work with are all the photographs from the forensic technicians who recorded the scene of death. We also have the photographs taken during the autopsy. It's far from perfect, but what I'm hoping we can do is to extrapolate enough information that will prove that Mr Robinson did not die voluntarily by his own hand and that the hanging was post-mortem. I believe he died through being strangled by someone from behind, probably by using the same cord that was knotted around his neck.'

'What will that require?' asked Van Rooyen as he got up to open his drinks cabinet and grabbed a bottle of whisky.

'It all comes down to the angle in which the pressure was applied around the throat, which we can ascertain from the ligature marks on the neck. When a person is hanged, the angles of the ligature marks are different to when a person is strangled.

She held her hand behind her head to indicate the pulling of an invisible rope. 'This is a crude way to explain it, but when you are hanged, the pressure is applied downwards because gravity pulls the victim down, and that's true whether it's a complete hanging when the person is totally suspended or a partial hanging, like in Mr Robinson's case. He was found on his knees, slumped forward and suspended from a cord tied to a door handle.'

Dr Nel moved her hand to a point directly behind the back of her neck. 'But when it's strangulation by a ligature, the pressure on the neck will leave horizontal marks. Through computer-aided design, we can make three-dimensional simulations that will show, quite conclusively, that there is a major difference in the pathology of both situations. Other signs suggest strangulation, the swelling of the tongue and the larynx, for instance.'

'Do we see a glimmer of light at the end of a very dark, evil tunnel, I wonder?' pondered Van Rooyen aloud.

'There's another fascinating point that they missed at the autopsy. When they photographed the back of Mr Robinson's neck, it showed distinct bruising. When someone is hanged, the ligature tightens and causes welts on the front and the sides of the neck, but not in the back of the neck.'

'So that bruising was caused by the killer's knuckles pressing on Mr Robinson's neck as he was being strangled?' asked Daniel.

'That's what I would argue', answered Dr Nel. 'Imagine when someone is garrotting a person, his hands are not going to be far away from the neck, as they apply pressure to get the necessary leverage, the murderer's hands are going to be close up and pressing against the nape of the victim's neck.'

'What will it take for you to do all the research work you need to do to prove our case?' asked Van Rooyen.

Well, it's not going to be easy, and I'm going to need the help of some colleagues of mine. I know some very clever people based here in South Africa, and some are overseas.

Van Rooyen finished pouring five rather large Scotches and began handing them out. "I think we all could do with a stiff drink after hearing that, Hanlie. A question for you: why do you think Dr Pillay missed a piece of evidence that could be so crucial in determining Joe's death?'

'I know Dr Pillay, a very competent and highly regarded pathologist. But he's fallible. I mean, who isn't? The workload that those guys must deal with is outrageous. And maybe luck has something to do with it', replied Dr Nel as she sipped the Scotch.

'The first autopsy I ever attended was on the body of a condemned prisoner. The man had been hanged that morning at Pretoria Central Prison. My professor, a wonderful teacher who inspired me to specialise in pathology, showed me the hyoid bone so that he could explain these phenomena that suggest whether the death was caused by strangulation or by hanging. That explanation took all of five minutes some twenty-five years ago. It was almost an aside from my old professor. Who knows, Dr Pillay's professor probably didn't tell him what my professor told me.'

Van Rooyen was the first to break the silence. 'So, as I said, there may be some light at the end of the tunnel. So where to from here?'

'Well, I certainly have my work cut out for me,' said Dr Nel.

'And I would like to return to Mr Robinson's house,' said Jacks. 'When I was there, I could see that security was tight, so I'm interested to know how someone got into the property.'

FIFTY-TWO

Nelson was concerned about his boss. Over the years, he had seen Fourie descend into black moods. And the only friend he turned to during those times was the bottle. Nelson was also worried that, besides some bits and pieces, he hadn't done a real job for Fourie since the hijacking. That was when they buried the guy's car in one of the fields on the farm. That had annoyed Nelson no end. It was virtually a brand-new car. All it needed was a change of licence plates, but Fourie would have none of it, stubborn bastard.

So, it was just as well for Fourie that Nelson found his cellphone in the long grass beyond the backyard the night he got so drunk and threw it into his back garden. Just as well, too, that it hadn't rained. As soon it was plugged in for recharging, Fourie found a text message from his bank confirming that fifty thousand rands had been deposited into his account.

Although not doubting that he deserved the additional payment for the Robinson job, Fourie felt a deep sense of shame that he'd lost control of his emotions. And more so, he had shown a weakness in his character to Smit, of all people. He vowed to cut back on the brandy.

The subsequent ban on canned hunting because of Mambo the Lion didn't look like it would ever materialise. He couldn't understand why he had panicked at what now appeared such a ludicrous story. He felt continually stressed and jumpy. And his anxiety levels seemed to be growing by the day. Unimportant issues seemed to amplify suddenly into insurmountable dilemmas.

Memories of the dark days kept flashing into his mind: his combat days deep in the bush, first in Zimbabwe, then later in Southwest Africa and Angola. The latter had been the worst. It was an incursion that demanded that all semblance of humanity be checked at the border.

Every so often, the recollections of Angola would catch him off-guard: memories of torching entire villages in the search for SWAPO insurgents, memories of machine-gunning everyone they could find, even when they could see from the helicopter gunship that women, old men, and children were being slaughtered with equal abandon; and memories of slitting of throats of Cuban soldiers who strayed too far from the safety of their camps at night.

Maybe he just needed a break; perhaps he should disappear to the bush for a couple of weeks and lose himself somewhere where there were no people, no cellphones, and no worries; some tranquil place. Nelson and William could take care of the cats. Hell, why not? He had nothing else to do that was particularly urgent.

He watched a litter of four cubs playing in one of the enclosures. They were imitating their parents' behaviours, trying to stalk each other in the long grass that would end in a boisterous mock fight. Fourie smiled as he watched the cubs. It was a shame that they would never be able to put to the test what they would learn as juveniles: the hunting skills and the social bonds that bind a pride together.

The moment was rudely interrupted by the ringing of his phone. 'Oh shit', said Fourie, seeing Smit's name on the screen. He let it ring for a while until he eventually took the call.

'Yes, Petrus, what can I do for you?'

'Hello, Fourie. First, you've seen that I have deposited the extra money into your account?'

'Yes', he answered curtly, embarrassed once again by his

drunken rant.

'Okay, well, let's not say anything more about that. Water under the bridge, hey?'

'Yeah, fine if that's how you want to play it. That's fine by me.'

'Okay. Look, I have another job for you. And it needs to be done ASAP.'

'Okay', said Fourie with little enthusiasm.

'Only thing. It's a woman.'

'I don't like jobs involving women.'

'I know, that's why I'm happy to pay you what I paid you for the Robinson job: a hundred grand. Think of it as your usual fee plus a fifty-grand bonus because it's a woman.'

Fourie was silent.

'I'm not looking for any complicated stuff here, no faked suicides or some pretend crime gone wrong like Jabu. Just a simple accident type of thing, you know, the kind of accident that can happen to anyone.'

'Does she also work for your company?'

'Not anymore. Her name is Debbie Peters, and she was Joe Robinson's PA. I had to fire her the other day, and she started to shoot her mouth off. She doesn't know anything', he quickly added so as not to alarm Fourie. 'It'll just be better if we get rid of her.'

'Okay, for a hundred grand then.'

'I have all the details, photographs of her and her address details. How shall I get them to you.'

'Leave it all in a sealed envelope at the reception desk at Janse-Mashele, and I'll send someone round to collect them. Fourie had no wish for a face-to-face meeting with Smit.

'Nelson', shouted Fourie. 'Come, we have a job we need to do.'

FIFTY-THREE

'Sawubona unjani Baba?' said Jacks to the security guard through his car window as he drove up to the boom gate. 'I am investigating the death of Mr Robinson, and I need to ask you guys a couple of questions.

'Ngiyaphila, unjani wena? Please park your car at the visitor's parking spot over there, Baba.'

Jacks did as he was instructed and walked back to the guardhouse. The three security guards who were on duty that morning introduced themselves.

'Mr Joe was a lovely man. We were so sad when we heard that he had died', said the oldest and most senior of the three, Edgar Motshekga. 'He was very good to us, always looked after us at Christmas time. He was a very generous man and full of fun. Eish, I don't know about these terrible things that all the newspapers say about Mr Joe.'

'Any of you on duty that night when Mr Robinson died?'

'Yes, I spoke to him when he drove in. He was very cheerful, and everything seemed normal, as always. Hello J Edgar, my old mate, he said when he came in. He always called me J Edgar. I don't know why. My name is just Edgar.'

Jacks smiled at Joe's corny joke. 'So, he was the same as he always was? Nothing unusual?'

'No, everything seemed normal.'

'And the people who came in and out of the complex during that day and night?'

'Well, we have all the videos of everyone who entered and left.'

Edgar pointed to the bank of CCTV monitors stacked on the back wall of the guardhouse, each with scenes of the complex's outer walls. 'We gave all the DVDs of the surveillance videos to the police. And everyone was accounted for, all the residents and a few guests visiting here.'

'And nothing unusual or out of the ordinary happened that day?'

'Only when that bakkie with the ladder on top buggered the electric fence.'

'Really? What happened?'

'Some idiot driving a bakkie did a three-point turn on the other side of the complex, and he managed to hook the wires of the electric fence on this big ladder that he had stuck high above the bakkie's cab. Having a ladder hanging off the vehicle like that wasn't right. It caused a short on the fence and buggered the whole section. We had to get an electrician here the following morning to fix it.'

'Did you tell the police about this?'

'Yes, I even showed them the footage, but they just said it was unrelated.'

'And the fence was deactivated that night?

'Just the one section.'

'Could you get the registration number of this bakkie?'

'No, the number plate was plastered with mud. It was a light-coloured bakkie, white or maybe silver, and the CCTV was only in black and white. But it looked like someone working in construction. Anyway, bloody fool ripped the wires and then just drove off.'

'Do you have a copy of the video?'

'The complex manager should have it; he wanted it to make the insurance claim.'

Jacks made a note to get in touch with the manager. 'Okay', said Jacks as he studied the monitors. 'And is the complex fully covered with this system?'

'Yes.'

'These cameras cover one hundred per cent of the complex?'

'Almost, yes.'

'What do you mean almost? It's either 100% or it isn't, not so?' said Jacks, careful not to appear too pushy.

'Well, it's almost a hundred per cent coverage. There's one corner in the back of the complex where the cameras don't reach, but that's only about ten or twelve metres along the wall.'

'Is it part of the section of the fence that was deactivated?'

'Yes, it is. Hey, I never thought of that.'

'Can you show me that spot?'

'Just walk along the wall until you get to the back of the complex, and you'll find a narrow alley. Walk along further until you get to some pine trees. That's the spot. If you like, call me when you get there, then I will tell you precisely where the cameras don't cover, said Edgar as he wrote his cellphone number on the corner of a newspaper page before tearing it off.

'That will be useful. Many thanks for your help. I'll see you later.'

'We'll be seeing you right now', laughed Edgar as he pointed to the monitors.

Jacks discovered that the complex was much larger when you had to walk around it, and he soon regretted leaving his car at the guardhouse. As he followed the perimeter wall, he saw the CCTV cameras attached to metal poles high above the electric fence and positioned every fifty metres. After about twenty minutes of walking in the mid-day heat, the wall turned a corner away from the major roads and followed a narrow alleyway virtually blocked with overgrown vegetation.

He pushed his way through clumps of weeds and thorn bushes that snagged on his clothes, leaving hundreds of tiny barbed, needle-like burrs impaled in his shirt and pants. BlackJacks. He knew that trying to wipe them off would be a futile effort. They would have to be pulled off, one by one, a tedious task when he got home. He continued negotiating past piles of litter and detritus that had probably accumulated over many years and human faeces that were more of a recent addition.

Eventually, he came to a stretch of the wall near the crop of pine trees that Edgar had mentioned. The distinct V-shaped kink in the wall detoured around an outcrop of dolomite that was probably too big and too hard for the builders to blast through.

Jacks pulled out the scrap newspaper Edgar had used to write his phone number and called him. 'Edgar, am I at the right spot?'

'Hi Baba', replied Edgar. 'You're almost there. Do you see where the wall kinks near those rocks? The spot the cameras don't cover is about ten metres along that stretch. Walk forward, and I will tell you exactly where the cameras don't cover.'

'Okay', said Jacks. Can you see me now?'

'Yes. Walk forward a bit . . . There, you're out of the picture now. Keep going . . . Keep going . . . Okay, stop there, you've just come back in shot on the next camera now.'

'Great. Thanks, Edgar.'

'Jacks studied the electric fence, but everything looked in order. It was a ten-strand industrial-grade fence that looked professionally maintained. No loose wiring and even the small warning signs were attached to the strands every ten metres as stipulated by municipal regulations. No, the fence seemed fine.

He looked around the area, but everything seemed unremarkable. After a while, he spotted a brick-built structure tucked away behind the pine trees. He pushed through a thicket of reeds and found himself standing before an abandoned Joburg City Power substation. He walked around the graffiti-daubed structure no larger than a garage that could house a single vehicle and found the heavy metal doors hanging off their hinges. After pushing the door as wide as the vegetation would allow it to open, he pulled his cellphone out of his pocket, switched on the torch app, and held it up to see inside the structure.

Suddenly, Jacks was confronted by a ghostly, disfigured white face barely a metre away from him. Jacks let out an involuntary shriek. 'Who the fuck are you?' He screamed in panic.

'It's okay, mister. It's okay', was the equally startled reply. 'Please, mister, I don't want trouble.'

Jacks jumped back to the sanctuary of daylight as he shouted: 'Come out now.'

'Okay, mister, but please don't hurt me', said the black man with albinism as he walked out of the sub-station.

Jacks was taken aback by the white, black face that confronted him. It was also deeply disfigured by a jagged scar that extended from the man's forehead down through where his left eye had once been and down further to his jaw.

'Please, mister, I don't want trouble, the man continued pleading.

'It's okay', said Jacks, holding up both hands in a submissive stance. 'I wasn't expecting to see anyone inside. You scared the shit out of me.'

'Oh, sorry, mister.'

'Who are you, and what are you doing here?'

'My name is Mbulelo, Mbulelo Sondlo, and I live here. I beg on the streets. Please, mister, please don't throw me out of this place, it's the only shelter I have.'

'Okay . . . Mbulelo, I'm not going to throw you out. I want to ask you some questions. Is that okay?'

'Yes, okay.'

'How long have you lived here?'

'I came up from the Eastern Cape from Ngcobo last year. After my mother died, and there was nothing for me there. I'm a white, black man, and I had a lot of trouble from tsotsis in Ngcobo. They said that my mother had slept with a white man and that the ancestors cursed me because my family had done bad things. They were always beating me up and threatening to kill me and sell my body parts to witch doctors.

'They did this to me', he said, pointing to the scar and the hollowed eye socket. They attacked me with an axe. After that, I left and came here. I thought I could find a job or something, but it didn't work out.

Jacks had had a friend at school who had albinism, so he knew about the prejudice many of them faced from ill-informed bigots. 'Do you sleep here every night?'

'Yes. I don't have anywhere else to sleep.'

'Okay, were you here last week?'

'Yes, I'm always here.'

'There was a man who lived in the complex over there', said Jacks, pointing to the wall. 'He was an old white man. He died. Did you hear anything about it?'

'No sir.'

'There were lots of police officers around the following day. Do you remember that?'

'Yes . . . Yes, sir, I remember that. I saw lots of police cars. That was the morning after the workman was here.'

'Workman? What workman?'

'There was a man here fixing the fence or doing something

with it. He came here just after dark, the night before the police arrived.'

'Was he alone?'

'Yes, he had a ladder, and he was standing there', said Mbulelo, pointing to the kink in the wall next to the rocks. He was a white man.'

'A white man?'

'Yes, and he was wearing overalls. He was standing there for a few minutes, maybe ten. Then, the alarm went off on the other side of the complex. He had a small box in his hand with wires coming out of it, which he stuck on the bottom wires of the fence. That must have switched the electricity off because he could squeeze himself through the wires when he climbed the wall without being shocked.'

A voltmeter to check that the fence was deactivated, thought Jacks. 'Then what happened?'

'Nothing happened. The man disappeared for a long time. Then I heard him coming back. That was late in the night. He squeezed himself through the wires again and left.'

'Would you recognise him if you saw him again?

'Maybe. He was a small, thin white man with short grey hair.'

'But it was dark. How could you recognise him?'

'I could see from the security lights where all the houses are, ' he said, pointing at the flood lights high above the cameras on the metal poles that ran along the perimeter wall.

'Okay. Thanks, Mbulelo. I may need to talk to you again. Where do I find you?'

'Here. I'm always here at night. If nobody kicks me out.'

Jacks pulled out his wallet and gave Mbulelo three one-hundred-rand notes. 'Here, get yourself some food. And don't leave here. I will come back to see you again, do you understand, Mbulelo?'

'Yes, yes, I understand. Ewe ndiyakuva, Tata, mdiyabulela kakhulu, thank you, thank you so much.' Mbulelo's single eye welled up with tears. Three hundred rand was more than he could make in a week of begging from motorists as they waited for the traffic lights to change. He was a white, one-eyed black man, yet, as a beggar, he was invisible to most of those drivers.

FIFTY-FOUR

After losing her job, Debbie's three younger sisters were determined not to let her wallow in depression. She had cried solidly for a day and a half, and that, they concluded, was more than those bastards at Janse-Mashele deserved. Therefore, as a tight-knit family who supported each other through thick and thin, they did what they always did when a family member met with some calamity: they went out and partied.

They had partied hard in the neighbourhood pubs and clubs over the weekend. By the following week, things were looking up for Debbie. She had been promised a job by a distant cousin who ran a haulage company. He needed someone intelligent and resourceful to keep tabs on his fleet of 22-wheelers spread throughout southern Africa. And, as he had stipulated, he needed someone tough enough to stand up to his argumentative drivers who were constantly moaning about their working conditions, vehicles, salaries, and just about anything you could think of, according to her cousin.

'You see, Debbs, when one door closes, another door opens', as one of Debbie's sisters had explained.

A trucking company may not have been as glamorous as an ad agency, but the salary offered to her was a good twenty-five per cent higher than what she had earned at Janse-Mashele. Besides, that place wasn't the same without Joe. And she doubted it ever would be.

There was also a new man in her life. He may not have been the best-looking guy in the world, but he was fit, athletic and had - as Debbie described - a body to die for. Being a farmer, he was also tanned and healthy-looking. And he had piercing blue eyes. So, Debbie considered him a decent all-round package.

They had met at one of the local coffee shops. He had sat at a nearby table when they struck up a conversation. At first, it was just a friendly chit-chat about nothing in particular. But then, after ordering her a second cappuccino, the topic switched to Debbie's new job. They discussed all the spectacular sights in and around Angola, Zimbabwe, Mozambique, Namibia, and Botswana for the next two hours.

The guy – his name was Chris - was well-travelled and interesting. He was telling her about the Zimbabwe Ruins when, out of the blue, he just asked her out for dinner. Just like that, Debbie had explained to her sisters. And even though none of her siblings had laid eyes on the mystery farmer, they were pleased she'd met someone so quickly after the trauma of losing Joe and her job.

Debbie had even splashed out on a new outfit for the occasion – a tight-fitting black mini dress that met with the approval of the Peters clan. She also had a new hairdo to disguise the white strands that seemed to be taking over from her blonde locks and a French manicure.

As she left home for the restaurant, her sisters were excited as they lined up by the front door to give Debbie the final inspection. The feeling that she looked like a million dollars was unanimous. She also promised to send an SMS when she arrived at the restaurant - Chris had arranged to meet Debbie at the Apollo Greek Restaurant in Greenside, one of the trendy areas renowned for its eateries. She also agreed to send a second text message informing her sisters when she was about to leave for home.

As she drove up to the roundabout located in the centre of Greenside's restaurant area, a white double cab bakkie pulled out in front of her, vacating a rarely found parking spot for that location at that time of night. It was directly in front of Apollo's. A car guard wearing an official yellow Day-Glo waistcoat stepped into the road to point out the space to Debbie. He then guided her as she reversed into the spot. Exiting the car, she handed over some coins with a smile. 'I'm lucky tonight to get a parking spot right here.'

'Oh, thank you, madam. Do you know that you have got petrol leaking out of the back of your car?'

'What?'

'Yes, madam, there's petrol dripping out of the back here. It's very dangerous.'

She looked at the side of her car where the fuel tank was located. 'I can't see anything. Where is it dripping?'

'No, Madam, it's here at the back, near the exhaust.'

Debbie stepped off the kerb in the narrow space between her car and the vehicle parked behind her. She bent over to look for the dripping petrol. 'Are you sure? I can't even smell petrol . . .'

Suddenly, Debbie was shocked as the man, holding a cloth, thrust his hand into her face. She tried to scream, but the fabric was held tightly over her mouth and nose. The man's left hand wrapped around her arms and upper body in a vice-like grip. She tried to wriggle herself out of the hold, but he was too strong. She was aware of a sickly, sweet, cloying smell. Then she could feel her legs buckle underneath her weight. Then, a blackness enveloped her as she passed out.

The white double cab drove up and double-parked next to Debbie's car. Fourie quickly leapt out, opened the back door, and lifted Debbie's legs as Nelson pushed her limp body into the footwell. Fourie grabbed a blanket from the back seat and covered Debbie's body before jumping back into the driver's seat and accelerating away.

Nelson picked up the car keys and the cellphone that Debbie had dropped just before she passed out. Within seconds, he had stripped the phone of its SIM card and battery, rendering it impossible to trace, before starting the car and pulling out of the parking spot. Then, following Fourie, he drove around the roundabout and into the night.

The kidnapping, which had taken less than 30 seconds in the middle of one of the busiest nightlife spots in the northern suburbs, was conducted unseen.

Book Three: Autumn 2012

FIFTY-FIVE

'Baby steps', said Bernie Van Rooyen as he leaned back in his chair before hooking his bright red braces with his thumbs and pulling them playfully. He glanced at the notes he had taken when Jacks had explained his encounter with Mbulelo. 'Having an eyewitness to events that possibly led to Joe's murder - or shall I say alleged murder - is another couple of baby steps in the right direction.'

'Could this not be the smoking gun?' asked Daniel.

'Oh, that hoary old cliché' cringed Bernie. 'If there's one thing I've learnt over my thirty-year career in crime, it's that if you want to see a smoking gun, best you be at the scene of a murder three seconds after it happened.'

Daniel held up his hands in submission.

Bernie continued: 'Anyway, let's just examine what we have here: an eyewitness to a suspicious event; a person or persons unseen accidentally, in inverted commas, damages the electric fence at Joe's townhouse complex, which deactivates it. Then someone climbs over that fence at the only part of the wall not covered by the CCTV cameras. That person disappears before reappearing some hours later. And during that time, Joe is allegedly murdered. So, is it reasonable to suggest that these two events are connected?'

'What else could it be?' asked Daniel.

'It's not impossible to suppose that he was a burglar attempting to break into another house, even though there were no reports of any attempted burglaries. It's not impossible to suppose that he was someone who was enjoying some clandestine affair with a married woman living in the complex.'

'That's stretching it a bit', scoffed Jacks.

'Well, that's the problem. A defence counsel can claim that our story is just as outlandish. We can only build our case - one piece of evidence at a time - or take baby steps, as I said.'

'We need to secure our witness', said Jacks.

'Absolutely. We can't have this Mbulelo chap living like a vagrant and begging for a living', replied Van Rooyen.

'Is there somewhere safe we can send him to?' asked Judith. 'A hostel or a charity or a church group or something?'

'I think I might be able to take him in. I have a rambling property in Craighall, and my gardener, Wilson, is getting so old that he can barely do half the work he's supposed to do, so at least while I keep him fed and provide a decent roof over his head, he can earn his keep. It won't be the Hilton, but I'm sure it'll be better than some reeking old substation.'

'How's the security at your property?' asked Jacks. 'If these people know that we have a witness, they will come after him. And you know as well as I do that these are professionals. Cold and very calculating professionals.'

'Oh God, yes, you're right, Jacks. I suppose I have an average level of security at my place. But then again, Joe's complex would be regarded by most people as being extremely secure, but none of that stopped Joe's murderer from getting in.'

'Be specific about what you have in the way of security.'

'Well, you know the usual stuff: electric fence, burglar alarm, armed response. Oh, and two bloody big boerboels who would bite the legs off anyone trying to pole-vault over my wall', added Bernie proudly.

'Good, big dogs help, as long as they're not poisoned.'

'God, Jacks, you are a barrel of laughs today.'

'You know me, advocate, I have to be realistic. I think our best chance of keeping Mbulelo safe is that no one beyond this room knows about him or anything about what he witnessed.'

'That's correct', agreed Bernie.

'Do we need to get a statement or something from Mbulelo?' asked Daniel.

'Getting a sworn statement is the first thing we do. I want to do this in front of a judge or, at the very least, a clerk of the court who can witness, sign, stamp and seal the document there and then. I also want him to tell his story in front of a video camera.

'We're going to have to find him and move him to your place as soon as possible', said Jacks.

'Yes, as soon as we can find him.'

'I'll go back and look for him at the substation. But he could be at any intersection around Sandton, ' said Jacks.

'I can search the streets if that will help', suggested Daniel.

'I can also drive around that area', said Judith.'

'Right then, you three go and find Mbulelo, and I'll go home and take care of the accommodation.'

FIFTY-SIX

To Mr Daniel Stein

C/O Janse-Mashele

Strategy Department

12 Alice Avenue

Sandton

Dear Daniel,

My young friend, what a lovely surprise to get your letter. I seldom get letters these days, and as you can imagine, emails and text messages are hardly an option for someone like me who is forbidden to have a cellphone or a computer.

It is a shame that we didn't get to chat while on the film set. (Look at me saying things like 'film set' – a term I had never heard of until a couple of weeks ago.) Like you, I was also looking forward to meeting up again, but the Department of Correctional Services must have rules and regulations, and as I am one of their treasured guests, I have to accept my lot in life, I suppose.

I must say, I did enjoy the whole filming experience. I never realised that so much work went into making a film, and as you mentioned in your letter, all for just 60 seconds. It boggles the mind, it really does. But I can't say I was very enthusiastic about wearing makeup. I can tell you, there were many laughs at my expense in my wing that night after the film shoot.

I am also delighted that everyone is happy with the finished commercial. I haven't seen it yet, and we don't get to watch television at C-Max. But I'm not one for TV anyway, maybe it's because I never grew up with it, so I can't say I'm too bothered.

Some prisoners have seen the commercial, and many guards have seen it, too. So, I have been teased a lot about being the next Harrison Ford!

One excellent thing that has come out of this whole exercise is that there has been talk that I might get transferred to somewhere that's a bit more relaxed than a maximum-security prison. Leeuwkop and Krugersdorp have both been mentioned. I hope it is Leeuwkop because they have a farm there, and I think I mentioned to you that it would be wonderful to work on the land again. Something I haven't done since I was a young boy. But then, I don't want to get my hopes up, only for them to be dashed if things don't work out.

Another great surprise was that when that commercial went on TV, I had a letter from my half-sister, Brenda, that I barely know. She wrote me a lovely letter to say that she wants to come and see me and that maybe we can be the family we've never been. Isn't that wonderful? I can't wait to meet with her.

I would also enjoy a regular correspondence with you. I'd find it stimulating and fun to be in touch with someone on the outside. Especially with all the modern technology, it'll be nice to have someone to explain it to me.

Today, the world is very different from before I was convicted. As you know, I read a lot, but it's not the same as experiencing things first-hand.

So, what else can I tell you? As you know, I had my master's in psychology last year, so I think I have exhausted the subject. This year, I'm thinking of studying something a bit more human. I picked up a book on sociology in the library here, and I found it very interesting. At the moment, I'm toying with the idea of a BA course in sociology through UNISA. Trying to make sense of society, human social behaviour patterns and social interaction would be fascinating.

Well, Daniel, my young friend. It's almost nine o'clock and lights-out time here at C-Max, so I had better sign off now. Please do write to me again soon.

Sincerely, your friend,
Riaan du Plessis

FIFTY-SEVEN

When Bernie arrived home, he quickly got to work with his gardener, Wilson, to clear out an old storeroom tucked away at the back of the property. It took them a couple of hours to empty the room of the accumulated jumble and cast-offs that had accumulated over the previous thirty years. Then, with the help of Adelina, Bernie's housekeeper, they swept, scrubbed, and disinfected the room until it was spotless. After moving in some bits and pieces of furniture, Adelina officially declared Mbulelo's new home clean and comfortable.

The timing was good because Jacks sent a two-word cryptic text message stating, *'On our way 2 U'*.

When Jacks and Mbulelo arrived at Bernie's, the day's first order was to introduce Mbulelo to Bernie's two boerboels. They viewed the new lodger with much suspicion, whilst Mbulelo viewed them with dread. Never in his life had he encountered dogs so big and powerful. But there was a general acceptance after Bernie insisted that Mbulelo give them both a pat on the head.

The next all-important task was a hot bath to soak and scrub away the months of rough living. Jacks had whispered discreetly to Bernie that he had had to wind down all the car windows plus open the sunroof, and he also had the fan on full blast, but the stink that emanated off Mbulelo's clothes was still unbearable. So, he detoured to the nearest Woolworths to buy the man some new clothes and toiletries. Including the largest can of deodorant he could find.

As Mbulelo languished in his first hot bath in several months,

Jacks walked around Bernie's property to inspect the security. 'Bernie, your electric fence is in a dreadful state. Are you sure there's still some current running through it?'

'Buggered if I know, Jacks. What's wrong with it?'

'Some of the wires have snapped, most of the insulators have deteriorated, and in places, half of the fence is covered in vegetation. When was the last time you had it serviced?'

'I can't remember it ever being serviced.'

'Well, how long ago did you have it installed?'

'I don't know, eight, nine, ten years ago?'

'Twelve years ago,' chipped in Wilson. 'It was in 2000 that we first had it installed.'

'Hell, Bernie, you need to have it checked out. And with Mbulelo here, you need to get it done urgently.'

'I'll get my PA to make some phone calls tomorrow.'

Later, while Adelina prepared the evening meal, Wilson took his newly acquired assistant on a garden tour to discuss the duties that would begin the following morning. Wilson not only liked the idea of having some help with the heavier work, but he also relished the thought of being referred to as 'Baas', as Mbulelo did instinctively and respectfully.

Adelina had prepared a meal fit for Xhosa royalty. The favourite staple of the Eastern Cape, Umngqusho - samp and sugar beans with onions, potatoes, and chillies, all of which were topped with a rich mutton stew. It was the first home-cooked meal Mbulelo had enjoyed for months. And on the three occasions he emptied his plate, Adelina would dish up more until, as Mbulelo claimed, his stomach was about to explode.

FIFTY-EIGHT

Debbie's sisters were desperate with worry. They were all adamant that if Debbie promised to send an SMS message, she would send it, with no ifs or buts. Even if the phone's battery died - or worse - if her phone had been stolen, Debbie would still find some way to contact her sisters.

And even if this Chris character turned out to be some Hollywood heartthrob who had swept her off her feet, nothing in the world would prevent Debbie from sending that message. Besides, Debbie was not the kind of woman who would stay the night with a man she hardly knew. As gregarious a party animal as Debbie could be, she was still a conservative person at heart.

The four sisters were as close as siblings could be. While still young girls – ranging in ages between three and thirteen – their mother had been diagnosed with cervical cancer. She had been in a hospital for many weeks, only to be sent home to waste away while she waited for the inevitable.

When it came to mothering, Debbie, being the eldest, took responsibility for her three younger siblings and her father. As his wife's condition worsened, so did his ability to care for his young family, and he was relegated to an emotional wreck in a matter of weeks. Also, earning a modest income, the Peters family did not have the luxury of maids and gardeners that serviced most middle-class South African families at the time. So, Debbie, barely a teenager, assumed several roles: she cooked, she cleaned the house, she did the laundry, she helped with her sisters' homework, and she read them stories every night. She became a mother and father to her sisters.

Eventually, when the end was near, her mother was moved to a hospice a few streets away from their home. Then, every day after school, Debbie would ensure the girls looked presentable before taking them to see their mother.

The last lucid conversation the mother had before the diamorphine muddled her brain was with Debbie. The young girl promised her mother she would care for her sisters forever. And she did.

The sisters were tormented about what could have happened to Debbie. The first and obvious question was who this Chris guy could be. None of the sisters knew anything about him other than the few vague comments that Debbie had made. She met him at one of the local coffee shops in a strip mall down the road. He was a farmer, or she thought he was a farmer. He was short. He had piercing blue eyes. He was well-built, fit, and lean. He seemed to have travelled well in and around southern Africa.

Then came the speculation about what they didn't know. Christ, he could be a serial killer, or a rapist, or a God-knows-what; there were just too many weirdos around.

But the sisters also knew full well that Debbie was no fool. She was a pretty good judge of character. After all, hadn't she vetted all her sister's boyfriends when they were growing up? The sisters often spoke about how Debbie would treat those who didn't pass muster: she'd throw the boys out of the house. And God help any boy who harboured any thoughts of mistreating any of her sisters.

The three siblings had stayed up waiting to hear from Debbie. But there was not a word. Eventually, at around four in the morning, Serena, the oldest of the three, decided to phone the local police station to report her missing. But the cop she spoke to sounded half asleep and disinterested in her plight.

'You have to wait 24 hours before we can open a missing person's file', said the cop.

'No, we don't', countered Serena. 'It's in your SAPS website, for Christ's sake. It says there is no waiting period to report a missing person! It's in red, and it's in big capital letters on your website.'

'No', said the cop dismissively. 'You have to wait for 24 hours.'

'No, I don't . . . So, stop bullshitting me . . . I want to report a missing person . . . My sister is missing. Do you hear me?'

But the cop didn't hear her as he'd already slammed down the phone.

'Arshole cop', screamed Serena in frustration. 'Couldn't catch a fucking cold anyway.'

Next, they tried calling the Bureau of Missing Persons, a specialised SAPS unit. But the numbers of both the head office and the Gauteng provincial office just rang until they went to recorded messages informing callers that regular office hours were between eight-thirty am and four-thirty pm.

Then, they tried the emergency rooms of all the local hospitals. But again, they drew a blank with each one.

FIFTY-NINE

Daniel was sitting in front of his laptop typing a brief for a market research company when Mashele stuck his head around the doorway.

'Got a second?'

'Hi Mac, of course. What can I do for you?'

'I wanted to discuss researching the Correctional Services campaign.'

'Doing the brief as we speak.'

'Great. I'm on my way out for a meeting. Would you mind walking with me while we chat?'

'No, of course not.'

As they walked, Mashele was his usual friendly self. He smiled and greeted staff members as they passed each other in the corridors. But as soon as they were alone, his demeanour suddenly changed. 'Look, we need to have a chat. A very discrete chat.'

'Okay', replied Daniel guardedly.

'You're being watched, and your phones are tapped. Spyware has been installed on your cellphones. You have two phones, correct?' Asked Mashele as they started walking down the Mashele stairs towards reception.

Daniel was shocked by this revelation. 'Yes, but who? What?'

'Keep walking and try not to look shocked', whispered Mashele. 'They can hear every call you make and read every text message you send or receive.'

As they reached the bottom of the stairs, he walked over to the reception desk to greet some clients who had just arrived for a presentation. After a few pleasantries, he and Daniel continued walking to the basement.

'Have you ever heard about LM-Plus?' Asked Mashele. 'It's one of our subsidiaries.'

'Yes, I have heard it mentioned. Isn't it some PR company? Joe said something about it.'

'Yes, I'm sure Joe knew about them. LM-Plus is not a legitimate PR company; it's a bunch of very dangerous people who do a lot of dirty work . . . Smit's dirty work.'

Upon hearing Smit's name, Daniel could feel his body tensing up, which Mashele immediately sensed.

'I despise him too, Daniel. Look, you and I may not know each other well right now, but I promise you one thing: we are on the same side, and I'm sure as hell I am not on the side of Janse or Smit.'

'Okay.'

'Look, we can't talk here. Let's meet tonight for a drink somewhere.'

'When and where?'

'Let's meet at the Terrace Bar at the Hyatt, say six-thirty?'

'Great, see you then.'

'One more thing, Daniel, and this is really important. Don't tell anyone about this conversation. And say nothing about our meeting tonight. I wasn't joking about your phone being tapped. Okay?'

'Yes, I understand.'

Mashele smiled warmly and shook Daniel's hand before he got into his Ferrari and drove off to his meeting.

SIXTY

'Fourie, it's crucial that you call me as soon as you get this message, okay? Very, very important, understand?'

Fourie had been helping Nelson and Willem skin and butcher some dead cart horses when Smit's call came through. Fourie guessed Smit might be enquiring about the last job but didn't want to pick up his cellphone with his blood-stained hands.

He ignored the message for a couple of hours until he finally relented.

'You were seen', said Smit as he answered the call after the first ring.

'What are you talking about?'

'The night you did the Robinson job, you were seen climbing the wall over to the townhouse complex.'

Fourie fell silent as he weighed up the consequences of this news.

'Fourie, you there?'

'Ja, I was just thinking... Who saw me? And what did they see?'

'You were seen near the place where you went over the wall... You had the electric fence disconnected. You had a ladder, which you used to climb over a wall. Then you came back a few hours later and disappeared...'

Fourie thought it sounded like Smit was reading some report, probably authored by LM-Plus.

'This is a terrible loose end, and you need to take care of it', said Smit emphatically.

'What do you know about this witness?'

'He's an albino black man with only one eye . . . And a big scar on his face. And that his name is Mbulelo.'

'Where do I find him?'

'We think he might be staying in the house owned by an advocate called Van Rooyen. It's somewhere in Craighall.'

'Okay, that's good enough for me, I'll find him.'

'Best you do, Fourie. And this one is for your own account.'

'Ja, fine, whatever', agreed Fourie dismissively.

'There are two people you need to be aware of that are making mischief for us. Judith Maponya is Jabu's sister. She's a young woman in her mid-twenties and an attorney. She's been dealing with this advocate.'

'Okay. Have you got details on her?'

'Yes, I do. The other person making trouble for us is a young guy called Daniel Stein. He works for us at Janse-Mashele. He was a friend of Joe Robinson. I want you to keep an eye on both people.'

'Leave the details on both at the usual place.'

'I will do. What about Debbie Peters? I take it that you have taken care of her?'

'Yes . . . She's taken care of', said Fourie.

SIXTY-ONE

From the moment Mashele told him he was under surveillance, Daniel felt agitated. He also felt deeply violated and was enraged at the thought that complete strangers were reading his text messages and emails, listening to his phone conversations, and watching his every move. It made him suspicious of everyone. Even the shop assistant at the neighbourhood takeaway café looked like she was taking too much interest in him as he queued to pay for a sandwich.

Other than popping out for that lunch, he had decided to lay low in his office for the rest of the day. He dreaded the thought of bumping into Smit in one of the corridors. He didn't know if he could trust himself to keep his mouth shut. Or trust himself not to throw a punch.

Disinterested in work, he bided his time scanning online newspapers. At least he was glad to see that the clamour about Joe had finally died down. He frequently looked at the wall clock as the dials inched their way - excruciatingly slowly - towards the sixth hour. When they finally did, he packed his laptop in his bag and left for the Hyatt.

Daniel was impressed with the opulence of the hotel lobby. Very Mashele, he thought. The man himself was already there, sitting in a quiet alcove at the Terrace Bar, a heavy crystal-cut tumbler of whisky in front of him. 'Ah, Daniel, I'm glad you could join me. Would you like a drink?'

'I'll just have a beer, thanks.'

'Can't I interest you in something stronger? They have a fine selection of malts here.'

'No, a beer will be fine, thanks, Mac.' Daniel was keen to get to the heart of the matter. 'So, you say I'm being watched?'

'Yes, shame, it must have been praying on your mind.'

'Yes, can't say I was in much of a mood to finish the Correctional Services research brief.'

'I wouldn't worry about that.'

'But it sounds like I have many other things to worry about?'

'Well ... If you put it that way ... Yes, I'm afraid there are things that you need to worry about.'

'JM-Plus?'

'JM-Plus, yes, and the people who do the dirty work for them: the private detectives and other assorted pond life.'

Mashele hesitated for the few seconds it took the waiter to pour Daniel's beer.

'Before we start, I have a question for you. Why do you feel the need to talk to me?'

'Good question, Daniel, and let me answer it as directly as I can.'

'I wouldn't want it any other way.'

'Of course not ... Daniel, you're going to help me change Janse-Mashele to Mashele and Associates.'

Daniel was shocked, 'Well, that certainly was direct. So how exactly am I going to help you achieve that?'

'By helping me to get rid of Janse and Smit.'

'What, just like that?'

'Yes, just like that.'

'Let me tell you about my position at Janse-Mashele. I have been with Janse for eight years now. It started off okay; maybe you could call it a symbiotic relationship: he had the infrastructure and the credibility, and I had the energy and the chutzpah to win over the clients. But things have changed. Janse became lazy.

Even though I am a full partner, in Janse's eyes, I'm just a useful darkie; some politically connected house negro to be paraded when clients need to be impressed. Janse is far too arrogant and paternalistic to treat me as a full partner.'

He paused to sip his Scotch. 'We were in a business meeting some time back, and the client, a deputy minister actually, commented on the lack of transformation in South African business. And just for a moment – a split second – I could see Janse rolling his eyes. He didn't get it. He still doesn't get it. People like Janse continuously block people like me. You see, Daniel, Janse's racism is so deeply ingrained in his psyche he can never change. He's an anachronism. He's a product of the apartheid system, and he can never truly accept what has happened in this country over the last 18 years – the death of apartheid. He can never get into the game; he stands on the touchline, heckles, nit-picks, and sneers, but he never gets involved.

With a hand signal, Mashele caught the attention of a passing waiter and ordered a fresh round of drinks. 'He pays me very well, although he doesn't like me to be seen spending my money. Boy, does that piss him off? One of the reasons I buy Ferraris and Porches is to piss him off.'

He chuckled at his quip, which he realised had gone over Daniel's head. 'The question I ask myself is this: do I still need Janse as a partner? No, I don't. He's a liability to me and a liability to the company. And I want him out of the business as fast as possible.'

'What about Petrus Smit?'

'Well, I have even less to do with Smit than with Janse. He's also a very ruthless, dishonest person with a chequered past. He can't build a company. He can't lead people. He can't win over clients. And it's inconceivable for Smit to be in this company without Janse. And whatever you hear about Janse being ruthless, he's not in the same league as Smit.'

'Joe said something like that.'

'Yes, and we come to Joe . . . Poor Joe. I liked him, you know.'

'He liked you, too. He always said that if you weren't running an ad agency, you should be leading one of these charismatic churches.'

'What?'

'Yes, Joe reckoned that you'd have a congregation emptying their wallets and bank accounts in minutes if you were preaching to them.'

Mashele laughed loudly. 'Did he really say that?'

'Yes, he did. He loved it when you rallied all the troops, as Joe called it. Thought you had more leadership qualities than anyone he'd ever come across.'

'Wow, I'm touched.'

They sat in silence for a moment, both thinking of Joe.

Mashele took a sip of his whiskey. 'They killed him, didn't they?'

'Yes, we believe they did.'

'We?'

'I'm involved with some people. But I'm not going to share their identities with you.'

'That's fair enough. They killed Jabu Maponya, too?'

'Yes.

'This is why they are tapping your phones and trailing your every move through GPS.'

'How do you know this?'

'Remember the conversation we had during the shoot at C-Max?'

'Yes.'

'Remember what I told you about protecting you against Smit?'

'Yes.'

'Well, a very good friend of mine has been helping me to do just that.'

'Who's your friend?'

'He's the deputy director general of the NIA. Do you know the NIA?'

'National Intelligence Agency?'

'Correct, he told me someone had tapped your phones and bugged them with spyware. Apparently, it's not complicated; you buy software online, and suddenly, you're a fully-fledged James Bond.'

'Oh my God', said Daniel as the awful realisation struck him.

'What is it?'

'I've just realised that if these bastards were listening to my phone conversations, then I have just put someone's life in danger. I need to make an urgent call.'

'Use the house phone in the lobby', suggested Mashele. 'I would let you use mine, but it's also bugged by the same people. Daniel, we'll talk again. But please believe me when I say we're on the same side. My motives were just to get them out of the company, but if they did kill Joe, then I'll do everything I can do to make sure they end their days in some hole.'

They shook hands quickly before Daniel walked briskly to the lobby. He picked up the landline phone and called Judith.

'Judith, hey, it's me. Look, do me a favour, write down this number and call me back on a different phone, okay? Please do it as quickly as you can. The number is 0-1-1 2-8-0 2-2-3-4. I'm in the lobby of the Hyatt Hotel in Rosebank.'

'Okay, call you back right now.'

It took two frustratingly long minutes for the landline in front of him to ring.

'Hi, I'm calling from a neighbour's phone. What's going on?'

'Hi, look, I've just been told that my phone has been tapped by people working for Smit and Janse.'

'Oh my God!'

'Yes, shit, remember the chat we had in our cars yesterday when we were looking for Mbulelo?'

'Oh yes.'

'Well, we need to get Mbulelo as far away from Bernie's house as possible.'

'I'll get hold of Bernie and Jacks. Oh, my God, I hope it's not too late.'

'I know. I will call you later. Okay?'

'Okay, bye.'

SIXTY-TWO

Mbulelo's first day at work had consisted of weeding, trimming the hedge, and mowing the lawn, all under the watchful eye of Wilson, who was pleased that his first-ever assistant had a natural affinity towards plant life.

'You're a white-black man with green fingers', Wilson had commented, much to his amusement. And he laughed uproariously every time he repeated his wisecrack, which had been several times throughout the day. Mbulelo enjoyed the attention, and it felt good to do some physical work instead of walking past lines of cars whilst being unseen by most drivers.

He was also delighted to be given not one but three substantial meals a day. Adeline felt sorry for the boy who had lost both his mother and his grandmother and had been so badly treated by those tsotsis in the Eastern Cape. She couldn't erase the trauma that Mbulelo had experienced, but at least she could feed the boy with plenty of good, healthy food to help him regain his strength.

The other privilege that Adelina treated Mbulelo to was some after-dinner TV entertainment. She, Mbulelo and Wilson were enjoying a lively game show when Bernie's boerboels started to bark. Mbulelo was still nervous about the dogs. And even though Bernie had taken the time to introduce Mbulelo to them as a friend, the youngster had felt intimidated whenever these 90 kg brutes came up to sniff at him, which they did several times on that first day.

The boerboels rarely barked. But when they did, Bernie, Adelina, and Wilson understood it wasn't for something frivolous. The barking was getting more intense until, suddenly, both dogs whimpered loudly and then went silent.

Also alerted by the barking, Bernie was halfway to the kitchen to see what was bothering the dogs when he heard the loud screeching of breaks in the road just outside his property.

Within a few seconds, he heard the doorbell ring, and seconds later, he heard Jacks' voice on the intercom. 'Advocate, it's me, Jacks, I've been trying to call you for the last thirty minutes ... Need to talk to you urgently.'

'Oh, so sorry, Jacks. I was in court all afternoon and left the bloody phone on silent. Come in', said Bernie as he pressed the gate button.

Bernie opened the front door. 'Jacks, what's all this urgency?'

'Mbulelo's security has been compromised. Daniel has been informed - supposedly on good authority - that his phone is tapped. He remembered that he and Judith chatted over their phones while looking for Mbulelo. Where is he now?'

'Mbulelo is at the back with Adelina and Wilson.'

'Okay, we need to get him out of here right now. I'll take him to a hotel until we can make permanent arrangements for him.'

'Oh, bloody hell, please come through.'

As they walked out through the back door, they were suddenly aware of two large, dark bodies slumped on the ground in the passage between the kitchen door and Adeline's room.

'Oh, my God, it's my dogs!' shouted Bernie in shock and despair.

Jacks stepped forward and reached inside his Jacket for the pistol he always carried in a shoulder holster. But as he cocked the weapon, two muffled sounds in quick succession rang out of the darkness in front of him.

Jacks suddenly seemed unsteady on his feet. He shuffled half a step backwards.

'Jacks? ... Jacks? Shouted Bernie. 'Are you okay?'

But Jacks didn't answer. His body swayed slightly on his feet before he collapsed, falling forward, flat on his face.

Bernie was stunned, confused, and scared. What was happening around him? First, the dogs and now Jacks? None of it made sense. Reality hit him only when the blood started pooling on the concrete surface around Jacks' head.

SIXTY-THREE

Her second night in the windowless room was stiflingly hot. She could only assume it was night as her watch was no longer on her wrist.

It was silent, too. Just occasionally, she could hear what she thought were wild animals roaring in the distance. But during the days, the sounds she mostly heard were the constant buzzing of bluebottle flies.

When she first awoke from her chemical-induced slumber, she had the worst headache she had ever experienced. Even though she felt groggy and dizzy, the torturous pain denied her the refuge of sleep. But eventually, after what seemed like an eternity, she cried herself into oblivion.

The headache was still there the following morning. The room was small, with no furniture except the old single brass bed, which squeaked at the slightest movement. There was also a hard-backed chair that looked too uncomfortable to sit on. Resting on the chair was a stack of old magazines - torn, ancient copies of Reader's Digest and National Geographic, Rooi Rose, Huisgenoot, and the Boere bible, Landbouweekblad. On the floor, next to the chair, was a dented enamel bucket and two toilet rolls.

After a while, Debbie could hear the distant footsteps of a person approaching the room. The footsteps were on a solid surface, possibly the same surface as the concrete that made up the floor in her room.

'Hello?' shouted Debbie as loudly as she could. 'Hello? Whoever you are, can you hear me?'

'Stop the shouting' was the terse reply. 'Take the pillowcase off the pillow and put it over your head. Do you understand?' It was an African accent that sounded like that of a middle-aged or older man. 'Have you put it over your head? If I come into this room and you see my face, I'll have no choice but to kill you, do you understand?'

'Yes, yes, I understand. I have done what you ask. I won't be able to see you, I promise.'

She heard a key wriggling in the door lock, followed by a creaking sound of the door opening.

'Okay, it's good that you have it on. It's very important that you not see my face whenever I come into this room. You must not be able to identify me. I am saying this for your own good. Do you understand?'

'Yes, yes, I understand.'

'While you are here, there are rules that you have to obey. I don't want any nonsense or bullshit from you. Do you understand?'

'Yes, I understand. I won't be difficult, I promise you. I just want...'

'Shut up', interrupted the voice. 'I will bring you food and empty the bucket that you use for a toilet. Do you understand?'

'Yes. But please, can I call my sisters to tell them that...'

Debbie was interrupted by the sound of the door closing and the key turning in the lock.

By the second day, a routine of sorts was established. The man brought her food three times daily: bread and milk for breakfast, bread and polony for lunch, and charred braai meat and mealie pap for dinner. On that first day, she didn't care that the food was barely edible as she had no appetite; she didn't care on the second day, either, because she was so hungry she would have devoured anything by then. Nor did she care that the man had to empty the bucket that she had to use to urinate and defecate. Usually, she would have been mortified at the thought of a man being exposed to her most private bodily functions. But her modesty paled in comparison to her anguish over her sisters. If only she could let them know that she was still alive, that she wasn't hurt.

She spent most of the first day and a good deal of the second day crying for her sisters and herself.

SIXTY-FOUR

Fourie was frustrated and angry with himself. He had seen the albino through the window of the maid's room at the back of the property. He'd been only a few metres away from his target, even had his weapon trained on him, and then the dogs started barking.

He'd been stupid. He'd slipped up. He had seen the *Beware of the Dogs* sign on the front gate but ignored it. He should have taken care of that problem first. He should have enticed the dogs to a quieter part of the garden by throwing some biltong over the wall before shooting them quietly. He had a silencer, for Christ's sake.

Then, the black guy came out of the house and tried to pull a gun on him. Fourie had no option but to fire his weapon. Both shots had been on target. The first hit the man between the eyes; the second was slightly higher above the left eye.

He had looked through the window again, but by now, the albino had moved and was standing behind the maid and some old guy, obviously alarmed by the barking and shouting outside. Fuck it, thought Fourie. He should have shot her, should have shot the old guy before shooting the albino, should have shot all of them. But the older white man, who walked out of the kitchen screaming about his dogs, was physically huge. Fourie guessed that stopping him would have emptied his magazine. So, he took the only sensible option – retreating to the sanctuary of darkness.

But Fourie didn't leave the scene altogether. He parked his double cab further down the street so that he could watch the goings on through binoculars. Within minutes, the private security vehicles arrived. They were soon followed by the first of many police and emergency vehicles, followed by private vehicles: plainclothes police, forensic guys and maybe friends and relatives, guessed Fourie. Then, the van from the morgue arrived.

From such a distance, it was hard to see what was happening. But after a couple of hours, he spotted what he'd been waiting for: his first sight of the albino. He was sitting in the passenger seat of an old Toyota Corolla that was being driven out of the property by some young white guy. The Toyota was moving towards him.

Fourie decided not to open fire. There were far too many cops just a few hundred metres away. He ducked under the dashboard as the Toyota drove past. Then, after waiting a few seconds, he started his engine and turned his vehicle around to follow the Toyota at a safe distance.

Within a minute, the Toyota arrived at a major intersection before turning onto one of the arterial roads that dissected the northern suburbs: Jan Smuts Avenue. Following some 100 metres behind, Fourie ignored the red lights as he got to the intersection and ignored the furious hooting from the minibus taxi that had to swerve out of the way.

Fourie felt confident that he was back in control. As the Toyota was driving at average speed, it was obvious to him that his vehicle had not been spotted. All he needed to do was to get into the inside lane, parallel to the Toyota, and as both vehicles rolled to a halt at a red light at an intersection, he could shoot the albino in the head.

Daniel didn't realise how lucky he and Mbulelo were that night. As he drove up to every intersection, the lights changed to green, not that he even noticed the clear passage continuously opening before him. His mind was too occupied with the night's murderous events, for which he felt responsible. He kept thinking about what he could have done differently. He and Judith should have changed the SIM cards daily.

Mbulelo sat silently with an old bag he had borrowed from Adelina, packed with the new clothes and toiletries that Jacks had bought for him. He was traumatised by the death of Jacks, and everything that had happened that night was so confusing. He didn't know what was going on. He didn't know what was going to happen to him. But he fully understood that his life was in mortal danger because if someone went to that amount of trouble to kill him, then it stood to reason they'd try again.

Little did he realise that what he feared was less than a hundred metres behind him. Driving down towards Rosebank, Fourie kept what he considered a safe distance, keeping his double cab three vehicles behind the Toyota.

Then Fourie's luck finally changed as the traffic lights ahead changed from green to amber. Pouncing on the opportunity, he pulled out to the right lane and passed all three cars in front of him before pulling into the left lane and stopping his vehicle parallel to the Toyota.

He could see the albino sitting quietly in the car's passenger seat barely two meters away. He had the gun held high, next to his ear, behind the double cab's door pillar. His window was open. It had to be now. Suddenly, just before Fourie could bring the gun down and out of the window, there was a tremendous roar, and a large, dark body suddenly obscured his view. A motorcyclist came to a halt between his double cab and the Toyota. Fourie dropped his hand to conceal the gun. It wasn't his night, he thought,

As the red lights changed to green, the motorcycle and the Toyota pulled away at an average pace. Fourie dropped back again, allowing a couple of cars to overtake him.

Sitting in the Toyota, Mbulelo didn't know where this stranger, Daniel, was taking him. At least he was Mr Van Rooyen's friend so that he could be trusted. 'Where are you taking me, sir?' he asked softly.

Daniel, still agonising over Jacks' death, didn't fully hear Mbulelo's question. 'Sorry, Mbulelo, what were you asking?'

'I'm asking, sir, where are you taking me?'

'I'm taking you to my place for tonight. I live in an apartment across town. You'll have to sleep on the couch, but at least you'll be safe there.'

'Okay, thank you, sir.'

'It's Daniel. Please call me Daniel.'

'Okay, thank you, Daniel.'

As he drove up to the next intersection, the lights turned amber, and then Daniel did something that was out of character - something that always had him swear under his breath when he saw other drivers do it - he put his foot down and accelerated through the intersection even as the lights changed to red.

Fourie's double cab, still boxed in behind three vehicles, had no choice but to stop.

'Fuck it', shouted Fourie in frustration as he could see the Toyota's rear lights disappearing around a corner.

By the time the lights changed, he had pulled out to the fast lane at the first opportunity and accelerated as fast as he could, but it was to no avail. There was no sign of the Toyota. Daniel had turned off Jan Smuts Avenue.

Fourie pulled over at a filling station and called Smit.

'That guy you mentioned. The one that worked with Robinson, what's his name?'

'Daniel Stein.'

'Okay, what kind of car does he drive?'

'Christ, how the hell am I supposed to know? We have 350

people working for Janse-Mashele.'

'An old Toyota?'

'Maybe, I don't know.'

'Then can you tell me where he lives?'

'You're going to have to wait. I'm at home, so I'll have to log into the company server to look at the HR records. I'll SMS his address to you.'

SIXTY-FIVE

The ordeal badly shook Bernie. It seemed like an age before the forensic technicians finally finished examining the murder scene just outside the kitchen door.

After Jacks' body had been taken away, and the detectives took the last statements, Bernie could finally sit in his lounge and talk to Judith, who had arrived minutes after the first police officers. Judith could see his hands trembling as he poured himself a large scotch.

'How the hell can you try to understand what happened tonight.'

'There is no sense to it, Bernie', replied Judith.

'Poor Jacks. What an absolute gentleman he was. I must have known him a good ten years. He was still in the Scorpions when we first met.'

'Did he do a lot of work for you?'

'Yes, Jacks did most of the investigative work on my cases. I think I was instrumental in getting him to become a private investigator in the first place. When they disbanded the Scorpions, he was at odds with what to do with himself. He didn't want to continue in the police services and had little time for the people heading up the newly formed Hawks. And he didn't want to go overseas like many of his ex-colleagues. I suppose you were still a law student when this happened, Judith, but the Scorpions had a hell of a reputation. And when they were disbanded, law enforcement agencies and police forces from English-speaking countries hired many of them. So, I suggested that if he did become a private investigator, I would give him most of my work. And I would recommend him to my colleagues in chambers.'

'Was he married?'

'No, divorced a few years back, never remarried, and no children. He told me that he was from a small town in Limpopo Province. His parents still live there. He also has a younger brother who lives somewhere here in Gauteng. Jacks said he was an accountant or something. I suppose the police will trace his family to give him the terrible news.'

'Yes, when Jabu, my brother, was killed, the police were excellent. You hear all these negative things about cops all the time, but they were professional and very kind to my mother. They sent a trauma counsellor who was a great help.'

'I suppose it's a sad reality of the bloody violence that we're all subjected to, but these trauma counsellors must be the hardest working people in the country.'

'Yes . . . Sad, but probably true.'

'I know this pales in comparison with what's happened to Jacks, but I'm going to miss my dogs, too. As old and as arthritic as the big softies were . . . God, I'll miss them.'

'I spoke to Adelina earlier, and she also cried for the dogs.'

'Well, Adelina always felt safe with them around. The dogs adored her. She'd fed them from when they were pups, so they never left her side during the day when I was at work.

'My boys were just young teenagers when those two arrived here as small pups. After losing my wife and the boys growing up and leaving home, the dogs were one of the few constancies in my life that reminded me of those happy days when I had my family here. Now, the boys are married and have their own children, and they only come here on odd weekends. God, the boys will be upset.'

Bernie broke down in tears, and Judith sat silently for a few minutes.

'God, I thought it was a terrible time when my wife Evelyn died seven years ago. But that was nothing like this; the violence is just so traumatic.'

He paused while he swallowed half of the scotch. 'You know, Judith, I've been dealing with criminal law for over thirty years, but it doesn't help when something like this happens to someone close to you.'

'Things like this are out of our control, Bernie. The only thing we can do is to help put the people responsible away in some cell for the rest of their lives. That's the only thing we can do, Bernie.'

'Yes. I think you're right', said Bernie as he finished the Scotch.

'So, what happened? Jacks told me that someone had tapped Daniel's phone?'

'Yes, they obviously heard a conversation Daniel had with me about Mbulelo.'

'Do you think that's how they knew he was here?'

'It must have been. These people are evil and desperate.'

'And how did Daniel know? Who told him all this about his phones being tapped?'

'Macdonald Mashele.'

'Of Janse-Mashele? But, surely, he's on the other side . . .'

'No', interrupted Judith. 'Daniel said Mashele approached him to say that he had valid reasons to see Janse and Smit put away.'

'Such as?'

'Apparently, he made no bones about hating Janse and Smit with a passion. He also suspects that they had some involvement with Jabu's and Joe's death. And, probably the biggest reason for wanting to see the back of them is because, with Janse and Smit out of the way, the company will become his to run as he pleases.'

'But can this Mashele fellow be trusted?'

'Daniel believes he can. We need to use him for our purposes. Besides, we don't have to tell him everything we know.'

'But Mashele must be up to his neck in all kinds of dodgy goings-on in that company. You can't be a partner in an organisation and not know that fraud is being committed.'

'But Bernie, assuming that he has had some dodgy dealings, if he seriously wants the other two in jail, then we should cut a deal with him.'

'Turn state's evidence, you mean?'

'Yes, give him immunity from prosecution. Let him spill the beans on the two people we want to put away.'

'If he's not in league with the other two, then how did Mashele know that Daniel's phone was bugged?'

'He told Daniel he's friendly with someone senior in the NIA. This person told Mashele that Daniel was being followed and that his phones were bugged.'

'My God, the NIA? The plot, as they say, thickens.'

'Apparently so.'

'So where do we go from here? A meeting with Mashele?'

'That's what I was going to suggest.'

SIXTY-SIX

Fourie drove through the open gates to the complex of apartments in Highlands North, just a few hundred metres away from another of the northern suburbs' arterial roads, Louis Botha Avenue. With no security measures, entering and exiting the complex couldn't be easier, thought Fourie. He drove past the rows of cars parked under the carports and quickly found Daniel's Toyota. Fourie drove to the nearest spot marked for visitors and parked his vehicle. He rechecked the address that Smit had sent him: Unit 36, The Willows, Norton Street, Highlands North. He then checked the magazine in his weapon before screwing on the silencer for the second time that night.

The apartments were typical of housing designed for younger professionals on the first rung of the property ladder: small and box-like with bland contemporary styling and housed in three-storey blocks, each comprising six units. Daniel's apartment was on the top floor.

Fourie immediately saw that the front rooms in all six apartments were in darkness. He then checked that no one was around before he got out of the double cab. Leaving the keys in the ignition, he closed the door quietly and left it unlocked; he was experienced enough to know that fumbling with keys when he needed to get away in a hurry wasn't an option.

He followed the brick-lined walkway around a well-tended lawn before finding the flight of stairs that would take him to the top floor of the block. As he walked up to the door numbered thirty-six, he could see the spy hole, which meant that ringing the bell would lose him the element of surprise.

He checked his watch: 01:25 am. Chances were that everyone would be asleep by now. He placed his ear to the door but couldn't hear a sound; there was no TV, music, or conversation. The occupants had to be asleep. He inspected the lock. It was a Privacy type with a keyhole inside the doorknob, a quick and simple challenge for Fourie. Pushing his weapon into the waistband of his pants, he took out a slim wallet from his inside Jacket pocket, opened it and amongst the miniature tools, he selected a straightened hairpin.

As the lock had a push-button mechanism, Fourie stuck the hairpin as far as it would go, then pushed it firmly to release the locking device, which resulted in a distinct click sound that was too loud for Fourie's liking. He twisted the doorknob and gently pushed the door open.

With the weapon back in his hand, he stepped into the apartment. In the darkness, he could make out a short passage that led to a small open-plan lounge and kitchen area. In the passage were two doors: one, presumably for the bathroom, and the other for the single bedroom.

His thoughts were in overdrive, so he decided to move towards the lounge first, where, in all probability, the albino would be sleeping. Then, the chances were slim that anyone asleep in the bedroom would hear the silenced shot through the closed door. Then, he still had the element of surprise when he kicked open the bedroom door to finish off the other guy.

He waited for a second or two so that his eyes could adjust to the darkness, then quietly took some deep breaths to steel himself for what he had to do, which was to walk silently towards the end of the passage. The lounge section of the room was brighter as the orange sodium streetlight streamed through the half-closed slats of the French blinds.

Fourie could see the body of a person underneath a duvet. He lifted his weapon, trained it on the chest area and fired a double tap before firing another two shots at the head.

No sound from the other room. Fourie didn't see the cricket bat that swung in a wide arc before it connected with the side of his head. The force of the blow propelled him halfway across the room and slammed him against the wall, where he smashed against some picture frames. Blood gushed in a torrent down the side of his face.

Seeing Mbulelo for the first time - his face a strange hue of pale orange from the streetlights - Fourie lifted his weapon. But the bat came crashing down on his wrist, cracking both the ulna and radius bones. He dropped the gun.

Fourie looked up as the cricket bat was about to crash down on him for the third time, but he lashed out with his foot, kicking Mbulelo hard on the side of his knee, which caused him to topple over and crash, shoulder-first into a glass-topped coffee table. He kicked again, this time catching Mbulelo on the side of his face. Fourie struggled up and saw his chance to escape down the passage. He couldn't risk wasting time trying to recover the weapon. He pushed himself forward with every ounce of strength he could muster before stumbling towards the open door.

Daniel woke to the sounds of Mbulelo screaming and glass breaking. He leapt out of bed and opened the door as a dark figure shot past. On hearing a groaning sound, Daniel ran into the lounge to check on Mbulelo. He found him bloodied from the broken glass and waving Fourie's weapon triumphantly in the air.

'I'm okay, Daniel; look, I have his gun', cried Mbulelo in triumph.

'Okay, just put that down before you shoot me or yourself', screamed Daniel.

As soon as Mbulelo placed the gun safely onto the floor, Daniel turned and ran for the front door. But, once outside, looking down at the car park area, he could see he was too late. The killer was already jumping into the double cab. Then, within seconds, he started the engine before roaring out of the complex as fast as the vehicle could go.

When Daniel went back into the apartment to phone the police, he could see that Mbulelo was bleeding from several minor lacerations on his shoulder and his back, where he crashed through the glass coffee table.

'What happened, Mbulelo?'

'I heard a noise outside. It sounded like someone was fiddling with the door lock.'

'Well, it's a good thing you're a light sleeper.'

'Maybe it's a good thing I was in fear for my life from those tsotsis.' He pointed to the scar on his face. 'When they did this to me, they also broke into my house in the middle of the night. You know, Daniel, when things like that happen, you learn to sleep with your ears open.'

SIXTY-SEVEN

Debbie had never heard of the term *Stockholm Syndrome*, in which hostages create a confused bond of loyalty with their captors. But she was shrewd enough to realise that she needed to cultivate a relationship with the black man who visited her thrice daily.

The pillars of this relationship rested on utmost respect and courtesy. Every time the man entered her room, she would greet him with a politeness that bordered on obsequiousness. And the tactic was working. She noticed that he started sounding less brusque when he spoke to her and began making minor concessions that made her life a little more tolerable. He brought her chicken polony when she told him she hated the ersatz pink variety. He brought her more magazines when she had exhausted the original pile. He also got her a small towel, an extra bucket of water, and a half bar of Lifebuoy soap so she could wash away the grime caused by the sweltering heat inside the room.

For Debbi, every concession represented a small victory that bought a modicum of hope that she would survive. The fact that the man insisted on her wearing the pillowcase over her head whenever he entered the room also gave her the belief that she would eventually be released. Slowly but surely, she was building her persona in the mind of her captor: that she was flesh and blood, that she had feelings, that she had a family, that she respected him completely, and that she didn't blame him for holding her in that small room against her will.

'Do you know my name?' she asked him one day, surprising the man.

'Yes ... no, I don't know', he demurred, not wanting to drop his emotional guard.

'It's Debbie. Please call me Debbie.'

'Okay', he conceded. 'Debbie.'

'Thank you. What is your name?'

'I'm not telling you my name. Are you mad or something? You're not going to know my name or see my face. If you do, I have told you that I will have no choice but to kill you.'

'No, please, you don't have to tell me your real name. Just give me a name, any name, so I can call you something and put a name to your voice.'

'Okay', he relented. 'Thomas, you can call me Thomas.'

'Thomas, thank you, Thomas. My father's name was Thomas', she lied, trying another subtle way of creating a closer connection with her captor. 'He was a kind man ... Such a good man.'

'Oh ... Okay', he acknowledged, without realising that she was trying to manipulate more compassion out of him that may lead to the ultimate act of kindness: her release.

During the long, hot days when the room transformed into an oven, Debbie tried to take mental stock of where she was and what she knew of her captor. She must be in some deep rural area – the bush, maybe – because she could hear lions roaring. Some nights, she had lain awake for hours listening to the low-pitch, throaty, rhythmic roaring of male lions announcing their dominance.

Occasionally, she could hear the distant sounds of a tractor engine. She could also hear what she guessed was a windmill, the galvanised metal type used to draw water found in their thousands on farms across the country. The whirring sound of the mill sped up when the wind picked up, so she guessed it had to be a windmill.

Then there were her captors. The man she was supposed to meet at the restaurant the night of the kidnapping, the man who called himself Chris, had to be involved in this somehow. But she had not seen nor heard anything of him. He had said he was a farmer, a claim Debbie found plausible from his weather-beaten complexion.

Then there was Thomas, or whatever his name was. Thomas sounded like a person of little education who lived a simple life. She surmised that he wasn't street-smart or worldly; he was probably a rural person. Could he have been the car guard? She had no way of knowing as she couldn't remember the man's voice before the abduction. Besides, he had only spoken a few words to her, and it all happened so quickly. She just remembered the car guard tricking her into standing at the back of her car where they were obscured from pedestrians before he smothered her with a cloth soaked in some chemical that knocked her out. But it was probably him; though she couldn't ask Thomas questions about the abduction, she didn't want to risk putting him on the defensive and annoying him. But Thomas had to be involved with Chris.

Of course, the big question that played in Debbie's mind was: Why? Why had she been abducted? To what end? If it had been a sexual thing, she would surely, have been raped by now. Thomas had told her on the first day that there was no ransom. So, again, why had she been abducted? The more she thought about it, the less sense it made.

The only thing she could do was to keep her sanity and establish some bearings to her existence in that small room. She had no actual way of knowing if it was day or night. She guessed that Thomas's three daily meals represented breakfast, lunch, and dinner. Also, that was when the room became stiflingly hot, so it had to be daytime.

Of great concern to her was the feeling of being watched. She knew she wasn't under constant surveillance, but there were sporadic hints of a presence nearby. At first, it was shuffling, maybe a rat or a mouse scurrying in hay outside her room. Then, one day – it was hot, so she assumed it was daytime – she heard what she thought was someone clearing their throat. Was Thomas watching her through the keyhole? Was it someone else? The mysterious Chris, maybe?

She shuddered at the thought of being in the hands of some unpredictable psychopath who was toying with her like a cat would tease a mouse, prolonging the agony for some warped, inexplicable reason. She moved the toilet bucket behind her bed to shield her modesty. But it was futile as she didn't know where the person watching her could be.

Or maybe there wasn't anyone watching her after all? Perhaps she was going mad, staring at four featureless walls, with no windows, and with only a rough estimation of when it was night or daytime.

SIXTY-EIGHT

It was unusual for Bernie to be the first person to arrive at his chambers. Colleagues used to joke about his lack of enthusiasm for early morning meetings. One character, an advocate of Bernie's generation, took great delight in comparing the cantankerous lawyer to his grandfather's ancient Morris Oxford. By all accounts, the car was a slow and stubborn starter in the mornings. Robust hand cranking of the engine resulted in nothing but the risk of a dislocated shoulder until it eventually spluttered and coughed indignantly into life. But then it would go on all day and all night, just like Bernie.

The new cappuccino and espresso machine - a stainless steel shrine to Yuppiedom, as Bernie had described it - was a technical ambiguity to him. 'I am an advocate, not a barista', he had once joked to a tea lady. But the quip had spiralled way above her head. Ignoring the coffee machine, he boiled the kettle and retrieved a long-abandoned jar of instant coffee that he found at the back of one of the cupboards.

On hearing the front doorbell, he walked to the glass front door to find that Judith, Daniel and Mbulelo had arrived together.

'Instant coffee is the best I can offer at this ungodly hour', he said by way of greeting.

'That's fine. Can I help you make it?' offered Judith.

'That will be very helpful, as navigating a kitchen is not my greatest talent.'

As they walked to the conference room, Bernie examined the Band-Aids on Mbulelo's face and neck: 'So you had even more excitement last night, I hear. Are you both okay?'

'Yes', answered Daniel. Mbulelo had a few cuts and bruises, but he also gave a damn good account of himself. He managed to hit the bastard with my old cricket bat.'

'Excellent! Was it a pull shot or a cover drive?' asked Bernie with a big smile, which confused Mbulelo.

'It was one God-almighty cow shot that caught the shit right across the side of the head.'

'Well done, Mbulelo; let's hope he's suffering this morning. And the police? What did they have to say?'

'Two uniformed guys came around a couple of hours later but were not particularly interested. No murders, no gunplay, just an attempted break-in, which was of little interest to those guys.'

He pulled the hitman's gun and silencer from his jacket pocket, which was inside a plastic freezer bag. 'He left this behind.'

'My God, that could be very useful evidence. But I doubt we'll get any prints on it.'

'Yes, I didn't trust the cops last night. As I said, they weren't particularly interested. I thought I would give it to you so we can be sure it gets to the right hands.'

'Good thinking, Daniel. I'll put it in my safe for now and ensure it goes to the right people. But the main thing is that you're both okay. This morning, we will have to talk about where we send Mbulelo and you for a couple of weeks while we start turning up some heat on these people. I was also awake half the night, thinking about our way forward. Anyway, I have some suggestions to make.'

Their conversation was interrupted by the doorbell. 'That must be Mashele', said Bernie.

Daniel looked surprised.

'Part of the musings I had last night', said Bernie, 'sorry to spring this on you, but we needed to get him on side as soon as possible.'

Daniel nodded.

'Let me fetch him and bring him into the conference room.'

David Tlale and two other men were with Mashele. 'I'm advocate Van Rooyen', said Bernie, surprised that Mashele had brought an entourage with him.

'Good morning, advocate. I am Macdonald Mashele, and this is an old and trusted friend, David Tlale, the deputy director general of the NIA, and these two gentlemen work with David.'

'Good morning, advocate', said Tlale. 'Would you please indulge my colleagues and me? They would like to quickly sweep for any electronic listening devces that may have been placed on your premises. It will only take a couple of minutes. Would you mind, sir?'

'Hell no, ' answered Bernie, 'nothing surprises me with the things that have happened recently. Shall we wait here in reception?'

'Yes, that will be fine.'

'Then I had better collect all the folks in the conference room.'

After a few minutes of introductions and polite small talk, the two technicians reappeared from the conference room. 'The room is clean, sir. Everything is fine in there.'

'Thank you', replied Tlale. 'You guys can go now. And thanks for meeting me here so early.' Then, turning to the others, he continued: 'Lady and gentlemen, before we go to the conference room and get started, can I please ask you all to take out the SIM cards from your cellphones and leave them here in reception?' As an example to the others, David Tlale pulled his phone out of his Jacket pocket and placed all the parts on the reception desk after disassembling it.

Once in the conference room, the discussion began earnestly, with Mashele taking the lead: 'Okay, now we all know that the people we are dealing with are amongst the most dangerous individuals imaginable.'

'I think lethal is a more accurate adjective than dangerous', interrupted Bernie.

'Yes, I was very sorry to hear about Jackson Msimang', said Tlale. 'I knew him vaguely from his days at the Scorpions. He was a good man, a principled man.'

'Yes, thank you, he was', replied Bernie.

'May I ask something? How does Mbulelo fit in all this?' asked Tlale.

'Mbulelo was, how shall I put it, living rough near Joe Robinson's townhouse complex. During the night that Joe died, Mbulelo saw a person climbing over the wall into the complex. We have proof that someone else had deactivated the electric fence. That person reappeared a few hours later. And it was during that time that Joe died, not, we believe, by his own hand, as was reported, but by the hand of someone else.'

'The person Mbulelo saw climbing over the wall, is there hard evidence linking him to Joe's death?' asked Mashele.

'Although, at this stage, it's hardly proof beyond a reasonable doubt, there is another link in a chain of evidence in the case we're building.'

'You're saying that Joe Robinson was murdered?' asked Tlale. 'But the autopsy supported the police's claim that he died of asphyxiation because of autoerotic strangulation.'

'We were about to have a second autopsy when Joe's body was illegally and abruptly cremated. We also have evidence that the official form authorising that cremation was forged.'

'So, they were getting rid of the body before the second autopsy could be performed?' asked Tlale.

'Exactly. But the forensic pathologist collaborating with us believes that there is enough evidence from the photographs taken at the scene of the crime and enough the forensic research that she has been conducting to support our assertion that Joe was strangled.'

'And Mbulelo here is a key witness?'

'Well, we believe there's a strong inference from what Mbulelo saw to connect these events. As I said, it's all part of a litany of evidence that we believe presents a different narrative about how Joe died.'

'We now have to link the man that Mbulelo saw - who we believe is a professional hit man - to the people who hired him.'

'Smit and Janse?' asked Mashele.

'Yes, the charges against them will be conspiracy to commit murder, which carries a mandated twenty-five-year sentence.'

Mashele looked shocked, 'I can't believe that people I have worked with for seven years could go around murdering people. I take it Joe was murdered because he knew something about Jabu?'

'Yes,' answered Judith. 'Joe knew about the evidence of fraud that Jabu had collected against Smit and Janse. But then Joe lost his temper with Smit as they were walking away from Jabu's funeral, and Joe said more than he should have said when he threatened to report them to the authorities.'

'Fraud? Can you be specific?' asked Mashele.

'We have documentary proof that Smit and Janse defrauded the Department of Trade and Industry out of several million rands', said Bernie.

'They were charging the department for advertisements that were supposed to have appeared in foreign newspapers but never did', added Judith.

'Oh, God, that was the TISA campaign. I introduced that client to the agency myself. The DG's a friend of mine. But there are far more important things to worry about than any embarrassment on my side.'

'Exactly', agreed Bernie. 'One of those important things is to get Mbulelo out of this town. Now, I have a hunting lodge in the Waterberg in Limpopo. It's been in the family for many years. I hardly go there these days, but it's quiet and reasonably comfortable, and I can't imagine anyone knowing about it. Mr Tlale, can we count on the NIA to help us protect Mbulelo?'

'We'll need to put him into temporary witness protection. I can talk to some NPA people who control the Witness Protection Unit. Mbulelo will be comfortable in one of our safe houses in a different part of the country. No one will know where he'll be, not even me.'

'Right, that's one big headache sorted', said Bernie.

'But I would also like to use this opportunity to flush out the hit man', continued Tlale.

'But how do we do that? This guy is a real pro', said Daniel.

'For the last few weeks, Smit and Janse's people have been bugging Mac's house and office. But they don't know that we know that his place is bugged. So, we need Mac to talk with someone to tell them where and when Mbulelo has been relocated to a safe haven. And that could well be your hunting lodge advocate. If they check up, it makes sense that the place is registered in your name. Then, some of my people will lay low on the farm and set a trap for him. If we need a decoy to be seen at the hunting lodge, we must find an agent with albinism to take Mbulelo's place. Or dress up one of our white agents to look like Mbulelo.'

'Can't we tap Smit and Janse's phones like they've tapped ours?' asked Judith.

'We have Janse's phone bugged, but he's cautious about what he says. He doesn't give anything away. On the other hand, Smit seems to change his SIM card every few days, making it virtually impossible for us to keep tabs on him, said Tlale.

'I have one question for you, advocate', asked Mashele. 'Even if we had all the evidence, how long will it take to bring these people to a court of law?'

'Realistically, convicting them could take a couple of years. Then, there would be appeals so that you can add another year to that, at the very least.'

'That's what worries me', said Mashele. 'With the greatest respect advocate, our justice system is virtually dysfunctional. And with the expensive, slick lawyers these two will hire, they'll be out on bail, and then there will be delay after delay, and we'll never hear the details of what these two have been doing.'

'I don't deny that', admitted Bernie.

'I think we should try them another way, something that will put them on the back foot', said Mashele.

'Trial by media, you mean. I'm not sure about that', said Bernie. 'Whilst, tactically, I like the idea of applying as much heat as possible onto those two, the court of public opinion is not my area of expertise.'

'But it is mine', said Mashele. 'Smit and Janse are not the only ones with friends in the media. I believe we can get the team at Probe to look into this.'

'Probe, the TV show on Tuesday nights?' asked Judith. 'Do you think they would go for it?'

'Yes. The executive producer is a friend of mine, and I know he'd be interested because it makes for one hell of a story.' Mashele's enthusiasm levels started to intensify. 'Just think about it: there's a fraud that leads to a murder, and then there's a second murder, then a third. And more than that, one of the victims is vilified in the media by being branded a paedophile. Then, he supposedly kills himself in some unthinkable sexually perverse act. And the evidence was manufactured by the people responsible for his death and manipulated by a bogus PR company made up of apartheid-era secret agents. And the culprits are the guys running the biggest independent communications group in the country. This, I tell you, is the stuff of Hollywood movies. Then, we can bring in some of the top investigative journalists to look into the case, too. God, my PR people are going to have a field day.'

'Couldn't Smit and Janse sue them?' asked Daniel.

'Sued? They will probably threaten the show's TV station and producers with a lawsuit, but I know the production guys will take that with a pinch of salt. This is what they do for a living. People threaten to sue them daily', said Mashele.

'Once the show gives them a right of reply, which is what they will have to do', said Bernie. 'Smit and Janse will be onto their legal team to try to get an injunction against the show's broadcasting. But that won't be easy for them because there will be an abundance of evidence, which will be pretty damning.'

'They will shit themselves', said Mashele, the grin widening on his face.

'The more we can rattle them, the more our chances of having one turn against the other. I said at the beginning that we need one of them to turn state witness against the other, ' said Bernie.

Within the hour of the meeting with Mashele and Tlale, a team of Hawk detectives from the NPA's Witness Protection Unit arrived at Bernie's chambers to take Mbulelo away so he could vanish from the face of the earth until the trial.

There were sad goodbyes, especially between Mbulelo and Daniel, as a friendship developed, similar to troops who had experienced combat together.

Even Bernie was sad to see Mbulelo go: 'When all this is over, you can come and work for me', he said, extending his hand.

'Thank you, Mr Bernie, I would like to work for you', replied Mbulelo as he shook Bernie's hand vigorously.

SIXTY-NINE

Daniel was driving away from Bernie's chambers when his cellphone rang. He pushed the speaker button: 'Hi, Daniel speaking.'

'Hi, Daniel, said a gravelly female voice that sounded strangely familiar. 'Daniel, you don't know me; my name is Serena Peters, Debbie's sister.'

'Oh, hello, so how is my dear friend, Debbie?'

'Daniel, Debbie has disappeared.'

'What?'

'Yes, a few nights back, she went on a dinner date with some guy she'd just met. She said she would call us when she arrived at the restaurant where they were supposed to meet, but she never did.'

'Oh, my God . . . Have you reported it to the police?'

'Yes, we've spoken to everyone we could speak to, but we're getting nowhere. We're even thinking of employing a private investigator . . .' the rest of the sentence descended into incoherent sobs.

Daniel hung on the line patiently.

'I'm so sorry', said Serena as she regained her composure. 'It's been an absolute nightmare for all of us. We don't know if she's alive or dead.'

'It's okay, please don't apologise. Look, can I come and see you?'

'Oh, yes, please, would you? My sisters and I would love that; we desperately need help to find her. I mean, it's as if we keep hitting a brick wall. Debbie has told us a lot about you; she's very fond of you.'

'And I'm very fond of her', said Daniel, conscious and relieved that they were both speaking about Debbie in the present tense. 'SMS me your address, and I'll come to you around lunchtime.'

Daniel abandoned the work he had planned to do that morning. He spent most of the time making calls – using a selection of landlines he had never previously used – to Judith and Bernie, getting advice on the way forward. They had agreed that now was not the time to mention Daniel's obvious suspicion that Smit and his hired killer were behind it all. Daniel shuddered at the thought of what poor Debbie was going through, all caused by that bastard Smit's ruthlessness.

By noon, having driven down the M1 and being guided through the southern suburbs by Google Maps, he found himself standing by the gate of a modest home that looked as if it hadn't changed since being built in the 1970s.

In response to the doorbell, all three sisters came out to greet him, each hugging him like some long-lost friend. There was Serena, who could have passed as Debbie's twin: same gravelly voice, same slight build, and same shoulder-length blonde hair. And the two younger sisters, Brenda and Alice, who were darker, taller, and heavier in build than their two older sisters. All three looked tired and had puffy red eyes.

'Thank you so much for coming all this way to see us', said Serena. 'We've been beside ourselves with worry ever since Debs disappeared.'

'Of course, you must be going through hell.'

'We lost our parents when we were young', said Serena as they walked through the passage into the comfortable front lounge. 'Our Mom was ill for a long time, and then a couple of years later, Dad died suddenly from a stroke. Both of those experiences were awful and shocking, but nothing has been as bad as what we've been going through these last few days'.

'Tell me, what happened?' asked Daniel.

Serena composed herself and answered: 'Debbie was supposed to be meeting some guy she'd met . . .'

'He said his name was Chris, and she met him at the Mug and Bean down the road', interrupted Brenda. 'She had spoken to him for an hour or so, and he asked her out for dinner.'

Serena continued: 'Look, as we told the police, we don't know if this Chris guy had anything to do with Debbie disappearing, but it does sound fishy.'

'What did she say about this guy? Did she give you a description of him?'

'Yes, she thought he was a farmer because he had that typical farmer's tan. She said that he had that, you know, weather-beaten look, like someone who works outdoors. She also said he was slim and well-built, had short grey hair, and was in his early forties.'

Daniel immediately thought of the description that Mbulelo had given Jacks: short stature, forty-something years old, short grey hair, slim, fit-looking, or at least athletic enough to clamber up a two-metre wall. Granted, it described a sizable portion of the middle-aged white male population in South Africa. Still, Daniel's inclination towards coincidences evaporated after his experiences over the last couple of days.

'Did she say anything about anyone from Janse-Mashele approaching her or phoning her or anything like that?'

'No, nothing', answered Brenda.' Other than you and a few other people, she didn't want to have anything to do with Janse-Mashele. She was devastated by Joe's death, and she believed that he was innocent of all those terrible things they said about him in the newspapers. Then she lost it that day and slapped that bloody woman who said all those nasty things about Joe . . .'

'And there was that row with that big fat pig Petrus Smit when he fired her', said Alice in a sudden outburst of anger.

'Yes, that bastard Smit who fired her. Do you know that he threatened to make trouble for her?' asked Serena.

'Yes, I know, I was outside Debbie's office, and I heard most of what was said', Daniel evaded the subject of Smit as he didn't want to divulge his feelings towards the man he was convinced lay at the heart of Debbie's disappearance. 'What did the police have to say?'

'Not much, they filled in some forms, they had us write a statement, and we supplied the most recent photographs of Debbie', said Serena.

'The guys at the police station were hopeless', added Brenda. 'But the Bureau of Missing Persons was much more helpful. They were interested in this Chris person she was supposed to meet that night.'

Serena continued: 'The one detective – a lady detective inspector – told us that they went to the restaurant, Apollo's in Greenside, where they were supposed to be having dinner. But none of the waiters remembered seeing Debbie.'

'Also, everyone who had booked a table that night showed up. There were no no-shows', said Serena.

'And no short, grey-haired white guys sitting alone who looked like they had been stood up', added Brenda.

'So, the police reckon that Debbie never arrived at the restaurant?'

'That's what the detective inspector believes', answered Brenda. 'And the restaurant didn't have any bookings that night for two people made by someone called Chris.'

'What about CCTV, outside the restaurant or on the streets of Greenside?'

'We're not sure if that has anything worthwhile. The detective emailed us a bit of footage, which shows a car parking close to the restaurant. The timing is correct, but there's no way of telling if it's Debbie's car. The image is very blurry and black and white, so we can't even identify the car's colour.'

'Have you got it here now?'

'Yes, would you like to see it? Serena opened her laptop.

While she was locating the footage, Daniel asked: 'And her car? Did the police put a trace on her car?'

'No', replied Brenda. 'And Debbie's car didn't have a tracking device, either.'

Serena turned the laptop around to give Daniel a better view. Grainy black-and-white footage of a static shot filled the screen. In the foreground, insects flying in front of the camera darted like wispy streaks of light. In the background, a blurred view of a large traffic circle. Marked at the bottom of the screen was the date and time. Then, a non-descript sedan enters the frame and drives slowly around the roundabout.

'Okay, this is the car that caught the detective's eye. But it's a normal sedan, you know, it could be anything: a Toyota, a Nissan, a Honda, anything.'

'What car does Debbie drive?'

'A red Honda Ballad.'

Suddenly, Daniel froze when he saw a light-coloured double cab bakkie pull out from a parking spot in front of the sedan before driving off. The sedan stops. There's the flashing of the indicator light. A man wearing a reflective safety waistcoat – a car guard – steps away from the kerb and guides the sedan into the vacant parking spot. A minute or so elapses before the double cab returns and stops parallel to the sedan. The driver gets out. There's some movement on the vehicle's far side, but it's too indistinct to determine what was happening. The driver of the double cab gets back into the double cab and drives off. A few seconds later, the sedan pulls out and drives out of the frame before the image is frozen on the screen.

Daniel could sense that all three sisters were staring at him, looking for some reaction. But he gave nothing away. Nothing about his fears about the double cab that looked suspiciously like the vehicle he saw driving away from his complex the night when the guy broke into his apartment and tried to kill Mbulelo. 'What else have you done to try and find her?' asked Daniel.

'You name it, we've done it', said Brenda. From handing out flyers in Greenside to contacting everyone we know on Facebook to offering a reward for any information. But nothing has worked. It's as if the entire world is conspiring against us. Debbie vanishes into the night, and no one knows anything.'

'No one except maybe this Chris guy, if that's his name', said Daniel. 'The flyer, please can you give me a copy? I'll scan it and email it to everyone in Janse-Mashele.'

'Thank you, anything and everything helps', said Serena.

'Call me if I can do anything. I'm not sure what else I can do for now', he lied.

SEVENTY

To Mr Daniel Stein

C/O Janse-Mashele

12 Alice Avenue

Sandton

Dear Daniel,

Good news! I am thrilled to tell you that I have been transferred to Leeuwkop Prison. And, as I'm sure you know, it's just down the road from your office in Sandton. My security classification has also been downgraded from Category C, C-Max, to Category B, Medium. I must say, the difference will take some getting used to. Most of the screws here at Leeuwkop are friendly, and the routine is a hell of a lot more relaxed than in Pretoria. That was 23 hours a day in solitary, but the cell doors are left open through most of the daylight hours here.

What's even better is that I can even do some work. I've been helping in the library. Also, I might be able to start assisting some of the younger boys with some therapy. Nothing too tricky, mind, just letting the guys know they have someone who can listen to them talk about their worries and psychological issues and give them some advice. So, I'm now able to help others, and that's something I haven't experienced in years.

I must say, I enjoyed the drive from Pretoria to Leeuwkop. I couldn't believe the amount of development along the highway. Joburg and Pretoria are practically one city now, and I find that remarkable.

Of course, one of the great treats for me is that I can now have up to four contact visitors a month, each for 60 minutes. Yes, I know I'm a bit cheeky, but if you have some spare time, I would love it if you visited me. Do you know where the prison is? Just down the end of Leeuwkop Road, next door to the Leeuwkop Golf Club. Where else would you find a prison next to a golf course, only in this crazy country, right?

The other morning, they must have been mowing the fairway because I could smell the freshly cut grass. That was the first time in 22 years that I had had that experience. My God, it was heaven.

Anyway, please write to me when you have a moment, or better still, come and see me anytime that's convenient.

Goodbye for now, Daniel. I hope to see you soon.

Riaan.

SEVENTY-ONE

Henk Janse was one of the first people at Janse-Mashele to spot copies of the flyer pleading for help finding Debbie. Daniel had pinned several copies the previous evening on every noticeboard throughout the building. Janse tore off one of the A4 leaflets and quickly glanced at Debbie's smiling face before making his way to see Smit.

'What is this?' he asked as he marched into Smit's office and threw the flyer on his desk. 'Joe Robinson's PA has gone missing. You've had her killed, haven't you? What did I tell you about laying low and staying out of trouble?'

Smit squirmed in his chair and blushed. 'Look, I was going to tell you...'

'Tell me? Tell me what? That you and that murdering maniac have completely lost it? Is that what you were going to tell me?'

'We had no choice but to get rid of her.'

'This is spiralling way out of control; it's unravelling. I mean, how many more people are you going to have killed before this ends?'

'Look', said Smit, raising his voice to Janse for the first time in the years they had known each other. 'This bloody woman was shooting her mouth off and had become a big threat to us.'

'A threat to us? Us? That's bullshit, Petrus, and you know it. You had her killed because she bruised your precious fucking ego. You've tasted power like you've never had before, so now you think if anyone pisses you off, you can call Fourie and have them bumped off.'

'Look, Henk, we can't . . .'

'Don't fucking look Henk me. You and that maniac Fourie are both out of control, and these murders have got to stop. I mean it . . . They must fucking stop! Do you hear me? Tiny bubbles of saliva had collected at the corners of Janse's mouth. He abruptly turned and stomped out of the office.

Smit didn't move for quite some time. His mind was blank. He hadn't expected Janse to attack him verbally. Here, he protected both their interests – and Janse would always make considerably more money than he ever would.

Here he was on the front lines, getting his hands dirty, and where was Janse? Always somewhere safe in the background. He was exposed to various personal risks here, yet Janse would never endanger himself. Janse never even signed anything. Janse never took risks. Janse never did any of the dirty work; Petrus Smit did it all.

Smit thought about what Janse had said. Maybe things were beginning to unravel, but not those issues that concerned Jabu Maponya, Joe Robinson and Debbie Peters. What was unravelling was his relationship with Janse. Janse's greed had continually exasperated him. Enough was never enough for Janse.

Then there was the Namibian matter. Some days earlier, Smit, reading some papers upside down on Janse's desk, discovered that Janse had offered to purchase a cattle farm in Namibia for thirty million rands. Of course, that was nothing remarkable in itself; Janse had bought and sold several farms over the years they had worked together. But Smit was suspicious of Janse's motives for a couple of reasons.

First, Janse had said nothing to him about the deal. Usually, when he bought a property, he would mull it over for weeks, and once the deal was done, he would boast about his new acquisition incessantly. But about this farm in Namibia, Janse had not uttered a word.

Smit's second concern was that Namibia would be the obvious choice if Janse needed a bolthole out of South Africa. The border was a 16-hour drive from Johannesburg, through country that Janse knew well. And when the South African authorities came for him, Janse would no doubt have a team of highly paid lawyers to stall his extradition before he could flee the country.

He was planning his getaway if things ever turned pear-shaped, thought Smit. Janse would leave him to face the music alone. The ungrateful bastard will never get away with it, he vowed.

SEVENTY-TWO

Mashele was sitting behind his desk when Daniel walked into his office. 'Daniel, what can I do for you?'

'Hi, Mac... I need to talk to you about a personal issue', replied Daniel hesitantly.

'Oh, I see', said Mashele as he rolled his hands to encourage Daniel to sound more fluent.

'Mac. I need to take some days off... A week... Maybe two.'

'Oh, why's that Daniel?' said Mashele, pointing to the underside of his desk to indicate the location of the listening device.

'I have a friend who has been in a spot of trouble...' replied Daniel, raising his voice to an unnatural level.

Mashele held his finger to his mouth as a warning to lower his voice: 'A spot of trouble?'

'Yes, this friend needs to get out of town... Oh, and I need to help him... Be with him, I mean.'

'Oh, I see, where are you going?'

'To the bush, to a friend's place in the Waterberg district... It's an old hunting lodge.'

'So why don't you just fill in a leave form like normal?'

'The thing is, I haven't been in the company long enough to qualify for the amount of leave I need. I thought you could help me by giving me a special dispensation or something.'

'I'm sure that won't be a problem.'

'Oh, that's great, thanks, Mac.'

'So, who's this friend with the hunting lodge?'

'He's an advocate . . . His name's Bernie Van Rooyen, and it's his old family farm that was turned into a hunting lodge years ago . . . It's called Kudu Lodge.'

'Kudu Lodge, really?'

'Yes, Kudu Lodge.'

'In the Waterberg, you say.'

'Yes, that's right.'

'Oh, I don't know that part of the world.'

'It's about 30 minutes from Bela-Bela on the Thabazimbi road.'

'Come with me, and we'll get a leave form from Monica. I'll write a note to HR approving the whole thing.'

As soon as they left the office, Mashele whispered: 'God, Daniel, whatever you do, don't give up your day job for an acting career.'

'Oh, I don't know, I thought I had some of that moody Johnny Depp kind of performance.'

'Johnny Depp, my black arse.'

SEVENTY-THREE

The briefing with the production team of the investigative TV series Probe was revealing. Hard-edged journalists who were well-versed in exposing the criminal underbelly of South Africa were astonished by the story's scale and intricacy.

What started as a prosaic tale of fraud - which sounded like dozens of stories that Probe had covered in the past - had quickly descended into a litany of frightening consequences. Murder and attempted murders by professional hitmen, abduction, sexual taboos, manipulation of the media, and industrial espionage using operatives from the apartheid security agencies.

Slowly and painstakingly, as if summing up the case for a judge, Bernie presented the evidence they had amassed, candidly pointing out what was circumstantial and emphasising the evidence that, as he reasoned, was irrefutable. The journalists and producers listened with rapt attention.

He stopped occasionally to refer to some detail in his notes, organised in the thick Lever Arch File. Or invite Judith, Daniel, or Mashele to elaborate on their first-hand experiences.

With little sign of emotion, Bernie took the assembled team through the physical evidence: the shoebox full of financial documents that presented a convincing case for fraud against the principals of Janse-Mashele that had started the whole sequence of events. Jabu's murder made to look like one of the many hijackings that occurred daily in South Africa.

Then there was the forensic pathology. Bernie handed that

part of the evidence to Dr Nel to explain. Her initial assertion that the bruising on the back of Joe's neck indicated strangulation and not hanging had been unequivocally backed by all the pathologists she had consulted with. They had also agreed unanimously about the ligature marks around his throat and the fractured hyoid bone. Then, there was Joe's medical condition that had developed into severe erectile dysfunction. Adding to that was the medication prescribed by Joe's GP that suppressed all sexual feelings and urges, rendering him completely impotent. Even though she had been unable to have the second autopsy, Dr Nell was emphatic in her belief that Joe had died as a result of murder and not by accidental auto-erotic asphyxia, as had been widely reported.

There was the disappearance of Debbie, which, quite possibly, had led to her murder. Here, Daniel elaborated on the CCTV footage Debbie's sisters had shown him and his suspicions that the double cab was the exact vehicle that had driven away from his apartment complex that night after the second attempt on Mbulelo's life. Daniel made a mental note that he would need to divulge all his suspicions to Debbie's sisters before the programme was broadcast.

Then there was Mbulelo, who witnessed a small white man with short, grey hair who climbed over the wall and through the deactivated electric fence before disappearing into the townhouse complex around the time of Joe's demise. His evidence would need to be on camera, which was a significant complication as he was now in the witness protection programme.

The lack of fingerprints on the child porn pictures, Joe's mainly, was also discussed by Bernie.

Mashele expanded on how certain individuals in the media were bribed and manipulated through a shadowy PR subsidiary of Janse-Mashele, JM-Plus, controlled effectively by Smit.

Details of the two villains of the piece, Smit and Janse, were reserved for the end of the briefing. Bernie spoke poignantly about how the murder of his friend, Jacks, and the two attempts made on Mbulelo's life indicated the ruthless desperation of these people.

After Bernie had finished presenting the case, the meeting broke into an impromptu question-and-answer session between the journalists and the group now referred to as Bernie's Team. The journalists had endless questions, and as over-excited people talked over each other, Glen Bryson, Probe's executive producer, took charge. 'Okay, guys, let's settle down for a moment.'

After everyone calmed down, Bryson turned to Bernie. 'Advocate, what you and your team have shared with us will make a hell of a programme. He then turned to his line producer: 'But we have so much material here, we've no option but to broadcast it as a one-hour special.' Bryson then explained that an episode of Probe comprised four stories, each edited into twelve-minute segments, including the live introduction by the in-studio anchor. All four stories made up the actual length of the show, which was 48 minutes, with the rest of the time taken by the ad breaks, or 'paying the rent' as Bryson explained it.

The executive producer spoke at length about the dangers of covering such a story. Extreme violence, including three, possibly four, murders, had been committed in attempts to silence witnesses. No chances would be taken. Bryson announced that the entire production team would be on a security lockdown. Confidentiality was, from now on, paramount. He would speak to the TV station principals to organise private close-quarter protection specialists for everyone involved: producers, journalists, and all members of Bernie's group. It was an order that raised the ire of some of the journalists, but Bryson was insistent. 'Yes, this is unprecedented, but so is this story', was his reply.

Witnesses like Mbulelo would need to be kept anonymous. So would anyone else who required it. Bernie, Daniel, Judith and Mashele immediately agreed they would not conceal or disguise their identities. And Dr Nel would also appear as herself.

'We have to give Janse and Smit the right of reply. Even offer an on-camera interview to both of them. Bryson said they would resort to their legal firm, which would apply for a high court interim injunction to get a gag order. 'It's what they usually do.'

'Considering that there's such a weight of evidence of several severe crimes being committed', replied Bernie. 'I don't fancy their chances with any judge.'

Bryson added, 'What we've noticed over the years is that these injunctions are seldom granted'. 'And as the print media and radio stations smell a rat, all they do is give us a huge amount of free publicity for the upcoming episode. Honestly, every time there's an attempt at an injunction, you can see a spike in our viewership figures. Wish every crook we featured tried to take out an injunction against us.'

'So?' asked Mashele. 'Where to from here?'

'We need to get into pre-production straight away. And I mean right now. We'll sit with our researchers, scriptwriters, and editors to work out the general structure of the story. And believe me, getting all this evidence into 48 minutes will be a tall order. Then, we'll need to set up interviews with you and all the other witnesses. We'll have to talk to the authorities to interview Mbulelo.'

'When do you contact Janse and Smit?' interrupted Mashele.

'The right of reply, you mean. We do have to give them a reasonable amount of time to react. We don't phone them ten minutes before the show goes on air; a couple of days should suffice. Now, working backwards from there, I think we'll be a week and a half away from the broadcast. He turned to his colleagues: 'Guys, best you call your loved ones and warn them that you'll be scarce for the next week and a half. Then advocate, Judith, Daniel, Dr Nell, and Mac will need all your help to tell this story.'

To finish off, Bryson slapped his hands and, with the excitement of a rugby coach just before the start of a cup final, said: 'Right team, let's go and create some ball-busting television.'

SEVENTY-FOUR

Fourie's mind was in turmoil as he drove along the N1 Highway towards Limpopo Province. Here he was, on a quiet three-lane highway that was as straight as the barrel of the rifle stowed in the back of his double cab, yet he felt as if he was stuck in a cul de sac.

His work for Smit depressed him. He hated the man. He hated having to do his bidding. He hated ending people's lives to satisfy Smit and Janse's greed. Besides, as the plaster cast on his injured wrist and the sutures in the side of his head testified, he was getting too old for this kind of work. He wasn't as quick or as agile as he used to be. He yearned for a simpler life, maybe meet a good woman and settle down before he got too old.

He knew that there was no chance of connecting with Debbie. He had taken to her when they were chatting in the coffee shop. She had a real spirit about her, thought Fourie, a sort of bugger-you-belligerence softened by a quick-witted sense of humour. But she wouldn't be interested in the likes of him. He hated the thought of having to eliminate her. But what other options did he have? He couldn't keep her locked up forever. He didn't have any answers. The only thing he knew for sure was that this would be his last job for Smit.

He drove off the highway at the Bela-Bela intersection. It had been years since he had last made this journey. As a kid, his parents would leave the farm for two weeks to take him and his younger brother to the spa resort in the middle of the small town. It was called Warmbaths in those days because of the natural hot springs discovered in the area by the Voortrekkers in the nineteenth century. By the 1970s, the apartheid government built an elaborate resort, one of a chain that offered cheap holidays reserved exclusively for the volk, who kept them in power. How he and his little brother had looked forward to those holidays: two weeks away from the farm's toil and loneliness; two weeks of swimming and playing touch rugby and cricket with new-found friends.

As he drove through the centre of town, the memories flooded back. These were the carefree, innocent days that existed before the price of that cosseted life had to be paid for with the brutality of the border wars and the mass insurrections closer to home.

What had started as Fourie's two-year stint of national service became his calling in life. His father had been proud of his success; the medals, the promotions, and the transfer to Special Forces had pleased the old man. Fourie had also been encouraged to enrol in the Permanent Force to make the army his career. So, what would his dead father think of him now, Fourie wondered. Would he still be proud of his son? Working for the likes of Smit and Janse? He doubted it.

As he drove along the heavily pot-holed road that linked Bela-Bel to the mining town of Thabazimbi, Fourie could see that virtually all the land was cordoned with electrified game fences. This was big five bushveld country, where traditional forms of agriculture had long been abandoned due to persistent droughts and poor soil. The land, left to grow wild, quickly regenerated back to its original state before the farmers reintroduced the game that had previously roamed the land.

Smit's people had found a map of the area that delineated the original farm boundaries; the large unproductive cattle farms had been divided into smaller parcels of land, which had then been converted to profitable game farms for breeding and hunting.

Eventually, Fourie saw what he was searching for, the sign

for Kudu Lodge. Driving slowly, he followed the perimeter fence for another five kilometres to the edge of the property. Running parallel to the fence was an unused dirt track. He drove slowly through the overgrown vegetation for a few hundred metres away from the main road until he came across a tree large enough to conceal his double cab. Fourie cut some branches off the nearby Mopani saplings and covered the roof of the double cab. Being involved with the hunting industry, Fourie knew that many game farmers used helicopters as a matter of routine. Poaching of game had become a big headache for these farmers, especially if they had rhinos on their properties. And an unidentified double cab found in the middle of the bushveld would immediately arouse suspicion.

Satisfied that the vehicle was well hidden, Fourie prepared himself for the task. He stripped off his shorts and T-shirt and dressed in camouflaged gear and heavy hiking boots. He grabbed his rucksack, in which he had packed enough water bottles, biltong, and dry sausage to sustain him for a couple of days, plus a ground sheet and a light sleeping bag. He also carried high-powered binoculars plus night goggles. Then, he unpacked his most important equipment for this job: a .300 calibre Winchester Magnum rifle with telescopic sights, plus a bipod to provide him with the most stable shooting platform. Fourie's thinking was simple - with enough firepower to bring down a large antelope from several hundred metres, his target wouldn't stand a chance.

From the map, he could see that the original farmhouse was in a small valley five kilometres from the main road. That would be as good a place to start looking for his quarry.

The wires for the electrified fence that ran along the border of Kudu Lodge reached down to the ground, as the bottom strands would deter Jacksals and the occasional honey badger from pushing their way underneath the fence. Picking up a heavy log, Fourie pushed it through the fence, causing two wires to touch each other, triggering an electrical short that deactivated the entire zone. Then, pulling the cables apart, he leopard-crawled his way into the farm. Even though causing an electrical short alerted a monitoring device that controlled the system, there would be no way of telling what kind of mammal had tried to push through: elephant, buffalo or human.

Fourie mostly kept to a route under a canopy of trees comprising Common Hookthorn, Wild Seringa and African Wattle. Other than the odd warthog, there was little game to be seen. No doubt most antelope could smell and hear him coming a long way off, so they made themselves scarce. The walk was a leisurely stroll through the flat country for the first couple of hours. But then the terrain became steeper, making the hike much more challenging in the mid-day heat.

The hilly terrain eventually turned into a steep sandstone ridge, a rocky edifice nearly three hundred meters above him. Another two hours of strenuous trekking elapsed until he found himself halfway up the ridge. Below him, he saw a cloud of dust being kicked up by a vehicle in the distance. Must be the road to the farmhouse, reasoned Fourie. He walked along the side of the slope into a riverine valley that had carved its way into the ridge, following narrow trails trodden by Kudu and other antelope favouring hillier country. After just a few minutes of walking, the farmhouse appeared beneath him.

Fourie settled himself between some large rocks and thick vegetation, making him virtually invisible from a distance beyond a few metres from his position. Pulling out his binoculars, he started to survey the scene. He could see three vehicles parked on the side of the farmhouse: an open-top Land Rover with a canvas canopy – a typical game drive vehicle – and two sedans. There was no movement around the house, but then the afternoon sun was still high, and there was no hint of a breeze.

Lying on the ground, he placed the rifle in front of him and adjusted the bipods so that he could get a clear view of the house through the rifle scope. The 32x magnification gave him a better view than his binoculars. Fourie could see that neither of the two sedans resembled the old Toyota he had chased that night he'd tried twice to kill the albino. These were both five-series BMWs, covered in dust that seemed incongruous in such a deep rural setting. Fourie pulled out one of the water bottles and some dried meat and made himself as comfortable as possible. He guessed he'd be in for a long wait.

As the sun started to sink beyond the mountain range to the west of him, Fourie could see some movement on the farm. Four men had moved onto the veranda that ran the length of the old house. Looking through the rifle scope, he could see what they were doing in more detail: one man was arranging firewood in the braai while the others were sitting around drinking beer and chatting. Two of the men were black, and two were white, or could one of them be the albino black guy?

One of the white men walked out from the shade of the veranda towards the vehicles. He opened the boot of one of the BMWs and took out what looked like a case of beer. As he did so, Fourie could see that this was not his target. Caught in the crosshairs was a big, heavy-set white guy with a shaved head, aged in his mid-thirties. Fourie also saw that the man carried a pistol in a shoulder holster. He focused the crosshairs on the second white man, but he was sitting so far inside the veranda that he couldn't see beyond his white legs and khaki shorts.

As the smoke rose from the braai, one of the black men walked out from underneath the veranda. He was also physically big and carrying a weapon, a pistol holstered on his waist. He lit a cigarette. These are cops, thought Fourie. If they're going to this length to keep the albino alive, he's obviously a credible witness; all the more reason Fourie could not afford to fail on this attempt.

Scanning the veranda, it looked like someone else was inside the house. The two men on the veranda laughed and conversed with some unseen person. There had to be a fifth person. Could that be the albino? There was no way of telling.

Fourie watched them for another hour before the shadows lengthened, and it became too dark to make out what was happening. He tried using his night vision goggles, but the magnification was weak compared to his rifle scope, so he packed them back into his rucksack. As he was unlikely to get an accurate shot in the darkness, he flattened out his groundsheet and his sleeping bag and settled down to catch some sleep, which crept up on him quickly.

The first thing Fourie saw as he woke with the dawn was a klipspringer standing on the rocks a few metres from him. The tiny antelope was curious as he stared at the unusual sight of Fourie lying in a sleeping bag. Then, the moment Fourie moved, the animal darted off in keeping with his Afrikaans name, nimbly leaping from one rock to another with a stiff gait that created the impression that he was on the tips of his delicate hooves.

Fourie scanned the scene below him through the scope. Nothing seemed to be stirring in and around the house. The few discarded beer cans strewn on the ground near the braai were a plausible suggestion that the men in the house would probably sleep until late in the morning.

With the klipspringer gone, nothing stirred on the ridge, either. Just flies buzzing around Fourie's head. It was then that Fourie was aware of another insect sound that resembled the high-pitched buzzing of a mosquito. But with the absence of water anywhere near him, the likelihood of mosquitos being close was remote. But the thin, screeching sound continued.

Fourie saw a momentary flash of silver in the sky. It was a drone. 'A bloody drone', said Fourie aloud. It's a trap, thought Fourie. The cops had laid a trap, and he had walked right into it.

His mind raced. If they were using a drone to spot him, chances were that it would have a heat-seeking infrared camera that could penetrate through dense foliage. He watched as the drone moved closer to him. Then, it seemed to stop and hover in mid-air. By now, it was only a few hundred yards away from him; it was hard to tell. He grabbed his rifle to look through the scope, but the drone suddenly veered away and flew away erratically. Could he have been spotted? Did the person controlling the device see that Fourie had trained his rifle on the drone?

He looked down towards the house. There was a sudden burst of activity: men running towards the cars, jumping in, starting the engines, speeding off in dust clouds. He must have been spotted. The controller must have informed the cops at the farmhouse and no doubt they would try and head him off.

Fourie grabbed his rucksack with his water bottles and rifle and abandoned most of his equipment. Then, as quickly as the rough terrain would allow, he made his way along the path. If he could get out of the valley and get around the corner of the ridge, there was a chance that he could shake off the drone.

After reaching a spot beyond the valley, Fourie hid under a large outcrop of rocks to catch his breath. He could no longer hear the drone. With a panoramic view of the landscape stretching out before him, the only activity was the dust trails of vehicles driving around various parts of the farm. They were probably dropping off men to search for him on the ground, thought Fourie. He was relieved that he could see no dust clouds where he had hidden the double cab.

After draining a bottle of water, he descended the ridge.

SEVENTY-FIVE

As soon as Debbie heard the shuffling sounds outside the door, and before her jailer, Thomas, announced he was about to enter the room, she had the pillowcase over her head.

Hearing the door being unlocked and opened, Debbie said in as friendly a voice as she could: 'Hi Thomas. Did you find some new magazines for me?'

'I have to take you away from here.'

'What! Oh my God, why? Please, Thomas, please, you're not going to kill me, are you? Debbie started crying as the fear gripped her.

'No', replied Thomas, his voice softening. 'I'm not going to kill you. I'm going to let you go.'

Debbie's mind was racing. She was unsure whether to believe him, even though she desperately wanted to: 'Please, Thomas, please promise me that you're not just saying that.'

'No, don't worry. It's time for you to go home.'

Debbie sobbed. She feared that he was just building up her hopes so that she would go quietly and willingly to wherever he was going to kill her. But the thought of this nightmare being over - that she could finally be going home, that she could see her sisters again - it was all so overwhelming. 'Okay. But please, if you are going to kill me, make it quick. I've suffered enough; I don't want to suffer anymore.'

'Come, Debbie. Hold your hand so I can take it to lead you out of here. You are going home; I promise you.'

Debbie complied with his request as he led out of the room.

The walk was short, just a few minutes, moving slowly over a solid surface like concrete. Was it a factory? Was it a barn? Then Debbie could sense that they had walked out into the open. She could feel the sun's warmth on her shoulders and a light breeze on her arms.

'Just a little further to your car.'

'Oh my God, my car. I haven't thought about my car since I have been here. Am I going home, Thomas? Really going home?'

'Yes, Debbie, you're going home. Stand still while I open the car door for you.'

Debbie could hear the door opening and felt herself being guided into the car seat: a gentle hand on her head encouraged her to crouch; a soft hand on her shoulder caused her to move sideways until she could feel the car seat. There, she sat down and swung her legs to the front.

She heard footsteps walking away from her and then some whispering between two men. She tried hard to listen to the conversation, but the men were too far away for her to hear anything that made any sense. The footsteps returned, and she could feel the car sway slightly as the man entered the driver's seat beside her. 'Thomas, is that you?'

'Yes, it's me. Don't worry, Debbie, you are going home.'

Debbie decided to keep a mental note of everything she could hear. Maybe it would be helpful later. Maybe not. At least it occupied her mind and stopped her thinking the worst. She could hear the jingling of her car keys with all those silly little mementoes she had added to the keyring. She heard the key being inserted into the ignition, the engine starting up, and then, after some gentle revving, the first gear being engaged before she could feel the car beginning to move.

It was apparent they were driving on a bumpy dirt road. Debbie had long figured that she was in some a remote rural area. She counted the time it took to reach the nearest tar road. The time passed slowly and the bumps in the road made it difficult to maintain concentration. After what Debbie calculated to be eight minutes, the car stopped, and the handbrake pulled.

'Stay in the car; don't move. I'm going to open a gate.'

Debbie made a mental note of what she could hear: the jangling of a chain against a tubular metal gate and the shrill squeal of a hinge badly in need of grease. On his return to the car, Thomas spoke softly: 'Okay, before I drive out and close the gate, I want you to crouch down so that no one can see you wearing that thing over your head, do you understand?'

Debbie pushed her legs forward as far as they would go and lowered herself into the seat. But as she felt the slight pain and stiffness in her lower back, she knew it would soon be too uncomfortable. So she turned around and kneeled in the footwell with her head resting on the seat. She looked as if she was praying, which, in some ways, she was.

'Okay, that's good. You must stay like that until I say so, understand?'

'Yes, I understand.'

As the car inched forward, Debbie could hear the indicator before she realised they were now on a tarmac road, as it was a much smoother, quieter ride.

Debbie was still concentrating on remembering as much detail about this journey as she could. What she guessed was thirty minutes passed uneventfully, then forty, and then, suddenly, she sensed the car slowing down, heard the indicator clicking, and the car pulling over to the side of the road.

'Okay, I am going to let you go here.'

'Okay', replied Debbie, her heart beating faster than she had ever experienced, excitement combined with fear.

'This is what's going to happen. I am going to help you out of the car. Then you will not move. You will count to one hundred as soon as I start driving away. Only then can you take the pillowcase off your head. When you do, you will walk towards the bridge, your way home. Do you understand?'

'Yes, I understand.

'I am sorry, but I will take your car.'

'That's okay, Thomas; you can have it. And thank you, thank you so much for letting me go.'

He helped her out of the car and onto the side of the road, where she could feel the long grass rubbing against her legs.

She heard him walk away, a car door opening.

'Nelson', said the man. 'My name is Nelson.'

She could hear the door closing and the car driving away. How strange, thought Debbie. She had tried to mark time for 60, 80 or 100 or so minutes since she had got into the car, and here she was, counting the last 100 seconds to her freedom.

By the time the car's sound disappeared, she had only counted 45 seconds, but she pulled the pillowcase off anyway. She looked around, collecting her bearings. The car was long gone, and nothing had moved on the road. It was a deeply rural area: fields of green maize stalks rustled in the breeze nearby. And she could see fields full of grazing cattle far into the distance. She spotted the bridge about a hundred metres in front of her. As she walked towards it, the sun's heat was unbearably hot on the tarmac, so she walked through the long grass on the side of the road. Even though it felt good to be free finally, the tears started to stream down her face.

Before she arrived at the bridge, she could hear the sound of a vehicle coming from some distance behind her. She turned around and saw that it was a minicab taxi. She stood in the middle of the road, her arms stretched out to stop the vehicle.

'Please help me, I've been kidnapped.' She shouted at the driver. Behind him, Debbie could see the startled eyes of a dozen preschool children, jostling and clamouring for a better view of her. She realised she must be a bizarre sight: a barefoot, dishevelled white woman in a grubby cocktail dress, alone in the middle of nowhere. Debbie added to the oddity by sobbing and laughing at the same time.

SEVENTY-SIX

As soon as the signature music reached its punchy crescendo, the studio lights faded up, revealing the silhouette of the person sitting in the chair, Probe's veteran anchor man.

'Good evening, and welcome to this week's special edition of Probe. I'm your host for tonight, Zenzo Tilo.'

He swung his chair around to face another camera in a tighter shot: 'Tonight's show features one story only. It's probably one of the biggest exclusives we have ever covered. But be warned, this story is not for children or sensitive viewers.'

Behind Tilo, a video wall comprising several TV monitors dominated the studio set—an image of Janse-Mashele's building on each.

'It all starts as a tale of alleged fraud, described by one of the investigators as being on an industrial scale. And a fraud, we believe, has been committed by the principles of one of the country's largest and most respected communications companies, Janse-Mashele.'

The screens in the studio cut to a picture of Jabu.

'The story starts with Jabu Maponya, a clerk in Janse-Mashele's finance department. Jabu was hijacked and murdered outside his home. Tonight, we will present evidence that Jabu was assassinated to silence him from being a witness against the perpetrators of these frauds.'

A picture of Joe flashed onto the screens.

'As was sensationally reported some weeks back, this man, Joe Robinson, also an employee of Janse-Mashele, was found dead at his home in the most shocking of circumstances. The authorities maintained that Mr Robinson died by his own hand as a result of auto-erotic asphyxia. Evidence of child pornography was present at the scene, strongly indicating that Mr Robinson was a paedophile, and for this, his memory has been vilified in the media. Tonight, we will present forensic evidence that strongly suggests that Mr Robinson was also murdered at the hands of a person or persons unknown. And that all the evidence of sexual perversions was staged with the express aim of destroying Mr Robinson's reputation.'

Up flashed a picture of Jacks.

'The lead investigator in both cases was himself murdered. Ex-Scorpions investigator Jackson Msimang was trying to protect one of the key witnesses to Mr Robinson's death when he was mercilessly gunned down.'

Debbie's picture, the same as the one used in the flyer, was then flashed onto the screen.

'And Debbie Peters, Joe Robinson's PA at Janse-Mashele, was a woman who believed that her late boss had been framed. She spoke openly and frankly about her suspicions before she was abducted.'

The screens cut to a sequence of shots from the CCTV cameras in Greenside when Debbie's car pulled into the parking spot.

'Ms Peters was held for several days before being released under mysterious circumstances. And we have an exclusive interview with Ms Peters.'

The silhouette of a nondescript person was flashed onto the screens.

'Some of the witnesses you will see on tonight's show must be disguised for their protection. But amongst those who have come forward to tell what they know, the one man who has risked everything is the partner in Janse-Mashele, Macdonald Mashele.'

The screens cut to Mashele's face.

'Mr Mashele will give an insider's account of what he knows about the nefarious activities that were going on right under his nose.'

The image on the screens was cut to the JM-Plus logo.

'And if all that isn't sensational enough for you, Macdonald Mashele will also expose what he knows about a subsidiary of Janse-Mashele, JM-Plus. Fronted as an innocuous PR company, JM-Plus is a company staffed by ex-apartheid security services operatives that are central to this story.'

The camera cut to a close-up shot of a smiling Tilo: 'It's all happening tonight on Probe. Stay on this channel; we'll return after these messages.'

Petrus Smit was alone in the darkness of his lounge. Sitting in front of the TV, he was whimpering quietly out of fear and shock. There was also anger that had been building up for days since the Probe production team had ambushed him with their cameras, asking for his comments about the allegations made about him and Janse. And just after that, Janse, the biggest beneficiary of Smit's activities, had disappeared.

Smit had tried calling him several times, but Janse's line was dead. Smit had even driven to his home in Pretoria, but the constant ringing of the house bell produced neither a sound nor a trace of movement that Smit could see. Eventually, one of the gardeners happened to walk out of the service gate at the back of Janse's property. When confronted, he volunteered that Mr and Mrs Janse had packed up the Landcruiser two days earlier and had left for a holiday, and the staff told to go home until further notice and that he was the only person left on the property so that he could keep an eye on things. That was all he knew.

Namibia. It had to be the new farm in Namibia, thought Smit. And he's gone without saying a word to me. Smit's anger was like a pressure cooker that was about to explode.

As the Probe returned after the commercial break, Smit sat on the edge of his couch. He felt sick; he needed to vomit.

'Welcome back. On tonight's edition of Probe, we have one of the most sensational local stories we have ever covered: fraud, corruption, murders, sexual taboos, and abductions. And linked to these crimes are these two men...'

Pictures of Janse and Smit flashed onto the screens.

'CEO and founder of the company, Henk Janse and finance director, Petrus Smit.'

Smit retched over the arm of the couch. But as he hadn't eaten for two days, all that materialised was bile and stomach acid that burned the back of his throat.

'Over and above the award-winning company, they also ran a more shadowy organisation called JM-Plus. Tonight, we will present evidence that JM-Plus is mired in illegal practices such as bribery and providing carefully orchestrated disinformation to damage the reputations of individuals and companies.

Smit picked up his phone and tried Janse's number again. *'The number you've dialled does not exist. Please check the number... The number you've dialled...'* Having heard the same haughty voice umpteen times over the last couple of days, Smit was tempted to throw his phone against the wall. But an old black and white photograph of him, taken some twenty-five years earlier, suddenly flashed onto the screen and caught his attention.

Tilo's voice described Smit's background in the security services and then the CCB. It explained how Smit had recruited operatives in the apartheid-era secret services to staff up JM-Plus, operatives who were well-versed in the dirty tricks of the apartheid regime. Another picture of him when he was younger, slimmer and more nerdish looking, flashed on the screen. Smit remembered that when the photograph was taken, he was in Angola to audit some specialised equipment that one of the covert units was using. Even amidst the bloodlust and mayhem, the finances still had to tally.

Smit lost track of the programme; the footage was reduced to a blur, and Zenzo Tilo's voice ebbed to a murmur. Besides, Smit knew the story; he knew it only too well. As he sat back on the couch, his mind turned to Fourie. Would Fourie take my call, or would he be aggressive and abusive? Would he be drunk? Smit felt he had no other option but to call Fourie. He scrolled through the contacts list on his phone until he found Fourie's name. He stared at it for a few seconds before he plucked up the courage to press the call button.

Fourie came on the line halfway through the third ring. 'Hello Petrus, is that you?'

Smit could hear a calmer tone in Fourie's voice; it was reassuring. 'Fourie, are you watching this TV programme? What the hell are we going to do, man?'

'Yes, I am watching it. We need a serious talk.'

'Yes, we need to talk. I don't know what to do; everything is happening so fast...'

'Look, the first thing you must do is take some time out. That way, you won't panic. And panicking is the worst thing that you can do right now.'

'Yes, you're right. But there's something else we need to do. Could you do a final job for me? I want you to kill Henk Janse.'

'Wow, Petrus, you want me to kill your boss?'

'It has to be done. Henk will stop at nothing to save his skin. He'll probably turn state witness and finger both you and me. I'm telling you, Fourie, we have no option.

'Okay. If you say so.'

Smit sounded flustered and panicky: 'Look, I have access to a lot of money, and I'll pay you well. Janse has disappeared and has left me to take the heat. But I know where he is. He's on a farm in Namibia. You could take a rifle and just shoot him from a distance: no bother, no bullshit, no complications. Just sit and wait for him to come out of the house and shoot him. What do you want, a million, two million bucks? I have the money, Fourie; I can make a deposit right now. How about a million bucks as a deposit.'

'A million bucks? Are you serious?'

'Yes, a million is right in your account now, tonight. Will you do it?'

'Yes, I'll do it. But Petrus, it would be best if you lay low yourself. The press will be onto you like flies on shit. You need to leave your place and disappear for a few days.'

'But where, Fourie? Where? I can't just go to a hotel somewhere; my face had been plastered all over the TV screen. Someone's going to recognise me.'

'Look, Petrus, I'll come and get you before dawn tomorrow morning, before the reporters come looking for you. Believe me, there'll be an army of them with TV cameras outside your house by mid-morning tomorrow.'

'Really?'

'Yes, then you can come and stay with me.'

'Come and stay with you?'

'Yes, I have a farm that's a three-hour drive from Joburg. You can come here and lie low for a few days, and we can work out exactly what you need to do. It's not too far if you need to get back to town to speak to lawyers or something. At least these bastards won't be hassling you and sticking a fucking TV camera in your face. Know what I mean?'

'Okay, I'll make the transfer right now for a million bucks.'

'Tell you what, Petrus; let's make it two million, and then the job will be fully paid.'

'Okay, if that's what you want, I'll do it now.'

'Don't forget now, 5.00 am outside Jane Mashele, I'll pick you up.'

'Great, see you at five. And, Fourie, thank you, my friend.'

When Smit switched off his phone, he felt a sense of lightness creep over his shoulders and the back of his neck. Also, his headache had gone, and his stomach had settled.

As he grabbed his laptop, he glanced at the TV screen to see the autopsy photographs of the bruising on the back of Joe's neck. Some female forensic scientist was describing the differences between strangulation and hanging, but Smit was too preoccupied to listen.

He opened his laptop and punched in the Janse-Mashele finance department server password. Years earlier, Janse had given Smit limited access to one of his bank accounts. But he didn't realise that Smit had hacked his way into all of them. He navigated his way quickly into Janse's accounts and entered the necessary passwords. The balance of the accounts totalled R145 million and change. He could also see that Janse had transferred the thirty-million-rand purchase price for the farm in Namibia a day earlier.

Smit giggled as he started punching the commands into his keypad. Within seconds, R144 million was transferred to one of his secret accounts. 'There, my friend, that should be a delightful surprise for you.'

He giggled again. He hadn't felt this good for weeks. His last task was to make the two-million-rand payment into Fourie's account. 'And this will also be a nice surprise, a bullet into your fucking ungrateful head.'

Smit's bank account was already healthy; the small amounts he had squirrelled away from the company had built up over the years. But to have it bolstered by an additional R144 million was the biggest bonus of his life. Smit couldn't stop thinking that Janse would soon find out about the money Smit had stolen. But what could Janse do? Have him arrested? Send his lawyers onto him? The cash in Janse's accounts would hardly stand up to scrutiny from the revenue services. Taking the money solved another problem for Smit; now he had the cash reserves he needed to pay for the best possible defence.

Maybe he should turn state witness against Janse. That was another option that he had. Besides, he could prove that he was not the primary beneficiary of any of the crimes - that was clearly Janse. He could admit to introducing Fourie to Janse, but that was the last of his involvement; he knew nothing about the killings and only managed the finances on behalf of Janse.

By now, Smit's mind was racing. If he admitted to the frauds he committed on Janse's behalf, he might get away with only serving a few years. All he needed to do was salt away Janse's money into an overseas account so that he would have an extremely healthy nest egg waiting for him when he exited prison.

He opened his laptop again and visited the Mauritian bank account, which he had kept on the back burner for many years. He had much work to do, and he'd probably not get any sleep before Fourie picked him up, but he didn't care; his mind was racing so fast he'd never be able to sleep. He continued working, unaware that Macdonald Mashele was on the screen, branding him a fraudster and a murderer to millions of people throughout Africa who were watching the show.

SEVENTY-SEVEN

As he stood outside the Janse-Mashele building waiting for Fourie, Smit could feel a wave of tiredness creep over him. But as there was no chance of sleep for many hours to come, he just settled for a loud yawn, which got the attention of the two men at the security kiosk next to the main gate. They had wondered why, at five o'clock in the morning, the finance director would drive to the building, park his car, and go to his office before reappearing an hour later carrying a box full of papers and a small suitcase, before standing outside the gates and waiting for God-knows-what. But they also knew Smit to be unfriendly, even hostile, so they didn't bother asking.

The reason Smit had arrived so early was so that he could retrieve some documents from his and Janse's office. He shouldered through Janse's office door even though he knew where Janse's PA kept the keys.

As he stood waiting with the box at his feet, he was relieved that Fourie was on time. Smit felt a sense of relief that things were beginning to go according to plan, which was just as well because if Fourie hadn't turned up, he would have had no plan B.

'Howzit, my friend,' said Smit as he climbed into the passenger seat of the double cab after placing the box and his suitcase on the back seat.

'Howzit Petrus', replied Fourie, who did a U-turn before speeding away.

'Thank you for coming to fetch me. I've been awake all night, so I don't think I would be in any shape to drive too far.'

'Couldn't sleep? Too many things to worry about, hey?'

'No, I had work-related things that I had to do.'

'Don't tell me that you were still doing work for Janse-Mashele after all that's happened?'

'Just doing things that had to be done', Smit felt uncomfortable about a night spent laundering the money and breaking into Janse's office to steal documents that he could use to incriminate his boss if he needed to. 'Did you get an alert from your bank last night?'

'Yes, I got an SMS. The two million was deposited. Thanks for that.'.

'Good. That's a lot of money. Have you thought what you're going to do with it?'

'I don't know. Maybe buy a faraway place and chill out for a few years. Who knows?'

They sat silently for some minutes, two socially awkward individuals who disliked each other and regarded small talk as anathema.

'Eventually, Fourie broke the silence. 'So, you say Janse's gone to Namibia?'

'Yes, he's bought a cattle farm a couple of hours outside Windhoek.'

'So, a long drive but an easy kill, you reckon?'

'Oh yes. Just drive there, shoot him and drive away; simple as that.'

'Nothing's as simple as that.'

'Well, you know what I mean.'

'Where is the farm exactly?'

'I have all the details in the box on the back seat, and there's even a map of the place.'

They sat in silence again until Smit could no longer stay awake. He sat with his head hunched forward, snoring loudly into his chest for the rest of the journey. It suited Fourie. He was in no mood to indulge the fat man's glibness about what it took to kill people. And he didn't have the patience to humour him for much longer.

Smit woke with a start as the double cab abruptly stopped.

'We're almost there, just got to open the gate to my property', said Fourie as he leapt out of the vehicle.

Smit was taken aback on seeing the warning signs. 'Christ Fourie, you said you had a farm; what are all these warning signs about lions?'

'I have a lion breeding business. Don't worry, Petrus, they don't just run around the farm like sheep or cattle. You'll be safe.'

'Lions scare the shit out of me.'

'Lions scare the shit out of everyone. But, as I said, you'll be safe. They're all fenced in, all behind lock and key.' Fourie laughed at Smit's discomfort. 'In fact, we'll be feeding them later. It's a hell of a sight; you'll enjoy that.'

Smit shuddered at the thought of a pride of lions gorging on some carcass. Ever since he was a small boy, he had been pathologically terrified of lions. His mother had taken him to Pretoria Zoo, and a big male had roared at him from the other side of a fence. It had scared him so badly that even in adulthood, he felt uncomfortable watching any large cats on TV.

'It's alright, thank you, Fourie, but I'll give it a miss.'

As they drove past the high-fenced enclosures that accommodated the lions, Smit felt a tinge of fear tingle down his spine. But as he stared at the lions, one pride after another, they were all lying about in semi-torpor. Even the cubs were listless as the heat of the day was beginning to intensify.

Smit wasn't surprised that Fourie's house would be so austere, but he didn't expect the place to be so tidy and clean. Then again, Fourie had been a soldier, and didn't they drum that sort of thing into the heads of the young troops?

Fourie was quite domesticated. He poured moer koffie, the traditional Boer coffee, in which ground coffee beans would be simmered over a fire in a tin pot for what seemed like an age. Fourie served the strong, sweet, milky beverage with rusks, the traditional twice-backed Afrikaner sweet biscuits dunked in the coffee.

The conversation, although not free-flowing, was at least civil. Fourie explained how he had transformed the business from mixed farming to the less labour-intensive lion breeding programme, giving him time for his other business.

As lunchtime neared, Fourie switched on his TV for the midday news. As expected, the revelation of the previous evening's edition of Probe was the first item. Shots of Janse and Smit continuously flashed onto the screen, with footage shot outside the building. Smit was shocked at the number of news crews covering the story; it looked like Fourie had been right. Then they cut to Brenda Isaksson, the head of PR at Janse-Mashele.

She looked stressed as she read a prepared statement: 'All I can tell you at this stage is that neither Mr Janse nor Mr Smit are in the building. And we do not know their whereabouts at this stage. We are aware of the allegations made on the Probe TV show last night, and of course, we are shocked and distraught by these revelations. Once Mr Janse and Mr Smit's whereabouts are known to us, we will be in a much better position to address these issues. I want to add that no one on the exco of Janse-Mashele was aware of any illegal activities whatsoever. Also, no exco member of Janse-Mashele had any dealings with JM-Plus besides the financial director and the CEO. We have also informed the authorities that we will do all we can to assist them with their investigations. That is all we can say at this stage. Thank you very much.'

Smit was shaking with shock and fear again.

'Come, Petrus. Come with me and let me show you around the farm. Come, a walk will do you good, take your mind off this shit that's going down.'

Without thinking of his fear of lions, Smit got up from his chair and followed Fourie out of the house.

'Let me show you some of the cubs.'

'No, no thanks, Fourie, I'm not comfortable...'

'For Christ's sake, man, these are cute babies. They're just like kittens. You're not scared of kittens, are you now?'

'Well, no...'

'So, come on, you'll love them.'

They walked up to the nearest compound, where Smit could see three cubs running around and wrestling with each other.

'See, here they are; how cute are these guys?'

'Yes, I suppose so.'

'Come, you can pat them.'

'No, that's fine. I'm happy to look at them from here.'

'No man, come on, they love being patted.'

Smit continued to protest, but Fourie had already opened the gate, and Smit felt compelled to follow.

'These guys are orphans, so I sell them to petting zoos. Kids love to play with them.'

Smit followed Fourie into the enclosure. Once they saw the two men, the cubs stopped their romping game and began to walk towards Fourie.

'Look at this little guy', said Fourie as he picked up one of the cubs. 'You're a real cutie, aren't you?'

As Smit crouched down, the two other cubs came running up to him. Nervously, he reached out, and the cubs licked his fingers.

'See, they won't bite your arm off, ' Fourie laughed as he watched Smit rub the belly of the one cub that had turned on his back.

'Oh, that little bugger always likes to have his belly scratched.'

Smit was quite relaxed at this stage. 'You're right, Fourie, they are like kittens.'

'They will even chase a ball of wool like kittens. But even fully grown lions will do that, too. Once, I saw a pride chasing an old football tied onto a rope and pulled by a Land Rover. Bloody unbelievable.'

Smit started laughing as one of the lion cubs started to take a particular interest in his shoelaces. 'Hey, leave that, you little bugger.' Smit sat down on the grass and began teasing the cubs. He didn't notice Fourie walking away from him towards the back of the enclosure near the gate.

Smit's shoelaces were getting much attention as the third cub joined the other two. Smit was enjoying the game so much that he didn't register the metallic clanking sounds of a gate being closed. Then he looked up and realised that Fourie had walked away from him. But it was confusing; somehow, Fourie was standing on the other side of the gate and walking around the fence.

'Fourie? What are you doing?'

Fourie didn't reply; he looked at Smit momentarily as he walked along the fence.

'Fourie, what's going on? Speak to me.'

Fourie walked up to another gate and started to open it.

'Fourie, tell me, what are you doing?'

'Just getting ma,' shouted Fourie.

'Ma? What the hell are you talking about? Didn't you say both your parents were dead?'

Then, in an instant, Smit knew exactly what Fourie meant. In the next enclosure, a young lioness roared aggressively. Smit struggled to get back on his feet. He could see Fourie, behind the fence, opening the gate that linked his enclosure with the section where the lioness was becoming increasingly agitated. Before the gate fully opened, the lioness pushed her way through and sprinted towards Smit.

'Ma is coming for her babies', shouted Fourie. But Smit never heard him; he desperately tried to run towards the opposite gate. But he was too late. The lioness's thunderous burst of speed – at just over 80 kilometres an hour – meant she covered the last thirty meters in seconds. Smit screamed and turned his back on the lioness but stood no chance. The lioness leapt in the air, and both paws came crashing down on Smit's shoulders. He felt the unbearable pain of the two-inch claws burying into his flesh and felt the weight of the lioness on top of him, which forced him to topple forward into the long grass. He tried to cover his face with his hands, but with one swift paw movement, the lioness spun him around so that he could face her. He screamed so hard that he expelled all the air in his lungs. And before he could inhale again, the lioness dug her canines deep into his throat, clamping her jaws and crushing his windpipe.

A second lion, a large black-maned male, sprinted into the enclosure, following the mother of his offspring and pounced on Smit. But at that stage, he wasn't aware of the male lion ripping into his belly with claws and teeth, devouring a portion of his guts. By then, mercifully, he had already passed out, unconscious and oblivious to being eaten alive as the lioness continued her suffocating grip on his throat. Within seconds, the rest of the pride had arrived, and the scene quickly descended into a wild, raucous feeding frenzy. As the pride tore Smit's body apart, they first devoured the soft tissue: the organs, the fat and the intestines; before ripping off the limbs to chew muscle; and lastly, they gnawed his bones to get at the marrow.

SEVENTY-EIGHT

As enjoyable as the event was sure to be, it would likely be the only coming home party for a kidnapping victim that Daniel would ever attend. Classic Debbie, he thought. As he retrieved a large bouquet and a bottle of French Champagne from the back seat of his car, he could hear the music pumping out of Debbie's house.

Due to the publicity generated by Probe, most newspapers, TV and radio stations covered Debbie's release. Daniel had watched, listened and read every interview that covered Debbie's story. When he finally had the opportunity to talk to Debbie, she invited him to her house for the party. He found the front door wide open and blocked by a crowd of revellers. He heard someone shouting his name from somewhere in the back of the crowd; it was unmistakably Debbie.

She pushed her way through to him: 'God, I can't tell you how good it is to see you', she screamed as she threw her arms around him, enveloping him in a tight bear hug. 'Oh Daniel, it's wonderful to see you', she screamed again.

'They kissed each other on the lips. 'Come; let's fight through this lot to get to the back garden; we can talk there.'

As she led the way, Debbie was stopped several times by friends who wanted to kiss and hug her or tell her how glad they were that she was finally home. 'It's madness in here, but I love it', she shouted. 'I think I've seen every friend I've ever had since my school days', said Debbie, revelling in all the attention. Walking through the kitchen, Daniel caught a glimpse of Debbie's sisters as they attempted to bring some order to the alcohol-fuelled bedlam by clearing up empty bottles, handing out platters of food, and washing dishes. Debbie grabbed a couple of glasses and led Daniel onto the back garden lawn.

'Hell, I was so worried about you', said Daniel as they sat down in the quietest part of the property.

'God, I tell you, Daniel, I was scared shitless. I didn't know if I was going to get killed at any minute or if I would ever make it back here to the girls. I tell you, I have never cried so much in my life.'

'Well, you're home now', said Daniel as he held and kissed her hand. 'When they took you, what happened? Was it the guy in the double cab?'

'As I said in the Probe interview, I have no idea. It all happened so quickly. 'The police first showed me the CCTV footage of that double cab. The bastard must have been involved somehow, but I never saw him. When I was being held, I kept thinking that it had to be that Chris guy I was supposed to meet that night. And the cops think so, too. But I never saw him.'

'Bloody shame.'

'The girls told me you were interested in this double cab. What do you know about it?'

'This is a seriously evil man. He's a professional hitman that I and some people have had some tussles with; he's the guy who killed Joe.'

'I knew all along that those things they said about Joe were untrue.'

'Yeah, so when I saw that double cab, I was scared that he had killed you. That's why I didn't want to say anything to the girls then. I didn't want them to lose hope.'

'They guessed something like that.'

'Look, it's a long story, and I will tell you everything, but first, I want to hear what happened to you.'

'Everything happened so quickly, and I didn't see the double cab. The only thing I remember is parking my car and this black dude, a parking attendant or something, telling me that my petrol tank was leaking. I went to the back of the car to check it out. Then he grabbed me, grabbed me so tightly I couldn't move. Then he stuffed some rag over my mouth and my nose, which must have been soaked with some drug or other. The police were not sure what it could be, so the district surgeon took some hair samples and told me traces of these kinds of drugs can stay in your hair for up to four weeks. All I know is that I was out like a light, and when I did wake up, I had the biggest headache I've ever had in my life. Jesus, it knocked me sideways.'

'And where did you wake up?'

'It was some small room with an ancient, shitty brass bed and a single chair. And the room had no windows, so I could never see if it was day or night. But I quickly sussed it out from mealtimes.'

'So, someone was bringing you food. You had contact with someone?'

'Yes, this black guy would come to the room three times a day to bring me meals, but I never saw his face. He had this system of knocking on the door before he opened it, which was the sign that I had to wear a pillowcase over my head before he entered. He made it very clear to me that if I ever saw his face, he would have no option but to kill me.'

'Bastard, did he threaten you like that all the time?'

'No, that was the weird thing. He was a bit strict at the beginning, but he mellowed. I don't know if he felt sorry for me, but after a while, he almost became apologetic about keeping me there. This sounds ridiculous, but he was kind to me in the last few days.

'Was it the same guy who grabbed you on the street?'

'You know, I thought about that, but I couldn't tell because I couldn't remember the guy's voice. But it could be him, but, as I said, the whole abduction thing in Greenside just happened so quickly. There was someone else, too.'

'The Chris guy, maybe?'

'Also thought that. I heard someone moving in the room next door. And I also had this creepy feeling that I was being watched. I promise you, I searched every square inch of the walls in that bloody room, looking for a peephole or something, but I couldn't find anything.'

'Could you hear anything else, anything out of the ordinary?'

'Yes, I could hear sounds in the distance. Things like tractor engines.'

'Like you were on a farm, maybe?'

'Yeah, but the oddest sound of all was the lions.'

'Lions? So, you were in the bush?'

Yeah, lots of lions, but not like you hear in the bush. You know, you might hear one or two of them roaring. It was a hell of a lot more intense than that.'

'How do you mean?'

'It sounded like a lion enclosure or a zoo or something. I had a friend who used to live in a cottage in Forest Town, you know, close to Joburg Zoo?'

'Yeah, I know it.'

'Well, I often stayed with her, and there were times when the male lions used to go at each other—real noisy shit fights between males in different enclosures. I mean, these guys would get very pissed off with each other, and they would roar like hell. It must have been a dominance thing. It was a hell of a racket, and it would go through the night sometimes. That's how the lions in this place sounded. It wasn't like the bush.'

'Jeez. And you told the cops?'

'Yes. But I don't think they're any of the wiser. I also told them about the calculations I made.'

'Calculations?'

'Yes, when the black dude let me go, I had to wear that bloody pillowcase over my head, so I tried counting how long the drive took, first on the dirt road, until we got to the property's main gate. And that was a bit over five minutes. Then, it took a little less than an hour to drive to where he dropped me off. Close to that bridge. I heard the car's indicator being used as we got onto the tarred road and again an hour or so later, when he pulled over to drop me off. And in all that time, the car didn't slow down or stop or use the indicators, which, I think, means that we didn't drive off the road, stop at an intersection, or join another road or anything like that.'

'So we need to find a lion breeding farm or something like that's no more than an hour's drive on the same road where you were dropped off?'

'I think the taxi driver who picked me up said it was called Groet Vlei River.'

'Someone needs to take a drive up that road.'

'Well, it sure as hell won't be me. And I don't want you going up there either, Daniel. Leave it to the police or the Probe guys.'

'Did you speak to the Probe reporters about this Lion farm and that car journey to your freedom?'

'Yes, I did. They interviewed me about it but didn't show it on the programme.'

'Maybe they held it back for another episode. The media is milking this story for all its worth.'

'Now', said Debbie, determined to change the subject, 'enough of all this nasty stuff. Open that bottle and tell me your story.'

SEVENTY-NINE

Navigating the visitors' security procedure at Leeuwkop was not as strict as Kgosi Mampuru II in Pretoria, as Daniel remembered. But it was still almost a two-hour process for a sixty-minute visit.

He first had to undergo a registration process, a form-filling exercise, and a verification of his ID before being given a visitor's tag, which the warders stressed he had to wear at all times. Then, there was a briefing by an official who discussed at length what was and what was not permitted. Throughout the process, Daniel was body searched twice and warned that he would be searched a third time once the visit was over. The warders explained that because Riaan's prisoner classification had been lowered to a B-Category Medium, which permitted contact visits, they needed to be extra vigilant to ensure that no contraband was being smuggled. At least they were friendly, Daniel thought, and the wardens revelled in telling Daniel about some of the contraband they had found over the years; no files in cakes, they laughed, but plenty of drugs, cellphones and SIM cards; precious currency in any prison.

Daniel was also allowed to buy gifts from the tuck shop. So he bought the maximum allowed: four bars of chocolate, a packet of tobacco, and the cigarette papers to roll them.

Waiting for Riaan to be located and summoned to the visitors' centre took another half an hour as he had been given work duties on the farm. But at least there was a cheery atmosphere in the large sunny visitors' centre as families were temporarily reunited with their fathers, brothers, husbands, and boyfriends. And the warders, who were keeping a discreet eye on events, were laid back and kept themselves in the background.

'Daniel, my dear friend, it warms my heart to see you', said Riaan, beaming as he extended his hand.

'Hello Riaan, great to see you.

'No, I'm being spoilt by visits between Brenda, my half-sister, and you coming to see me.'

'You've mentioned her before. So you're both in touch finally?'

'Yes, thanks to you and that TV commercial you made.'

'That's wonderful. You look fitter and healthier than I've ever seen you, Riaan. Is that a suntan I see on your face?'

'Yes, my face got a bit sunburned', laughed Riaan, 'but working outdoors after all these years is a wonderful feeling.'

'What have they got you doing?'

'Oh, just a bit of weeding in the veggie patch. I wouldn't call it hard labour.'

'Well, with the job on the farm and access to the library, life is a lot better than C-Max, I can tell you.'

'Glad to hear it. Oh, I got these for you', said Daniel as he handed over the gifts.

'Oh, that's very kind of you', said Riaan as he tore the cellophane off the packet of tobacco.

'Anyway, Riaan, sorry I didn't come sooner, but I've had a lot on my plate recently.'

'Of course, I saw that programme on the TV. That's a privilege I didn't have before. And everyone watches Probe in here. I think it's because the guys want to know who will soon be joining us', Riaan chuckled at his joke. 'What was your company called, Janse something?'

'Janse-Mashele.'

'So, tell me, with all these goings-on at your company, did it affect you in any way?'

'Bloody hell, Riaan, I've been up to my neck in it. I don't know where to start?'

'Start at the beginning; tell me what happened.'

Riaan deftly rolled a cigarette as Daniel started to relate the story: the fraud that Jabu had uncovered and how they had murdered him; how Joe, along with Jabu's sister, had discovered the truth; then Joe's found dead in his home, and the false accusation of sexual perversions levelled against him; the independent forensic pathologist had been able to prove that he had died from strangulation and not hanging.

After Daniel had finished, Riaan remained silent for a few seconds. Then he took a long drag on his cigarette before sharing his thoughts: 'Hell, Daniel, trying to stage something like this isn't easy, believe me, I know. Listen, Daniel, you don't want to mess around with someone like this. He's a pro, a professional hitman.'

'Yeah, I know. I've already had what you might call a close encounter with the bastard.'

Daniel then explained what Mbulelo had seen on the night of Joe's murder and how he was still in the witness protection programme. Then there was the murder of Jacks and the two attempts on Mbulelo's life. 'The cops tried to lay a trap for him; they made out that Mbulelo was being kept safe at a hunting lodge in the bush. They almost got him, too. But he got away.'

'A guy like him is in a different league from cops. So, he's still out there somewhere?'

'Yes. And God knows where.'

'And if this Mbulelo fellow can identify him, he won't be safe. Neither are you, Daniel. Guys like this don't just give up.'

Daniel then told him about the only good news story throughout the whole saga: Debbie's freedom after being kidnapped. 'It was weird as hell. She had been abducted and held for several days, but then, suddenly, they released her.'

'Did she know where she was held?'

'All she knew was that she was in some rural area or on a farm that bred lions because she could hear them roaring nearby.'

This caught Riaan by surprise: 'Lion's you say?'

'That's what she said. And here's a curious thing she sussed out. Debbie said the lions she could hear were not in their natural state in the bush.'

'But how would she know that?'

'She said that she had a friend who lived close to the Joburg Zoo, and it was the same sounds: male lions roaring at each other from different enclosures.'

'Enclosures', repeated Riaan, lost in thought.

'Anyway, at least she's alive, thank God.'

'Indeed. She was very lucky. But Daniel, I'm worried about your involvement in all this. As I said, this is a very dangerous individual. I mean, he's a professional killer, for Christ's sake.'

Before Daniel could reply, he was interrupted by the warder standing behind them for most of their chat. 'Sorry, gentlemen, please start thinking of ending the conversation now. Your sixty minutes are nearly up.'

'That went quickly', said Daniel.

'Look, I can give you an extra five minutes, but no more', said the warder as he winked conspiratorially.

'Well, Daniel, my friend, it was great seeing you. Thank you so much for coming to see me, and thanks again for these, ' said Riaan as he scooped up his chocolates and tobacco.

'You're very welcome, Riaan. It was good seeing you. I'll come again in a couple of weeks. Let's make every other Saturday afternoon a regular date.'

'That will be wonderful, something to look forward to. And Daniel, don't forget what I said. Be very careful; don't get tangled up with this killer.'

EIGHTY

When Henk Janse discovered that R144 million had been withdrawn from his account, he became apoplectic. The thought that such a trusted friend would steal from him had shocked him to the core of his being. And more bad news was to follow. The Assets Forfeiture Unit, a division of the National Prosecution Authority, froze all of his assets. Or at least the assets they could identify amongst his labyrinthine web of finance. But not all was lost. He had funds even though Smit was unaware he had deposited them in various overseas accounts.

His high-powered team of lawyers in Johannesburg drained his resources, but he had little option but to engage their services. The team had tried to negotiate a deal that would see him pleading guilty to the frauds, and he would turn state's witness against Smit if the Police ever apprehended him. But the NPA was not buying into it. This depressed Janse.

As his lawyers had made this last-ditch effort, he had reconciled that he could handle about five years in jail. Anything above that would mean being too old to enjoy whatever he had left of his life. Besides, as the NPA had pointed out, even the fraud charges alone would result in a mandatory sentence of fifteen years. Then, as they further explained, there were the other charges he would inevitably face: three counts of conspiracy to murder, three counts of murder, two counts of attempted murder, and one charge of abduction, not to mention the list of bribery and corruption charges that the police still needed to investigate. The South African media had been quick to denounce Janse. It was obvious to him that this hostility was born out of the guilt that editors and journalists felt because of the ruthless way they had treated Joe Robinson.

He would be safe in Namibia for now, but he wasn't hopeful it would last. Janse-Mashele's downfall was a big story, and the police or the press would find him. Then, pressure would be applied on the Namibian government to hand him over, even though there wasn't an extradition treaty between the two countries.

The thought of being a fugitive filled him with dread. And even though there were many other countries without the necessary treaties – even neighbouring countries like Botswana, Mozambique and Angola, where he would have some level of refuge – none was to his liking. At least in Namibia, his mother tongue, Afrikaans, was still the first language for well over half of the white population, so it offered a reassuring sense of familiarity.

But, while his lawyers tried to cut a plea bargain deal with the NPA, the farmhouse offered a reasonable level of comfort. He began to enjoy his new life as a farmer, which took him back to his youth.

Over and above the land and the buildings, the purchase had also included the farm implements and the livestock, which resulted in Janse becoming the owner of the largest herd of pure-bred Afrikaner cattle in the area. It was an acquisition that soon became his new pride and joy.

As he walked amongst the cattle in the kraal, he couldn't help but admire the prize-winning bull before him, quietly chewing the cud. He was a magnificent example of a breed of cattle native to southern Africa long before the Portuguese and the Dutch colonists arrived in the seventeenth century. Deep red, with a prominent hump, and horns that spread out far beyond its flanks, the Afrikaner bull started to paw the ground with his hoof, scraping the earth and sending plumes of dust into the air.

Janse was in awe of the colossal strength of the beast. The bull was uncomfortable with Janse's presence in the kraal, and the rest of the herd sensed his skittishness. They were becoming more restless. They started lowing loudly and pacing aimlessly around the kraal. Janse thought it wiser to leave so that the cattle could calm down. It was the moment when he placed his foot on the bottom rung of the fence that the bullet pierced his right temple and exited a little above his left ear. He never heard the shot. He was dead the nanosecond the bullet exited the side of his head, thrusting his body sideways. The sudden movement further startled the bull, and his flurry of angry hoof-stomping panicked the rest of the herd.

Five hundred metres away, lying amongst some bushes on a small koppie, Fourie watched the scene through the scope of his rifle. He could see blood spattered on the fence post near where Janse had been standing, but his body had disappeared underneath a cloud of dust and flailing horns.

'There you go, my friend', whispered Fourie. 'The last job, done and paid for.'

EIGHTY-ONE

It was a sweltering day to be working in the vegetable garden. As the prisoners shuffled around lethargically, most guards sat under whatever shade they could find to escape the heat. Guarding the work details on the farm was considered one of the least demanding duties for a warder. All inmates trusted with work privileges were in the low-risk security categories. Also, quite a few were elderly, and none gave any trouble.

Whenever the temperature climbed, the warders carefully ensured that prisoners on outdoor work details had as much water as needed. The previous year, one old lifer had fainted from a combination of heat and dehydration. Without applying the sense of urgency that heat stroke requires, the warders carried him indoors, where they did no more than splash some water on his face to bring him around. But the high body temperature, coupled with his advanced age, brought about the inevitable, and he went into cardiac arrest. By the time the prison doctor arrived, the old lifer had finally completed his sentence.

The top brass at Leeuwkop had reacted with fury. Such an incident always resulted in a mountain of paperwork. But worse was that they had to face the coroner and their bosses at Correctional Services to explain why such a preventable death had been allowed to happen. Consequently, all the warders on duty in the vegetable garden that day were disciplined and demoted. So, the warders were particularly careful that the prisoners were kept hydrated on hot days. To do this, they commandeered a wheelbarrow that carried a large plastic bucket filled with water and ice. That day, the wheelbarrow was pushed by another elderly lifer, Lucky Cele.

During the 1980s, Cele had been a one-person crime wave. As a gangster, bank robber and burglar, he had terrorised a good portion of Alexandra, the township in the northeast of the city. But his flourishing career came to a sudden and deadly end during a shoot-out with the police. A young constable was shot in the head and killed. Cele always maintained that he had not been responsible, that the hapless officer had been shot and accidentally killed by one of his colleagues. But the cops took the easy way out by blaming Cele.

Found guilty of a capital crime, he was on death row in Pretoria Central when, some three months before he was due to hang, President FW de Klerk announced a moratorium on the death sentence. And Lucky Cele's sentence was commuted to life. As many fellow inmates agreed, he was living up to his forename.

But now that he was in his seventies, he was something of a broken man: his arthritis and badly stooped back took their toll, and he also showed early signs of dementia. Cele had stopped living up to his name.

Riaan winked at Cele as he pushed the wheelbarrow towards him: 'So Lucky, you ready then?'

'Ja, man', replied Cele, with a chuckle 'You sure you want to do this?' He handed Riaan a plastic cup of water.

'Of course, why the hell not?' said Riaan as he emptied the cup in one swallow.

'Man, like me, you're way too old for this kind of thing.'

'I know, Lucky, but we must keep trying, right?'

'But you like it here, you're in the fresh air, the food's not bad, even the screws are pretty decent.'

'I know, but hell, I think they've had me long enough. I don't want to outstay my welcome.'

At this, Lucky Cele laughed aloud.

'Now lucky, don't draw too much attention to us now. Is Thato ready for this?'

'Yes, Thato is a good man. Like me, he thinks you're mad. But don't worry, Thato and I will be convincing, even though we'll have some fun.'

'Okay, so let's do this then.'

'Just one thing, Riaan, it's been a pleasure knowing you, man. Good luck and Godspeed.'

'Thanks, Lucky. Thanks for all your help in doing this. You keep well, my friend.' Knowing that a handshake would have looked odd to any warder, they made do with a discreet bump of the shoulders.

The old inmate pushed the wheelbarrow towards a group of prisoners a few metres away. They dropped their hoes and their shovels and gathered around Lucky's wheelbarrow.

Thato Sekeze had also been an ex-career criminal before his work had been cut short by an eighteen-year stretch for robbery with aggravating circumstances. He'd also spent most of his sentence at Pretoria Central, where, having shared a cell with Lucky for a while, the two had formed a close friendship.

The slight nod from Lucky was all the cue Thato needed. His sudden move forward pushed the wheelbarrow, causing water to slop over the side of the bucket.

'Hey, take it easy, you fucking idiot. Stop spilling the water,' shouted Lucky.

'Who the fuck do you think you're talking to, you old bastard' replied Thato, with equal venom. He then raised the quickly increasing stakes by throwing a cupful of water into Lucky's face.

With speed and agility that belied his age, Lucky swung at Thato, and his fist caught the man right on the chin. Thato wheeled backwards, spat some blood out of his mouth and retaliated with a kick that connected with Lucky's left knee. Thato stepped closer still to deliver a punch at Lucky's bowed head. But Lucky reared up and caught Thato with a head-butt on the chin, followed by a punch in the stomach.

All four warders had assembled under the shade of a large wild peach tree when one spotted the fight. They quickly leapt out of their deck chairs and ran towards the melee.

By now, Thato had recovered from the head-butt and punched Lucky in the ear with a haymaker. Both fell to the ground, where they wrestled with each other in what had now turned into a layer of mud due to the water bucket having been tipped over.

Pushing the other inmates aside, two warders tried to separate Lucky and Thato, but both combatants were too strong. So, the remaining two warders jumped in to help their mud-stained colleagues. After a few fraught minutes of grappling, applying headlocks, and threatening blue murder, the four warders eventually managed to subdue Thato and Lucky and handcuff them both.

As all this action was playing out, Riaan had walked to the far end of the garden towards a small rainwater harvesting tank next to the hut where all the implements were stored. The prisoners had drained the water from the tank to lighten it as much as possible. Riaan toppled it over with one push and rolled it towards the perimeter fence. Then, after pushing the tank back into an upright position, he clambered onto the flat top of the tank before leaping over the fence.

Underneath his orange prison-issue overalls, Riaan was wearing a pair of shorts and a khaki shirt, the collar of which had been folded inside the shirt to keep it hidden from the warders. The shirt also had the distinct green and gold Correctional Services crest on each shoulder patch, which, from a distance, was a passable imitation of the real thing. Riaan quickly stripped off the overalls. He then retrieved the small wire cutters, which Lucky had donated that he had hidden between his buttocks.

Walking up to the second fence, he swiftly cut through the bottom three strands of wire and crawled into a small field that accommodated the overflow from the staff car park. He saw the car some of his trusted fellow inmates had suggested he should steal: a 1998 Nissan Skyline owned by a warder on Riaan's wing, Donald Visage. Being the oldest vehicle, Riaan's fellow inmates had reasoned, it was the least likely to have an alarm or an immobiliser.

Riaan pulled out the homemade Slim Jim car lock pick strapped around his waist. It was a long, thin strip of metal with a hook on the end that an inmate who worked in the metal workshop had made for him for two packets of cigarettes and R150 cash.

Even though it had been 25 years since he'd last used one, Riaan quickly managed to slip the Slim Jim between the car window and the rubber seal. Then, pushing it down inside the door, he manoeuvred the hooked end to catch the rod connected to the lock mechanism. Within five seconds, the Nissan driver's door was unlocked. It was also years since he had ripped out the cabling under the car's dashboard to hotwire a vehicle. Again, it was an exercise that took no more than a few seconds. 'Just like riding a bike', said Riaan to himself as the ancient Nissan spluttered to life.

Before reversing the car from the parking spot, Riaan pulled the last props inside his shirt: a warder's khaki cap, complete with a homemade Correctional Services badge. Riaan then drove the car out of the parking area and onto the road that led to the prison's service entrance, which was normally used by prison staff.

Driving up to the gate, he saw the officer in the guard house fanning himself with a folded newspaper: 'Howzit', shouted Riaan through the open side window. 'You should tell them to get you an air-con unit or a fan at least; bloody ridiculous not having one on a day like this.'

'Howzit', replied the bored-looking guard. 'You know what it's like trying to get anything out of the bosses in this bloody place.'

'Donald asked me to drive his car to the garage down the road for a service', said Riaan with an easy smile.

'No problem', replied the guard as he pressed the button, and the heavy grille gate slowly trundled open along its rail.

Driving through, Riaan lifted his thumb at the guard, suppressing his desire to scream at the top of his voice that he was finally free after 22 years.

EIGHTY-TWO

As the spirited Probe signature music faded, the on-screen image cut from the opening titles and the Probe logo to presenter Senzo Tilo standing beside a road in a remote bushland area next to a small bridge. 'I'm standing next to the bridge over Groet Vlei River, the spot where Debbie Steyn was released after being abducted. Debbie, as we all know by now, was the woman who worked for Jense Mashele during the time of infamous criminality of fraud and corruption that led to three murders, two attempted murders, and the elaborate faking of paedophilia charges against one of the murdered victims, Debbie's boss, Joe Robinson. These crimes allegedly involved the senior management of the multimillion-rand communications group, Jense Mashele.'

The camera panned across to reveal a straight road stretching far away. Tilo's voice continued off-camera. 'Debbie believes she was held on a farm, possibly a lion breeding establishment or a wildlife sanctuary, at a location that she guessed was between one and two hours away from this location and along this road. Let's see how Debbie explained it.'

The image suddenly cuts to a headshot of Debbie being interviewed in a featureless studio. 'I was forced to wear a pillowcase over my head so I couldn't see where we were going. I just know that the initial part of the journey was on a dirt road for several minutes. Then the car stopped, and the driver, a black man called Nelson, who was one of two men who kidnapped me, got out of the car to open a gate. Then we drove on a tar road for what I'm guessing was a bit less than one hour. And I don't think we left that tar road until we got to that bridge.'

The interviewer's off-camera voice asked, 'How do you know that, Debbie?'

'Because this Nelson fellow didn't stop the car or use the indicator, which he did when we got onto the tar road and again when he pulled over by that bridge. Those were the only times I could hear the indicator, so I believe we stayed on that road until he released me and told me to count to a hundred before taking that pillow case off my head so I couldn't see him.'

The image cuts back to Tilo standing by the bridge. 'If there's one thing these kidnappers didn't count on, it was the smart thinking of their victim, Debbie Stein. So Debbie believes that somewhere along this road, maybe an hour's drive from here or a two-hour drive, is the location where her abductors held her for several days. Stay with us on Probe while we track down the location.'

The camera pans again to reveal a helicopter in a field beyond the bridge. Slowly, the rotor blades began to turn. The next shot was of Tilo inside the helicopter, sitting beside the unseen pilot. 'We have estimated that with this Nelson character driving at an average speed of one hundred kilometres an hour, we would find a lion farm. There's only one problem. According to the South African Predators Association, which governs breeding and hunting pursuits in South Africa, there are several accredited lion breeding farms and a dozen or more lion hunting parks in an area that fits within Debbie's estimation.

As Tilo continued describing the difficulty in identifying where Debbie was held captive, the camera zoomed in on various lion farms, which were immediately identifiable from the fenced enclosures holding groups of lions lying on the ground.

As the helicopter flew over a particular farm, the camera

momentarily focussed on some outbuildings next to an old farmhouse. Then, behind the house, caught a glimpse of a man standing between a small caravan and a red sedan. He looked up as the helicopter flew past.

As the programme paused for a commercial break, the mixed-race lady walked into the lounge carrying two mugs of tea. 'You enjoying this, Riaan?'

'Well, Brenda, the company that made that TV commercial was this Janse Mashele. And that my friend Daniel, whom I met that time, worked with that Joe Robinson who got murdered, and this Debbie lady.'

'My God, but it's terrible what's happened. I hope they catch those men who caused all these murders.'

'Yes, Brenda, it is terrible. All this killing just because of greed.'

'Those two men at the company?'

'Yes, those and other very dangerous men.'

'Well, at least the two men who ran that business are filling up the front pages of newspapers. The story of you escaping from that prison is only on page four of the Telegraph. Here have a look at it', she said as she passed Riaan the late edition of the paper.

Riaan looked at the headlines that covered the first four pages: *Janse and Smit gone to ground'; 'The price of doing business Janses' way: 3 murders, 2 attempted murders, 1 kidnapping'; 'Janse's attorney's claim not to know his whereabouts'; 'Janse, Mashele lose clients, fires staff.*

And tucked halfway down on page four, the headline above an old prison-issued picture of Riaan: *'TV prisoner escapes Leeuwkop!'*.

He read aloud: *'As an additional twist to the Janse Mashele saga that's currently filling news pages and TV and radio airtime comes another puzzling development.*

Riaan du Plessis, the former apartheid special forces assassin who was serving a life sentence for several murders, amongst other serious crimes, has made a daring escape from Leeuwkop prison.

The Department of Corrections Services has yet to issue an official statement regarding an escape that must greatly embarrass the department. The prisoner recently appeared in a TV commercial that praised the department's efforts at rehabilitating prisoners to prevent them from reoffending.

Adding to the intrigue is that Janse Mashaba produced the commercial.

When asked by Telegraph reporters about this development, the Department of Corrections spokesman refused to comment other than to say that it was purely coincidental and that there was no link to the Janse Mashaba case.

However, social media is awash with conspiracy theories claiming that Janse Mashaba's influence stretches to political leaders at the ministerial level.

This is a developing story that Telegraph staff reporters are investigating. More information will be published as soon as it is made available.'

'So there we have it. I'm famous', said Riaan with a chuckle.'

'Anyway', said Brenda as she took a closer look at Riaan's picture in the newspaper, 'it's a good job you shaved off that beard. No one is going to recognise you.'

'Your idea to shave off my hair was also good, even though it looks and feels funny, having had hair on my face and my head for most of my adult life.'

'It makes you look much younger, Riaan, and you look nothing like this picture. So, what now? What are your plans?'

'Well, I'll be leaving you tomorrow, Brenda. All I need to do is pop out later to find car registration plates I can swap with the ones on this old Nissan. Then tomorrow, I'll be off to find some old army friends who can help me lie low somewhere until all this dies down.'

'Well, Riaan, you'll always be welcome here. And even though we look different, we are and always will be brother and sister.'

EIGHTY-THREE

The media frenzy surrounding Smit and Janse's disappearance was at a fever pitch, as a throng of TV news crews and journalists were massed outside the Janse Mashele office, attempting to interview everyone who entered or left the building. Other than vitriolic comments from people who had lost their jobs, the only useful remarks had come from the company's security guards stationed at the security kiosk next to the main gate. They confirmed that two of their night shift colleagues witnessed Smit getting into a vehicle early one morning. A few of the more dedicated reporters waited for the night shift guards to come to work later that evening to interview the two witnesses.

As the security guards arrived for their shift that evening, they were surprised to see lights and a TV camera pointed at them.

'Gentlemen', asked the young female TV reporter, 'we believe that you saw Petrus Smit, Janse Mashele's financial director, here very early in the morning when he disappeared. Can you tell our viewers exactly what you saw?'

Enjoying the attention, the first guard replied: 'As we told the police detectives, we saw Mr Smit at around four thirty in the morning.'

'He's usually early', added the second guard, 'but not that early.'

'Yes, he drove his car into the underground car park. Then, some 30-minutes later, he came outside .'

'He was carrying a box and a small suitcase', added his partner.

'He then waited on the pavement here and looked annoyed.'

'But every time we saw Mr Smit, he always looked that way.'

'What happened then?' asked the reporter.

'After a few minutes, a white double cab bakkie arrived, driven by a white man. Smit got into the vehicle before it made a U-turn and drove away.

The camera shifted onto the news reporter as she addressed the camera: 'So, who was the driver of this mysterious white double cab? And where did he take Petrus Smit? Questions that have to be answered if we are to solve this horrendous case of multiple murders.'

For one viewer watching the news report, it was no mystery. Daniel knew it had to be the same double cab he'd seen on the CCTV footage of Debbie's abduction. And the same vehicle he saw making a speedy getaway after the attempt on Mbulelo's life at his apartment.

He called Judith. 'Hi, did you see the report on the news just now?'

'Yes, the white double cab makes yet another appearance.'

'Exactly. And it's probably going to that lion farm where Debbie was taken.'

'I spoke to Bernie today. He thinks we should get together to chat about these developments. How's your diary at the weekend?'

'Good either day.'

'Then let's meet at Carlo's for brunch on Saturday. I think that's Berni's favourite meeting place.'

'Carlo's it is, see you then.'

The days at the office were depressing for Daniel. The work had ground to a near halt, and he was expecting to be fired any day as the company had always followed a last-in-first-out policy during retrenchments. His saving grace was that the strategy department of Jense Mashele was understaffed. Daniel spent most of his day doing what most staff members did: trawl through the recruitment company website for suitable job openings.

The entire staff complement was furious about the crimes that Janse and Smit had committed. Smit had never been popular, but by now, he was utterly detested. As for Janse, his name was literally besmirched as some of the younger people in the creative department had spray-painted over his name wherever it appeared on company logos throughout the building. Even the metre-high company name on the reception desk had not been spared. And to add to the defilement, they had chosen red paint.

Most of the clients had fired the agency, citing reputational risks to their brands by being associated with Janse Mashele. And the only visitors to the company were a steady stream of police officers and forensic technicians who carried out searches and took away computers from the finance department and Janse's office.

'Daniel', shouted Mashele as he stormed into Daniel's office. 'Stop looking so downhearted, and stop looking for another job.'

'I'm not', lied Daniel.

'Then you must be the only person in the building that isn't.'

But If you are, stop because you have a job. A bloody good job that's going to pay you a damn sight more than you're being paid now.'

'Sorry, Mac, but I don't understand. What's going on?

'You've just been hired by a comms group called Lazarus.'

'Lazarus? I've never heard of the company.'

'Of course not, because I've just thought of it. And my guys are registering the company as we speak. An appropriate name, don't you think?"

'Yes, Lazarus, the resurrection and all that. But what about clients? Do you have any?'

'That's the best part: about half of our old clients have agreed to sign up with us if we expunge all traces of Janse. So we'll be out of this building.'

'What about this case? Are there any comebacks for you? Obviously, Mac, please don't think. . . I'm not implying . . .'

'Relax, Daniel. It's cool. Everything is cool. Thanks to Advocate Van Rooyen, he's negotiated with the prosecutors that I will be a state witness in all the cases as soon as those bastards are finally caught. He's a brilliant lawyer that Bernie.'

'Yes, he is. Wow, Mac, that's amazing. We're going to be back on our feet.'

'We will be, and far sooner than you think. Oh, and another thing. We've got to get Debbie back, so please call her for me and tell her and persuade her to join us at Lazarus.'

'That's amazing. I think she'll be delighted.'

EIGHTY-FOUR

If one thing clearly defined Advocate van Rooyan, it was that he was a creature of habit. Sitting next to Judith at a table at the busy Carlo's restaurant, he was devouring an omelette that seemed to contain the content of the kitchen. He wiped his mouth with a serviette as he stood up to shake Daniels's outstretched hand. 'So good to see you, Daniel.'

'You too, Bernie', replied Daniel as he hugged Judith.

'So how's life at Jense Mashele? It's miserable, I'm sure, ' said Van Rooyen.

'Yes, it's miserable. Most of the clients have dumped the agency. Many staff members have lost their jobs. It is staggering how a company of the size and stature of Janse Mashele can ride on the crest of a wave one day and plumb to the dark, cold depths the next.'

'Well, it was hardly run based on good governance, now was it? Said Judith, sipping her lemon tea.

'No, it wasn't. It was crooked from top to bottom, and we had no idea. Anyway, I chatted with Mac the other day, and there is a dim shred of light at the end of this long dark tunnel.'

'Yes, I have been talking to Mac, and he's shared the good news with me. And I must say, I'm happy for him, you and Debbie, and those who can still earn a living.'

'What? Is Mac starting a new company?' asked Judith.

'Yes, Lazarus Communications.'

'Lazarus, as in the resurrection? That's very appropriate', said Judith. 'The bringing the company back from the dead.'

'Yes, well, there's someone who won't be coming back from the dead', interrupted van Rooyan.

Both Daniel and Judith were suddenly taken aback by Van Rooyen's statement.

'This is why I wanted to get together with you both, as I didn't want to share it over the phone. It's Janse.'

'Janse's dead?' asked a shocked Daniel.

'Yes, I had a call from one of his lawyers a few days back. It seems that he was assassinated at a farm he had just bought in Namibia. By all accounts, it sounds like a sniper shot him from some distance.'

'Good God', said Judith.'And when are they announcing all this?'

'His lawyers have informed the authorities, and everything is in the process of being checked out and confirmed officially by the Namibia police and Ministry of Justice. His lawyers reckon that the police here in Joburg will announce on Monday.'

'A sniper, you say, no doubt an army-trained sniper. Or should I say an apartheid-army trained sniper', said Daniel, whose anger seemed to be rising.

'Most likely, I would guess. Janse was inside a paddock full of cattle, who were spooked, and they trampled over his body. So it was just as well that he died instantly. It was a headshot, I was told.'

'So the bastard never faced justice for killing my brother, Jabu.'

'Or for killing Joe', said Daniel.

'Or for killing my friend, Jacks', added Van Rooyen.

'It's bloody infuriating when nasty, callous, murderous bastards get to escape justice like this.

'And what about Smit, any news about him?'

Nothing, Daniel, I haven't heard a word about his whereabouts.

But trust me, he'll show up at some stage.'

EIGHTY-FIVE

After spending a few days of solitude in the vast, empty Namibian desert, Fourie returned to his farm in darkness. Nelson's caravan, parked at the back of the house for more years than Fourie cared to remember, was gone. No doubt, it was towed by Debbie's car to Zimbabwe.

Fourie was sorry that Nelson had sneaked off without saying goodbye. With Smit's two million rand in the bank, Fourie was wealthier than he had ever imagined, and he had planned to give Nelson enough to make him financially secure for the rest of his life.

But he and Nelson had grown apart of late. Nelson disapproved of the way Fourie lived his life, especially the drinking and the black moods. On several occasions, Nelson had asked Fourie why he chose to work alone. In the old days, they had worked as a team, and as Nelson had reminded him, they had worked well together. But now, even though Fourie claimed it was nothing personal, Nelson saw it as being side-lined and took it as an insult.

Fourie also realised that kidnapping the woman was probably the final straw for Nelson. He had complained bitterly that it was wrong. And that it would have been much better and safer to kill the woman in Joburg in the first place. A bullet in the back of the head with a silenced handgun while she walked on the street in Greenside that night. It would have been quick and straightforward, and nothing could have linked either of them to the murder.

But this business of keeping her as a hostage just complicated matters. And a complication like that, as Nelson had said on several occasions, was bound to trip them up. At least, she had not seen their faces, so she could never identify them. Fourie had Nelson to thank for that, not that this miserable white man never thanked him for anything.

Before unpacking the double cab, Fourie lit the braai on the veranda at the back of the house. He then poured himself a large brandy that he topped with Coke. His last chore for the evening was to clean his rifle. A quick job he could do while the coals of his braai fire died down. He took the gun from its case and left it on the kitchen table.

He then went out to check on the fire. He stood watching the flames taking hold as he finished his brandy. He was about to go to the house for a refill when he heard the sound that was familiar to every old soldier; the sound of his rifle being cocked.

'It was very careless of you to leave a loaded weapon lying around like that. You've lost your touch, Sarel.'

The voice came from behind him, from the doorway to the kitchen. Fourie froze.

'My God, Riaan, Is that you? Or have I finally gone mad?'

'Turn around very slowly, and you'll see you're still sane. But put your hands on your head where I can see them. And no sudden moves now, Sarel.'

'No one's called me Sarel in a very long time', said Fourie as he turned around. 'My God, it really is you, Riaan.'

'Ja, it's me.'

'Warrant Officer Riaan de Plessis.'

'That's right, Captain Sarel Gerhadus Fourie, sir.'

Fourie smiled. 'So, they finally let you out then?'

'No, I walked out of my own accord.'

'But why? You couldn't have had much more time to serve? How long have you been inside now, twenty years?'

'Twenty-two.'

'Shit man, that's a long time.'

'Never mind that now. Pull up your shirt so I can see that you're not carrying a weapon. But do it carefully now.'

Fourie pulled his shirt up from his waist and turned around slowly to reveal no handgun stuck in his belt. 'Are you pissed off at me because you got caught and served time, and I didn't?'

'Hell no, you were just a dumb soldier like me, but you were luckier. I was pissed off with the generals and the fucking politicians who got away with it scot-free. But even they don't bother me now.'

'Yeah, well, I'm still pissed off with those guys. But why this, Riaan? Why are you pointing my rifle at me?'

'Sit down, Sarel, so that we can talk.'

'How about me getting the brandy bottle first?'

'You want a drink? Okay, let's both of us have a drink. But slowly now.'

As Fourie walked slowly into the house, Riaan followed as he trained the rifle on Fourie's back. Fourie picked up the bottle on the kitchen table, but then, with a sudden burst of energy, he kicked a chair backwards towards Riaan to distract him before throwing the brandy bottle towards Riaan's head. Riaan reacted by swinging his body around, and using the butt of the rifle; he struck Fourie on the side of the head. Fourie crashed onto the floor and lost consciousness.

Minutes passed until Fourie came around. As he gathered his senses, he saw Riaan sitting next to the kitchen table, the rifle on his lap, pointing straight at his stomach. He tried to move but realised that his wrists were tied to the armrests of a kitchen chair and both his ankles tied to the chair legs.

'Hell, Sarel, you've slowed down. You must be getting old.'

'You're older than me, you bastard.'

'Let me help you so we can both sit at the table, talk, and drink like civilised men. And please, Sarel, don't try any shit like that again. Do we understand each other?'

Fourie nodded. Riaan placed the rifle on the table, bent over, and pulled Fourie and the chair upright. He then grabbed a glass that he'd filled with brandy and held it to Fourie's mouth so that he could take a sip.

'You're looking after me like I was a baby now.'

'Well, we looked after each other for years, didn't we?'

'We did. We had some good times, too?'

'That's true.'

'So, what's this all about, Riaan? Why all this? Why the gun in my face?'

'Who have you been working for, Sarel? Is it that big fellow Smit?'

'Yes, he used to be a client of mine, but he is not anymore. I didn't know you knew him.'

'I didn't know him. I saw him a few times years ago. I knew he worked for the CCB and that you had to deal with him as head of the unit. Then when this big story was splashed all over the TV and the newspapers, I recognised him. I remembered him from the old days. I also remembered that you hated his guts.'

'I did.'

'So why are you still doing work for him?'

'I've stopped working for him.'

'Then why did you do work for him?'

'Because he paid me well and was the last of my clients.'

'Clients for what? Killing people?'

'Oh, for fuck sake, you're not getting moralistic on me, are you, Riaan? You've killed enough people in your time.'

'Yes, I did. And it was wrong. It was wrong then, and it's wrong now.'

'Look, we were soldiers, and we were following orders.'

'That's kak. We weren't soldiers; we were no more than hired killers. People like you and me were conned into believing that we were serving our country, conned into fighting a stupid fucking war fought for stupid fucking reasons. And we were led by crooks.'

'Well, I won't disagree with your last point.'

'Can't you see Sarel, just as we were serving crooks then, and you're still serving crooks now, people like Smit and this fellow, Janse.'

'So, is this about Smit? Is Smit the reason you connected all this to me?'

'No, it's someone who works for Smit. Daniel Stein.'

Fourie smiled: 'Ja, I know who he is. He was a youngster who got in the way.'

'Daniel and I have become friends.'

'So, what's that got to do with me?'

'You've tried to kill him. You killed his friends. And you kidnapped another friend.'

'I don't deny any of that. But let me ask you something, Riaan. How did you figure out I was connected to all this?'

'The woman you kidnapped.'

'Debbie?'

'That's right. She told Daniel she could hear lions roaring at night when you held her here. She also sensed that the lions' sounds were so intense and constant that they had to be inside some enclosure.'

'Smart lady.'

'Ja, as soon as I heard this, I knew it was you.'

'How come?'

'I remember you telling me that if you could get your life back together after all the shit we had to do in the CCB, you fancied the idea of turning the old family farm into a lion breeding business.'

'Ja, well, I did it. I've got forty-eight breeding females and five top black-maned males. You can hear them now.'

'It's got to stop. Sarel. You can't go on killing people. Those times are over. Our time is over.'

Picking up the rifle, Riaan walked out of the house. As he poked the braai fire, he could hear the male lions roaring in the nearby enclosures, each male aggressively trying to establish his dominance. He listened to the lions for a while before returning to the kitchen. Seeing Fourie sitting there with his back towards him, Riaan raised the rifle to his shoulder, aimed at the back of Fourie's head, and pulled the trigger.

The noise of the shot was deafening. Riaan had forgotten how loud a gunshot could be. He glanced at Fourie's body, slumped forward in his chair. A fountain of blood gushed out the hole in the back of Fourie's head before brain matter started oozing out.

'Yes, Sarel, my old friend, our time is over.'

Riaan re-cocked the rifle and sat down in the chair opposite Fourie. After draining the remains of the brandy, he then placed the weapon between his legs and rested his chin on the barrel. Leaning forward, he reached down with his right hand until he could feel the trigger guard. He then placed his thumb on the trigger before pressing it down as hard as he could.

End

Printed in Dunstable, United Kingdom